SPIRIT'S
CHOSEN

ALSO BY ESTHER FRIESNER

WITHDRAWN

SPIRIT'S CHOSEN

ESTHER FRIESNER

Fitchburg Public Library
5530 Lacy Road
Fitchburg, WI 53711

RANDOM HOUSE 🏠 NEW YORK

This is a work of fiction. Names, characters, places,
and incidents either are the product of the author's imagination
or are used fictitiously. Any resemblance to actual persons,
living or dead, events, or locales is entirely coincidental.

Text copyright © 2013 by Esther Friesner
Jacket art copyright © 2013 by Larry Rostant

All rights reserved. Published in the United States by Random House
Children's Books, a division of Random House, Inc., New York.

Random House and the colophon are registered
trademarks of Random House, Inc.

Visit us on the Web! randomhouse.com/teens

Educators and librarians, for a variety of teaching tools,
visit us at RHTeachersLibrarians.com

Library of Congress Cataloging-in-Publication Data
Friesner, Esther M.
Spirit's chosen / Esther Friesner. — 1st ed.
p.   cm.
Sequel to: Spirit's princess.
Summary: As Himiko traverses ancient Japan in order to free enslaved
members of her clan, she encounters members of many other
tribes and emerges as the leader who will unify them.
ISBN 978-0-375-86908-2 (trade) — ISBN 978-0-375-96908-9 (lib. bdg.) —
ISBN 978-0-375-89991-1 (ebook) — ISBN 978-0-375-87316-4 (pbk.)
[1. Sex role—Fiction. 2. Shamans—Fiction. 3. Clans—Fiction.
4. Magic—Fiction. 5. Spirits—Fiction. 6. Slavery—Fiction. 7. Japan—
History—To 645—Fiction.] I. Title.
PZ7.F91662Srf 2013   [Fic]—dc23   2012027690

Printed in the United States of America
10 9 8 7 6 5 4 3 2 1
First Edition

Random House Children's Books supports
the First Amendment and celebrates the right to read.

For Daryl, Georgia, Scout, Elliott, and Charles,
grandchildren of Allen and Brenda Lewis:
May all of life's adventures bring you joy.

CONTENTS

PART 1
KIN

1

IN THE WAKE OF WAR

The first flakes of an early snowfall drifted from the sky as Kaya and I began our descent from the hillside above my village. I took deep breaths of the cold air and knew that autumn had slipped away at last. The final steps of the dance that I had just performed for the spirits still echoed through my bones. The lingering scent of summer from the thick pad of fallen pine needles in the forest behind us clung to me like a swirl of ghosts. I was going home.

"Kaya?" I paused partway down the slope and turned to her. She was being unnaturally silent and it troubled me. I was the daughter of the Matsu clan's chieftain and her mother was chieftess and shaman of the Shika, yet our equal rank as princesses of our peoples was not what bound our lives together. We had become friends when I'd wandered into her village, many years ago, but neither she nor I could say exactly why we'd taken to each other so quickly. Perhaps we each recognized something in the other that we lacked, some quality that made the two of us better, stronger, happier together than we could be on our own. Even if she or I had been born to a family with no noble blood at all, we still would have been the best of friends, and more than that: we were sisters in spirit.

"Kaya, what's wrong?"

"Nothing." I could barely hear her response, muttered under her breath. She wouldn't look at me.

I refused to let her stay silent. "You're a bad liar." I spoke gently so she would know I meant no real insult. "You're so quiet. Something *is* bothering you. What? Are you worried about what we'll find down there?" I gestured to where my village lay, or what was left of it.

We were the Matsu, the pine tree clan, as strong and steadfast as the venerable tree that was our guardian spirit. Our village was protected by a sturdy wooden palisade, ringed by a wide ditch, and barricaded behind massive gates. A tall watchtower gave our sentries a good view of the surrounding countryside so that our warriors could rush to defend us when an enemy force appeared in the distance.

It hadn't been enough. The Ookami—the wolf clan— had brought war to our land, and they won.

Our gates were smashed, our watchtower pulled down, our palisade broken, the dirt walls of our moat undermined until they'd collapsed. Many of our houses were now no more than smoldering piles of blackened timbers and ash. Worse, the ancient pine that was the living symbol of our people had been toppled and destroyed, leaving nothing behind but a splintered stump, a shattered blade that thrust at the heavens and stabbed at the heart of the Matsu.

"Are you afraid the Ookami haven't gone?" I persisted. "Let me go ahead alone, then. If I don't come back for you, you can—"

"As if I'd let you risk yourself like that!" she snapped. "If the Ookami are still in your village, we'll face them together. Do you think I'm a liar *and* a coward?"

"You know I didn't mean such a thing. And a coward would never have left the safety of her own village to travel here with me," I replied evenly. "I'd never question your courage, but I have to question your silence. It's not like you. What's stolen your tongue?"

She looked at her feet again.

"Kaya, if you don't speak up, how can I—?"

"It's *that*." Her eyes flashed with anger as they met mine. She gestured sharply at the wand of cherrywood in my hand.

Her words startled me. I turned the smooth stick slowly between my fingers. The glossy, dark brown bark looked almost black in the pale light of an overcast sky, but all along its length were frothy clusters of pink flowers. With the world poised at the gateway to winter, this thin branch was cloaked in blossoms of spring.

"This?" I was honestly bewildered. "This is what's troubling you? But it's a *good* sign, Kaya; we both know that."

"Maybe *you* do." My friend turned her gaze to the uphill path. "You're a shaman; you're at ease with things like this. *I* don't know what to make of it. You had that twig with you on the day Sora brought you into our village, when you were lost and half mad with thirst and hunger. It's been nothing more than a sliver of dead wood for many seasons since then, yet suddenly it bursts into bloom right before our eyes! You might feel comfortable with a miracle just—just"—she flung her hands up—"just *leaping* out at you, but I'm not!"

"Kaya—" Her distress was plain. I wanted to comfort her, but I couldn't find the words.

She wrapped her arms around her body and closed her eyes. I thought I glimpsed the trail of tears on her cheek, but she turned away too quickly for me to be sure. "You were right, Himiko," she said in a strangely choked voice. "I am a bad liar, and I'm a coward too. I *am* scared. You're holding a miracle in your hands, I don't understand it, and I've never been so frightened in my life."

"I know." I put my arm around her shoulders, holding the blooming branch away from her. "These flowers—at first I felt almost certain they were a message from the gods telling us not to despair, but now . . ." I gazed at the snow falling on the trembling blossoms. Each delicate white flake caused another pink petal to lose its hold and tumble to the earth. "Does this mean that we should hold on to hope, or that it's something too fragile to survive? Look, the twig is turning bare again." As I spoke, the last petal dropped. My eyes followed its fall.

It touched the earth and vanished.

I gasped and clutched Kaya, driving my fingers deeply into her arm. "Did you see that?"

"Ow!" She jumped away and spun around to confront me. "That *hurt*. Why did you—?"

"It's gone," I said. "They're all gone, all of the petals, as if they'd never been. I didn't notice before, but . . ."

I shivered, though I wasn't cold. "The last one, just now, I

saw—I saw it melt away instantly, like a snowflake falling
into a fire. Look. There's not a trace left of any of them."
I motioned to the ground. Though my wand had been
thickly laden with blossoms, not a single sign remained.
My recent words echoed through my mind—*"hope . . . too
fragile to survive"*—and I felt a hard, sour knot twist my belly.

"Himiko?" Kaya gave me a peculiar look. "You've
turned white as frost."

"I—I'm scared," I replied simply.

"Because the flowers vanished?" she asked. I nodded,
which made her scratch her head. "Huh. And they frightened me when they *appeared.*" Her familiar smile crept
back. "It sounds like our fears are playing mirror games."
She chuckled.

I tried to join in, but my false laughter was weak and
fled as suddenly as the fallen petals. I gazed at the bare wand
and passed my fingertips gingerly over the wood. "Nothing
is left. Nothing."

I began to weep without a sound. Tears bathed my face
before I realized I was crying. When the first sob broke
from my throat, Kaya already had her arms around me, my
face resting against her shoulder.

"You're not talking about the blossoms, are you," she
said. It was not a question. "I understand. Don't worry,
Himiko. Whatever's waiting for you down there, you won't
face it alone. Those flowers carried a message from the
gods, and messengers don't linger once their job is done.
The news they bring doesn't change after they leave. You

called those flowers a *good* sign, right?" I nodded. "So we've *still* got favorable omens on our side. Don't you dare deny it!"

I raised my face and had to smile. It was good to hear my friend sounding like herself again: Lady Badger was back in all her gruff, stubborn glory. My distress let her set aside her own misgivings to help me through mine.

"I won't," I replied. "But . . . suppose I was wrong?"

Kaya snorted, sending the snowflakes flying crazily around us. "Next thing, you'll be claiming that none of it ever happened, that it was another one of your visions."

"It might as well have been a dream," I said. "There's no way to prove it was real."

"Oh, it was real enough, I'll swear to that. Maybe *you* could imagine something so fanciful, but not me, never. I'm a hunter, Himiko. I don't jump at shadows, and I only see what's there. Once we bring you home, you're going to tell everyone in the village about what we saw here. Who's better than their shaman to bring such cheering news? The gods know, they'll need it."

"I'm not their shaman, Kaya," I whispered. "Have you ever heard of any clan with two?"

"Maybe . . ." My friend took a deep breath. "I don't like saying this, but maybe your people no longer *have* a shaman."

"No!" I pushed Kaya away so violently that she staggered. "Don't say—don't even *imagine* such a thing! Master Michio's alive. The Ookami wouldn't dare kill a man who can command the spirits."

My friend looked at me with pity. "Himiko, it was war.

The wolf clan wouldn't have hesitated to strike down anyone in their way, shaman or not."

"Stop it!" I cried, clenching my fists so hard that I drove
the cherrywood wand painfully into my palm. "I don't want
to hear this!"

"But you'll have to face it soon," Kaya said.

"I know that! I know, and I'll face everything—our
plundered storehouses, our ruined homes, our wounded
and . . . and our dead. I won't hide from any of what's waiting for me, but until I *must* do so—" I fought to calm myself
again. "Until I *must* see who's missing, let me go on believing that everyone dear to me survived. *Please,* Kaya."

She came back toward me and took my hand. "If that's
what you want."

We continued our way down the hillside. As we walked,
Kaya spoke about countless matters, great and small. I
think she wanted to distract me from fretting over the fate
of my clan. I had my own way of doing that. Though reason
told me that each step I took brought me closer to a bitter
reality, my heart persisted in believing I would find a fresh
miracle waiting within our village gates: in the midst of
war's destruction, my family would be untouched.

I pictured my welcome home exactly as I wanted it to
be. Father would scowl when he saw me and give me a harsh
tongue-lashing for having run away. Strange, how strongly
I hoped he'd turn the full force of his temper against me.
It would mean that the Ookami conquest had not broken
him completely, that a spark of strength still glowed in his
heart, and most important of all, that he'd survived.

As for the rest of my family, Mama's warm greeting

would interrupt Father's scolding as she took me into her arms while his junior wives, Yukari and Emi, looked on, smiling. Our three little ones, Takehiko, Sanjirou, and my special favorite, Noboru, would try to swarm into my lap long before I could sit down. My older brothers would be there too, though someone might have to go fetch them from their work. Masa would enter the house still smelling of the smoke of the blacksmith's forge, but Shoichi and Aki would carry in a strong confusion of scents—the keen air of first snowfall mixed with the reek of sweat from their labors rebuilding our village.

There was only one part of my imagined return that filled my heart with pain: the inevitable moment when I'd have to tell Aki that his beloved wife, Hoshi, was gone.

When I'd first found the Shika clan, my father and eldest brother had come to bring me home. That was when Aki encountered Kaya's sister Hoshi and fell hopelessly in love. She returned his feelings with all her heart, but there was little hope that they could be together: Father nursed a burning distrust of anyone not born a Matsu, and would never consent to his heir marrying outside of our clan. In spite of this, Aki and Hoshi wed in secret and lived apart. He and I shared high hopes that a time would come when Father's hostile attitude changed, but before that day could dawn, a great sickness swept through the Shika village. I used the healing skills taught me by our former shaman, Lady Yama, and while I was able to help many recover, Hoshi died. As much as I blamed myself, I prayed that Aki wouldn't blame me more.

As I let my imagination dance, Kaya and I reached the

road leading to the ruined village gates. I could see the rice paddies, bare and cold at that time of year. The harvest was gathered in, but how much of it remained with my people? I could tell myself that all my family were waiting for me, but I couldn't pretend that the Ookami had left without taking our stores of rice for themselves. The phantoms of imminent hunger and desolation loomed over the land, banishing the last of my comforting fancies.

No one challenged us as we crossed what was left of the moat, no one greeted us as we entered the gates, no one was there. The smell of smoke hung on the chill air, but not the welcome aroma of cooking fires or the sharper tang of the potter's firing kiln or my brother Masa's forge. This smell carried a hint of dreadful things, vague horrors whose ghostly voices whispered all around me. Their message was too faint to understand, but its meaning was somehow still starkly plain: *Lost, lost, lost! So much destroyed, so much gone forever, so much darkness left behind!*

I stopped about ten paces inside the village border and felt tears sting my eyes as I took in the sights. Some homes still stood—a random number of the raised houses belonging to the Matsu nobility and the thatch-roofed pit houses where simpler folk lived—but many were scarred by fire. A few were nothing more than blackened holes in the ground. I couldn't look at the charred ruins without picturing the people who had lived in each one and wondering—fearing—what had become of them.

Kaya took my hand and squeezed it. "You're seeing it the way it was, aren't you?" she asked. I could only nod. A fresh sob was rising in my throat, choking me. It was one thing to see my clan's fate from a distance, another to stand in the midst of it, where every toppled structure and every obliterated home was haunted by the faces of my kin. Whether they'd loved me or scorned me, they were still a part of me. How many of them were alive?

I hadn't seen a single person since entering the gates. Only the faint sounds of activity coming from the nearest remaining houses proved that some of my clanfolk still lived. But my family . . . where were they in all this desolation? The time for telling myself cheerful fantasies was over. Only truth reigned here.

"Come, Kaya," I said, forcing myself to speak firmly. "We're going to my house now. I have to see who—"

"Himiko?" A familiar voice sounded weakly from the shadows of a pit house. Master Michio peered out into the milky light of that snowy day. He took one uncertain step forward, then another. He looked haggard and exhausted, his eyes rimmed with red and sunk into dark circles, but once he realized he was seeing me and not a vision, his face became radiant with smiles. "Ah, it is you, my dear! You've come back to us, may the spirits be praised. How are you? Where have you been? When did you—?"

I raced to him so swiftly that my bad leg nearly tripped me up. I staggered, but he hurried forward to save me from a fall. My relief at finding him alive was so great that I couldn't help laughing, but my joy echoed strangely in the pall of emptiness hanging over our village.

I took a deep breath and steadied myself, then stepped back from him and bent to retrieve my wand. It had fallen from my hand when I'd stumbled. The twig so recently bright with miraculous blossoms was now covered with dirt. I brushed it clean before securing it in my sash. Only then did I clap my hands in the prescribed gesture of respect for greeting my friend and teacher.

Master Michio observed all of this and chuckled. "So formal? That's not how things were between us. What did I do to offend you?"

"I am the one who has offended," I replied. "I went away because Father would never consent to my being a shaman, and when you spoke up for me, you suffered for it."

"Suffered? I wouldn't say so much myself. However . . ." Master Michio turned his face to the sky and peered up into the dancing snowflakes. "However, if we three stay outside in this weather much longer, my bones will suffer for it. Come to my house and let me offer you something to eat and drink." He gave Kaya a friendly smile. "Then you can introduce me to your charming friend."

"Master Michio, I think I should return to my own home first," I said.

He looked serious again. "There will be time for that. You're back, and your house is waiting. Be happy in knowing it still stands."

"And my family—?"

He spoke up sharply, cutting me off. "Himiko, I have never asked you for any favors. Now I do ask for this: let me be the one to bring you back to your kin. When the war came, I couldn't do enough to help our people. No matter how loudly I implored the spirits for aid, none came, and we were conquered. The Ookami spared my life out of respect for my calling, but that didn't stop them from pulling down our sacred tree. Every time someone looks at what's left of Grandfather Pine, I can almost hear them thinking, *What good is our shaman if he couldn't even save you?* That knowledge is a stone weighing down my heart.

"Give me the chance to redeem myself by taking credit for your safe return. It won't be a *big* lie; I did pray daily that the spirits would guide you home again. Our clan's losses have been terrible, but if the people can believe my power over the spirits is great enough to accomplish *this*"— he made a sweeping gesture, indicating me from head to toe—"they will take hope for our future. Please . . ."

"Of course." I bowed my head, though my heart ached to rush home.

His smile returned, weary but warm. "Thank you."

Kaya and I trailed after him through the village. It was hard for me to see so many homes destroyed or badly damaged, but I took a bit of comfort from noticing that the Ookami had not devastated everything. Many houses bore only minor signs of harm, and a few remained entirely untouched. The thatch of Master Michio's pit house had been torn in a few places, but the structure was intact otherwise. Kaya and I stooped to follow him inside, and soon we were sharing a meager meal of cold rice and a few scraps of dried meat so tough it was impossible to name the animal that had provided it.

As we ate, I introduced Kaya to my teacher and friend. "The Shika clan, eh?" Master Michio's eyes twinkled. "I remember my mother speaking about the deer people, but she never said they gave birth to such beautiful daughters."

Kaya laughed into her fist. The shaman spread his

hands and pretended to be confused. "Did I say something funny?"

"Well, *I* don't think so," I said. "But Kaya prefers to picture herself as Lady Badger: tough, stubborn, and always ready for a fight."

"Can't you be all that and pretty too?" the shaman asked Kaya in an innocent voice.

"Since when are badgers pretty?" my friend asked with good humor.

"Since the first day of creation," Master Michio replied. Then he added: "Just ask another badger."

We all laughed, and our laughter carried its own special magic. While it lingered, lifting our hearts, it pushed aside everything else. If that merry sound could have lasted forever, the world would hold only joy. But that was impossible. Like the tumbling petals that had once adorned a slender branch of cherrywood, the notes of laughter faded, fell, and were gone.

I was the first to fill the silence left in their wake. "Master Michio, thank you for welcoming us. It is good to be here with you again, but when can we go to my family? Do you want to speak with them first, before I show myself?"

"That might be the best idea," Kaya put in. "They don't know what happened to you, whether you're alive or dead. Happy tidings can be as big a shock as bad ones if it comes out of nowhere. You don't want your poor mother fainting because she thinks she's seeing your ghost."

"Little chance of that," Master Michio said under his breath. Before I could question him, he went on: "The pretty badger is right. Some news must be broken gently, gradually.

It's the kindest way. I promise that we'll go to your house soon. Meanwhile, I could use your help. The battle with the Ookami left many men here gravely hurt. I met you just as I was leaving one of them. He needs fresh salve for his wounds and a potion to numb pain, but my supplies have been used up. The sooner we work together to make more, the sooner he'll have some relief, poor fellow."

What could I do but consent? With Kaya lending a hand too, Master Michio and I mixed dried herbs and other ingredients into medicines for our people. While I knelt to grind roots into powder, he chanted spells, seeking the spirits' assistance, calling on them to strengthen the plants' healing qualities. I had learned the same incantation from my first teacher, Master Michio's half sister, Lady Yama, but though I could have joined my voice with his, my throat closed. I was choking on a rising flood of questions, and if I let one slip out, the others would pour after, interrupting our shaman and perhaps making him lose the goodwill of the spirits.

At last he was done. A row of bowls filled with healing compounds lay on the ground between us. Master Michio looked content.

"Thank you, girls," he said. "Many people will bless you for helping their loved ones rest more comfortably tonight."

"How many?" Kaya asked. Master Michio gave her an inquiring look. "How many of your men were wounded? How many died?"

"Lady Badger has a blunt tongue." The shaman frowned. "Why do you ask such things? What good will it do to give you an accounting? Will it satisfy you to know that we lost *too* many of our people?"

"How many is too many?" Kaya replied. She held up both hands, her fingers spread. "This many? Less? More?"

Master Michio's disapproving look deepened. "Why don't I take you with me through this village so you can ask the widows and orphans to tally their dead just to feed your childish curiosity? Or if you insist on an accurate count, wait a few days. A few more may die by then. Some wounds I'm treating won't heal, no matter how much I labor over them. Will that satisfy you?"

"Master Michio, she didn't—" I began.

"*Shame* on you." Kaya sat back on her heels and drew herself up with dignity. Her gaze did not falter as she met our shaman's hostile stare, and I heard echoes of her chieftess mother's commanding voice in every word she spoke. "I have good reasons for my questions. Himiko is my friend, my spirit's sister. Her pain is my pain; her clan's loss is mine! I didn't come all this way with her out of curiosity. I won't leave until I know that this clan can survive. I ask how many died because I want to know how many still live. Do you have enough food to take all of them through the winter? Will you have enough able-bodied people to tend your fields when the planting season comes? More important, how many of the Ookami are still here? How are they treating your chieftain in defeat? What will they do when they learn that another member of his family has appeared?" She seized my hand. "Himiko wanted to go home, but I won't leave her side until I know her home is *safe*."

Master Michio's scowl softened. "A blunt tongue, but sharp teeth." He sighed, and that sigh melted into tears. I watched in horror as our shaman covered his face and sobbed like a heartbroken child. With a small cry of sympathy I rushed to throw my arms around him while he shook with weeping.

Kaya was stunned at the effect her words had produced. We had both grown up with the knowledge that a shaman must be as brave and strong as any warrior. It takes courage to confront the spirits, to entreat them, to command them, to summon and banish them. Some are kindly, but there are also malicious ones that need to be placated or even fought. Sometimes we shamans were all that stood between our people and the wrath of these powerful, harmful beings. Master Michio had stood guard for many years on the border between darkness and light. Why should a young girl's words, no matter how biting, reduce him to this?

"I—I'm sorry," Kaya stammered, her face pale. "I didn't—didn't know—didn't want to—Oh, I'm *sorry*!"

Master Michio raised his head and forced a smile. "No, Lady Badger; you have no need to apologize. You did nothing wrong. It's my own fault. I'm like a little boy who meets an *oni* on the road and thinks he can hide from that horrible mountain ogre just by covering his eyes. He tells himself, *If I can't see it, it can't see me, and when I open my eyes again, it will be gone.*" He shook his head. "But the *oni* is still here, and I must face it."

My hands were still resting on his shoulders. He shifted sideways, away from me, and turned so that we faced each other. "There is much to tell you," he said. "If I only knew where to begin . . ."

"Start by telling me one thing," I replied. "Was it my fault that we were conquered?"

Master Michio blinked rapidly, confused. "Was it your—? By the gods, child, what makes you ask such a thing?"

I clasped my hands in my lap. "When I decided I couldn't stay here any longer, I joined a group of boys and girls who were going into the forest to gather nuts and mushrooms for the winter. As soon as I saw my chance, I slipped away from them. I'd spent a lot of time before that asking many questions about the Todomatsu clan, the seacoast people with whom you used to live. I did it to leave a false trail, so that when Father realized I was gone, he'd send a search party down the wrong road to find me and I'd be able to get away. Tell me truly now, Master Michio, did Father send men after me, men who should have been here to help fight the Ookami?" My voice rose shrilly. "Did my trickery cost our clan its freedom?"

"Ah! No, no, put such thoughts out of your head at once!" he exclaimed. "Your plan might have worked, but when your father ordered your eldest brother to lead the men, Aki argued with him. He insisted you hadn't gone to the Todomatsu and begged your father to let him track you down on his own. You can imagine how well your father liked being contradicted. The whole village heard him yelling at Aki, commanding him to do as he was told. Your mother, poor lady, begged him to let your second-eldest brother, Shoichi, lead the search party. All she wanted was to have you back, but the argument had become a contest of wills between father and son. When the Ookami struck, no one had left the village. Every fighting man of our clan was here."

He looked at the ground. "For all the good it did. We fought fiercely, but there were too many of them. They threw torches over our walls, set fire to our gates, and when our men rushed out to meet them in battle, they overwhelmed us."

"Are they still here?" Kaya asked.

Master Michio shook his head. "They didn't linger. Why would they? Could you sleep securely in the midst of your enemies, even if you had defeated them? Once they were victorious, their chieftain ordered his men to pull down Grandfather Pine and made every one of us watch while they burned him to ashes."

Their chieftain . . . , I thought. *Ryu.* The name called up angry memories. Many seasons ago, before the Ookami had brought war to our gates, they had come to offer the chance to unite our peoples. Ryu's father was their ruler then, and while he and his men met with our nobles, I was told to entertain the Ookami chieftain's son. As we walked, I quickly learned that his handsome face hid a callous and arrogant heart. He saw other people as his playthings, his tools, his slaves, their lives worth only what they could do to serve his desires. I was able to save myself from him with the spirits' help, but the memory of his ruthless words still lingered.

And now this ruthless man had led the conquerors of my clan. I shivered.

"When the Ookami had done their work, they left, taking whatever they liked from us," Master Michio went on. "Who was left to stop them? We'll have a hungry winter, but it won't be the last one. When we harvest the rice we plant next spring, they'll send warriors back to claim as great a share as they please." He sighed. "We serve the Ookami now."

I clenched my hands so tightly that the nails bit into my palms. "It isn't true," I said. "It can't be. They defeated us, but we will not let them rule us. We will recover from this and cast them out of our lives. My kin are no one's servants. Father, Aki, and Shoichi will rally our fighters and—"

"No, Himiko." Master Michio's voice broke with sorrow. "No more. No . . . no more."

I could scarcely breathe. When I spoke, it was a hoarse whisper. "They are . . . gone?"

My teacher said nothing, made no sign. He let silence confirm the horrible truth. Bitter cold seeped through me from my skin to the marrow of my bones. I felt Kaya's arm encircle my shoulders, though I hadn't seen her move. I saw nothing. I was alone in a dark place, a land of awful shadows and taunting laughter.

2
A TANGLED MIND

Some time later, I realized that Kaya and I were by ourselves in Master Michio's house. My friend still held me as a mother holds her drowsing child. I lifted my head from her shoulder slowly and looked around, confused.

"Where is Master Michio?" I asked. My voice sounded distant and fuzzy.

"He went out a little while ago," Kaya answered.

"Did he? And without a word to us? How strange . . ."

"He tried speaking to you, but you didn't hear him." My friend's eyes were sad. "I don't think you could, after the shock he gave you." She hugged me. "My poor Himiko. I wish I could have saved you from that."

"I'm surprised it hit me so hard," I said. "Our clan was attacked. Father is—was our chieftain, Aki and Shoichi were grown men. They'd be the ones leading our warriors against the enemy. What was I expecting to hear? That by a miracle they would all survive the battle unharmed?

I knew that was impossible, and yet"—a sigh shuddered
through me—"and yet I still hoped for it. If that was wrong,
the gods have taught me a hard lesson. Not one of them
lives, not one."

I got to my feet and looked down at Kaya. "Will you
come with me?"

"Where are you going?"

"I have to go home. I need to see what's left. And then
I must perform the rites for the spirits of my kin."

"But it's getting dark outside, and Master Michio told
us to wait here," Kaya protested.

"I've waited long enough. Come with me or stay behind, but I'm going." I headed for the doorway.

I had just ducked my head and stepped outside when I
stumbled into our clan shaman returning from his errand.
He was not alone.

"Himiko?" My brother Masa looked like a ghost in the
wintry twilight. It was too dim to see his expression, but
his voice held a mixture of disbelief and joy. "Himiko, it *is*
you! When Master Michio told me, I couldn't believe—Oh,
thank the spirits, you're safe!"

I fell into his arms and clung to him, shaking. I felt that
if I let go, a whirlwind would sweep in and carry him away
from me too.

"What's going on out there?" A gray-haired woman
peered out of her nearby house and stared at us. A second house, this one with part of its roof gone, produced
a young mother with a wide-eyed toddler on her hip. A
grimy-faced little boy edged past her to get a better view.
Before long a small crowd had formed around Masa and

me. They were mostly women, children, and the old. It was a comfort to find myself among the familiar faces of my clanfolk, but I mourned to see how few of these belonged to our young men, our nobles, our hunters, and all those who would have defended our village.

"It's Lady Himiko!" someone shouted.

"Truly? Where's she been?"

"I heard she got lost in the mountains."

"Lost and eaten by wolves, that's what I was told."

"Huh. We were *all* eaten by wolves," a glum voice declared, meaning the Ookami. "She looks like she came out of it better than we did."

"Where have you been, Lady Himiko?"

A whisper hissed past me: "Does she know about her family? About her father and the rest?"

Another one replied: "*Shhh!* If she doesn't know yet, better if the news comes from Masa. It will be kinder that way."

"Why should *she* have special treatment?" I recognized Suzu's harsh voice at once. When we were children, she had bullied her way into becoming leader of all our agemates. We played together, but she resented me for being a chieftain's daughter and she turned the rest of the girls against me. "She's been spared enough! She wasn't here when the wolf clan came; she didn't have to *see* her father die! I had to *watch* while they took my little sister away with the rest of the slaves, but she gets to be sheltered from it all? Is the pampered little princess too weak to meet the truth? Does she melt in the rain? Is she—?"

A sudden slap rang out, followed by a yelp from Suzu, then silence.

"Don't hit her!" I called into the gathering shadows.
"She hasn't said anything wrong. I was *not* here when we
were attacked. I know that my father and my two eldest
brothers died in battle. All I want is to go home to mourn
them properly, and to give thanks for the family I have left."

The people murmured their approval, yet there was a
strange note in their voices. I thought I caught a few more
whispers—*"soon enough, poor girl . . . tell her now or . . . Masa
should be the one who . . ."*—but before I could question anyone, Kaya stepped out of Master Michio's house and the
crowd moved their attention toward her. By the time I introduced her to my clan, night had fallen. Even though the
snow had melted, a cold, cutting wind reminded us that
we faced a long time until spring. Everyone retreated to
their homes, leaving Masa, Kaya, Master Michio, and me
behind.

The shaman clicked his tongue and exchanged a look
with Kaya. "Not a worthy welcome for you, Lady Badger,
but cold always gets the better of curiosity." He hunched
his shoulders. "I could use some warmth myself, now that
I've placed you in Masa's hands. We will talk again in the
morning." With that, he ducked into his house.

Masa looked at Kaya. "Lady Badger?" he repeated.

"I'll explain later," I said. "Right now—"

"I know; you want to go home. I'll escort you there."
He started walking the well-remembered path.

I matched him step for step. "Masa, I know the way
myself. There's no need for you to go out of your way like
this. Won't your wife have your evening meal waiting? In
this weather, you should eat it while it's hot."

"Hot or cold, there's not that much of it," Masa replied. "Don't worry about Fusa. She knows I won't be back until I see you well settled at home."

"Why would you have to do that?" I asked.

Kaya answered for him: "Maybe he needs to give your mother some warning. She's been caught in a landslide of tragedies, so many losses crashing down on her all at once. She shouldn't have a fresh shock."

"Yes, exactly, your friend is right!" Masa exclaimed a little too quickly. "That's why I need to be there when Mother sees you, to make sure it's not too much for her."

It was useless to argue with him. I let Masa conduct me home as if I were as much of a stranger there as Kaya. He climbed the carved ladder ahead of me and dashed into the house before I could set foot on the high wooden platform in front of our doorway. As I turned to offer Kaya a hand up, I heard him talking to Yukari, the youngest of Father's three wives. Her gasp of surprise was loud, but then she immediately dropped her voice to an almost inaudible murmur. I was about to enter the house to find out what was going on when I heard her clearly say, "Let me tell her," and she stepped out of our doorway onto the platform.

"Tell me what?" I asked.

"Ah! So you overheard." My younger stepmother sounded beaten down by weariness. "We've missed you, dear one. All of us were terribly worried when you didn't come home that evening. Your father and Aki argued about where to look for—"

"I know all that from Master Michio," I said evenly. "If there's nothing more, can we please go inside? This is

Kaya, daughter of Lady Ikumi, who is chieftess and shaman of the Shika clan." I waved to where my friend stood
waiting at the edge of the platform. "We've come a long way
since daybreak, and it's getting colder."

"Oh, Himiko, forgive me!" Yukari exclaimed. "And
you, Lady Kaya, I beg your pardon for such rudeness. It's
only that there is something my daughter should know, a
warning I must give her before she sees—before she is prepared to see—"

A terrified shriek sounded from within the house. A
small shape came running out onto the platform so fast that
it would have plunged over the edge if Kaya hadn't snagged
it and pulled it back to safety. It squealed and thrashed in
her arms, desperately calling, "Mama! Mama! Save me!"

"Takehiko?" Clouds veiled the moon, leaving me little
light by which to see the face of Yukari's son, one of my
three younger brothers.

"May the gods have mercy, not again, not now!" Yukari
cried, retrieving her boy from Kaya and scooping him up
into her arms. She was weeping.

"It was my fault." Masa stood in the doorway, flicker-
ing firelight at his back. "I should have watched her more
closely. I only turned aside for a moment when she grabbed
him."

A shadow rose behind him, and I heard a wail so desolate it was barely human. Had Master Michio failed to perform the proper rites for Father, Aki, and Shoichi? Was our
home now haunted by their spirits?

"What did I do to you, my sweet little boy?" the shadow
groaned pitifully. Pale hands thrust themselves past Masa,

grasping the air, and a gaunt face with dark smears for eyes and mouth leaned heavily against his side. "All I wanted to do was hold you on my lap and feed you your evening meal. Why did you run away from me, my darling? Tell Mama. I'll give you whatever you ask. Don't you leave me too, my precious Noboru!"

With an extraordinary effort, my mother shoved Masa out of the way and lurched through the door. She lunged for Takehiko, crooning my brother Noboru's name. The child screamed and buried his face against his mother's shoulder. Yukari drew back without looking, coming perilously close to the platform edge.

"Mama!" I shouted and threw myself on my mother, wrapping my arms around her from behind and pulling her close. As she struggled to escape me, I spoke urgently in her ear: "Mama, what's wrong with you? Stop, I beg you, stop, you're scaring Takehiko. Oh, Mama, please let me help you!"

As if my words held magic, my mother ceased struggling and relaxed completely. "Himiko?" Her voice wavered. Without releasing her from my embrace, I gave her enough freedom to turn and see my face. Even in the darkness, her smile was radiant. "Oh, my darling daughter, I thought I'd lost you too!" She collapsed against me, laughing and sobbing.

I spent a restless first night home. As tired as I was from my journey, I could only catch a few short, troubled periods of sleep. Whenever I felt myself sinking into dreams, a host of demons sprang up to jolt me awake. They leered and clashed their tusked jaws, chittering like a cloud of bats as they reminded me over and over of all the appalling things I had faced in the short time since I'd returned.

I finally decided to give up any hope of real rest and rose to prepare myself for the new day. I sat up and looked around. Bright sunlight was streaming through the door, and the air was crisp and refreshing, and not as cold as the previous night. I took a deep, hungry breath of it, reveling in the familiar smells of my home, my village, my place in the world.

Still asleep in the bedroll to my right, Kaya snuffled and muttered, then flung herself onto her back with a snore that made me giggle. Mama lay to my left, her hand knotted in the fabric of my bedroll. I took care not to disturb her when I stood up and began the morning chores.

"Himiko?" Yukari's sleepy voice called out softly as she rolled over to face me. She had stowed her son in the corner of our house that lay as far as possible from where Mama slept and had passed the night curled protectively around him, a human palisade.

"Good morning, Yukari," I said as cheerily as I could, kneeling beside her. "Shall I make our breakfast?"

"You'd better let me do that," she said, pushing her way out of the bedroll.

"Why? You're making me feel like a stranger. Kaya's our guest, not me."

"It's not that, dear one. I welcome having you back to help me with the household duties. It's just that I want to show you the changes we've been forced to make since—"

"Changes?" I recalled the scanty meal Master Michio

had served last night. "Oh. Of course. You don't want me cooking more food than we can afford."

"What a smart young lady." Yukari smiled sadly. "You'll learn quickly about the way we do things now, and soon I can spend my days at leisure while you take care of all the housework." It was good to hear her laugh, even if it sounded halfhearted.

I leaned closer. "Yukari, I've only been able to get bits and pieces of what happened here. Before Mama wakes up, can you tell me everything?"

She looked confused. "But you said that Master Michio already—"

"Not about the battle. Tell me what happened *here,* within *these* walls, to *this* household." I clasped her hands. "To us."

Yukari tilted her head back and stared at the beams of our house as though seeking beloved ghosts in the shadows. "When the Ookami first broke through our gates, I was outside on the platform with Takehiko. We weren't supposed to be there. Before your father went forth to face the enemy, he ordered us to stay inside, out of sight, but Takehiko refused to be pent up. He kept squirming away from me and dashing out the door, time after time. I think he would have scrambled down the ladder and straight into the heart of the battle if I hadn't caught him and dragged him back. Finally I gave in and said he could watch things from the porch as long as I was with him. Your mother scolded us both, but stayed where she'd been told, indoors with Emi and their little ones."

She closed her eyes and her body sagged with a great

weariness. "That was why Takehiko and I were the first to see the moment when our men lost the fight. I pray that my boy didn't see *too* much of what happened there below, but I know that he must have seen something of the horror: he didn't resist at all when I swept him up into my arms and held his face against my shoulder. I remember shouting back into the house, 'They've won, the wolf clan's won, our men are falling! We have to get away! Hurry, hurry, run!'" She looked at me again, her pretty face transformed with sorrow. "I don't know how I managed to race down the ladder while carrying my son. Perhaps the spirits gave me strength. I ducked under the house where we keep the big storage jars and put Takehiko inside an empty one, then hid nearby."

"Weren't you afraid that the Ookami would discover him when they came to steal our rice?" I asked.

She shook her head. "I thought of that. Strange, how calm I became when I was trying to protect my boy. It was as if I were planning what to do on an ordinary day—clear away the bedrolls, clean up after breakfast, tidy the house, first this, then that, one, two, three." Tears slipped down her face. "Before I put Takehiko in the empty jar, I rolled it to where we pile the broken ones and heaped shards over it. I reasoned that shattered jars don't hold rice, so the Ookami would ignore them. At first he clung to me and balked at going into the jar, but I screeched at him like a crazy"—she glanced at my mother's sleeping form and guiltily snatched back the word—"like a wild creature. I terrified him into obedience, then found another pile of debris away from the full jars and hid myself. Then we waited for it all to be over.

"That was the hardest part. I had managed to scoop pottery fragments over myself, but knew I wasn't completely covered. All I could do was lie in the dirt, my face in my arms, my lips moving constantly in silent prayer, and hear our enemies' shouts of triumph come closer and closer, listen to them pounding up our ladder, to the sound of heavy footsteps on the floorboards above my head, to more of the wolves laughing nearby as they swarmed around the pillars of our house, ordering our own people to trundle out the filled storage jars from underneath. Perhaps it was a blessing that they made others do their dirty work: it meant that the Ookami didn't come near my hiding place, and if any of our clanfolk caught a glimpse of me, they didn't betray my presence. The debt I owe them can never be repaid."

Takehiko whimpered in his sleep. The sound made Yukari lurch toward him as though a rope bound her and the end of it was in his tiny hands. At the last possible moment she stopped herself from seizing him, sat back, and gave me a sheepish look.

"I'm sorry. He suffers from nightmares and I've gotten into the habit of rousing him before he can scream himself awake. I often mistake the sounds of ordinary sleep for the onset of those evil dreams, and then we're both fretful from lack of sleep."

"I understand," I said, patting her arm. "Do you think he'll wake soon? You still haven't told me—"

"—what happened to the others?" Yukari's glance darted toward the doorway, as if she were contemplating a fresh flight. Her once-pretty face was wan and strained.

"Himiko—" Her voice rasped. "Himiko, do you hate me too?"

The question took me off guard. "Where did you get such an idea? You and Emi raised me with as much tenderness as Mama ever did, and I love you!" I hugged her fiercely. "Why would I ever hate you?"

She pushed me away and hunched herself over until she seemed as small as a girl. "Because it's my fault that our family is broken," she said. "When danger came, I saved my son and myself, but I left everyone else behind."

"Yukari, you did everything that you could for them," I reassured her. "You saw the enemy coming and gave them as much warning as you had for yourself. It's not your responsibility if they didn't heed you."

She shook her head violently. "I should have done more. I should have stayed with them. We are a *family*. We must all share the same fate. What's wrong with me? Do I really believe that I am better than they are? Am I a coward? Did I—?"

"Who said such things to you?" I asked softly. But my heart knew the answer.

Yukari looked like a remorseful child. "It doesn't matter; it's true. I lay hidden under the pottery shards until nightfall, then coaxed Takehiko out of his refuge and carried him away to my aunt's house. It's very small and out of the way, so I thought it would be safe. I didn't want the Ookami to know that Takehiko was a chieftain's son."

"That was very wise of you."

"It was selfish too."

"Yukari, you were *not*—"

She wouldn't listen to me. "When the Ookami left, I went home. Your mother was the only one left. Our enemies had taken many slaves back to their village. They took Emi because she was our chieftain's wife. They took Sanjirou and Noboru because they were his sons."

"Not Masa?" I asked. "Not Mama?"

"They never guessed Masa was nobly born because he works as a blacksmith. As for your mother . . ." Yukari nibbled her lower lip nervously. "When I returned, she was— she was acting the same way you saw her last night. She threw herself at me, shrieking and clawing at Takehiko. My screams brought our nearest surviving neighbors and Master Michio. While he calmed her and cared for her, someone else told me what had happened while—"

"Himiko?" Mama's plaintive cry came from across the room. "Himiko, where are you? *Where are you?*" Her voice rose sharply and turned shrill with panic.

I rushed to her side, taking her into my arms to reassure her. It was as if some wickedly playful spirit had cast a spell to turn me into the mother and her into the child. She was shaking badly, her fingers gripping me so tightly I yelped with pain. The sound startled her into letting go.

"Oh! What have I done to you, my precious one?" she exclaimed, gently cupping my face in her hands. "I'm sorry, I must have been suffering from a bad dream. You must be hungry. Let me make breakfast. It's so good to have you home again!"

By the time Kaya awoke, yawning, both Mama and Yukari were busily at work preparing our morning meal.

My mother had countless questions for Kaya, and though
our provisions were now limited, she saw to it that my
friend was offered the best of what little we had to share.
She behaved with the poise and dignity befitting a chieftain's widow, and spoke briefly about how she had supervised the proper burial of Father, Aki, and Shoichi.

"It was not easy—we had many dead to bury and not
enough able-bodied men to break the ground—but I led
the women who helped complete that task. I will show you
where they lie, Himiko, but not today. For some reason, I am
very tired this morning, even though I had a restful night."
She folded her hands in her lap. "I always sleep well, knowing I have done my duty to my husband and my sons."

Takehiko's wide-eyed, fearful stare whenever he looked
in Mama's direction was the only sign that yesterday's outburst had happened. Everything seemed normal, but a frozen pond can seem strong enough to walk on until the thin
ice breaks and you plunge in.

After we finished eating, Kaya attempted to clean up,
but Mama wouldn't hear of it. "You are our guest and we
owe you thanks for bringing Himiko back to us," she said.
"You are welcome in this house for as long as you like. I
wish we could give you better hospitality, but you know our
circumstances."

"If you won't let me clear away the dishes, maybe I can
fill them for you," Kaya said, a toss of her head indicating
where she'd placed her bow and quiver. "I don't know how
much game you have around here at this time of year, but I
think I can manage to bring down something."

"We would appreciate that." Mama smiled faintly. "The

Ookami have not left us many hunters, nor many weapons for them to use. If you do have good luck, I hope you will bring down enough game for us to share with a few of our neighbors. Some of them are in a much worse situation than we are."

"I'll pray that the spirits will favor me in the hunt," Kaya said cheerfully.

"The spirits . . ." Mama's face turned hard. "The spirits are for fools. The spirits are ashes and air." She spoke with so much icy bitterness that I shivered to hear her.

Kaya looked at Mama uneasily. "Well, I should go," she said. "The light doesn't last long in this season. The longer I have to hunt, the better."

"Go with her, Himiko," Mama said. She was smiling again, but such an unnaturally taut, artificial grimace that it was more disturbing than her grim expression. "We won't need your help for anything today." She looked directly at Takehiko, who pressed himself against his mother.

A sudden inspiration struck me. "Little Brother, would you like to come with me?" I asked him mildly. "I've missed you." With a small cry of relief, he rushed into my arms.

"Where are you taking my sweet boy, Himiko?" Mama asked, her words trembling on the chill air. "You shouldn't go. You should stay here, where your father told us to wait. It's not safe out there. The enemy is coming!"

Yukari touched my mother's shoulder. "The enemy is gone. It's over. Let the children go." I had never heard her sound so old.

"Gone?" Mama looked momentarily lost. She blinked rapidly, then nodded. "Ah, yes. They are. I forgot. Well, go, then. Go." She rose to her feet and began gathering up the breakfast dishes. Kaya and I exchanged an uncertain look, but Yukari made urgent shooing motions, so we left, my half brother clinging to my neck all the way out of the house and down the ladder. When I set him down, he latched on to my hand with an astonishing grip and walked as fast as he could, putting distance between us and home.

In the morning light the remains of our sacred pine tree stood as a painful reminder of what had happened to my village. It made my heart ache to see it, even in passing. The ghost of the towering tree rippled before my eyes. I had climbed his branches when I was small, trying to prove to my adored big brother, Aki, that I was worthy to be taught the hunter's way. Just when my moment of triumph seemed assured, I lost my hold on the high limbs and plummeted toward the ground. All that saved me was a pair of curving branches like outstretched arms that interrupted my fall.

You saved me, Grandfather Pine, I thought. *I wish I could have saved you.* Silently I made a promise to dance for the pine tree's spirit, since that was all that I could do for him now.

"That was strange," Kaya remarked as we walked to the ruined gate. Her words jolted me out of my musings.

"What was—?"

"Back there. In your house." She looked at me over the top of Takehiko's head and mouthed: *Your mother.*

"I know. One moment she seemed perfectly normal, and the next—" I winced. Takehiko was holding my hand so tightly that it hurt. "Little Brother, you're going to break my fingers."

"Sorry," he muttered. "Don't take me back. I'll be good."

I picked him up and bounced him on my hip, smiling. "We're not going back until it's time to eat again, I promise. I do want to spend some time with you."

"Thank you, Himiko," he said, and buried his cold little nose against my neck.

"Are you two going to come on the hunt with me?" Kaya asked.

I shook my head. "We'd scare off all the game. Besides, I still have much to find out about what happened here, and things that I need to do." *Like visiting graves,* I thought sadly. *Though I doubt I can do that while I have Takehiko with me.*

We saw Kaya off at the gateway. My little brother regained enough courage to raise his head from my shoulder and wave to her as she strode away. He even called out "Good hunting!" in his reedy voice.

"Well done, Takehiko!" My praise made him beam with pride, and soon he was fidgeting in my arms, eager to be set down so that he could run about on his own. He was giggling and frolicking in ever-widening circles around me as I made my way to the blacksmith's forge. I had some questions for my remaining older brother, Masa.

As Takehiko and I walked through our village, I saw my clanfolk hard at the day's work. Many were diligently engaged in mending the houses that had not been completely destroyed. Others were heading out the gateway, some probably in search of material for those repairs, more of them likely on their way to gather whatever wild edibles the fields and forests would yield. If we Matsu were to survive the approaching hunger of winter, we would need to find whatever foods we could to replace our stolen rice.

I greeted everyone, but was surprised and hurt when their responses were cool at best, silent at worst. Why was everyone scowling at me? What had I done? I decided to seek out Master Michio, to see if he might have some explanation for everyone's odd behavior.

"He's probably not at home," I murmured to myself. "He'd be out, looking after the wounded, but if I find him, perhaps I could help—"

"What did you say, Big Sister?" Takehiko asked.

I stooped to his level. "I said that since I'm back, I can help Master Michio take care of people. Would you like to do that too?"

"Maybe . . ." Takehiko looked ill at ease.

"What's the matter, Little Brother?"

"I—I don't know if I can be—be near Master Michio. He's our sha-shaman. He talks to the spirits. Papa's a spirit now. What if I do something wrong and Master Michio tells Papa and Papa comes back and yells at me? What if Papa looks diff-different? Like—like an *oni*?" He shuddered when he mentioned the mountain ogre whose terrifying appearance—horned, tusked, towering, grotesque, and brutish—haunted children's bad dreams.

"Master Michio is too kind and patient to do such a thing to you, dear one," I comforted him. "And your papa would never let you see him as a monster. He loved you very much, and his spirit will protect you always."

Takehiko seemed reluctant to accept that. "How do you know?" he challenged me. "Can *you* talk to the spirits?"

I took his hands in mine. "Yes, I can."

He gaped at me, then yanked his hands away and

"You can*not*!"

"Yes, I can," I repeated. "I'm a shaman like Master Michio, and I have spoken with the spirits. Not with our papa's spirit," I hastened to add. "I don't know if I can do that until I try, but I have spoken with others."

My little brother frowned. "Oh, you *liar*," he declared. His fear was gone, burned away by indignation. "I'm telling my mama, and she'll tell *your* mama, and then you'll be in trouble!"

He was a small ball of fury, buzzing at me like a wet wasp. I forced myself not to laugh, though I did smile at him. "Will you believe me if Master Michio says the same thing?" I offered him my hand.

He pursed his lips and took it. "Maybe."

"Then let's go and talk to him right now. I was going to go see our brother Masa first, but I think that can wait."

"Yes." Takehiko nodded. "Master Michio's house smells better than Masa's forge. It's scary, but it's not as hot and noisy. Good."

We walked toward the shaman's house, passing more of our clanfolk. No one greeted me unless I spoke first until we encountered one of Father's old friends, Lord Hideki. One of the gray-haired noble's arms was thickly bandaged and swung limp at his side, but he still had the powerful stride of a much younger man and moved purposefully to intercept us. Planting himself in our path, he narrowed his eyes at me and glared.

"May the gods forgive me for doubting my neighbors, it's true," he snarled.

"Lord Hideki?" I wavered, so taken aback by his bare-faced ill will that I neglected to greet him with the proper deference. Even though I was a chieftain's daughter, I owed this man some show of reverence for his age and position in our clan.

"Look at you." His scornful gaze swept over me. "Traipsing along as if nothing happened, no more heart in you than in an empty eggshell, not a single sign of respect for your father and brothers! Did their deaths really mean so little? Or do you fancy that you're too good to share in our mourning?"

I gasped, suddenly aware of what this man's words meant. I had been so tired from my trip home and so shocked by my mother's affliction that I had not exchanged my ordinary clothing for the hemp garments we wore to honor the spirits of our beloved dead. Glancing to either side, I only then noticed that everyone in our village was wearing hemp, even little Takehiko.

"My clothes!" I cried, clutching the front of my dress. "Oh, Lord Hideki, I'm so sorry, I didn't—! I wasn't—!" Without another word I fell to my knees and pressed my forehead to the dirt, consumed with shame.

As I huddled there, I heard my little brother begin to whimper, but I was too mortified to stir. A mean-souled burst of laughter came from somewhere, but Lord Hideki barked a command that silenced whoever was enjoying my humiliation.

I heard a woman's persuasive voice say, "Lord Hideki, could it be that she isn't properly dressed because . . . because of how things are in her house, these days? There was another incident last night, over this little boy again. After such a homecoming—"

"All right, all right, never mind." Lord Hideki sounded impatient and irritable. Strong hands touched my bent back. "Get up, Lady Himiko," he said gruffly.

I lifted my head slowly, my vision blurry with tears. Takehiko was also weeping. "Lord Hideki, I apologize with all my heart for—"

"No." He looked embarrassed. "No apology, none, unless it is mine. I have known you since your birth. I should have also known that you would never act with such disregard for the spirits of your father and brothers, especially Aki. Everyone in our clan saw the bond between you two. I am a short-tempered old man who should learn to hold his tongue."

I rose to my feet and beckoned Takehiko to my side. With one arm sheltering my little brother, I replied, "You were one of my father's closest friends and most valued counselors. Right or wrong, you were angry at me for his sake. I can understand that. I will go home at once and put on more appropriate clothes."

The older man gave me a stern but approving look. "Your father was right to cherish you, Lady Himiko. Please let me atone for my outburst. Your house might not have any hempen garments to fit you, but I still have my late wife's clothing, including her mourning dress. Will you accept it as a token of friendship between us?"

I smiled at him. "It would be an honor, Lord Hideki."

It did not take long for Lord Hideki to bring us to his home, though it was not the same one he had inhabited

before the Ookami came. As a noble, he had enjoyed the
grandeur of a house like ours, raised high on sturdy pillars. The place to which he brought us was one of the
common pit houses, and one with a badly thatched roof.
When he caught sight of my questioning expression, he
shrugged and said: "My home was ruined. I was lucky that
they didn't order it burned as well as knocked to pieces and
pulled down. I was able to rescue most of my belongings
from the wreckage. I am living with my cousin until we can
rebuild in the spring, if the gods allow it."

Takehiko and I followed him into the small house.
Lord Hideki's cousin was a plump older woman who was
usually one of the liveliest people in our clan. When we
entered, however, she was still curled up in her bedroll, her
whole body shaking with a bad cough. Her wheezing breath
filled the house.

Lord Hideki clicked his tongue. "Poor woman. It will
be a miracle if she lives to see the cherry trees bloom again."
He spoke quietly, so that she would not be able to overhear
his pessimistic words.

I cocked my head in her direction and listened to the
rasp and squeak as she inhaled and exhaled. "That doesn't
sound *too* bad," I murmured for his ears only. "Master
Michio has cured our clanfolk of worse coughs." *And so
have I,* I thought, recalling all of the times that my teacher
had allowed me to be the one to diagnose his patients in
secret and compound the medicines that made them well.

"Master Michio has more pressing matters than one
old woman's cough." Lord Hideki was grim.

"Ah. The wounded." I nodded. "How many?"

"Every house that is still standing holds at least one," he told me. After an uneasy pause he added: "Except yours. But your roof shelters its own troubles."

He motioned for Takehiko and me to stay where we were, in order not to disturb his ailing relative, and went into a corner of the house to seek the mourning garb he had promised me. When he returned with the hemp gown draped over his good arm, we went back outside.

I held the dress up to my shoulders. "This will fit me very well," I said. "Thank you, Lord Hideki."

"No thanks are needed," he replied. "Only your pardon for having misjudged you so badly. Our world has been turned on its head, but that is no reason to treat one another unjustly."

"Takehiko! Takehiko!" A little boy came running up to us. "Izo found a toad, a *big* one, and it's only got one eye, right in the middle of its head! Come and see!"

My little brother looked up at me. "Can I go, Big Sister? Please?" He asked politely, but he was already trying to twist his hand out of my grasp and was pulling away from me.

"Go, but promise me you and your friends won't torment the poor animal."

He looked offended. "We're only going to *look* at it."

"That's all right. Enjoy yourselves. Just make sure you don't return home before finding me again. We left together and if we don't come back together it will make your mama fret."

"Oh, I'll *never* go back without you, Big Sister," he said, his eyes like an owl's. "I don't want to be there alone." With that, he and his friend ran off.

Lord Hideki's eyes remained stony, but he managed a smile. "It is very good to see the children returning to their games, especially your little brother."

"Everyone must know how things are for him at home now," I said.

"We are all kin, all part of one clan," the old nobleman replied. "This village is not large enough to hide many secrets."

"Then why has nothing been done about it?" I demanded. "Why doesn't Yukari take her son to live with her aunt until Mama is well again? The child is terrified!"

"She tried to leave once. Your mother ran after them, howling like a beast in agony and threatening to summon your father's avenging ghost to destroy the whole clan if those two did not come home."

"What ghosts could she summon? My mother is no shaman!"

He shrugged as well as he could with a wounded arm. "No one wanted to put that to the test. The council of nobles—those of us that remain—urged Yukari to go back, and she did. Maybe it was fear that convinced her, but I think it was compassion for one she loves. She did not witness what happened to your poor mother, but she was told all about it. A heart of iron would feel pity." He gritted his teeth. "I should have killed them."

"Lord Hideki?"

"Even with only one useful arm, I should have *tried*."

No need to ask who he meant when he said *them* with so much venom.

"What good would that have done?" I hesitated to speak bluntly to the old warrior, but I felt the need to do so, and to take the consequences. "Your death would have been a useless sacrifice. Use your life to help my mother heal. She has lost her husband and two of her sons in battle. Her youngest is lost to slavery. If you died trying to avenge all that, they would still be gone, and her spirit would carry the fresh burden of losing a good friend."

He sighed deeply and shook his head. "You were not there, child. You didn't see what else they did to her; I did. I was wounded early in the battle and was brought back for Master Michio to bind my arm. He had just finished when we heard the roar as the enemy broke through the gates and overran our village. We ran outside to see what was happening and stood by, helpless, as they invaded your house and dragged everyone outside.

"The Ookami leader gloated over your family, taking a demon's joy in telling them how your father had died. Emi burst into sobs, but your mother held herself steady. She spoke with wonderful dignity, telling that young monster, 'When the time comes for your death, pray to the gods that you will die as well as my chieftain died today.' Her words galled him to the bone; his face became a thundercloud. He wanted her tears, and when she refused to surrender, he took a step toward her, spear in hand, most likely intending to kill her where she stood. She met him eye to eye, unflinching, as great a warrior as your father ever was. But then . . ."

Lord Hideki bowed his head and rubbed his temples with his usable hand. It took him a few breaths before he could continue: "One of the wolf chieftain's men who'd been rummaging through your house came out onto the platform crying, 'Look at this, my lord!' There was a wolf's skull in his hands."

I tensed. I hadn't thought about that relic for ages. It was just another part of the furnishings of our house, a hunting trophy for which all three of my older brothers shared responsibility, each in his own way: the wolf was stalking Masa when Shoichi's arrow grazed its shoulder to make it turn, only to have Aki give it the death wound. My family saw that skull as a proud reminder of hunting skills, but the Ookami would not view it that way. The wolf was their guardian spirit, and they would see the wolf's skull as . . .

"Sacrilege," I breathed.

Lord Hideki inclined his head in agreement. "The Ookami were infuriated. They began shouting for their chieftain to order all of your family put to death to atone for the crime. For one awful instant it seemed as if he was going to heed them. He ordered his men to tear your youngest brother, Noboru, out of your mother's arms. She fought so desperately that it took two of them to do that, and two more to hold her back. He raised the skull above his head like a club, poised to strike the child down. May the gods spare me from the memory of your mother's scream!" He uttered a shuddering sigh. "In that moment, her mind shattered."

"But what about Noboru?" I cried, seizing his arm.

"Did Ryu—the chieftain—harm him?" Yukari had told me that my youngest brother was a slave, but what if she'd said so to shield me from worse news?

To my relief, Lord Hideki said, "Thank the gods, no, he did not hurt the child. I don't think he ever intended to do so. The Ookami chieftain has a cruel streak in his spirit, but once victory was his, he did not use his power over us brutally."

"Death and slavery and threatening to kill a child are not brutal?" I countered angrily.

My father's old friend looked at me with weary eyes. "There are crimes that happen in the wake of war, Lady Himiko. You are too young and inexperienced to know about them, and I pray you never do. The Ookami chieftain ordered many evils against us—taking our food, taking our people—but he gave *other* commands. Our women . . ." He closed his eyes and inhaled deeply. "Our daughters, our wives, our sisters, not one of them was touched by his men. He forbade it and they obeyed. He is young, but I could see that his warriors fear him. That fear was our good fortune. For that mercy, at least, we are grateful."

"I see." I bowed to Lord Hideki. "Thank you for this." I held up the hempen garment. "I will put it on as soon as I find Takehiko and bring him home."

This time my path through the village was a better one. My clanfolk saw me carrying the proper clothing for honoring the dead and no longer treated me coldly. Many of them left their chores to speak to me and express their sympathy for the losses our family had suffered. I was once more welcome among my kin.

As I looked for Takehiko, I thought about what the old warrior had said about Ryu's unexpected act of kindness in keeping his troops from attacking our women. My own experience with the wolf lord had been different. When his father, Lord Nago, had come here to propose an alliance between the Matsu and the Ookami, it was my role to entertain Ryu while the chieftains talked. The handsome wolf prince took a fancy to me, but his attempt at courtship failed when it revealed his selfishness, arrogance, and cold heart. He reacted to my rejection by trying to force himself on me. I made him pay for that, but I had the sour feeling he remembered how I had humiliated him.

I pressed my hands to my sash. It hid a small figurine, a clay image of a woman whose arms encircled a golden stone. A woman . . . a goddess, the goddess who had appeared to me in a marvelous vision not so long ago, a goddess who held the sun, a goddess who held us all in her heart.

Was this your doing, lovely one? I wondered. *If I had been here when Ryu attacked, instead of with the Shika clan, what would have become of me at his hands? I was spared that, but . . . was I spared for a greater purpose? Guide me, sweet lady! Let me find the path I am meant to climb and let me bring my people with me, to healing, to light!*

I found Takehiko with three other small boys. "How did you like the one-eyed toad?" I asked.

"Stupid thing had two eyes after all," one of the children replied sulkily.

I turned to my brother. "I must go home and change my clothing. Do you want to stay here and play with your friends? I'll come right back."

"Oh, you don't have to do that, Himiko," Takehiko said, dismissing me with a born lord's grand manner. "I can go home myself when it gets dark. I'm no baby."

"As you wish, Little Brother." I made an exaggerated gesture of reverence and left him there. It was good to see him acting like an ordinary child, free of fear if only for the time being.

No one was in our house when I returned. Mama and Yukari must have had work to do elsewhere, perhaps helping our neighbors. I took a deep breath of the familiar smells of home and basked in the feeling of peace those walls now contained. Would it be asking too much if I begged the gods to let this sense of harmony last?

I removed my dress and put on the hempen gown, securing my wand and the image of the sun goddess carefully with my sash before venturing outside again. There was something I had to do, a promise I ached to keep, an oath I could not fulfill while minding Takehiko. This was my chance. My brother was safe with his friends, and in this chilly weather I doubted the children would leave the village to go exploring. Besides, if they tried, there were many watchful eyes on them, many hands poised to drag them back from danger. My clan looked after its children.

I was not a child. Someone might see me leaving the village and casually ask where I was headed, but no one would forbid me to go. That was good. I did not want to speak about my destination. I was afraid that if I named the place, I would break down into helpless tears.

There were many fresh graves in our clan's burial ground; too many. Most were humble, but one stood out,

broad and high. A chieftain's tomb must reflect his status.
My father's resting place was not as large as some of the
others belonging to his ancestors, but its size was a testi-
mony to the respect of his people. In the midst of their own
grief, they had taken the time and given the labor to honor
him. The beaten earth walls had the look of being cast up
in haste by hands not used to this sort of project. Most
of our strongest men were dead, wounded, or enslaved, so
this tomb must have been the work of the very old, the very
young, and the women. It was a monument to a leader who
had been loved.

I laid my palms against the wall of my father's tomb
and whispered a farewell. There were two smaller tombs
beside his, also freshly built and higher than most of the
other grave sites. Was this where my brothers Shoichi and
Aki lay?

Aki . . . I closed my eyes and called out to his spirit. *Oh,
my dear big brother, are you still near? Can you hear me? When
I was on the homeward path I walked weighed down with sadness,
dreading the moment I would have to tell you that your beloved
bride, Hoshi, is dead. I thought that I had failed you when I could
not heal her. I shrank from the thought of seeing your grief, but
now . . . now I will never see your face again in this world. I can
only hear your laughter in my memory. I reach for your hand, but
all I touch is cold earth and empty air.*

"Aki!" My shout was loud and piercing as the sound
of rock striking rock. A flock of crows nested in a nearby
stand of pine trees took wing at the sound, cawing hoarsely
across the winter sky. "Aki! Father! Shoichi, hear me! I will
serve your spirits with love. I will make the offerings to ease

your passage into the unknown lands. I will sing the spells and perform the dances to honor you. And always—*always,* I will carry your lives with mine, in my memory and in my heart."

With the words of the first song of leave taking on my lips, I danced for my lost ones there, under a sky of iron, through a mist of tears.

3
READING THE LEAVES

My first teacher, Lady Yama, once told me that there are as many lessons in life as there are leaves in the forest. She was right; I could not count the number of things I learned in the cold days between my return home and the springtime. Some were pleasant surprises, some were enlightening, but one was this: terror is not gone just because you wish it so or because you fail to see it waiting in the shadows. The deer does not always know the hunter is there until he feels the shock of the arrow's strike and sees the feathered shaft quivering between his ribs just before he dies.

I returned from the burial ground and tried to settle myself back into the life of our clan. It was not the same life I had left behind me when I'd run off to Kaya's people. The day after my dance, the snow returned. It was a long winter for us all. Hunger made it so, although what we suffered was a far cry from starvation. The Ookami had not taken all of our food stores, not out of compassion, but cunning.

All of us Matsu were their slaves, whether we had been led away to their village or remained inside our own walls. They would take a share of all the crops we grew from now on, so it was in their best interests to leave us enough rice, beans, and millet to plant for them as well as barely enough to keep us healthy. Famished workers are weak and weak workers cannot raise good harvests for their masters.

Though the Ookami did not leave any of their men behind to oversee our labor, there was no doubt they would send a messenger from time to time to make certain we were behaving ourselves: a messenger, entering our gates boldly, or a spy, observing us secretly without our ever knowing he was near. If he saw any suspicious activity, any hint that we were plotting to throw the wolf clan's foot off our neck, it would be reported and would cost the lives of our kin who were their hostages. We were powerless, and the aggravation of facing our weakness day after day was infuriating.

Since we could not strike out against our enemy, some of us struck out against each other. There were more quarrels among my kin than I recalled ever having seen, vicious spats over trifles. Some of us turned our fury inward so that it ate away at our hearts, leaving behind only resignation and despair. It was a blessing that the children ignored their elders' bad choices. They did their chores and played their games as if little had changed, although sometimes they became the source of more frustration among the grown-ups. What could a mother or father do when their child pleaded with them for food that could not be spared? Frayed nerves kindled fresh disputes, and many

Matsu seemed to use their rage to keep themselves warm that winter.

The only people in our village who seemed immune from the plague of misdirected anger were Master Michio, Lord Hideki, Masa, and me. I did not have our shaman's good nature, the old warrior's steadiness, nor my brother's meek willingness to let others win any fight as long as they left him alone afterward. If I kept clear of the countless small storms seething through my clan, I owed it to their influence, their help, and above all, to my friend Kaya.

She returned from her first hunt with a trio of pheasants and the news that she'd seen fresh boar tracks in the hills. The Ookami had driven off all of our pigs, so this was important. Kaya remained with us for five more days, going off to track game every morning, always coming home with something for the pot. On the sixth day, she announced that she was returning to her clan.

"I will miss you with all my heart," I said, pressing my cheek to hers as we made our farewells at the gateway. "But I understand: you have to go back before the weather gets worse. You know, Masa volunteered to travel with you. He is still willing. Won't you reconsider his offer?"

She gave a bark of laughter. "And then who will bring Masa back here? Your brother is a good man, but I know the ways of the forest better than he. He's needed here, as a blacksmith and a peacemaker."

I made a wry face. It seemed as if he spent as much time at home, settling arguments between his wife, Fusa, and his sister-in-law, Toyo, as he spent working at the forge. Always generous, he had opened his home to Shoichi's widow while forgetting how bossy and shrewish she could be. Once her grief faded, Toyo tried to take over the running of the house. Fusa would not stand for that, and the battle was on, with Masa trapped in the middle.

"You should still let him go with you," I said. "He would welcome a few days of tranquility."

"And supposing he loses his footing on the path home and falls off a cliff?" Kaya teased, making a gesture to avert just such a catastrophe actually happening to my brother.

I performed the same warding-off sign as I replied: "Well, what could be more tranquil than that?" We parted with laughter. I did not expect to see my friend's face again until spring.

How surprised I was twelve days later when a clear, frosty morning brought Kaya back to our gates. She was carrying her faithful bow and arrows, but she also had a large, heavy-looking bag slung on her back beside the quiver. Her return attracted a crowd of curious onlookers. By the time I heard that my friend was back, it took me some effort to work my way through the crowd.

"Himiko!" Kaya called out cheerfully. "At least *you're* glad to see me, aren't you?"

"Of course I am, but"—I glanced at the faces ringing my friend. I saw many questioning expressions, but mostly suspicious looks and a few outright scowls—"I didn't think I would see you again so soon."

"Heh. The only reason I went home was to let my mother know I was going to be staying here for as long as I could be of help to you and these fine people." She made a sweeping gesture that included the now-grumbling crowd.

"She told me that I could remain with you for as long as I like."

"Isn't *that* generous," one of our women said scornfully. "One less mouth for her clan to feed this winter, one more for ours to fill, when we've got scarcely enough food for our own bellies."

"Hush!" someone else chided her. "Lady Himiko's friend is as highborn as she and a fine hunter. You didn't complain about her presence before, when she showed up at your door with a nice pheasant!"

"And what if her luck doesn't hold?" the first woman countered. "What if the game moves farther off, or vanishes? She'll have no kills to share with us then, but we'll still need to feed her."

"Actually, I was hoping this would help," Kaya said, letting the sack she was carrying fall to the ground. She opened it to show the precious contents to the crowd: "Rice. I'm sorry, but that was all I could carry on this trip. If the weather allows, I'll go back and see about bringing more."

The woman's attitude changed radically at the sight of Kaya's gift. "You did this for us? We aren't even your kin!"

"Do you want me to take the rice back, then?" Kaya asked, grinning. The woman goggled at her a moment, then realized she was being teased. The two of them burst into laughter.

No one questioned Kaya's presence after that. She was made to feel as much a member of the Matsu as her mother, Lady Ikumi, made me feel a member of the Shika. It didn't hurt matters that Kaya's luck in the hunt remained good.

Some of our remaining men recovered from their wounds enough to join her on the trail. Her talent as a tracker and an archer left them no room to question whether a girl belonged in a hunting party. Lady Badger's position was unassailable!

As I watched her come back from a successful hunt, laughing and joking with her companions, I couldn't avoid a pang of envy. *That was the life I wanted for myself, when I was small,* I thought. *Now I cannot imagine being anything but a shaman and a healer. Did the spirits guide me to this path, or was it always within me, dreaming, waiting for the right moment to awaken?* I shook my head. *Never mind that. I am no hunter, but I am also necessary to my people. Let that be enough for me.*

It was true: I *was* necessary to the Matsu clan. After that first awkward day after my return home, I woke up early and went straight to Master Michio. I found our shaman already up, preparing for his work. He was startled to see me awaiting him just beyond his threshold.

"Himiko? What brings you here? Is it your mother?" He had the look of a man bracing himself for bad news.

"She is well, Master Michio," I said, setting his mind at ease as quickly as possible. "She was her old self all day yesterday."

"I hope that will be the way of things from now on. Your return may be just the medicine her spirit craves in order to be healed." He cocked his head at me. "So, why *are* you here?"

He was carrying a basket filled with salves and other supplies. I took it from him and balanced it on one hip.

"I'm going to help you. We have so many wounded here that you have no time to look after any of our clanfolk with other troubles. The first thing I want to do is make a potion to help Lord Hideki's cousin breathe easier."

"Ah!" Master Michio wore an embarrassed smile. "I heard she wasn't well, but I haven't had the chance to see her yet."

"Of course not," I said. "One healer alone can't take care of everyone, but if there were two . . ."

" 'If'?" He beamed at me. "There *are* two, Himiko. As far as I'm concerned, this clan has been blessed with two healers for quite some time."

That first day, I accompanied Master Michio as he went from house to house, looking after the wounded. In the first home we entered, our patient was too weak to notice my presence, but his wives were both deeply shocked to see me. While they stood dumbstruck, my teacher turned to me and said, "I think you can handle this, Lady Himiko."

"With the help of the spirits, I can," I replied. I knelt beside the ailing warrior and raised a chant to invoke healing, then examined the man's bandages, changed one that was too worn for my liking, cleaned the wound, applied salve and a new dressing, and rose to my feet once more. The two women stared at me in silence for a moment, then started chattering so many questions that they made my head whirl. They had watched me grow up, but I wager they never expected to see me grow up to be a shaman!

"Enough, good ladies, enough!" Master Michio stepped in front of me and raised his hands. "Lady Himiko will be caring for your husband from now on. How fortunate you are to have her aid! And what an honor for you, that a Matsu princess will restore your beloved partner to health!"

The women heard him out, exchanged a look, and immediately began overwhelming me with thanks. As we departed, I turned to Master Michio and whispered, "Why did you have to make such a great deal out of my being a princess? That has nothing to do with my ability to heal!"

"No, but it might help some of our people accept your new status more easily," he replied. "Even in these sorrowful times, people remain people. The harmless little victories they score over one another give them pleasure. Those women might object to an untried *girl* attempting to heal their husband, but a *princess*? Wait until they tell the neighbors!"

"Won't I be helping their neighbors too?"

"I should hope so," he said serenely. "Starting now." He led me to the next house and the next, until every family that needed a shaman's help knew that none would be neglected.

Once they saw that I knew what I was doing, our people accepted my new role with remarkable ease. With two healers to tend to them, the wounded received better treatment and recovered more quickly. Those who suffered from other ills no longer felt shunted aside. Most important, my family had no trouble acknowledging what I had become.

Yukari was the first to confide her feelings: "Takehiko and I can rest easier knowing you have the power to heal, dear Himiko. Your mother has been much better since your return, yet who knows if it will last? Ah, but with a

shaman right here, at our own hearth—! I'll finally be able
to sleep nights without keeping one ear alert and one eye
open for any trouble."

Mama *was* doing better. When she heard about how I
was working with Master Michio, she said, "I understood
why your father was so opposed to this, but that doesn't
mean I agreed with him. You are my daughter too, and I
know you are no Lady Tsuki! May the gods witness the
truth—I think the only reason she has the biggest monument in our burial ground is to make sure she *stays* there!"
We shared a laugh, and in that moment I dared to imagine
our home had found peace once more.

It was a wonderful pleasure to be able to practice my
arts openly. What joy is there in singing a song in a whisper? Lady Tsuki's twisted nature had left Father with a
bone-deep suspicion of all shamans and forced me to spend
my time of training in secrecy, but that was over. I was free
to be my true self.

*If only it could have happened in some other way! If only Fa-
ther could have lived and been able to share my happiness!* These
were the thoughts that haunted me more than any ghost.

I mustn't think about that, I told myself as I went from
house to house, caring for the men who had survived battle
with our enemies. *He's gone, he and Shoichi and . . . and Aki. I
can't change that. Even if I had been here when they fell in battle,
I couldn't have done anything to alter what happened. Someday I
will see them again, but now . . .* I took the small and precious
image of my goddess from my sash and held her tenderly in
my cupped hands. *Sweet Lady, guide my eyes. Turn them to see
what* can *be changed. Let me look after the living.*

And so I found my place in the life of our clan that winter season. As day followed day I saw my duties as a healer dwindle. One by one, the people who received my care no longer needed it. I thanked the gods for every time I was able to tell a man, "I won't be coming back to see you tomorrow. Look, your wound is healed!" I sorrowed when my abilities were not enough and all that I could tell his family was, "I'm sorry," before I began to sing for the dead.

Master Michio advised me that the best way for the two of us to divide our duties was at random. "I mentioned your position as our princess in order to clear the way for you as a healer," he said. "Now that's accomplished, we don't want individual families competing to have you and only you to care for their sick and ailing. Since the Ookami left us with so little, some of our clanfolk grab any scrap of status to make themselves feel loftier than the rest. There's enough bickering in our village as it is; you mustn't add to it."

What he said was true. I'd noticed it myself. My former playmate, Suzu, had always carried an envy-born grudge against me, but since I'd been recognized as a shaman, she came seeking my exclusive help for her family. Oh, how she wheedled, pretending we'd always been the best of friends! Worse, she tried to win me over by muttering against Master Michio: *"Save us, Himiko! Don't leave us in that man's hands. He's growing old and inept; he makes dangerous mistakes, I'm sure of it! I swear, my poor cousin was worse after Master Michio took 'care' of him. Promise that you will be the only one to tend us? Pleeeeeease?"*

Kaya made a face when I told her about this. She was accompanying me into the forest to seek medicinal roots that might be hiding under the snow. "What nerve, talking about Master Michio that way!" she exclaimed. "I wish I'd been there. I would have given her a *reason* to need him." She slammed her fist into her palm.

"Tsk. Now poor Suzu's in trouble," I replied. "Lady Badger's going to tear her to shreds."

"Hmph! Lady Badger wouldn't soil her paws on that creature." Kaya looked haughty. "But you should have given her a swat with your wand, at the very least."

"My wand is *not* a weapon."

"Who says it is? Just hit her over the head with it and call it a blessing! A *hard* blessing." Her teeth flashed in a mischievous grin. "A blessing that would give her better manners."

"Ugh. I'd rather stay away from her than try to change her. You should have seen her when I said I couldn't promise to be her family's sole healer! That simpering mask vanished faster than you can blink."

"I can guess what was underneath it," Kaya said. "What a scowl that girl's got! She must be part *oni*."

"At least I'm used to *that* look on her face. It's honest, even if it's nasty enough to blight rice. I prefer it to her fake sweetness."

Kaya grabbed my arm and dug her chin into my shoulder. "Ohhhhhh, Himiko, don't say such awful, *awful* things about me!" she cooed in a too-accurate parody of Suzu's voice. "I can't *bear* thinking that you don't like me just because I turned all the other girls against you. You didn't really *mind* that, did you? Aren't you my dearest, most precious, best-of-all best friend in the *whole world*?" She tilted her head coyly and batted her eyelashes until we collapsed, laughing.

It was good to laugh. Little by little, my clan was rediscovering the way back to a world where we laughed more often than we wept. Laughter gave us strength to rebuild our houses. It comforted our bellies when our scant supplies fell short and let us look beyond the hardships of each dull winter day to the hope of a future springtime. The Ookami had broken our walls, collapsed our moat, torn down Grandfather Pine, but as long as we could laugh, they had not destroyed our courage, our heart, or our soul.

New homes rose. Old homes were repaired. Snow fell less often, then stopped. The flinty scent of the dead season's cold air began to carry a hint of returning greenery. Life was coming back to our village by many roads.

One morning I was awakened by a frantic child who dragged me to his mother's side so that I could help her give birth to a healthy baby girl. The young mother was one of our many recently made widows and her little son took his new responsibility as man of the house very seriously.

As I brought the new child into the light, the infant gave such a strong cry that it crossed the border between our world and the spirits' realm. For a moment, I sensed the presence of her departed father. "You have a fine daughter," I murmured, holding up the baby, and caught the flicker of his smile as he returned to his rest.

The infant's lusty cries roused the whole village and before any of us knew it, we had turned the occasion into a full-fledged festival that took place around the memory-haunted roots of Grandfather Pine.

The gods must have approved: Kaya decreed that no celebration was complete without good things to eat. She and the other hunters dashed off into the forest and returned with half a dozen wild pigs that they surprised in a narrow cleft in the hillside.

"Sorry they're so scrawny," Kaya said as the unlucky beasts were turned over to our cooks.

"Never mind that," came the jovial reply. "They're fat enough to be a banquet for us!"

"A banquet?" one old woman piped up. She nudged her sister and the two scuttled off. They returned carrying clay jars that turned out to contain rice wine.

"There's a few more hidden between the back of our house and the village wall," one of them announced. "Those filthy Ookami never even thought to search there!"

"Ha! That was *my* idea, stowing them there," her sister declared smugly. "The day I can't outsmart *that* flea-bitten pack of mongrels, I'll take myself to the burial ground!"

The addition of wine made our celebration seem even more like something from the happy days we'd known before the war. People sang and danced with abandon. Masa and his household sat with ours. His wife and sister-in-law were behaving as if they had been best friends since girlhood, with no bickering between them. I nudged Kaya and whispered:

"Look, little Takehiko's gone to sit in Mama's lap! You know what this means?"

My friend smiled. "He's not afraid. I *thought* I noticed him warming up to her."

"He used to adore her. Thank the spirits, she's healed! Now we can have our old lives back. Things will be different with the Ookami lording it over us, but who knows?

Someday we may find a way to break free of them. Things change; that means they can change *back* too." I looked at Takehiko, who was singing a song while my mother bounced him on one knee. My heart was bright with happiness.

I rejoiced too soon. I forgot the full meaning of words I'd just spoken: *Things change.*

The celebration went on, growing more boisterous by the moment. The newborn child who was the unwitting cause of so much revelry slept content in her mother's arms until one merrymaker got a little too close to the baby and bawled, "What're you gonna name her, eh?" The little one's startled yowls sent the man staggering back, knocking a bowl of wine out of another fellow's hand. Soon they were fighting.

The brawl spread. All the petty disagreements and frustrations that had been building up among my clanfolk erupted. The new mother looked on, horrified, but still too spent from childbirth to be able to get away quickly. Her infant wailed louder, which added to the rising din. Her son tried to protect his family, but he was much too small. I rushed to help them, Kaya close behind me. Together we stood guard over them, watchful in case any of the ongoing clashes came too close for comfort. Time after time we shoved and stiff-armed and blocked pairs of scuffling villagers. We shouted ourselves hoarse, trying to make them stop fighting, but our voices were too high-pitched to get anyone's attention.

"I wish I had one of Master Michio's bronze bells," I told Kaya as we struggled to remain standing in the midst of growing chaos. "*That* would get their attention."

"How—how do you mean?" she replied, panting for breath. "Ringing it or using it to thump a few empty heads? I know which *I'd* choose!"

Fortunately for my people, the set-to ended before Lady Badger could get her paws on any kind of weapon. A deep, authoritative voice resounded over the noise of battle: "*This* again? Stand down, you fools! Stop before I break your empty heads!"

Old Lord Hideki strode into the midst of the crowd, swinging a heavy piece of firewood. The brawlers scattered before him like rice husks in a high wind. I don't know if he ever intended to club his own kinsmen, but no one present was stupid enough to find that out the hard way. Within the time it takes for three breaths he was the only man left standing. The rest were sitting meekly with their families while their wives and sisters scolded them or exclaimed over their bruises and scrapes, *then* scolded them.

The men retreated, but Kaya and I remained standing while Lord Hideki ranted at our clan: "What is *wrong* with you? Are you trying to finish what the wolves started? Haven't we lost enough men? What is worth fighting over like this?" A few people tried to mutter shamefaced excuses for their behavior, but a single glare from the old warrior's eyes silenced them. His questions did not want answers.

Then, like the ash-covered ember that suddenly kindles into flame again, a woman spoke up: "I'll tell you what's worth fighting about!" she cried, pointing at the two elderly sisters who had provided the drink that had loosened my clanfolk's tongues and fogged their common sense. "Why did *they* have all that wine, eh? Why were they keeping it secret from the rest of us all this time? Come to think of

it, what else do you suppose they've been hiding? Why not rice wine *and* rice? While the rest of us starve, those old lizards have been gobbling good things all winter long! I say we go search their house and—!"

"Take one step that way and you'll find yourself taking the next one out of our gates!" Lord Hideki shouted, brandishing his cudgel. The woman flinched and hurriedly stepped back as he continued to berate her. "How dare you speak to your elders with such disrespect? You're not starving! A starving tongue doesn't have the strength to clatter like yours." Abruptly he turned to glare at my brother Masa. "*Now* do you see the truth of what I tell you?" he thundered. "This is your doing!"

Masa recoiled as if the older man's words were blows. Most of our people exchanged bewildered glances and began whispering furiously to each other, wondering what this was all about. The only ones who looked neither surprised nor confused by Lord Hideki's accusation against my brother were our remaining noblemen. Before the Ookami came, they had been Father's valued counselors. Now their stern eyes were focused on Masa. He squirmed under the burden of so many hard looks. His lips parted, but he could not find a voice to raise in his defense.

I could.

"Lord Hideki, what do you mean by speaking against my brother like this?" I asked. "He's done nothing wrong. I saw him trying to *stop* fights, not start them."

"Himiko, please . . ." Masa's cheeks were blotched red with embarrassment. "You don't know anything about this.

I'll speak with Lord Hideki about this later. It doesn't involve you."

"On the contrary, it involves all the Matsu!" Lord Hideki declared. His arms spread wide, embracing our gathered clan. "See what has become of us: we can't even mark a happy occasion without falling into more of these stupid little quarrels! It was never like this while we had a chieftain to direct us as one people, one kindred. Why have we fallen apart this way? Because the one who *should* lead us, the one whose ancestors have always guided this clan"—he glared at Masa—"says no."

I turned to my last remaining older brother. He looked ready to sink into the earth. "I have good reason for my choice, Lord Hideki," he said so quietly that it was nearly impossible to hear him. "I told you so already. Why do you keep at me like this?"

"Your father was my friend; we were close as brothers," came the grim reply. "He loved this land. He loved our people. The Matsu always came first in his heart. You are his son. How can you be too selfish and lazy to accept the responsibility of his heritage: to be our chieftain!"

"That's not why I refused! Why didn't you *listen* to me?" Masa's despairing plea rose shrill and loud, startling those nearest him. Takehiko took fright and tried to climb from my mother's lap into Yukari's arms but Mama enveloped him in her embrace, rocking back and forth until he sat with her calmly again.

"My brother is right," I said. "He should not lead us."

The old lord tightened his lips. "No one asked for your opinion."

"You *never* ask, Lord Hideki," I responded. "You decide. You direct. You choose and then you force your choices on everyone else. Why not choose to become our chieftain?"

His shaggy eyebrows came together. "I should slap that insult from your lips, girl. Do you think I am a thief to take what isn't mine? Your family has ruled the Matsu for as long as any man here can recall. The line of your blood is unbroken, and on my honor as your father's friend, I will see to it that this remains so!" he roared at me. "The wolves killed this clan's chieftain and two of his heirs, but as long as one survives, I will not rest until he accepts his obligation to his kin!"

If he thought he could make me back down with such a ferocious outburst he soon learned I was as stubborn as he. "Did you ever *listen* to Masa's reasons for refusing to be our chieftain?"

"Pff! They weren't reasons; they were excuses. He claims he can't be our chieftain and our blacksmith too." He dismissed this with a curt wave of one hand. "His wife's father was our blacksmith before, and he isn't too old to take up the job again. Your brother also insists he knows nothing about how to use weapons. We lost the war! Why would our chieftain need to fight for us now? Last of all, he wants us to believe he can't make others follow him. Ridiculous! Why couldn't he make others obey him—?"

"—when they won't even pay attention to him?" I asked evenly. "*You* don't."

"It's true," Masa said, eyes downcast. "I know who I am. I'm a good blacksmith, a good neighbor, and—and I hope I'm a good husband." He glanced at his wife Fusa, who gave him a loving look and squeezed his arm protectively. "I would not be a good chieftain. I don't deny that we need one, I'm just saying it shouldn't be me."

"But you are our chieftain's only living son!" one of the other gray-haired nobles shouted. He should have said *"grown* son," but was too eager to take Lord Hideki's side to speak accurately.

Such a small slip of the tongue shouldn't have been important. I noticed it, but imagined I was the only one.

"Only . . . living . . . son?"

The words were slivers of ice melting against my spine. They trembled on the air as my mother rose to her feet, clutching Takehiko close, and stepped toward the man who had spoken. Her eyes glowed with a strange brilliance. She looked like something from another world, a place of eternal night and unending horror. The clan elder was no coward, yet he backed away at her approach. Takehiko squirmed and kicked, whimpering for his mother, but when Yukari tried to take him from Mama's arms she got a vicious kick that sent her staggering.

"Keep away from us!" Mama screamed, tightening her grip on the terrified child. "You're insane! You want to hurt my precious Noboru, but I won't let you! I'm a good mother; I'll never let anyone take my baby from me. I will always protect him, *always*! Just because your child is gone, you think you can steal mine? And *you*!" She made a blood-chilling face at our gathered clan. "She's turned all of you against us. I know! You think I don't hear the lies? You call *my* son by *her* son's name! There's only one reason I've allowed you to get away with such hatefulness, such falsehood: because we know the truth, my precious Noboru and I. Isn't that right, my love?" She pressed her lips to the top of Takehiko's head.

My little brother uttered a half-smothered protest, then jerked his head up. "I'm not Noboru!" he yelled in Mama's face. Small as he was, he fought and pushed his way out of her arms and ran to Yukari. My stepmother seized her son and darted to Lord Hideki's side, seeking protection.

Mama stared at her empty arms, then collapsed into a wailing huddle of pain and misery. "Demon, demon, give me back my boy! Have mercy, pity me, give him back!" She stretched out her hands to Takehiko. "O my youngest, my dearest, my lastborn treasure, my Noboru, why do you flee me? What has this madwoman done to turn your heart away from your own mother?"

I threw myself onto my knees beside her and once more tried to bring her back from the depths of renewed delusion. "Mama, you know the truth," I murmured, hugging her. I had not seen her in such a bad way since the evening of my homecoming. "That's Takehiko, not Noboru. Noboru is with Emi and Sanjirou, among the Ookami. He isn't here, but he's alive. Do you understand me? *Alive.*"

Her lips were trembling as she looked up at me. "Alive?" she repeated. I could sense nothing but emptiness behind her eyes. She lived, but her spirit was wandering. I had to bring it back.

"Master Michio!" I called. I didn't need to say anything more. Our shaman was with me in an instant, his strong arms supporting my mother. I was free to reach into the folds of my sash and take out my wand and talisman.

I touched the clay image of the sun goddess to Mama's brow and tilted my head back, beginning a chant for restoring balance and calm.

My incantation wove a spell that embraced my mother but also drew me into its rhythmically beating heart. The words and their deep, entrancing melody swirled around us. I could almost see them taking shape, becoming graceful, dancing creatures of mist and music. I felt my mother slump into my lap as Master Michio gently released her from his grasp. Her body moved with the deep, regular breath of peaceful slumber.

"Everything will be all right, Mama, you'll see," I whispered, cradling her limp body. "When spring comes, I'll find a way to bring Noboru home again, I swear it. I don't know how, but I'll try, and with the spirits' help—"

". . . not fair." The words were uttered in a low, dangerous growl.

I blinked. Had she spoken? "Mama?"

"It's not fair!" She punched both fists into my chest, knocking me over backward, and was on her feet before I fully realized that her tranquil slumber was a trick. "Why should *her* son live when mine are gone? Let her know my suffering!" She sprang away so suddenly and so fast that Lord Hideki hardly knew what was happening when she wrenched the firewood cudgel from his hands.

"You took my son!" she screeched. "I'll take yours!" She brought the bludgeon down on Takehiko's head. We heard the sickening crack of bone.

Yukari screamed.

4

A PATH OF PROMISES

I scrambled after my mother, but I was too late. Lord Hideki had recovered from the shock of her assault and tore the cudgel from her hands while my stepmother Yukari's shrieks and sobs echoed through the wintry air. She lay curled up on her side, a ring of helpless, confused onlookers hovering over her, too ignorant to know what to do, too stunned to move away.

Beside her, miraculously unharmed, my little brother Takehiko stared at his mother's unnaturally bent right arm, the one she had thrust into the path of the descending club to shield her child.

Master Michio moved with astonishing speed, his expression grave as he examined the broken bone. I should have run to fetch the supplies he would need to help her, but I could not leave my mother; not now.

"Kaya . . ." I only had to speak her name and my friend was there, poised to help me. As briefly and accurately as possible, I described the things that Master Michio would need and where he kept them. She nodded crisply and was away.

I wished our clanfolk had behaved half as helpfully. In the wake of this scarcely averted tragedy, only a few of them did anything actually useful. While Shoichi's widow took charge of my weeping little brother, Masa's wife, Fusa, saw to it that the new mother, her infant, and her little son were taken home safely. Masa himself remained where he was, shocked by what had happened, yet ready to take a stand for our mother's sake.

The rest of our clanfolk gathered to gawk at her, now limp and whimpering in Lord Hideki's unyielding grasp. The old warrior's face was flushed scarlet, though I couldn't tell if it was from rage or the humiliation of having a woman disarm him. When her legs folded under her, he didn't relax his grip, letting the weight of her body dangle painfully by one arm. Her sobs could have melted stone.

"I'm sorry, I'm so sorry, I didn't mean to hurt Yukari, forgive me, I don't know what happened to me, I can't . . . I can't . . ." She gasped for breath and covered her face with her free hand, filling her palm with tears.

"Let her go," Masa said, his lips a small, taut line. "You're hurting her."

"After what she did?" Lord Hideki snarled. "If you want to talk about *hurting* someone . . ."

"I'm done talking." Masa seized Lord Hideki's wrist and squeezed. My big brother had a blacksmith's strength. Mama's captor grunted in pain and released her. Masa caught her as she fell and swept her into his arms as if she were a child. She clawed at the front of his tunic and moaned. "It's all right, Mama," he said kindly. "I'm taking you home." He turned and began to walk away.

"You *dare*—?" Lord Hideki thundered.

Masa paused and looked back. "You wanted me to be a chieftain, to make decisions for our clan. This is my decision."

"This? Treating her as if she did nothing wrong? She tried to *kill* that child!"

Mama heard his words and uttered a cry so terrible my heart flinched in pain. "She didn't know what she was doing!" I protested. "She isn't well."

"For a sick woman, she has a demon's strength," Lord Hideki countered. He lifted his chin at Masa. "Go now, but see to it that she is ready to face the consequences of her crime tomorrow."

My older brother shrugged. "So be it." He carried Mama away just as Kaya returned with the supplies needed to care for Yukari.

As Master Michio and I examined my stepmother's broken bone as tenderly and effectively as we could, Kaya took charge of Takehiko. His recent ordeal had left my unhappy little brother wide-eyed as an owlet and nervous as a mouse between the fox's paws. At first he refused to be parted from his mother, but Lady Badger had her clever ways of conjuring smiles and kindling laughter. She soon had him riding on her shoulders while Yukari received the care she needed.

My stepmother was fortunate: the break lay just below her wrist. It was simple to set, and with the spirits' help

would heal more quickly than if it had been the wrist itself
that took the brunt of the cudgel blow. Master Michio sent
for a bowl of boiling water, steeped some crushed herbs,
and had her drink the mixture to dull the pain.

I had just finished tying Yukari's bandage when I became aware of the muffled hum of voices all around me.
Bits and scraps of words flew through the air like petals
swooping on the dawn breeze. Time and again I heard my
mother's name, but never once spoken with anger or condemnation: only pity.

They understand! My heart sang with blessings. *Our
clanfolk* know *she was not herself when she attacked Takehiko!
They don't blame her for it.* I wished I could embrace them
all for such wonderful compassion. *If anyone is at fault for
what happened here today, it's me. I should have watched her more
closely. I wanted to believe she was well again before that was so. I
won't make that mistake again. Tomorrow I will begin her healing
anew, and this time I won't pretend that she is better until it's true.*

Master Michio gathered up the remains of all the items
we had used on Yukari's broken arm and carried them back
to his house. I stood and helped her to her feet. My stepmother cast anxious eyes all around. "Where is he?" she
quavered. "Where is my son?"

"It's all right; he's with Kaya," I soothed her. "Let's
walk home and wait for them while you rest."

"Home . . ." Yukari drove the fingers of her good hand
into my arm. "Oh, Himiko, will *she* be there too?"

I saw the desperate fear in her eyes and wanted to weep.
My mother and Father's junior wives had been as close as
sisters. They shared joys, turned their backs on foolish

jealousies, and offered one another comfort in times of grief. They had made our home a place of harmony and love.

Now it was a dark haven of dread.

I took a deep breath. "I think Masa will keep her at his house. He was heading in that direction. Fusa and Toyo are good daughters-in-law; they'll see to it that she's well tended. You and Takehiko will be safe tonight."

"Yes, tonight . . . but tomorrow?" She shivered. "What are we to do, Himiko? We can't banish her from her own home, but if she's there, how can I close my eyes for an instant, knowing that the madness could change her again, without warning?"

"We will do everything we can to prevent that." I spoke as if I were the mother and she the child. "Perhaps we can have Toyo come live with us just to look after her. That would help keep the peace in our house and Masa's." I gave her an encouraging smile.

Yukari relaxed and let go of my arm. "Thank you, dearest child. I'm sorry for acting like such a rabbit. Your mother was kind to me from the first day I entered her home. I want nothing more than for those good days to return, but . . ." She sighed. "But I must protect my boy. Oh, Himiko, if only the Ookami hadn't taken her Noboru! It was hard enough for her, having to bury two sons and a husband, but to have her youngest torn away—! Do you think they will ever permit him to come back to her?"

"We can hope for that," I said, though I didn't believe it. I knew that my littlest brother was much too young to be of any value to the Ookami as a slave, but he was a precious hostage. "When that day comes, we'll see her fully restored. Noboru's return will heal her mind far better than any shaman's chants or potions. Meanwhile, Master Michio and I will do what we can for her and pray that the spirits show mercy."

I brought Yukari home and insisted that she lie down on her bedroll. I was preparing a warm herbal drink to promote the swift healing of broken bones when Kaya and Takehiko came in. My friend had performed wonders, changing our scared little mouse back into a glad-hearted, laughing boy. By the time we all went to bed, the only reminder of the day's turmoil was my mother's absence.

The spirits were compassionate to me that night. Though my waking mind was filled with concern for Mama's fate, I found serenity in sleep. More than that, the night's journey carried me to a place where I had once known the greatest happiness, the realm where I had heard prophecy from the sun goddess's own lips and found the one I loved with all my heart. I woke still filled with the delight of my dreams.

Kaya was also awake, lying on her side with her cheek resting on one hand. "Ha! Watch that grin before you blind someone with it, Himiko," she said. "Good dreams, eh?"

I bobbed my head, unable to stop smiling. "I saw him, Kaya! I saw Reikon again."

"That spirit prince of yours?"

"You remember him?" I don't know why I was so pleased to hear it.

"Just his name. You never introduced us," she responded.

"How could I? He isn't human, and you—Oh. You're teasing me."

"I am not," she maintained with a comical offended look. "I'm feeling left out, that's all. You told me about him, but that's not the same as getting to *meet* a handsome prince of the spirit world. Did you even think to ask him if he's got a brother or a cousin who might be interested in me? *Hmph.* Some girls have nothing but luck, and never share with their friends." She feigned a melancholy sigh.

"Kayaaaaaa . . ."

"Stop bleating like a sick fawn." My friend rolled over onto her stomach, both hands now propping her chin. "Tell me about your dream." She leaned toward me a little more. *"All* the good parts."

"It wasn't like that."

"Too bad."

"Ugh, you're awful, and you're going to be disappointed: I've never dreamed about Reikon that way. In fact, I haven't dreamed of him at all until now."

"I *don't* believe that!" Kaya objected, raising her head sharply.

"Believe it or don't, it's true. There's a difference between thoughts and dreams. He never left my mind or my heart, but no matter how much I wish to see his face again, to walk with him through the light and shadow of his world, it hasn't happened."

"Except for last night."

I smiled a little wider. "Yes."

She waited for me to say more, and when I stayed silent, she exclaimed, *"Now* who's teasing? Tell me all about it or suffer Lady Badger's wrath!"

"I'll tell, but you'll still be disappointed. I dreamed he

found me following a steep path somewhere in the mountains. He took my hand and we walked on together. We
didn't speak." I shrugged. "Then I woke up."

Kaya pursed her lips. "You were right, Himiko: I'd call
that dream a big letdown, yet it's got you grinning like a
well-fed fox. If you can make a feast out of such a dried-up
crumb, you *must* love him."

I lowered my eyes. My smile faded like the last lick of
flame from a dying fire. "Do you think I'm a fool, Kaya?"

"What for?"

"For yearning after a spirit. For setting my heart on an
impossible goal."

She thought about it a while. "I've used the same bow
for years, Himiko. I know how far it can shoot, and how
foolish it is to waste good arrows. Yet there are times when
I'm hunting that I see prey that's out of range—a big kamoshika, a plump pheasant about to take wing, a wild boar so
fat and tempting that just the sight of him makes my mouth
water! What do you think I do then?"

I gave her a sideways look. "You shoot?"

She nodded once, emphatically. "I shoot. And what
happens?"

"You hit the target?"

"No. Not usually. But sometimes I do, and even when I
miss, I feel better to have tried and failed than to have failed
without trying. Who knows if it won't turn out the same for
you? You've entered the realm of the spirits. Maybe someday your prince will find his way into our world."

Kaya's heartening words were a comfort to me on a
day when I would need much comfort. We had all barely

finished cleaning up after our meager breakfast when Masa appeared in the doorway. He looked dejected and did not bother to give any of us a morning greeting. His eyes met mine for a moment and all I could see in them was despair. Then he turned his gaze to Yukari, seated on the floor with her son.

"They're waiting for you."

My stepmother blinked as if taken by surprise. "Why do they want me? To tell what happened? Anyone who was there yesterday can do that!"

"It's Master Michio's idea. Until we have a chieftain, he must make all of the great decisions for our clan. He says that no matter how many others saw the attack, you will give the most accurate version of things because you alone experienced it. The truth lives with you."

Yukari shook her head rapidly. "No. No, no, no. I can't go. I won't. I'm afraid." Her nervousness affected Takehiko, who began to whimper and cowered behind his mother.

"There's nothing to fear," Masa told her. "Takehiko doesn't need to be present for this. Fusa and Toyo are waiting outside, at the foot of the ladder. They will take care of him in our home. And as for Mama . . ." His face grew even longer. "She won't be able to raise a hand against you. Lord Hideki himself came for her this morning. He was accompanied by all of Father's remaining counselors. Two of them linked their arms through hers while the other formed a guard around her and marched her to Master Michio's house. I left her there, surrounded. Even if she weren't so confused and fearful, she'd never be able to get past all of those men to hurt you."

"But that's not why I don't want to testify!" Yukari exclaimed. "I know she won't hurt me again but . . . but what if I say something that hurts *her*?" Takehiko wailed.

I knelt and stretched my arms wide enough to embrace them both. "Then go and say something that will help her," I told her. "We are her closest kin, her family. No one in this village knows Mama better than we do. Don't leave her fate in ignorant hands."

Yukari bit her lower lip, then gave her consent. We turned over Takehiko to my sisters-in-law and walked to the shaman's house.

A crowd awaited our arrival. Nearly every able-bodied member of our clan was gathered around Master Michio's doorway. Men and women jostled one another, striving for a better view of the shaman, of Lord Hideki and the stern-faced elders, and of my unhappy mother, surrounded by her guards. When the people noticed our approach, their whispers soared and swooped like bats at twilight, but at least they had the courtesy to stand aside and let us pass.

"There you are, Lady Yukari." Master Michio stepped forward. "How are you feeling? Has the pain been too much for you?"

She bowed her head and mumbled, "It's all right."

"I hope you aren't saying that just because you think it's what I want to hear," he said warmly. "Of course I *do,* but only if it's true." He chuckled.

The familiar, benevolent sound worked its magic: Yukari took heart and smiled shyly. "My arm hurts, Master Michio, but it's not too bad. Himiko has looked after me very well."

"As I would expect of her." He gave me an approving look, then patted my stepmother's uninjured arm. "You know, if we're going to help you heal, you mustn't be afraid to speak up when you feel pain."

"*Pain?*" Lord Hideki's loud sarcasm turned every head in his direction. "You think *that* is what she fears? She saw her only child savagely attacked before her eyes, and the one who did it remains among us! If she fears anything, it's that the same thing will happen again."

"I did not realize that the gods had given you the power to read other people's hearts, Lord Hideki," Master Michio said dryly. "Would you care to tell me what *I* fear too?"

The stern elder ignored our shaman's jibe. "Lady Yukari, I cannot look at you without shame, knowing that I was partly accountable for what happened, but I swear before everyone gathered here, I will atone for it."

He left his place with my mother's guards and got down on his knees before Yukari, pressing his brow to the cold ground. She was unnerved to see such a revered member of our clan abasing himself to her. "Lord Hideki, please get up! This is needless. What happened was . . . was nothing any of us could have foreseen or prevented. How can you be guilty of that?"

He looked up at her with a face of stone. "If I had held my weapon in a stronger grasp, as a man should, she never would have been able to take it. You would not have been so gravely hurt while saving your boy's life. Worst of all, I would not be here today to witness a good woman—wife of my honored chieftain, widow of my beloved friend—be condemned to die."

In the astonished silence that fell over all of us, Yukari's gasp was as explosive as a clay pot smashed against a boulder. "No, oh no." Her uninjured hand muffled her mouth. "Condemned to die? It's not right. How can you say such a thing?"

"Yes, Lord Hideki, how?" Master Michio's usually affable smile was gone. "Have you forgotten that the final judgment here rests with me?"

The clan elder stood up, swatting dirt from his knees, and confronted our shaman belligerently. "And have you lived among strangers for so long that you've forgotten how we Matsu live? This clan has never tolerated murderers."

"My mother is no murderer!" I shouted, barging my way in between the two men. "You were always our family's friend, Lord Hideki: why do you slander her with an abominable name? No one is dead! No murder took place!"

"Only thanks to Lady Yukari," he responded. "This wasn't the first time your mother has run wild. Can you swear that she will never raise her hand against another innocent? Can you promise that there won't be a death the next time?"

I straightened my back. "I can."

"Why? Because she is your mother? That's not enough." His tone softened, and he gestured to where Mama sat, imprisoned by a living wall. I could catch glimpses of her, back bent, updrawn knees, face buried in her folded arms.

"I am not speaking as her daughter," I answered. "I speak as a shaman. I give you my word, she will be healed."

Lord Hideki was unmoved. "I don't want your word:

I want proof. You claim you'll heal her. When? This whole winter was not long enough for you to succeed in casting out her madness. And you, Master Michio!" He turned to face him. "You have had even more time to make her well. Have you?"

Our shaman met Lord Hideki's challenging stare with one of his own. "If I have failed to cure her, let *me* be punished for it."

"What good will that do?" The old warrior threw his hands in the air. "There is only one way to prevent another tragedy, and that is to follow what our laws demand of us. Listen: when I was a boy, there was a great tumult in our village one night. A man had been caught in another's home, a knife in his hands. The two were rivals for the same woman. If the intruder had not roused his victim by stumbling in the dark, he would have committed murder. His intentions were clear. Our chieftain said: *'The hawk that misses one kill and flies away still wants blood. He will try again. If I have the power to protect my people from his talons and do not use it, I am the guilty one when he returns and succeeds.'* The man died. Our clan's way calls for the death of those who seek the lives of others, whether or not they accomplish their purpose. It has always been so; it must be so now."

A flurry of horrified whispers ran through the crowd. Lord Hideki turned his fiery gaze on the people. "I only speak for our ways, the rules that our ancestors handed down to us since this land was newly born. Do you think I *want* this woman's death?"

"What you want does not matter," I told him. "None of

this is up to you." I had never spoken so boldly to an elder of a clan. I have no idea what power possessed me. A great strength and a greater certainty filled me, body and spirit. *My people must not go down this dark path,* I thought. *It leads to a place without mercy, where there is no justice, only law.* "Let Master Michio speak. Let *him* give us a decision."

"He'd better not free her just because he feels like it!" one of the guards shouted stridently. "Any decision he hands down must obey our ways!" There were a number of approving murmurs. Not all of our clan were blessed with sympathetic hearts.

"You forget, my lords, my people," I said softly. "I am a chieftain's daughter. I know our clan's ways as well as you, or better. Father spoke about them often, from the time I was too young to understand. He discussed our laws with his counselors, when there was a quarrel to settle, but there were times I overheard him speaking with his friends, wondering aloud why some of our customs were so harsh, like one that decrees a murderer's fate is death—"

"Ah-ha! So you admit this!" the guardsman exclaimed an instant before I concluded:

"—and death for every member of the murderer's family."

The uproar was tremendous. The people's voices rose in noisy protest. Even those who might have stood by and let my mother die were shocked at the thought of her death causing so many others. Yukari stood speechless, her mouth agape, and began sinking to her knees without realizing it. Masa rushed to hold her upright. From behind the wall of guards, my mother howled like a suffering child. Master Michio struggled to restore silence, then looked at me like a man dazed by a hard blow to the head.

"Himiko, are you sure of what you're saying?" he asked in a pleading voice.

"You know I am, Master Michio, because you know our laws too," I replied, unafraid. "If I had not mentioned it, someone else would have, sooner or later." My eyes rested meaningfully on Lord Hideki.

"No." He shook his graying head slowly. "I never would have done that."

"Why not?" I pressed on. "That *is* the full measure of the law against murderers. If my mother is condemned, so is our family. We are spared only if she is spared. Which will it be?"

I saw the first glimmer of uncertainty in Lord Hideki's eyes. He began to waver visibly. I sensed he was on the verge of abandoning his stance and I held my breath, praying for his surrender. He was not a cruel man, and faced with such a dire choice, was likely to take the side of compassion. All he needed was time enough to reconsider and listen to his heart.

He did not get the chance.

"Well, how about it? You heard Himiko!" Kaya's strong voice smashed the momentary hush. "Come on, be sensible. Do you honestly believe her mother's a willful murderer? You'd have to be blind or a fool or—"

"This is not your business, girl." Lord Hideki spoke through gritted teeth. Kaya's unwise words had turned his doubt to cold rage.

"That shows how little you know," she countered.
"Himiko is more than a friend to me: I count myself her
sister just as surely as if we were born to the same parents.
If she dies, I will die with her!"

I seized her arm. "Kaya, *think* about what you're saying," I said urgently.

She ignored me, still intent on Lord Hideki. "Listen to
me well, old man: I *will* live or die as Himiko's sister, but if
I do die, it will also be as a chieftess's daughter! My mother,
Lady Ikumi of the Shika, will hear of it, and she will avenge
my death against all of you! If Himiko's mother dies, I will
go hand in hand with my sister, my friend, into the darkness, but we won't wait long before every one of you comes
down that same path after us!"

Kaya finished her speech on a note of triumph. It did not
last long. Lord Hideki growled an order and my friend found
herself set upon by a group of our strongest remaining men.
She fought them fiercely, but soon found her hands lashed
together before her and her arms bound tightly to her sides.
When she tried to kick at one of her captors he tripped her,
and several loops of cord were wrapped around her ankles.

Master Michio was livid. "This is unspeakable, Hideki!"
he exclaimed. "This young woman is our guest!"

"Not for much longer. She's arrogant enough to think
her threats will make us bend our necks to her orders. She
needs to be sent back home and learn manners."

"Send me home like this and you'll see what my clan
does about it!" Kaya shouted, thrashing futilely on the
ground. I knelt at her side to help her sit upright. "One
more battle will finish you!"

One corner of Lord Hideki's mouth lifted slightly. "Even if you are their princess, I doubt that the Shika will go to war for the sake of one girl's humiliation, especially since you brought it on yourself. Ah, Lady Kaya, I take no pleasure in that thought. What made so much foolishness spill from your lips? A momentary madness?"

"A momentary madness?" I echoed, standing up. "Is that how you see this, Lord Hideki? Then why can't you see my mother's case in the same way? Have you never once lost control of your actions because of overwhelming anger or grief? Have you never . . . never . . ."

"*Never . . .*" An uncanny feeling came over me. As I spoke, the sound of my words began to change, to become something . . . visible: a wisp of fog, a twinkle of sunlight, the ghostly face of a lovely woman. Her lips moved, and the words flew from my mouth to hers, each one building on the last, forming her hair, her neck, her shoulders, her arms, and every part of her body down to her small bare feet.

"*Never . . . never . . . never . . . you never stopped loving me, Hideki, not for a day, not for a moment, not for a single breath, not even after I died. You loved me better than yourself, and yet there were times when some irritation or problem or trouble made you bellow hurtful things at me. You were sorry afterward, when you were calm again. You begged me to forgive you, and when I did, you said you didn't know why I wasted mercy on a witless creature. How did I answer you then, beloved? Tell me what I said to you, my only love. . . .*"

The apparition faded and I found myself looking into

the old noble's ashen face as he spoke: "You said . . . you said *'Mercy is never wasted,'* Haru." He covered his face with his gnarled hands and began to weep. We all watched as he turned from us and walked away.

In the stunned silence following his departure, I became aware of my clanfolk's solemn gazes shifting to me. "What is it?" I asked. "What do you want? I don't know what came over Lord Hideki or why he called me by that name. Who is Haru?"

"Haru was Lord Hideki's wife," Master Michio said. "I was still living in this village when they married. He adored her, but she died too soon and he never took another bride. All this happened long before you were born. You never knew her, yet when you spoke to Lord Hideki just now, it was her voice we all heard. That is, all of us here who are old enough to remember the sound." He took my hands and squeezed them gently. "She spoke through you, Himiko. Not even I have been given so much power over the spirits of the dead."

I drew my hands from his grasp and went to untie Kaya's bonds. No one stopped me, but no one helped me, either. The knots were tight and complex; it took me some time to loosen them. I worked in silence. I could not find an adequate way to respond to what Master Michio had just told me. I could not believe what had happened to me.

The silence was everywhere. The only sounds I could hear were the stirring of a breeze through dead grass, the barking of a dog somewhere in our village, the distant cries of birds, summoning the springtime. Even Kaya was mute and stiff. My strong-willed, independent friend was not even able to look me in the eyes steadily. What had I become?

When the last cord fell from Kaya's wrists, we stood up together. Every face around me was a mask of awe. Only Master Michio had the ability to bring the Matsu back from that awful stillness.

"May the gods witness what I say," he intoned, raising his palms. "I speak without a chieftain's authority, but pray I have a chieftain's wisdom. I will not condemn an entire family to die because only one of them attempted to commit a grave crime."

Most of the people murmured their agreement, but a rumble of objection sprang up among the men surrounding my mother, most of whom were clan elders, noblemen who had served Father as counselors in happier days. One of them shouted: "So that's how things will be from now on? Our laws will be kicked aside because of some shaman's deception? Some of us remember how things were when Lady Tsuki reigned! She had a way of calling up the dead when it served her. Even then, I wondered if she *really* had such power, but I thought I was too young to dare question her. And what use would one lad's protest have been, when she had our whole clan too scared to raise a whisper against her?"

His speech conjured up small ripples of discontent here and there among our clanfolk. Like the outspoken guard, many of them recalled Lady Tsuki. My chieftess-shaman aunt was long dead but still infamous for having used her otherworldly powers to intimidate the people. The stares directed at me became hostile.

Another one of our nobles spoke up: "The Ookami took everything from us, but at least they let us keep our customs, our *heritage,* given to us from the time this land was new! If we deny them, we deny ourselves. If we abandon them over a girl's trick, we dishonor our ancestors and tempt the displeasure of the gods."

The crowd buzzed with fresh muttering. My opponents accused me of trying to terrify the people, yet they were doing just that themselves. If Master Michio spared my mother's life, there was a chance that our clan would rise up against him and carry out their own judgment. They might hold back from enforcing the cruel full measure of the law, but there was no guarantee of that. At the very least, they would make Master Michio suffer for having taken a stand against them.

I can't let that happen, I thought. *Not to Mama, not to Master Michio. If I let my people shed innocent blood, then the gods themselves will condemn them to a murderer's fate. No. Never. By my life, with the spirits' help or without it, I will not let that be.*

"My lords!" I called out, opening my arms to all my people. "I swear before you that what happened here was not my doing and certainly no trick. I know as little as you do to explain what happened. Yes, I have walked in the realm of the spirits, but I never once tried to summon the dead. If I do possess that power, I give you my sacred and binding oath that I will never misuse it in Lady Tsuki's fashion. I have not served you as a shaman for very long, but even so, have I ever used my skills except to help you?"

The unfriendly tone of the whispers softened. My clan knew I spoke the truth, but most of them were still afraid to take my side. The seed of their fear was planted deep: *Deny the law, and you dishonor the ancestors. Dishonor the ancestors, and you displease the gods. Displease the gods, and you doom the Matsu.* I would have to work hard to root out such a deadly weed.

"I do not tell you to discard our customs," I went on. "I only ask that we follow their guidance with mercy and understanding. When you are gripped by a fever, can you control it? Can you compel your body to stop burning and trembling? Then you must understand how it is with my mother: She cannot control the madness that has made her ill from the day the Ookami stole her little son. Were our ancestors heartless? They would feel pity for her grief, her shattered heart, her tangled mind. If we fail to show her the same compassion, *that* is how we truly dishonor their spirits. If we do not show mercy now, why should the gods ever grant mercy to us?"

I lowered my arms. My whole body wanted to shake, but I forced myself to stand firm and keep gazing steadily into the eyes of the clan elders in charge of my unhappy mother. These were men who had seen me grow up from a nursing infant to a boisterous child to a friendless girl. I had tugged on their whiskers and made them laugh when I grasped their fingers with small, sticky hands. They might never accept me as their equal in authority, but I needed to make them hear me speak as someone worthy of their respect. Standing there, waiting, I overheard many whispers telling me that my words had moved many of our clan, but they were from commoners, accustomed to let the nobles

guide their lives. I had to make these elders see things my
way. I had to hold my ground.

The old men looked away from me and began to confer
intently among themselves. One of them beckoned Masa
and spoke to him briefly. I wanted to sing with joy when I
saw my older brother nod, then kneel to pick up Mama and
carry her away.

They heeded me! She's safe! Thank the gods, she's—!

My elation was not to last. In Lord Hideki's absence,
the most venerable of the remaining nobles took charge.
"We will speak with Lady Himiko and Master Michio privately," he declared. "The rest of you may leave. There is
plenty of work awaiting your hands."

"But what about Master Michio's judgment?" one
woman called out. "We want to hear it!"

"You will be summoned to hear it when it has been
determined. You have spent too much time in idleness already. Go!" He made a sweeping gesture and, true to the
way they had always lived, my people submitted and obeyed.

The nobles and I followed Master Michio into his
house. He did not look happy with the way things were
proceeding, but his displeasure was nothing next to Kaya's
when she was told she could not accompany me.

"This is Matsu business," the leading elder told her
curtly as he barred her entry.

"But Himiko is—!" she began.

"Yes, yes, your sister in all ways except the only one
that counts. Wait outside or go elsewhere."

"It's all right, Kaya!" I called to her. "Yukari will need

your help at home." My friend made a face, but gave in, grumbling loudly as she stamped away.

I had never seen Master Michio's house filled with so many people. The elders were acting as if this were their first time visiting the shaman's home. They reacted with suspicion and a touch of nervousness to everything they saw and wrinkled their noses at the concentration of unfamiliar smells. One by one they settled themselves on the floor, hands on knees, facing the two of us.

"Well, my lords?" Master Michio said gruffly. "You demanded privacy; you have it. Speak your minds."

The leader raised one hand. "We are not here as enemies, Master Michio. Our goal is yours: to preserve and restore this clan, to give our kin renewed stability in a world that has suddenly turned upside-down and buried them." His eyes shifted to me. "The Matsu are without a chieftain, so it is our responsibility as clan elders to guide them onto the right path. Our lives have become precarious; we cannot afford a single misstep. Lady Himiko is very eloquent for one so young and has earned our gratitude for her healing skills, but—"

"—but you are afraid that if you pardon my mother and her madness returns, the people will lose faith," I finished for him. "They will claim it's the gods' vengeance on the Matsu for not keeping the customs of our ancestors."

"Exactly!" The elder beamed with relief. "May the spirits be praised, you are a *sensible* girl after all! At last you see the wisdom of accepting what we *must* do about your mother."

"I know very well what we must do about her." I

forced myself to sound calm and in command. "We must heal her."

"*What!*"

For an instant, the elder's roar of outrage brought back hard-edged memories of Father when his blazing temper ruled our home. My first instinct was to cringe, then to do or say whatever it would take to douse those angry flames.

Then I regained control of myself. I was no longer a child, easily intimidated by an all-powerful grown-up. I was Himiko the healer, Himiko the shaman, Himiko the warrior who fought without spear or bow, yet won. I would win this battle; for my mother's sake, I had to.

I stood up to the furious old man. "My lord, be reasonable. Even the most powerful shaman who ever lived could not heal anyone if she did not have the right remedy for the sickness. If you have a griping stomach and I give you plain water instead of *kihada* bark, you will not recover. My mother's mind will be restored solely when we can give her the proper medicine."

"By the gods, why didn't you *do* it? What were you waiting for?"

I spread my hands. "We could not give her what we did not have. Unfortunately, the only source for her cure is far away from our village."

"Ah, and with the winter weather there was no possibility for you to gather it, so you tried treating her with the potions you *did* have and hoped for the best, eh?" He was pleased with himself for puzzling that out.

I did not contradict him. Leaning forward, I pressed my forehead to the ground. "My lords, as my father's daughter,

I ask this favor of you all." I sat back on my heels again. "Let me have one last chance to restore the harmony of the home he died defending. If you will just give me the time I need to fetch what I *must* have in order to perform this healing, I promise that my mother *will* be cured when I return."

The aged leader of the nobles gave me a searching look, then sighed. "If you can do that, Lady Himiko, you will solve all our problems. As soon as we *know* your mother is restored and no longer a danger to our people, we can find a way to excuse her attack on Takehiko and Lady Yukari. That would certainly please *me*." He turned to his comrades. "What do you think?" They were eager to agree with him. "And you, Master Michio?"

"Nothing would make me happier."

"So be it." He redirected his attention to me. "Lady Himiko, if you fail this time, do you promise to accept *any* verdict concerning your mother's fate?"

I reached into the fold of my belt where I kept my talisman and held out the lady's image for all to see. Even in the dimness of Master Michio's house, the dragon stone in her hands glowed with its own radiance. "You have my word. I swear it by the never-failing light of the sun goddess."

"And you have our promise too: no harm will come to your mother until you return and attempt one final healing." The old men joined their voices in an oath made on their lives and the lives of all our people. It was their right as clan elders.

The exchange of solemn promises was accomplished. Master Michio struck one of the sacred bronze bells and

called upon the gods to witness our words. With the formalities completed, the elder who had spoken for all of
them let out a huge gust of breath and changed from a fire-
spitting flint-face to a benevolently beaming grandfather.

"You will have to see me before you set out to gather
those roots or leaves or whatever it is you need for your
mama's medicine," he said. "My daughter-in-law makes the
sturdiest baskets in our clan. I want you to have one. It will
bring you luck."

"Thank you," I replied, bowing slightly. "I can use
both the basket and the luck."

"How long do you think it will take you to bring back
what you need?"

"That depends. . . ." I folded my hands in my lap. "How
far is the road to the Ookami?"

5

ONE ROAD,
MANY FOOTSTEPS

Two days later, without having said a word about my intentions to Kaya or anyone in my family, I woke up before dawn and stole through the village to our shaman's house.

"Master Michio?" I whispered before entering.

"Come in, my child," he responded. "I'm just adding the last things to your travel gear."

"Thank you for that." I bent my head a little as I slipped through the doorway. "I couldn't get ready for this trip at home. It will be better this way, with no one in my family knowing about my plans until after I'm—" I raised my eyes and froze in midstep. There on the floor, beside the supplies our shaman was packing in a bag for me, sat Lord Hideki.

"Good morning, Himiko," he said. "Or should I say 'Good journey'?"

"The elders told you, didn't they," I stated. I was angry. One of the things that I had settled with those old men was my desire for initial secrecy. I insisted that no one in our village find out where I was going or why until I was already on the road. They gave me their word. They did it with bad grace, but they *did* it. Now this betrayal?

"You will forgive my friends," Lord Hideki said calmly. "They have not told anyone else about your plan and they broke no promise by telling me. The oath they swore was on behalf of *all* the Matsu elders. Whether you like it or not, that includes me." He chuckled. "I do wish I had been there when you fooled them into making that promise. When you let them know your actual intentions, did their faces look like this?" He scowled like an *oni*. "Or this?" He opened his eyes so wide that his eyebrows vanished into his hair. "Or was this more like it?" His jaw dropped, making him look so comical that I giggled in spite of myself.

"Amazing," Master Michio said, laughing along with me. "That is precisely how they all looked, Lord Hideki. You must have been there, but so sly and silent that we failed to notice you."

"I wish that were so," he replied. "Hearing about it afterward is not the same. I was informed that my colleagues called you all sorts of unflattering names for your part in what happened. That can only mean you outsmarted them in an argument."

"The main credit is Himiko's," the shaman said graciously. "When she revealed that the 'medicine' she was going to bring back was actually little Noboru, they were so shocked that their heads exploded like badly fired pottery. It made quite a mess of my humble house, I can tell you! She picked up the pieces and put them back together, reminding them that they had already sworn to let her go. I merely swept up the few crumbs of clay she missed."

"Fine gratitude I got for repairing those old crocks," I said with a wry smile. "As soon as they recovered, they struck out at me, demanding to know why I was going to free no one except my little brother. What about my other stepmother, Emi, and her son, Sanjirou? What about the rest of our people, enslaved by the Ookami? Was I just going to leave them to their fate? They made me feel ashamed."

"That was their intention." Master Michio shifted his shoulders. "Think of it as their way of paying you back for making them feel foolish. You *did* mislead them into giving their oath."

"You sound as if you don't approve of the girl's tactics," Lord Hideki remarked, stroking his beard. "And yet I heard many bitter descriptions of how you defended her."

"All I told our revered nobles was that they sounded as if they *expected* that Himiko had the power to free all of our captives. If that were so, why were they wasting time trying to set up her reluctant brother as our chieftain? Why not give the leadership of this clan to someone truly formidable?" He rubbed the back of his head sheepishly. "I think I might have gone a bit too far when I threw myself on the ground at her feet and acclaimed her as princess, shaman, and chieftess of the Matsu."

"Mmm, perhaps a *bit*." Lord Hideki grinned.

I ventured to touch the old warrior's hand. "Thank you for coming here to wish me well," I said. "I appreciate your goodwill now, especially because I know you wanted— because I know what you felt *had* to be done."

He was still smiling, but his eyes were sad. "So you do understand my reasons for speaking so . . . coldly at your mother's judgment. That is good. I would not want my chieftain's daughter to go on believing me to be a monster. I will pray every day for your success and safe return. When you take back your little brother, may the spirits give you stealth, strength, and swiftness. May they cast dust in the eyes of the Ookami and make the very earth rise up to trip their feet!"

"My lord, I'm grateful for your prayers, but there is another thing I would appreciate even more: look after Mama while I'm gone. She will be living with Masa, closely watched. It must be so for her own safety and for Takehiko's sake, but please do what you can so that she doesn't feel like an imprisoned criminal. She's going to find out about my departure, so when that happens, reassure her that I'll be all right and that I *will* come home. Will you do this?"

"With all my heart." He pressed my hand and let it go. "And more: I did not come here this morning just to wish you well, Himiko. I came to give you two parting gifts." He took a knife from his belt and handed it to me with both hands. Even in the twilight of Master Michio's house I could see the glitter of its keen edges. "My father gave this to me when he declared I had reached manhood. He claimed that the blade captured a guardian spirit who favored our family from the days when we first came to this land. I would like that spirit to watch over you now."

I was humbled by such a generous gift. "Lord Hideki, I can find no words good enough to thank you for this," I said, a catch in my throat.

"Himiko—Lady Himiko, I should say—you gave me a far greater gift than this." His eyes were touched with tears. "You let me hear *her* voice again, my sweet Haru's voice. I always thought I would go to my grave alone, but when her spirit spoke in front of so many witnesses, I saw that she had never wandered far from me since the day she died. You restored the only real joy my heart ever knew"—he smiled faintly—"even if she did return just to give me a good scolding."

"Lord Hideki, I don't know what I did to make your wife's spirit speak through me that day," I admitted. "I never summoned her, but if—when I return, I will try to call her back for you once more." I mirrored his smile. "Maybe this time she'll have kinder words for you."

"Perhaps." He stood up and grunted as he rubbed a touch of stiffness out of his lower back. "To be young again . . . When I was your age, there were no such things as mountains. I climbed them as easily as if they were flat fields of millet. Pick up your pack, Lady Himiko. It's time you and I set out on this journey."

My brows bunched together in surprise. "My lord?"

He laughed at my bewilderment. "Don't worry, my dear, I am not coming with you for very far. I am only going to put your feet on the right road." He seized the bag of supplies Master Michio had prepared and ducked out of the doorway, saying, "Make your good-byes and meet me in the old watchtower's shadow."

Still baffled by the old warrior's words, I appealed to my teacher for help. "Master Michio, what's he talking about?"

Our shaman was amused. I never knew I could be

so entertaining just by not knowing what was going on. "Didn't you hear what he said about his youth, Himiko? He and I were talking about it before you arrived. He was quite the adventurous lad, always exploring, always wandering farther and farther from home, always coming back with marvelous tales about the places he'd been, the monsters he'd conquered, the other clans he'd encountered."

"Others clans . . . like the Ookami?" Master Michio nodded. "Ah, so he knows the way there!"

"And he will describe it to you so clearly that you will swear you can see every pebble on the path. Following his directions will make it much easier for you to find the Ookami than . . . than . . ." He paused and cocked his head. "By the way, how *were* you planning to reach their village?"

I blushed. "I was going to rely on information from the other elders."

"How long ago did they travel there?"

"They didn't. All they knew came from things they overheard the wolf people say during their occupation of our village, and each elder had a different tale to tell me. The only things they all agreed on were that the Ookami live in a mountain settlement, that I would have to walk toward the setting sun to reach it, and that I would find other clans along the way."

Master Michio scratched his cheek. "That's not much to go on."

"I know, but it was all I had until Lord Hideki came to my aid." I sighed. "I shouldn't keep him waiting. Master Michio, I—"

My teacher hugged me before I could say anything

more. "Now I know what it is like to bid farewell to the daughter of your heart. I will miss you, Himiko. May the gods go with you and guide your footsteps." He took a step back, holding me at arm's length by the shoulders, and added: "And next time you need directions to somewhere far away, perhaps you should ask the spirits which way to go. It might be more help than asking our elders." With a final, quick hug, he let me be on my way.

I found Lord Hideki waiting for me at the appointed place. He had a very small bag cupped in one hand. "A little something for the road," he said, giving it to me.

I thought I felt smooth, shifting grains inside. "My lord, what is this?"

"A ration of rice from my household. Don't look at me with such alarm, child! I'm not going to starve for lack of so little, and you will be very glad to have it. Now let's be on our way."

We walked out of the village together, crossing our ruined moat, heading through the still-unplanted rice paddies. The rising sun behind us sent our shadows stretching out toward a distant stand of pine trees and the mist-veiled mountains beyond. I said a silent prayer that my strength would be equal to the journey ahead. Though the leg I'd broken in childhood had healed imperfectly and sometimes pained me when I overburdened it, it gave me no trouble when I walked along the steep paths and through the dense forests on the way to the Shika clan. Unfortunately that had no bearing on my present situation. According to Lord Hideki, the trip now facing me was many times as long.

"I gave my word to the elders that I would be back with Noboru before harvest season," I told him, worried. "Will that be enough time?"

"Don't fret, Lady Himiko. I have no way of knowing how long it will take you to rescue your little brother, but your travels should not take much more than a dozen days in each direction."

"Is that how long it took you?"

"Ah, well, that's hard to say. First of all, many years have passed since I was that young man, and even if I did recall the exact number of days I took the road to the Ookami lands, my path there and back was not direct. I had no *purpose*, as you do. I was exploring the world, you see, stopping whenever I discovered something interesting, and enjoying my freedom."

"Then you are only guessing when you say the journey takes about twelve days."

"True. But as for what marks your trail on that journey . . ." He smiled. "*That* is something I know, and no guessing about it."

I listened attentively as Lord Hideki spoke about all the details of his youthful expedition to the Ookami village and beyond. Sometimes I had him listen while I repeated what he'd said. I wanted to be certain I had it right.

We did not spend the whole time talking. Often we walked in silence, guarding our own thoughts. The farther I went from home, the more I became haunted by the bittersweet memory of my last night under our roof:

I had gone to Masa's house to see how Mama was

doing. My sisters-in-law had done their best to make her feel welcome and comfortable, but her recent ordeal had made her retreat deep within herself. She was huddled in one corner of the house, wrapped in her bedroll like a caterpillar in a cocoon. Toyo glumly reported that she had not uttered a single sound since Masa brought her back from the interrupted judgment procedure.

"At least she eats and drinks what we give her," Fusa chimed in. "And she keeps herself clean too, which is a *great* relief for us. She just won't talk."

I knelt in front of Mama and spoke to her tenderly. I was very happy when she looked up at the sound of my voice, but it was a short-lived joy. A momentary flicker of life touched her eyes and vanished, leaving her staring at me with a fish's flat, expressionless gaze. I tried and *tried* to rekindle that first spark of attention—with words, with gentle touches, with melodies the two of us had sung while sharing housework—and I failed.

This might be a hidden blessing, I thought as I bid Masa and his family good night. *If Mama doesn't notice when I'm here, perhaps she won't notice when I'm gone.* It was a feeble attempt at comforting myself, but I clung to it.

My dejection weighed my steps all the way home. I crossed our threshold and listlessly announced, "I'm back."

"By wind and by fire, *another* miserable human?" Kaya sprang toward me on hands and knees, snarling and champing her teeth ferociously. "What gives you furless fools the nerve to invade my burrow and steal my treasure? I'll bet you've come because *he* summoned you." She made a scornful gesture at Takehiko, who stood holding a bundle of tall

dry grass in one fist and a strand of his mother's beads in the
other. "Badger-Slayer the Mighty Hero, he calls himself. Ho,
ho, what sort of hero needs help? My magnificent fangs and
claws will tear him to shreds!" She made a fake charge at
Takehiko, who let out a squeal of pretended fear and scam-
pered out of her reach.

"Don't come near me, Lady Badger!" he shouted. "I've
got a magic sword"—he waved the bunch of grass—"and if
I hit you with it, you'll become a frog."

"A frog? Me, a frog? Never!" Lady Badger sprang
toward him again and got a smack on the snout for it.

"Ow." Kaya sat down abruptly, one hand covering her
nose. "Not so hard, Takehiko. You're stronger than you
think."

"Frogs don't say ow," my unrepentant little brother instructed her. "And I'm not Takehiko, I'm Badger-Slayer the
Mighty Hero."

"And *I'm* ready to feed you all," Yukari announced from
her place by the cooking pot. "Come help me. It seems I can
prepare a meal with one hand, but serving it will be harder."

Kaya and I both rushed to her aid, but before my
friend could get off the floor, Takehiko shrieked a war cry
and threw himself on top of her, slinging one leg over her
back and proudly proclaiming that now he was to be called
Badger-Rider the Undefeated, known and feared throughout the land.

"How can you call yourself Badger-Rider?" Kaya asked
archly. "Aren't you forgetting that you turned me into a frog?"

"No excuses, lazy badger! Go, go, go!" Takehiko cried
gleefully, bouncing on her back.

"Ride her hard, Little Brother," I said dryly while Kaya snorted and snarled. "It can be her punishment for not helping your mother with the chores."

"Lady Badger doesn't do chores," Takehiko said gravely, dropping his "sword" and his "treasure" in order to wrap his arms around Kaya's neck and press his cheek to hers. "She's too busy digging criss-cross tunnels to trap her enemies. They all go in after her and get lost, and then she eats them right down to the *bones*. But she didn't catch me, and you know why?" He went on chattering about what a clever hero he was. He was so caught up recounting his valiant exploits that he didn't object when his badger steed delicately removed herself from his embrace and joined me in serving our modest dinner.

It was the image of my dear friend and my little brother playing together so happily and so carefree that returned to me now, as each step I took carried me farther and farther away from them, from the rest of my family, from all my kin, from everything I had ever known. Though I told myself repeatedly that I would return, an icy presence at the back of my mind persisted in whispering: *Will you? Will you even be able to reach the Ookami lands? Will you outwit the wolf chieftain in his own den? Will you ever again embrace the ones you love . . . or only watch them from your place among the spirits of the dead?*

Only the gods know what will be, I thought. *All I know is that I will try.*

Lord Hideki and I did not part ways until we left our clan's fields well behind us and entered the shade of the pines. I began to worry that he had decided to make himself my escort for my whole journey and was not going to tell me until I confronted him with it.

He would see it as a good deed, I thought. *I'm sure he's telling himself "I'll stay with my old friend's little girl, lead the way, protect her from harm, rescue her if she gets in trouble. The poor, weak creature could never hope to make such a trek by herself." I had better say something about it.*

I took a deep breath, bracing myself for the argument that was sure to come. "Lord Hideki, isn't it time for you to turn back?" I asked casually.

"Is it?" He raised one brow. "I was not aware you disliked my company so much, Lady Himiko."

"It's not that; it's just—"

"There, there, I am only teasing you. You are quite right: it is time for me to leave you. All I wanted was to bring you this far." He pointed to a thicket of ferns, newly uncurling after the winter's hardships. "Unless my memory has turned to dust, those plants mark the banks of a brook."

"Ah! The first landmark?"

"Just so." He nodded. "I have not walked this way for many years, but I hope you will find it unchanged."

"Ferns like water," I replied confidently and quickened my pace until I was standing among the bright green fronds, looking down into the rushing water of the brook. "It is here, Lord Hideki," I called back. "Just as you said it would be. Come see."

The old noble made no move to join me on the bank. "Good, good. That means my memory of the journey is likely to be reliable. I can say farewell to you now and be easy in my mind. That is"—he added after a moment's hesitation—"as easy in mind as possible, thinking about how far you have to go."

I rushed back to him and hugged him tightly. I didn't care if he thought my gesture didn't show the proper respect for his status as a clan elder and scolded me for my impudence. "Thank you for everything, Lord Hideki," I whispered.

His arms were around me suddenly in a strong, protective embrace. "May the gods go with you, my dear child," he said solemnly. "And may you return in safety and joy."

We released each other and I walked back to begin following the brook upstream, according to what he had told me. I did not look back until I was certain he was well out of sight. Then I leaned my back against the rough black bark of a young pine and cried.

I felt better after a while and resumed my path. I had not walked through the forest alone for a long time. The last occasion had been my most recent journey to the Shika village. Kaya was with me on my return home, and as much as I appreciated my friend's cheerful companionship, there was something about being by myself in the heart of the woods that filled my soul the way a bowl of rice filled my belly.

Every step I took was an invocation, a prayer to summon the presence of the spirits. Winter was slowly losing its grip on our village, drawing its dank fingertips over earth and air as it reluctantly gave way to spring, but here that chill, unfriendly season was long gone. Twigs grew red with rising sap. Moss sprang to green life on the stones. I even saw a wink of brown and white hiding in the shelter of a great oak and knew that there would soon be mushrooms to gather.

Soon . . . if I'm lucky, I thought. Early spring fed my heart with hope, but hope needed company in the cooking pot. My bag of supplies had a reassuring weight and held other things to eat in addition to Lord Hideki's generous gift of rice, yet how long would it be before I was faced with an empty bag and an empty stomach?

It would help if I knew exactly how far I have to go. Then I could portion out what I've got, but as things are . . . I sighed. Lord Hideki had told me the road to the Ookami lands took twelve days to cover, but had been quick to add that he was not sure about that number. I knew all too well how easily a journey could take on a will of its own, like a child.

Hadn't I experienced this very thing firsthand years ago, when I'd gone by myself to visit a grove of blooming cherry trees less than a day's walk from our village? It was a simple outing, but one that became an unsought adventure because I lost my way home. Though that was the journey which guided me to Kaya's people and to my first encounter with the spirit world, I could not afford such a detour now.

This is no time for timidity, I told myself. *I am not the child I was then, the girl who nearly starved in the forest. Now I know more about the hidden treasures of the wild lands. There will be no useless fretting over whether I have enough to eat. Either I provide for myself or I go hungry, but I will not rely on what I carry and I do not depend on anyone but me.*

My first day traveling was unremarkable. The path was

clear, the weather was cool but not uncomfortable, and I did not encounter any dangers. *O gods, if it could only be such easy going all the way to the wolf clan lands!* I thought with longing. There was no harm in wishing for impossible things.

When daylight began to fade, I made camp within a grove of camphor trees, their crowns bright with clusters of white flowers. The brook I had been following was wider now, and as I lay in the shelter of the fragrant branches, the sweet sound of rushing water lulled me to sleep.

The next two days passed in much the same way. The weather favored me, as did the land. According to the directions that Lord Hideki had given me, I had a few days to travel before I had to face a steeper trail into the hills, and I was able to cover that unchallenging terrain at a fast pace that did not put a strain on my less-than-perfect leg. At the end of the second day I found the next landmark Lord Hideki had described: an ancient oak tree whose roots had grown up over the top of a great boulder like the fingers of a gnarled hand clutching a stone.

Wonderful! I thought, grinning ear to ear. *I'm on the right road. Better still, this means Lord Hideki's memory is true, even after so many years.* I patted one massive curved root. *And through all of those seasons, you waited here to meet me, Lord Oak. No wildfire touched you, no insects or illness ate a way into your heartwood, no flood weakened your hold on the earth, no quaking shift of the dragon's spine uprooted you from your home.* Laying my cheek to the cool flank of the boulder I added: *And you, Lady Stone, thank you for sustaining your husband all this time, for the strength you give him to stand firm, for the unending bond between you. May the gods renew your spirits, may your embrace endure for ages.*

I continued on my way, my heart light. Birdsong filled the branches above my head. Darting wings delighted my eyes with sudden flashes of color. When I stopped to drink from the brook, an old frog on the bank gave me a severe stare. Clusters of soon-to-hatch eggs glistened in the water below his sun-warmed seat, and I heard his spirit reprimand me with a rumbling, *Be off! Be off! Begone before my children see you, monstrous creature!* A squirrel scolded me from her perch; tall, tufted ears flicking in my direction while her fringed tail trembled with indignation. I laughed and begged her pardon for invading her home and promised that I would not linger. I walked with determination to cover as much ground as possible by sunset, but also with a gentle tread. Life was dancing all around me and I could not bear the thought of a blundering step on my part disturbing the dancers.

That night I ate well thanks to finding a thick growth of new ferns thriving in the damp earth beside the running water. I was so hungry that I did not go to the bother of building a cookfire but ate the tightly coiled green shoots raw. They filled my stomach, yet left me unsatisfied. I wanted the taste of meat—only a little! Though I carried some preserved strips of wild boar, the prize from one of Kaya's successful hunting parties, I held myself back from eating so much as one bite. I might come to a point in my travels when that dried meat would be the only thing between me and *real* hunger. It would be foolish to eat it now, just to indulge my yearnings.

I went to sleep in a bad mood, made worse by a teasing wisp of scent that reached my nostrils just as I was about to drop into dreams. It was the unmistakable smell of meat cooking over an open fire, the savory droplets of melting fat sizzling when they hit the flames. My mouth watered beyond my control. I couldn't help wondering whether it would be a good idea to get up and follow the tantalizing aroma to its source and see if the unknown cook would be willing to share.

Stop that! I told myself. *You're imagining things. There is no cook and no cookfire anywhere nearby; there* can't *be! Remember what Lord Hideki told you? The first village you'll encounter is at least a day's march farther on, maybe more. Do you want your greedy gut to lead you astray in the dark? Lie still, close your eyes, and don't be a fool!*

I forced myself to find sleep, but it was not restful. I woke up the next morning feeling oddly tense and on guard. The smell of roasted game still haunted me, now so faint that I could believe it was nothing but the remains of a dream. *A very* provoking *dream,* I thought testily as I rose to wash my face in the stream.

The crisp-skinned leg and thigh of a bird was waiting for me when I returned. It lay on a bed of tender young oak leaves spread over a flat rock. I stared at it for a long time, then cast searching glances left, right, and all around, seeking answers to this mystery. Even though I had woken up hungry, my appetite was gone. The delectable scent, now strong again, had lost its power to tempt me.

It looks like a pheasant's joint, I thought, extending one finger gingerly. I half expected to have the apparition vanish at the slightest touch, but it was solid enough, the browned skin cold and shiny with grease. I brought my hand to my mouth and licked my fingertip. Delicious! I wanted to sink my teeth into the meat then and there.

No, better not. At least not until I can find out where this came from and why I'm being favored like this by some invisible giver. I folded my hands in my lap and gazed at the roasted leg as though it were a puzzle to solve. *That taste . . . That first taste seemed to be all right. It didn't make me sick. Maybe I could have just a pinch of the skin and see how that sits on my stomach.* I leaned forward, my hand trembling just a little as I reached for the meat. *Just the smallest bit of skin and meat to find out if—*

"For the love of all the gods, *eat* it already!"

Kaya strode out of the trees, scooped up the food, and shoved it into my hands. With a loud snort worthy of Lady Badger, she plopped down beside me, glaring. "Do I have to tell you how to do *everything*?" she demanded. "I thought you'd know enough to feed yourself, but it looks like I was wrong. Honestly, Himiko, it's a good thing I'm coming with you on this trip, or you'd starve to death in the middle of a chieftain's wedding feast!"

I gaped at her for a moment, then burst out laughing. "How long have you been on my trail, Kaya?"

"From the moment Lord Hideki came back through the village gates and I knew my path was clear. Don't worry: I told your stepmother my plans. That way, if my mother should happen to send a messenger to your clan in order to see how things are with me, he can tell her I'm fine, just . . . elsewhere." She spread her hands.

"This journey to the Ookami lands is a *big* 'elsewhere,'" I reminded her.

"Pff! As long as it's big enough for two, it's where I belong."

"I must admit, I'm happy to have your company," I told her.

"You'll be happier to have this"—she pointed at the large sack she'd been carrying—"and this." She jabbed a thumb at her bow and arrows. "What were you going to do to protect yourself on the road?"

I showed her the blade Lord Hideki had given me. She raised one eyebrow skeptically and asked, "Do you know how to use that?" When I gave her an *Are you serious?* look, she made haste to add: "I *meant*, do you know how to use that on something that's still alive and dangerous?"

I pursed my lips. "If you keep talking to me as if I were a child, you'll get the chance to show me how *you* handle something alive and dangerous." That made her laugh first, apologize second.

Almost apologize.

"A thousand pardons, O great shaman!" Kaya exclaimed, raising her hands as she bowed her head to the ground. "Surely the spirits will make the wild boars and the wolves and every other perilous creature flee before you the instant that you throw herbs at them."

She was still bent over when I sprang forward and sat on her back, pinning her down. She squawked and struggled, but I was not so easy to dislodge. "Now you listen to me, you flattened badger," I said with good humor. "I might not know how to use Lord Hideki's blade to protect myself, but I do know that it's no match for wolves or wild boars or any big animal. I wouldn't try to make a stand against them. As for smaller dangers, I *used* to have a good friend with some skill as a fighter. I was hoping she'd give me a lesson or two, but I heard she's been spending most of her time talking to earthworms, so there's really no hope she'll ever—"

Kaya took a deep breath, thrust her fists against the ground, and bucked. I fell off her back, giggling. Scowling, she wiped the dirt off her face and chest, then declared: "I must be seven kinds of fool for wanting to help you when I could have stayed safe at home or nice and comfortable in your village."

"Don't you mean *in your village with Yari*?" I asked, looking sly as a well-fed fox.

Kaya's face turned red. "What do *you* know about Yari?" she said.

"Well, he *is* one of my sister-in-law's brothers," I replied. "Fusa told me that they were never close, yet he always seemed to find a reason to see how she was faring whenever you and I were visiting my brother Masa this winter. And wasn't he the one who came by Mama's house with firewood every chance he got? Firewood that he never managed to carry up the ladder himself. Somehow you were always the first one to dash out the door, ready to help. I wonder why it took so long to bring up the firewood even with two pairs of hands working at the task." I grinned.

"You're awful," Kaya grumped at me, chin tucked in. She sounded so unhappy that I felt a pang of remorse for teasing her.

"I'm sorry, Kaya," I said, touching her arm. "I shouldn't make fun of you about this. The truth is, I'm glad you and

Yari are . . . getting along. I'm hoping that when we return home, maybe the two of you will, well . . ."

"He wants to marry me," Kaya said. She spoke so low that I had to ask her to repeat her words, to make sure I'd heard them correctly.

"He does?!" I clapped my hands. "That's wonderful! You know that I count you as my sister, but once you take Fusa's brother for your husband we'll *really* be kin!"

She lifted her chin and regarded me uncertainly, as if checking to see if this were a fresh joke at her expense. "You like the idea?"

"I welcome it!" I cried, hugging her. "And I welcome your company on this journey more than ever. With your cleverness and skills as a hunter, we'll be able to travel faster, find a way to rescue my little brother more easily, and go home sooner so that *I* can perform your wedding rites!" Joy possessed me. I couldn't help but leap to my feet, draw my wand, and begin to dance, offering the spirits a prayer that was part thanks, part praise, and all hope for my friend's happy future.

Kaya shook her head. "You're *never* going to eat that pheasant leg, are you?" She sighed.

6

LADY KARASU
AND LADY IYOKO

I think that in spite of her protests, my friend Kaya was as much of a shaman as I. She was the master of a magic spell that transformed our path from a journey through unknown lands into a pleasant outing. When the road we were on began to climb the foothills leading into the sunset mountains, her jests and songs and funny stories distracted me from the ever-increasing challenge of the route.

At least that challenge was solely on account of the terrain. We did not have to deal with the added trouble of not knowing which way to go. Lord Hideki's directions held true, his memory was accurate. He gave us many landmarks by which to guide our footsteps, mostly rocks or other enduring features of the land, but sometimes trees or other plants whose appearance or location made them stand out.

Whenever I announced something like, "Next we have to look for a pair of 'man-and-wife' cedars," Kaya became uneasy and snappish.

"Why did Lord Hideki have to choose *trees* as trail markers? They're too easy to destroy! Even a 'man-and-wife' pair, with their branches knotted together, can't stay standing if a really big storm washes out their roots or hits them with a bolt of lightning! He should have relied on rocks and rivers. Nothing ever happens to change them."

"I agree with you," I said mildly. "I don't believe in landslides or droughts, either."

She snorted and threw a fallen pinecone at me.

One day, we both caught wind of the unmistakable scents that could only come from a village. It lay in a wide highland meadow where spring flowers bloomed pink and white and blue. Thatch-roofed houses just like the ones we knew from our own villages peered over the top of a wooden palisade, but there was no encircling moat and no watchtower. As we came downslope, we saw terraced fields rising along the flank of the farther hillside. We lingered in the shelter of the trees, watching the people go to and fro and waiting for the right time to reveal our presence.

"It might be best if we entered the village now," I said in a low voice. "There are so many people in the fields that probably not too many will be inside the walls. If they don't like strangers we can go on our way without causing too much fuss."

"Do we have to go into the village at all?" Kaya asked. "Our bags are still fairly heavy, you've managed to forage plenty of fresh food, and I've been having lots of luck hunting. We don't *need* these people for anything."

"But we *do* need to cross their land. If we try to do that

by night, we'll get lost, and if we go slinking along by day and they spot us, we'll look like we were up to no good. I'd rather deal with introductions than explanations. Let's go." I stepped out of the trees and went about ten strides before I realized Kaya was not right behind me. Turning in my tracks, I peered back at her and softly called, "Kaya? What's wrong? Are you afraid?"

She emerged from hiding with small, reluctant steps, her expression both shamefaced and grim. "I'm being *careful,* not afraid," she said gruffly. "And you would do better to learn a little caution. What are you planning to tell these people, once you're inside their walls? 'Excuse me, but we're on our way to visit the Ookami. They enslaved my little brother, so I'm going to steal him back. I don't have any idea if you're friends or enemies with the wolf clan, so why don't we make a bargain? If they're your enemies, we'll all sit down together and chat about how horrible they are. What fun! But if they're your friends, *please* don't send a messenger ahead to warn them about our plans, all right? Thank you *so* much, and now feed us.'" She ended with an infuriating Lady Badger smile.

I folded my arms. "That was not what I had in mind to do," I said crossly.

"Is that so?"

With an exasperated sigh I grabbed her shoulder and told her exactly what I had planned. She listened wide-eyed, and by the time I finished speaking, her smirk had become an excited look of admiration. "That's *perfect.* I love it. Let's try it right away. Where do you get these ideas, anyhow?"

"Not down badger burrows," I told her, and we both giggled.

A short while later we were at the village gates. At that time of day they stood wide open, and though there was no watchtower, there was a middle-aged man standing guard. He looked bored and was so inattentive that we were less than five arm-lengths away before he noticed we were strangers, not members of his clan.

"Stand where you are!" he shouted, shaking his spear. "Who are you? What do you want here?"

I stepped aside and let Kaya address him. "Greetings, great warrior," she said smoothly. "I am called Karasu and this is my lady Iyoko. We have traveled for many days and are tired and hungry, yet we want nothing more than to know if the spirits have led us to a place of blessing or a cursed land. We will not trouble you long with our presence, for my lady is called to continue on a pilgrimage far into the west, even beyond the lands where the Ookami rule."

"The Ookami?" The guard shuddered slightly. "What business do two girls have with that den of wolves?"

Kaya gave him her most bitingly scornful look. "For your information, Lady Iyoko is both chieftess and shaman of the badger clan, with a voice so powerful that every word she utters summons the spirits of this world and those of the shadowy realm of the dead. If this *girl* were to open her mouth and speak your name, you would be surrounded by the avenging ghosts of every person you ever offended, disappointed, or angered!" She narrowed her eyes and with a wicked smile added, "Would you like to see her prove it?"

The guard shivered even more violently than he had at the mention of the Ookami. "No, no, not at all!" He raised his hands in a warding-off gesture. "There's no need to bother the dead over trifles. Let them enjoy their rest undisturbed. Ladies—*noble* ladies, you are welcome in the land of the willow clan. Follow me, if you please. I will bring you to our chieftain's house so that his wives can make you comfortable."

"We are in your debt, great and *wise* warrior," Kaya replied.

Our escort made haste to fulfill his words. Soon we found ourselves in the care of two overawed women who heard "Karasu's" account of my pilgrimage and my powers and accepted it all without question. We were offered food and drink, and while we refreshed ourselves, one of the ladies sent the guard off to fetch her chieftain husband. He was a wiry man, his tattooed face marked by a thick white criss-cross scar on his left cheek. I glimpsed a sacred bronze mirror at his belt and knew I faced one who was both chieftain and shaman.

"Lady Iyoko of the badger clan, I am Lord Tsuru of the willow people. You honor us with your presence; be welcome," he said. "I am told that despite your obvious youth, you can command the spirits almost *too* easily to be believed. I am likewise informed that because of your incredible power, you cannot say a single word, for fear that we shall all be buried in a landslide of departed ancestors. What a pity. I was hoping to speak with you directly, not through the mouth of your slave." He indicated Kaya.

"I am *not* her slave!" Kaya blurted, indignant. "I am her sister, Lady Karasu!"

"So you say," the willow chieftain replied with a slight smile. "But if your mistress must stay silent, we have only your word on that. What if I choose not to accept it? This clan may be subject to the Ookami, but after their victory, they allowed us to keep our own traditions. One of these dictates that slaves may not eat or spend the night under the same roof as their masters. If we fail to maintain the practices of our ancestors, the gods will punish us, so I am afraid I will have to ask you to take your meals and your rest elsewhere, just to be—"

"That will not be necessary, Lord Tsuru," I said calmly. "I assure you, she *is* my sister."

He grinned at the sound of my voice. "Ah, but now the question is: who are *you*? Are you truly Lady Iyoko, the almighty shaman? But I was told she summons swarms of spirits with every breath." He made a great show of looking all around, then opened his arms in a gesture of confusion. "If you are Iyoko, where are your obedient ghosts? Are you the only one who can see them? Or could it be"—his eyes twinkled—"could it be you are nothing more than a not-so-very-clever liar?"

If he imagined that his childish tactics would make me break down and confess to being a cunning trickster, he was wrong. I remained composed. "My lord Tsuru, forgive my sister," I said placidly. "She exaggerates my abilities, but she does not lie outright. I am a shaman."

"And I am a butterfly," he replied dryly.

"Prove it," I said with a sharp lift of my chin. "But

before you flap your wings and soar away, tell me what you
want me to do to demonstrate that I am what I claim to be.
I will do it or become your slave if I fail."

The willow chieftain chuckled. "You would make a
bad slave, Lady Iyoko. You have too much backbone. How
would *you* choose to prove that you are a shaman?"

Wordlessly I opened my travel sack and produced the
different packets of medical herbs that Master Michio had
provided for my journey. I named each one and described
everything about it: the best places to find the plant, the
most favorable time to harvest it, the illnesses or injuries it
would heal and the way to administer it. Last of all, I produced my own bronze mirror and held it out to Lord Tsuru
reverently.

"Shall I show you that I know how to use this too?" I
asked.

"Put it away, my lady, if you please." He no longer
mocked me. "Pack up all of your things. The sight of them
shames me. I apologize for doubting you."

"My lord, we are strangers here," I replied. "I don't
blame you for mistrusting us. My father was a chieftain
and his first duty was the protection of the clan. It made
him more careful than other men, suspicious of anything
or anyone that might harm us. So you see, I understand
you."

"And I believe I understand you as well," the willow
chieftain said. "Two young women, traveling alone . . .
Some people would see you as helpless fawns to be hunted,
others as meek little mice, to be kicked aside." He turned
to Kaya. "You are very clever, Lady Karasu. Your tales of

Lady Iyoko's terrifying powers protect the two of you like a turtle's shell."

Kaya managed to look demure. "It's better this way. It keeps me from wasting my arrows."

That made Lord Tsuru guffaw. "Better to be feared than loved, eh?"

I spoke up again: "If we can't be respected, yes. We have far to go, my lord, and not everyone we encounter is as good-hearted as you. We must do what we can to take care of ourselves, and to persuade others to treat us properly."

"Why *are* you traveling like this, Lady Iyoko? Your home must be very, very far away: I have never even heard of your clan until today."

"Not everything my sister told you is untrue," I replied. "We are on a pilgrimage. I wish I did not have to leave my home, but if I am ever to find peace and restore harmony to my people, I must complete this journey."

"And is it also true that your goal lies beyond the lands of the Ookami?"

I nodded. "There was a time when I did not know their name, but when my mind fills with the image of a wolf stealing a child, I know I must track it to its lair and rescue the innocent from its jaws."

"Ah, a vision!" Lord Tsuru interpreted my words in his own way, and I let him. "The gods have chosen your path for you. They will be obeyed." He sighed. "I have pretty, young daughters of my own, Lady Iyoko. It pains me to think of you and your sister on such a perilous adventure, but I will try to help you as much as I can. My home is yours; stay with us as long as you like."

"Thank you, Lord Tsuru," I said. "We will not take advantage of your hospitality for more than one night."

"Then we will send you on your way with fresh water, as much food as we can spare at this time of the year, and some advice about the road ahead."

I smiled. "Food and water are welcome, but advice is a treasure. May the spirits bless you and your clan, my lord."

We passed a peaceful night among the willow clan. Our presence drew a throng of the curious who surrounded their chieftain's house, hoping to catch sight of us, or should I say of *me,* the "deadly dangerous" shaman. The guard we first encountered had wasted no time to scurry all around the village with the tale of my powers. How he must have loved the attention he got for being the bearer of such a hair-raising story! When I stepped out of Lord Tsuru's home to greet the people, all of the women and most of the men shrieked, moaned, and begged me not to say a single word, for fear that I would call up the dead. Even when Lord Tsuru reassured them that they had nothing to be afraid of, rumor overruled him. I resigned myself to a silent visit.

Dawn found us back on the road. Kaya and I were both in high spirits, and the beautiful spring weather added to our cheer.

"It worked!" Kaya exclaimed, dancing along the path. "It worked, it worked, it *worked*!"

"What worked?"

She looked at me as if I'd grown horns. "Your *plan,* silly. What do you think I'm talking about? It was brilliant. I can't wait to try it again at the next village! 'Bewaaaaaare the invincible, indescribable, incredible shaman Iyoko! Her spells bind both the living and the deeeeeead!'" She chortled. "I wonder if we should try telling that to the Ookami and scare them into releasing your brother *and* all the rest of their captives?"

"Why not?" I replied, straight-faced. "I've always wanted to know what it's like to have a spear stuck through me."

Kaya made her finest *Lady-Badger-is-fed-up-with-you* face. "I wasn't *serious*."

"I know." I threw one arm around her shoulders. "But wouldn't it be wonderful if it were that simple to save Noboru!"

"Maybe it will be," Kaya said hopefully.

I shook my head. "The Ookami are strong, and the strong are not so easily frightened. In the time since Ryu's father invited mine to unite our clans, their rule has spread over the land like a water stain on silk. Lord Tsuru's clan is only one of many they've conquered. Some gave up without much of a struggle, like the willow people. They lost their freedom and have to pay heavy tribute to the Ookami, but aside from being forced to tear down their watchtower and surrender most of their weapons, they lead their old lives."

Kaya became thoughtful. "Himiko . . . do you ever regret that your father refused to ally your people with the wolves?"

"If that idea ever comes to me, it dies quickly. Father had good reason to reject the Ookami offer. He didn't trust them. They were too . . . hungry. He didn't want our clan to be their friend today, their prey tomorrow."

My friend considered this, then asked: "When they

did attack your clan, do you think he should have acted like Lord Tsuru and surrendered? It would have spared lives and the Ookami probably wouldn't have destroyed as much of the village. Your people could have gone on living as they were, and your family—"

"No." I cut her off, my face grim. "We might have pretended that everything was as it used to be, but the truth? The truth would be that the Ookami could show up at our gates at any time, demand anything they wanted—crops, animals, people—and get it. Think, Kaya: Lord Tsuru said he had young and pretty daughters, but where were they? The willow folk are the wolf clan's slaves in everything but the name. They put their necks under Lord Ryu's foot docilely. We fought to stay free."

"But you lost," Kaya said in a small, compassionate voice.

"Yes." I looked past her, back in the direction of my village, my family, my people. "For now."

The road we followed changed, taking us deeper into the mountains. The weather was mostly fair, but not always kind to us. More than once we had to take insufficient refuge from wind and cold and rain. There were days when Kaya's arrows provided plenty to eat and other times when we had to be content with half-empty bellies. There were nights when we slept as peacefully as though we were in our own homes and others when evil dreams disturbed us, when we were kept awake by the sounds of prowling creatures, and when we awoke with the aching bones of grandmothers.

I lost count of the days we traveled. Lord Hideki had admitted he was only guessing about how long it had taken him to reach the Ookami lands. Lord Tsuru had little useful information to add. He had never ventured farther from home than the range of a hunting party. All of his knowledge concerning different clans came to him secondhand, from the stories other people told him. When Kaya and I did encounter settlements along the way it was either thanks to Lord Hideki's memories or by pure chance.

"I could get used to this," Kaya said as we left another village behind. "I forgot how good it is to sleep with a roof over my head."

"Well, I hope you'll remember that when we return," I said playfully. "Yari will be pleased to know his new wife won't be running off into the forest on any more hunting trips. She'll stay right where she belongs, taking care of her house and her husband."

"Ha! I'll leave that to Yari's *junior* wife, thank you very much," Kaya replied. "I'd rather put up with a little discomfort when I'm out making a kill than a lot of bother cooking it!"

Whenever we stayed the night in a village, we did so using the names that I had created for us before we approached the willow clan. We became so accustomed to introducing ourselves as "Lady Iyoko" the shaman and her sister, "Lady Karasu," that I frequently found myself calling Kaya by her false identity when we were on a rocky trail or crossing a mountain meadow. If Kaya teased me about it, I reminded her that she did the same thing to me.

"I suppose it's a good thing, all in all," I remarked. "Better to call you Karasu by accident out here than to slip up in some village and call you by your real name. That could be disastrous."

"Oh, it wouldn't be so bad." Kaya shrugged off all the consequences of having our true names revealed. "You'd find a way to explain and excuse it. You're getting very good at such things, Iyo—Himiko."

Getting better at telling lies? It wasn't a pleasing thought. I consoled myself by reviewing how many aspects of our ongoing deception were the truth: *I am a shaman and this journey is a pilgrimage . . . of sorts. It's not wrong to introduce Kaya as my sister, even if we weren't born that way. When orphaned children are taken in by new families, don't they call their adopted kin brother and sister? And ever since we visited the willow clan, Kaya stopped talking about me as though I've always got one foot in the spirit world and a handful of ghosts! So really, the only actual falsehood is our names, and that's a necessary deception, for our own protection. We have nothing to be ashamed of after all.*

I wish I could have believed that.

One afternoon, I saw a marvelous sight: plumes of white smoke rose from the hillside above our trail, wispy threads twining upward into the sky where rainbows played between them.

"Look, Kaya!" I cried, pointing. "Those must be the hot springs."

"What hot springs?" my friend asked.

"Oh, that's right, I never told you, did I? Lord Hideki mentioned them to me, but his passage through these mountains wandered much more than ours. I assumed he'd found them while exploring a far-off trail. I never expected to see them this close to our path!"

Kaya shaded her eyes and gazed uphill. "They don't *look* that close." She dropped her hand and grinned. "But they *do* look interesting. Do you think we should try to see them closer?"

"I think we should do more than that," I replied. "We'll have to make camp fairly soon anyway. We might as well do it up there."

It wasn't too difficult to reach the springs. A narrow game trail brought us there. They lay in a clearing where the steaming water formed a wide pool overshadowed by a rock ledge. Plants thrived all around, from lowly mosses to towering pines. I inhaled deeply, relishing the taste of mountain air that was fragrant with evergreen, tangy with the breath of earth itself.

I knelt beside the pool and ran my fingers through the water. "This feels good," I said. "*Very* good." I sat down and paddled my feet. "Ah! Hot!"

"How hot?" Kaya asked.

I flashed her a smile. "Not too hot to keep me out. What about you?"

For her answer, Kaya dropped her gear, yanked her dress off over her head, and was up to her neck in the middle of the pool before I could undo my sash.

We soaked blissfully in the hot spring until our fingertips wrinkled and the shadows of the trees around us stretched themselves long across the clearing. The fading

light finally jolted me out of my daydreams and sent me
scrambling to gather fuel for a campfire. Kaya dragged herself out of the water long enough to help me kindle a flame,
then walked right back into the pool.

"What about dinner?" I called after her.

"I can eat any day."

"Remember, it's going to get colder soon."

"Not where I am."

"You can't spend the whole night in there! You'll
drown."

"Drowned, warm, and happy," she replied, sighing
with contentment. "Just fish out my body in the morning,
will you?"

"You're impossible!" I shouted, and began preparing
my own meal. The hot springs had a peculiar taste, so I
used half the contents of my water gourd to cook a small
portion of our rice, adding savory wild greens and a bit of
dried venison for flavor. By the time it was ready, Kaya was
out of the pool, dressed, and shivering in the rapidly chill-
ing air.

"Changed your mind?" I asked archly. "Had enough
of a soak?"

"Y-y-yes," she said. "Un-until tomorrow."

True to her word, Kaya was chin-deep in the pool by
the time I woke up the next morning. Her eyes were closed
and there was a look of perfect peace and enjoyment on her
face. I was heartily tempted to follow her example. I was
also afraid that if I succumbed, we would lose a whole day
on the march. The hot springs were a welcome diversion

from the hardships of travel, but it was time to get back on the road to the wolf lands.

"All right, Kaya, that's enough," I said amiably. "It's time we were on our way."

Without bothering to open her eyes, she answered: "I disagree."

"Kaya . . ."

"What's that?" She raised one hand languidly from the water and cupped her ear. "Is it the spirit of the mountain I hear, calling my name, telling me to stay here and serve him as a hot springs maiden? O great spirit, how can I refuse? I'm yours forever!" She flung her arms high and slipped her whole head under the water, blowing a small storm of bubbles.

"This is not funny," I said when she emerged again. "We have to *go*."

"Yes, but we don't have to go *now,* do we?" she wheedled, pushing her dripping hair out of her eyes. "I'm not going to stay here the whole day; just until noon."

"Noon is too long."

"Half the morning, then."

"Don't try bargaining with me, Kaya. You have nothing to trade."

"And don't try playing chieftess, Himiko," she shot back with a hostile glare. "You have no way of forcing me out of the delectable water until *I* decide I'm ready to go." She closed her eyes once more. "Lady Badger has spoken."

I made a face that my friend could not see and contemplated my choices. I could wait for her to get out of the water, I could give up and join her in the pool, I could leave her where she was and continue on the road alone until she decided to catch up, or . . .

A short while later I stood at the edge of the flat stone outcrop over one end of the pool, my hands behind my back. "Kaya, dear sister?" I called in a too-sweet voice.

She opened one eye. "What?" she said, suspicious.

"It's time."

"So you said." She closed her eye and made a rude noise with her lips. "And *I* said, I'm not moving."

"Please don't. Stay right where you are. You're in just the right spot to help with the washing."

Now she had both eyes open wide and was sitting up straight.

"Himiko, what are you babbling—?" Then she saw what I had whipped out of hiding and was holding over the steaming pool. "My arrows!" she wailed. "My bow! The water will ruin them!"

"It might," I admitted. "We'll find out for sure if you don't get out now."

"You wouldn't *dare*. That bow is the best weapon we've got. It's our protection. It's been feeding your lazy belly for this entire trip. Put it down!"

"I will," I said. "On the ground or in the water, your choice."

"Are you out of your mind?"

"No, just out of patience."

"Fine, fine, stop pestering me, I give up." She levered herself out of the hot spring to sit on the lip of the pool just below my perch. Wringing water from her hair, she grumbled: "I'll be ready to go soon. Just let me—"

"Kaya, don't move!"

She looked up at me, exasperated. "Himiko, will you *please* make up your mind?"

"Don't . . . move." I spoke urgently, in a low voice, and gestured with her bow.

The scaly reddish-brown body, splotched with black-rimmed areas of gray, was coiled on the bank less than an arrow's-length from where she sat. The heavy triangular head looked as big as the palm of my hand. Kaya froze, staring into the black, unblinking eyes of a *mamushi,* a serpent whose poisonous bite never failed to kill.

"Hi-Himiko . . . ?" she quavered, her voice scarcely more than a thin whisper. "Himiko, can you get your blade?"

My blade? Ever since learning that Lord Hideki had given me an impressively made knife, Kaya had taken every opportunity to teach me how to use it . . . to no avail. No matter how long we practiced, I could never master a fighter's skills. Her attempts at teaching me how to throw it with accuracy were our greatest failures. Maybe it was a fault in me, maybe the spirit of the blade had no taste for being flung rather than wielded in hand-to-hand battle, maybe both; who could say? The fact remained that I was not born to be a warrior.

Now this.

"Kaya? Kaya, what do you want me to do?" I was dreadfully afraid I knew the answer.

"Do?" she echoed. "Throw your knife the way I taught you. Draw it slowly. Don't let the *mamushi* see you move too suddenly, or it will bite."

And what will the snake do when my blade flies wild? I can never hit it at this distance, at any *distance! O gods, why am I so clumsy?* I thought in desperation.

But I had to try.

I patted my sash and felt the familiar outline of my wand, the small, comforting roundness of my goddess, yet as for Lord Hideki's gift . . .

"I haven't got it," I said softly, apologetically. "The knife—the knife is in my bag."

"Oh." Kaya's breath came out as a sigh of hopelessness. We both knew that to reach the campsite where I'd left my gear, I would have to climb down from my ledge and walk past the place where the *mamushi* held my friend captive. The snake would see me, take fright, and then . . .

"Stay where you are," I said, trying to encourage her. "The creature knows that you're too big to be its natural prey. Soon it will lose interest and go away."

"I don't think so," my friend answered in a distant voice that sounded as though it were already coming from the world of the spirits. "See how it's coiled, how it stares at me? It's waiting. It will wait as long as it takes for me to move, and then . . . then it will strike. When that happens, Himiko . . ."

I did not hear what else she said. My mind retreated, turning inward, seeking the glowing path that came to me in visions. The vapors of the hot springs swirled around me and I shared their breath, the breath of dragons. The sunlight turned them from white to gold and I wrapped their essence around me, cupping their warmth and strength in my hands.

I saw the serpent's spirit through the gleaming mist. It was a tightly coiled, jagged shape of black and scarlet, like a basket woven of thorns. I reached out to it, coaxing the creature with honeyed words and softly spun threads of song. I praised its beauty, its unchallenged strength, its prowess as a hunter.

You who rule this mountain, mighty chieftess whose whole body embraces the earth, turn aside from the helpless creature before you! I pleaded, spirit to spirit. *Show mercy.*

Mercy? The word came back to me in a crackling jumble of witless pain and terror from the serpent's mind. *No, what, how, this? Burn! Burn, hurt, burn!*

I drew back, trembling, assaulted by so much panic and anguish. My vision sharpened and I saw a tiny seed lodged in the *mamushi*'s flat skull, a diseased speck already sending out tendrils of decay to devour the creature's mind. Its suffering was unbearable. Its mind howled for revenge against a tormentor it could not see—*strike, eat, fight, hurt, strike, strike, strike!*—but its spirit wailed for release.

I do not know where I found the stone or how I was able to lift and throw something so cumbersome and heavy. I was still lost in the realm of spirits, vainly trying to comfort the serpent in its agony, when I heard Kaya cry out and saw the *mamushi*'s presence flare up white-hot, then sink into the misty ground.

I returned to the waking world and saw my friend gaping up at me, dumbstruck. The limp, lifeless tail of the *mamushi* stuck out from under the huge flat rock that had crushed the rest of the creature.

"Forgive me," I whispered, and crumpled to my knees on the ledge.

As soon as Kaya and I recovered from what we had just experienced, we resumed our travels. It didn't take my friend long to go back to being her old, jolly self, and to recover her courage by turning her near-tragedy into a joke.

"I wish you would have told me why you're so awkward with that knife, Himiko," she said. "You can't teach a spearman how to use a bow, and you can't teach the way of the blade to a—a—a rock girl!"

"Is that what you're going to call me now?" I asked with a half smile.

"Maybe." She shrugged. "We should find a storyteller to recount the adventure of how Rock Girl saved Lady Badger's life from the dragon's poisoned breath by uprooting a mountain and crushing the monster! The children will love it."

"I think we've already *got* a storyteller," I said, giving her a meaningful look. "One who can turn the simplest event into a heroic tale. Kaya, I dropped a big stone on top of a snake. That's all."

"And saved me," she pointed out.

"All right, and saved you." I linked my arm through hers and squeezed it affectionately. "But I only did it for selfish reasons, because I couldn't stand the notion of a world without my Lady Badger."

The longer we traveled, the more my thoughts became haunted by doubt. The aches of walking so far, for so many days, became as much a part of my everyday existence as breathing, but the dark thoughts crowding into my mind brought pain that no hot spring could relieve.

What if we go astray? What if we can't find the Ookami settlement? What if it's so closely guarded that we can't find a way to steal inside the walls? What if it's so big that we can't find my little brother? What if there's no way to rescue him? What if we get through the gates and into the wolves' lair only to find that Noboru is . . . gone?

O gods, how that last possibility tore my heart! I had grown up with the hard truth that children died. Before they gave birth to Takehiko and Sanjirou, my stepmothers had each buried an infant son. My own mother had lost two daughters before I was born. Sickness and accident could claim children's lives even when they were in the care of those who loved them best. How much easier for death to find them when they lived enslaved among strangers!

I was held fast in the grasp of these dire thoughts when Kaya and I reached the village of the Inoshishi clan. At first there was nothing to distinguish our stay with the boar people from any of the other stops we had made along the way to the Ookami. Kaya no longer puffed up my shaman's art with ghost stories when she introduced us. However, we still received extraordinary hospitality. I could tell how extravagant it was by the sullen looks our host's clanfolk shot our way when he ordered them to fetch the makings for a feast in our honor.

"There's no need for this," I protested. "A simple meal will be enough."

"It would not," the boar chieftain replied firmly. Like all of the clan leaders we had encountered on our trip, he was also a shaman, but he went about the village decked out in enough beads, bells, mirrors, and feathers to furnish Master Michio, Lady Ikumi, me, and half a dozen more of us with all the spell-weaving tools we would ever need. "I will not hear of it, Lady Iyoko. You are a great shaman on a sacred pilgrimage. If we do not show the proper respect to those of us who make peace between our people and the spirits, it would be a lamentable state of affairs."

Meaning that if I am not given special treatment—whether I want it or not!—your people may start asking themselves why you should have it, I thought.

We ate our meal in the company of the Inoshishi nobles. The chieftain's house was large enough to shelter such a gathering, but it seemed rather bare inside. A young man seated to my left noticed my curious glances and murmured, "You should have come here many seasons ago, my lady. Our chieftain's house held many beautiful things, in those days. We are a small settlement, but we always produced enough extra rice to trade. When I was still riding on my mother's hip, I saw our men set out carrying jar after jar of rice and come home laden with woven silk, burnished bronze mirrors, and countless other wonders!"

"What happened?" I asked. "When did your harvests fail? Was there a blight? Fire? Locusts?"

His eyebrows met. "Wolves."

I understood.

"I hear that your pilgrimage must take you through their territory, Lady Iyoko," he said. "You will be pleased to know that you don't have too much farther to travel. We are the last village until you reach the Ookami settlement, though you still need to get through a mountain pass that might be rough going." His frown deepened. "I wish it were impossible."

"You disapprove of my journey?" I could not help speaking to him a little sharply. In every village we had visited, Kaya and I always heard negative remarks about two girls traveling alone, everything from dour predictions of the disasters awaiting us to expectant gloating: *And when it does* happen, *it will serve you right!* I was tired of it.

"I was talking about the pass, not your pilgrimage," he said stiffly. "Your journey is not what brought the Ookami streaming down upon us, overwhelming us, giving us no choice but to serve them or die. The rice we used to trade now goes to fill their storehouses. So do as much of our other crops as they care to take. We live hungry now."

He made a sweeping gesture over the food spread out before us. "It pleases our chieftain to pretend as though we are still our own masters and can entertain guests lavishly. My fellow nobles will not say one word to dissuade him. Why should they? We don't get to eat this well every day. Our common-born kin, on the other hand . . ." He let his words drift off.

I recalled the hard looks directed at Kaya and me, and the hunger-pinched faces. "I am sorry for them," I said. "For them and for you. My path here led me through many clans conquered by the Ookami, but the Inoshishi were the first. You have suffered their greed longer than any other people."

"No, Lady Iyoko," he said solemnly. "We were the second." He got to his feet, made a gesture of respect to me, and left the chieftain's house.

I wanted to go after him and ask what he meant by that. Hadn't he asserted that the Inoshishi were the last clan we would meet until we found the Ookami? It made no sense. Unfortunately, when I tried to rise, the boar chieftain took notice and made such a fuss that I had to resume my place and endure the feast until it was over.

I passed an uncomfortable night and woke up groggy but eager to be gone. Kaya gave me a sour look when I roused her, but once she wiped the sleep from her eyes, she shared my impatience to begin the last part of our journey.

At my suggestion, we agreed to break our fast later that morning, to avoid delay. We crept out of the chieftain's house stealthily, while his wives and children slept soundly in spite of his thunderous snores.

"He even *sounds* like a wild boar," Kaya whispered. I shushed her.

We stepped into a cold mountain morning, damp and gray, but already beginning to blush with the first light of dawn. A thin mist still lingered, making the Inoshishi village look like an abode of ghosts.

"I hope the gates aren't barred," I murmured to Kaya, then remembered: the Ookami did not allow their subject clans to have any. The wolves preferred vulnerable prey. Kaya and I were swiftly through the open entryway, the sun at our backs, forceful strides carrying us farther and farther from the Inoshishi.

7

ENCOUNTERS

"Look, Himiko, a fox shrine!" Kaya pointed at a flat-topped boulder by the roadside. A prettily carved wooden image of a seated fox perched on the stone, with a tiny pinch of rice sprinkled between its forepaws. Even when every grain was precious, people never failed to make an offering to the spirit that protected the crops. The shrine was sheltered in a stand of pine trees. We had climbed to the highest limit of the Inoshishi clan's terraced fields and were about to venture farther up the slope, to where the path narrowed into a mountain trail. The trees in the distance grew thick and plentiful, but no timber remained so close to the cultivated lands except the fox spirit's grove. I thought I heard a small, contented voice whisper *I like the scent of pine needles. You people were very wise to spare my trees.*

"We should leave something too," I said. "The fox is a very clever spirit, and we're going to need all the cleverness we can get."

"What about some more rice?" Kaya nodded at my sack. We had divided the responsibility for carrying our supplies, but the way things happened, I was the one carrying all of our rice. "It wouldn't have to be a lot."

"Yes, but it's too easy. I want the spirit to know that we gave some *thought* to our gift."

"All right," Kaya said gravely. "I'll wait here; you catch a mouse."

I twisted my mouth at her, then showed her my back as I cast about for an appropriate offering. There were poor gleanings, nothing to see but the common grasses waving along the border of the new plantings. I was just about to start searching the path at my feet for an especially pretty stone when something drew my eyes to the shadows beneath the shrine's guardian trees. A flash of bright green caught my attention, a sprig of blossoms the color of a fox's eyes. I gave a happy cry and raced to pick them, throwing myself onto my knees among the tangle of ancient roots.

"Lady Iyoko, forgive me!" A high, frightened voice startled me. I glimpsed bare feet peeking out from behind the same great tree trunk where I knelt, my fingers clutching the fox-eye flowers.

"Who's there?" I called. "Show yourself." I heard a muffled creak at my back and a low hiss, the familiar sound of Kaya stringing her bow and drawing an arrow from her quiver. "We won't hurt you," I added, praying that my friend would take the hint and let our unexpected visitor come out of hiding.

A wide, pale face came into view. The young woman confronting us looked ready to burst into tears. "I'm sorry,

Lady Iyoko, I truly am. I should have spoken as soon as I saw you and Lady Karasu on the trail, but—but I must have drowsed off, waiting for you to come this way."

She stepped into full view. There was no mistaking her condition: the front of her dress bulged with a child waiting to be born.

Soon, by the look of things, I thought. "You were *waiting* here for us?" I asked, incredulous. "It was hardly light when we left your village. You mean you were here for part of the night?"

"The whole night," she said, averting her eyes.

"With *that* belly?" Kaya demanded, unbending her bow. "Are you out of your mind?"

"I thought I was safe enough," she replied with a rueful smile. "The fox spirit has always been a good guardian to my family . . . almost always. You know how it is with foxes." Kaya grunted agreement. "Besides, I had to come here to meet you. I couldn't ask this favor if we were still down in the village."

"What favor?" I asked.

She went back behind the tree, returning with a bulging sack bigger than her head. When she handed me the bag, I encountered the familiar feeling of many small grains shifting under my fingers. "Rice?" She nodded. "Where did you get this?"

She looked alarmed. "Oh! I didn't steal it, if that's what you mean. Every family in our clan is given a ration of rice from our stores throughout the winter. My husband and I have been putting aside a part of our share every day."

"This isn't right," I said, shaking my head. "You're going to have a baby. You should be eating as much as you can get, to build up your strength. If you don't take care of yourself—"

"But I am!" she interrupted. "Otherwise I wouldn't ask you to take this offering to the fox shrine on the other side of the mountain. I'd go myself."

"This is . . . a very generous offering. Especially when your clan has so little to spare."

"It's *my* rice, and I can do what I want with it!" Our timid friend turned hard-faced and stubborn. "This *must* be taken to the other fox shrine. My grandmother told us that the spirits turn away from impure hearts. You're a shaman; the spirits speak to you, which proves I can trust you to do this, but if you refuse—"

"—you'll do it yourself?" I concluded for her. She nodded again, her mouth a tight line. She put on a brave front, but I could tell that she was afraid, for her unborn baby's sake. I beckoned Kaya and handed her the bag of rice. "Tell us where to find the other fox shrine."

Her face beamed with relief. "Oh, that will be easy! It lies about halfway down the other side of this mountain, in the middle of a meadow marked by—by many burnt trees." She grabbed my hands and bowed deeply over them. "Thank you for doing this, my lady. The gods will bless you. They will protect you. They will keep the *oni* deeply asleep in his lair when you pass by."

Kaya shifted the big rice sack to her hip and frowned. "What *oni*?" My usually bold friend looked agitated at the mention of that terrible monster, the mountain ogre. I didn't blame her for that.

An *oni* was twice the size of a full-grown man and had at least five times his strength. Their skins were deep blue or bloodred, they had horns on their heads, tusks jutting from their lower jaws, claws and talons sprouting from their hands and feet. It would take a team of hearty warriors to lift the *oni*'s favorite weapon, a spiked iron club. The brutes wore loincloths made from the hides of ferocious beasts and liked nothing better than to waylay travelers, crush their skulls, and devour them, flesh and bone.

Or so we'd been told.

"Yes, what *oni*?" I echoed. "Are we likely to cross paths with such a creature?"

The young woman hesitated, one hand resting protectively on her protruding belly. I could almost read the thoughts forming behind her worried expression: *If I say yes, they might decide to turn back, and then I'll have to bring my rice offering to the other fox shrine myself. But if I say no, I'll be lying; lying to a* shaman! *The gods will punish me for that.* Finally she said, "I don't *think* so. No one has even spied him this early in the spring. He lives on the other side of the pass and he has never ventured near the shrine you'll be seeking."

"Ah, so once we reach it, we'll be safe?"

"Ummm . . ." She licked her lips. "The *oni*'s den is farther down the slope than the fox shrine, so you will still be in his territory after you leave the offering. Oh, but you mustn't worry! He made his dwelling well away from the trail. I think he's as eager to avoid people as we are to avoid him. Even if he is ranging farther than usual, he's a clumsy thing. You can hear him crashing through the woods well before he reaches you, and that makes him easy to dodge or outrun."

"You sound like you've actually seen him."

"Oh yes, many times. So did everyone in our village."

Kaya and I exchanged an astonished look. "How is that possible? I thought you said he lives on the *other* side of this mountain," I said.

"I—I have to go," she said, ignoring my question. "My husband will be awake soon. Thank you for doing me this great favor, Lady Iyoko. I won't forget it." She picked up the hem of her dress and ran down the terraced hillside, in spite of her pregnancy.

Kaya wanted to go after her and compel an answer, but I said, "Let her go. I think she's already told everything useful, and we need to travel on."

"Useful? Huh!" Kaya picked up the young woman's rice bag. "All she did was warn us about an *oni* lurking some-where on our trail, but she couldn't even tell us for certain which side of the mountain he haunts. Now I'm not going to be able to relax on the way up *or* on the way down!"

"Well, better to know there is an *oni* living on this mountain than to trip over him," I remarked. "And it's al-ways best to be on guard, *oni* or no *oni.*"

She snorted. "Easy for you to say. You're not the one who's got to defend us from the monster." She indicated her bow and arrows.

"Don't make any wagers about that," I returned. "I could always drop a rock on him. I'm good at that." We continued on our way in the excellent company of shared laughter.

As we had been told, the path above the Inoshishi fields soon became steeper and narrower, threading its way through rugged forest. The trees grew close together, a massive palisade built by the spirits themselves. Birds called to one another from the branches above our heads and the underbrush stirred with the comings and goings of small, furry creatures, their minds set on finding food while steering well clear of the two-legged beasts invading their territory.

The day was sunny enough to fight off the chill clinging to the upper reaches of the mountain. We walked briskly, only feeling the cold when we stopped to take a drink from a glimmering rivulet or to rest our feet. Midday brought us to a little clearing, where we decided to have something to eat. I was just unpacking my bag when we heard the sound of heavy footsteps approaching from the slope below.

Kaya had her bow strung and an arrow nocked before I could whisper, "Do you think it's the *oni*?" Her jaw was set and perspiration dewed her brow, but she held her aim so steady that she might as well have been the image of a hunter carved from solid rock.

"Hello? Lady Iyoko? Lady Karasu, is that you?" A man's deep, confident voice reached us. "Don't be afraid, please. I'm a friend and I've come to help you!" Two breaths later, he emerged from between the trees, saw Kaya's arrow pointing at his chest, and jerked back. "Er, I *said* I'm a friend."

"People say a lot of things," Kaya replied evenly, but she lowered her bow. "We usually know our friends by name. I can't say that about you."

"Pardon me, please. I am Gori of the Inoshishi clan." He knelt hastily and pressed his hands to the earth, showing us respect. He was a broad-chested, brawny fellow who looked big and imposing even when he crouched submissively. "I apologize if I frightened you."

"Did I *look* frightened?" Kaya snapped.

He began to stammer a jumble of explanations and apologies. Kaya *had* been scared—so had I!—and she clearly resented Gori for giving her a fright, even if it was only temporary. She would have let him go on babbling excuses forever, just to soothe her wounded pride, if I had let her.

"Lady Karasu and I are happy to accept your apology, Gori," I said, putting an end to the awkward situation. "Now tell us why you're following us. Your clan has its own shaman, so I doubt you need my help for a healing."

Gori got to his feet. "I came after you to offer help, Lady Iyoko, not to ask for any. I am one of our clan's best hunters. I know these mountain paths very well. When I found out you were heading this way, to reach the Ookami homelands, I thought you could use my knowledge and my protection." A sideways glance at Kaya's stormy face made him add: "Well, maybe you won't need my *protection*. You're more than a match for the *oni*, if you ask me."

"What do you know about the *oni*, Gori?" I asked. "Are you one of those who has seen him?"

"Only from a distance. I was on the other side of the mountain, tracking a kamoshika, when I got a peek at him." He grinned nervously. "He saw me too. I'll never forget how he roared and shook his club! The kamoshika was caught between us, took one look at him, and bolted back uphill, right into range of my spear. It was too good a kill to pass up, even with a monster so close, so I acted fast. My quarry didn't have a chance to hit the ground before I slung the body over my shoulders and ran!"

Kaya narrowed her eyes. "Hunters' tales. Bah. I'm surprised you didn't claim to kill the kamoshika and the *oni* with the same spear-thrust! Speaking of spears, where's yours now? What kind of a hunter takes to the trail without his favorite weapon? And how were you expecting to . . . *protect* us without it?"

Instead of quailing under my friend's sarcastic attack, Gori stood tall. "It was a *small* kamoshika. I've run with heavier burdens on my back. I didn't bring my spear because I no longer have it. The shaft broke and it hasn't been repaired yet. And I didn't come after you unarmed." His hand dropped to the double-edged sword at his side. "Lady Karasu, you are a formidable young woman. I did not pursue you and your sister because I thought you were helpless females. I admire your courage for having undertaken this challenging journey. I don't think I could have done something so brave. All I want is to share one small part of your adventure by getting you through the mountain pass and beyond the *oni*'s territory. Will you allow it?"

Kaya and I looked at one another, silently contemplating Gori's offer. I motioned her closer and whispered, "He would only be with us for a few days, and he does know the road."

"What's there to know about it?" Kaya hissed back.

"Whether it survived the winter," I responded. "What if there's been a rockfall or a place where the path's washed out? He's hunted both sides of this mountain. He'd be able to guide us to the Ookami lands by following game trails."

"He *says* he's a hunter."

"He'll have to prove it soon enough. We'll let him come with us, but we're not going to feed him."

Kaya grinned. "Agreed."

Kaya's skepticism about Gori did not last the day. The big man showed himself to be deeply familiar with the route we traveled. Every so often he would pause to point out a place where a few early mushrooms had sprouted, or where a spring of fresh water bubbled just off the path, hidden unless you knew it was there. Once, he climbed a tree and came down holding a nest full of eggs. The mother bird came swooping down at him, but his answer was to grab a rock and fling it at her with deadly accuracy.

"Not much meat," he said, holding the little feathered body by one leg. "But I've eaten less and worse." He stuck the creature into his belt and offered us the eggs. Kaya accepted, but my mind echoed with the plaintive lament of the desolate mother's ghost and could not bring myself to stomach such a meal.

By the time we made camp for the night, Gori and Kaya had reached an accord and were beginning to banter back and forth like old friends. There were even a few mildly flirtatious words and looks between them. When he excused himself for a necessary trip into the woods, I nudged her and teased, "Do you think Yari's going to like it when you bring *that* one home?"

"The only one who'll have to like it is me." She smirked.

Though I had gotten up before dawn and walked all day on steep paths, I could not sleep that night. All my worries about what I would find when we reached the end of the road to Ryu's lair danced and swayed around me. I saw a wooden palisade ringing the wolf village, but the logs took on new life, sprouted branches and leaves, and began to grow until I faced an impenetrable fence of cedar trees keeping me out. To make things worse, I could hear my little brother's voice calling to me from the other side, weeping, screaming, and then . . . silenced. I threw myself against the unmoving tree trunks, clawing at them until my fingernails split and bled, crying, *Noboru! Noboru, don't give up! Don't despair! I'm here! I'll save you!*

He cannot hear you, Himiko, said a voice behind me. My heart leaped at the cherished sound but I froze where I stood.

What is it, my princess? Why won't you look at me?

I am afraid.

What do you fear?

That when I turn, I won't see you. I don't know if this is a vision or a dream. I didn't seek it, so I must have wandered into sleep, but if that's true . . . I took a steadying breath. *If that's true and I'm dreaming, I am afraid that when I try to see you, I will wake up and you will be gone.*

A strong hand closed gently on my shoulder. *How can that happen, when I am yours in dreams as well as visions, as much a part of you as wishes, love, and memory? I am here. Turn to me, Himiko.*

I did, and once again saw his face: Reikon, my spirit prince, my heart's home.

His arms folded around me and I inhaled a dizzying fragrance of the deep forest, of soft moss, ancient trees, and immortal stones. *If this is a dream, never let me wake,* I thought. *If this is a vision, let it carry me away forever.*

My love, you know that cannot be. He stepped back, breaking our embrace, shattering the moment. His eyes held my heartache.

Yes. I lowered my head. Mama's mad, distraught face swam in the air between us, and Noboru's image, innocent and smiling.

You are afraid you'll fail them, Reikon said. *You imagine monsters standing in your path, and you have no sword mighty enough to slay them.*

A sword? I uttered a brittle laugh. *I don't even know how to fight using my knife!*

Yet you will know how to use it well enough, when you must.

Yes, at mealtimes.

I mocked myself, but he looked as wounded as though I had spoken cruelly to him. *You will see, my princess. You will learn to have more faith in yourself. Perhaps you were not meant to win your greatest battles by bloodshed. You might not need a blade at all. Maybe—*he cocooned my hands tenderly in his—*maybe all that you are fated to wield is this.*

His fingers uncurled, revealing that I held the radiant image of the goddess. I began to smile, welcoming her, but suddenly all my joy fled. Something was wrong. The dragon stone in the goddess's arms shone as gloriously as always, but within the whirlpool of light I saw darker threads arising to entwine with the swirls of gold. I gazed deeper into their dizzying dance and tasted sour fear in the back of my throat as the central vision took the shape of a serpent's head, jaws wide, fangs about to strike.

You thought you killed me, Himiko, the *mamushi* hissed. *But I only shed my skin and came back to claim my rightful prey.* The heavy head darted out, the fangs struck, and I heard Kaya cry out in pain, terror, and despair.

I awoke breathless, staring up through pine branches at a sky full of stars, my heart pounding so loudly in my ears that I thought my head would shatter. *Oh gods, what a nightmare!* I thought. *I hope I didn't scream and disturb . . .*

"Don't. Please, don't."

What was that? It was Kaya's voice, but so quiet, so cowed that it didn't sound like her at all.

"Shut up, I told you," a second voice whispered, harsh and intense. "Wake your little friend and I'll have to kill her. Is that what you want?"

"No."

"Then lie still."

I turned slowly onto my side and peered into the darkness. My friend's bedroll lay a short distance from mine, just beyond the ashes of our fire. We usually slept side by side, but the terrain for this campsite was a maze of tree roots and rocks with few places comfortable enough to settle for the night. Now I saw two shapes lying together where only one should be. For a moment I imagined I was still the captive of my evil dream.

But this is no dream. All useless thoughts and feelings left me, banished by one decision, hard and sharp as a sword's edge: *I must . . . I will save my friend!*

I moved soundlessly, calling on the spirits to guide me, to clear dead twigs from my path, to disguise the muted rustle of my steps as the natural noises of small, night-prowling creatures. I implored the phantom of my brother Aki to lend me his stealth as a hunter and begged the ghost of his bride, Hoshi, to keep her sister Kaya safe until I could reach her.

The spirits were good: Gori didn't know I was standing over him until I seized him by a thick loop of hair, yanked his head back, and held Lord Hideki's sword under his chin. He tried to shriek but could only gurgle in fear. The blade's bite let him know that if he struggled at all, he would fall forward and cut his own throat.

Starlight shimmered over the knife he still clutched in his right hand. "Drop that," I told him. He obeyed instantly. "Kaya, can you see where it fell?" The time for "Lady Karasu" and "Lady Iyoko" was past.

"I've got it." How wonderful to hear my friend speak normally, no longer a victim pleading with her attacker, her strength restored! "He had it against my neck; a fine way to wake up! I think he even cut the skin a little. Hold him still, Himiko, and I'll let him find out how that feels."

"No. Not unless we have to." I turned my attention to

Gori. "You are going to move just enough to let my friend get out from under you. *Slowly,* understand?"

Automatically he began to nod, but my sword reminded him this was a bad idea. "Y-yes, my lady," he croaked, and cautiously supported his weight on his arms so that Kaya could crawl clear of him.

"Get your bow and train an arrow on him," I told her once she was on her feet again. "We have to talk about what to do with this carrion eater, and I don't want to hold him still like this forever."

"Well, if that's the case, you'll have to kill him now and be done with it," Kaya spat. I could almost feel the white-hot force of her justifiable rage against Gori. "The bastard cut my bowstring! He taunted me about it, while he had me pinned. You should have heard him, playing the big man! '*If* you please me, pretty one, I'll let you two girls go, but I don't want to find one of your arrows in my back when I head home, so I've taken care of that.' He told me he was going to make off with everything we had, and it wouldn't do us any good to come back to his village and complain, because he'd get there first and split whatever he stole with his clan leader."

"What? The Inoshishi *sent* him to rob us?"

"Pff! No. But this filth was going to drop enough gifts into the boar chieftain's lap so that we'd *stay* robbed! He's a brute and a coward and a miserable thief and—"

"—heavy," I finished for her. "Where's your bow?"

"I *told* you, he cut the—"

"Even a cut bowstring has its uses," I said with a smile. Shortly later, Kaya and I stood contemplating the man who had claimed his only reason for following us was to be our helper and protector. He lay on his stomach, face in the dirt, ankles tightly bound together and hands secured behind his back.

"You tie very impressive knots," I remarked to my friend.

"That was the best bowstring I ever owned," she grouched. "*Now* what good am I?"

"You still have your knife, and you can keep Gori's. Unlike me, you do know how to throw a blade."

"But I'm better with a bow and arrows." Kaya rubbed her chin thoughtfully, then pulled out Gori's knife and dropped beside him. He squealed in fear, expecting the worst.

To be honest, so did I.

"Kaya, don't—!" I spoke too late. The blade slashed, the deed was done, and my friend was on her feet again, brandishing her trophy.

"Would you *look* at this, Himiko?" she insisted, waving her hand under my nose. Her fingers clutched a remarkable length of shining black tresses, no longer bound up in the men's traditional style but trailing down her arm. "He's got nicer-looking hair than me! It's not fair." She grinned. "But it just might braid into a decent bowstring."

We left Gori trussed up and helpless. If he was lucky, he might find a way to wriggle out of his bonds, or maybe someone from his clan would notice his absence and have the Inoshishi hunters track him down before thirst or hunger or predators did so. Part of me felt that he deserved whatever hard fate the gods chose, a suitable punishment for what he had tried to do to Kaya. Another part of me hoped he would be saved and live to regret what he'd done.

Kaya did not have any such divided thoughts.

"I hope the mountain ogre finds him and devours him piece by piece, from the toes up!" she declared as we met the sunrise at the top of the pass.

"If you keep talking about him, he's always going to be with you, like a sickness that can't be cured. You'll never be able to forget how powerless he made you feel," I told her. "Whether he lives or dies back there, kill the memory of him once and for all."

"How do you suggest I do that?" she countered defensively.

"I don't know. Picture him as the *mamushi* that was trying to kill you and drop an imaginary rock on his head."

"At least the *mamushi* was honest," Kaya growled, but a little while later I saw her take Gori's severed hair and drop it beside the trail that took us down the mountain, into the Ookami lands.

8

THE HIDDEN ONES

We found the second fox shrine by midmorning of our first day descending the mountain path. It was much larger than the modest altar where the young Inoshishi woman had entrusted us with her carefully gleaned sack of rice. The image of its guardian spirit was elaborately painted and adorned with pretty pebbles and bits of turtle shell and perched atop a platform made of many heavy stones. They were built up high enough for us to look directly into the fox's eyes. As we had been told, the altar was waiting for us in a meadow with many burnt timbers standing around it. However . . .

"These are not trees," I said, glancing uneasily at the charred ruins of what once had been the elevated homes and storehouses of a village.

"See there?" Kaya indicated several large, regularly shaped depressions in the fresh spring grass. "Those were pit houses, I'm sure of it. They must have collapsed a long time ago; they're filled with wildflowers! Why would that young woman want to send such a generous offering to a deserted shrine?"

I was at a loss to explain it. "She's expecting a baby. She might have made a vow to the fox spirit and she's afraid to risk breaking it, for the child's sake."

"Then why couldn't she just leave the rice at the shrine near her own village?" Kaya argued, hefting the bag. "And if she's really worried about her baby, she should have eaten all this herself!"

There was an abrupt rustling from within the nearest ruined pit house. A scrawny, wrinkled, white-haired woman rose from her hiding place, groaning a little as her ancient bones balked at obeying her desires. She wore a weathered cloak made of dried grass, a crude garment that had helped her remain unnoticed until now.

"Yes, exactly!" she cried in a cricket's piping voice. "You are right, stranger, my Nazuna should take better care of herself, especially this close to her time! She will need strength to get through the birth, and afterward she'll have to make good milk for the infant. *'You can't do that living on air and prayer,'* I told her the last time she came here. I thought she took my advice, but I see I was wrong. Stupid, stubborn girl."

"Grandmother . . . ?" I faltered, addressing her with the respect due to someone of her age. "Grandmother, what is Nazuna to you?" I half expected her to turn to mist before my eyes and blow away on the breeze, a ghost encountered in a place that must harbor many more.

My question appeared to amuse her. "Just as you say,

girl: she is my eldest grandchild. You speak her name as if it's something new to your tongue. Why?"

"I never heard it until now."

"That's true," Kaya said, backing me up. "We're strangers in these lands, just passing through on a pilgrimage. Your granddaughter found us at the Inoshishi fox shrine, gave us this, and told us to leave it here."

"Is that so?" Her thinning eyebrows rose. "Pregnancy is making that child a little *too* trusting."

"I think you can see that her trust was not misplaced," I said, taking the rice bag from Kaya and holding it out to the old woman. "If you'll accept it, we can be on our way."

Nazuna's grandmother looked ashamed as she received the rice. "Forgive me, girls. Don't go so soon. The little ones and I seldom see other people. We cannot give you suitable hospitality, but we can give you somewhere comfortable to rest. We also know of a small hot spring nearby, very good for washing away the dust of travel and soaking tired feet."

"Oh *yes,* please!" Kaya exclaimed. I was happy seeing that my friend's close call with the *mamushi* was not going to spoil all hot springs for her.

The old woman chatted with us genially as she led us away from the ruined village. The need for concealing our identities was over: we introduced ourselves to her by our true names and clans, though I did not mention my calling. Some people, like my father, mistrusted shamans. Others were terrified of our powers. Until I knew this woman better, it was enough to be no more than Lady Himiko of the Matsu.

"I am Ayame of the hawk clan," she told us. "*Lady*

Ayame, if you please." She tittered, then sighed. "That high-sounding title is worth little to us now, when I fling stones to kill sleeping owls to eat and rob squirrels of their autumn hoards. Whenever we eat Nazuna's rice, it pains me to the marrow of my bones knowing that each bite comes out of her mouth, but what can we do? A few grains are sometimes all that keep us among the living."

"How did you know to wait by the fox shrine for our arrival with the rice today?" I asked.

"I didn't, until Isamu told me. You will meet my grandson soon, and his sister, Yuri. He's becoming quite the accomplished guard, always keeping an eye on the trails through here."

By this point in the conversation we had left the haunted meadow and were in a woodland of oak and evergreen. I spied what looked like a pile of forest debris at the base of a large tree and was startled when a grubby-faced little girl popped out of it like a bright-eyed little field mouse. When we came closer, I saw that the tumble-down heap of branches and grass was actually the top of a roughly built pit house. The girl shouted happily when she saw Lady Ayame approaching and ran to greet her, unconcerned by us two strangers in her grandmother's company. Another child watched our approach with more wariness. He looked only slightly older than the girl, but with the tired eyes of a long-sorrowing man. Both of the children were thin as grass stalks.

"Isamu, my beloved boy, you were right!" Lady Ayame called out to him. "You are a true son of the Taka clan, born with a hawk's eyes! See, these are the two girls you saw coming down the path—Lady Himiko of the Matsu and Lady Kaya of the Shika clan. They bring us more rice from Nazuna."

"Why didn't Nazuna bring it herself, like always?" Isamu asked, staring at Kaya and me as though the mere sight of us put a sour taste in his mouth. "What happened to her?"

"Tsk. What a question!" His grandmother stroked his hair, which was ungroomed and badly tangled. "She's going to have her baby soon. Do you want her to give birth while trying to get over the mountain?"

"No, oh no!" little Yuri cried. "We don't want that. What if the *oni* was out hunting and caught her and her baby? He'd *eat* them!" With a shy, sidelong look at me, she added, "Did *you* see the mountain ogre, Lady Himiko?"

"No, my dear." I smiled at the child, but it was hard to do wholeheartedly when her bony body and pale face filled my heart with pity. "Your sister Nazuna warned us about him, but he never crossed our path."

"Oh, Nazuna's not my *sister,*" Yuri informed me with a grown-up's dignity. "We had different mamas. Hers was a des—a des—a *despicable coward.*" She pronounced the offensive words with assurance, but I would bet she had no idea what they meant.

"Yuri! Don't say such things!" Lady Ayame scolded. "Nazuna's mother was your father's senior wife and the daughter of my heart. When your mother died, she treated you like her own children."

"I would never want to be *that* woman's child," Isamu said angrily. "When the Ookami came and destroyed us,

Father fought, but *that* woman ran away. She abandoned us all."

"*Isamu!*" Lady Ayame's reproof rang out like a slap. "You will *not* speak ill of our family. Our guests will think that I am failing to raise you well. Do not shame me!"

The boy was abashed. "I'm sorry, Grandma," he muttered.

"Then show it. Lady Kaya and Lady Himiko want to bathe after their travels. Lead them to the spring."

"Can I go too, Grandma?" Yuri bounced on her toes, clutching the old woman's papery hand. "Please, please, please?"

"But if you do, who will help me make room in the house for our visitors?" her grandmother asked mildly. The child's face fell.

"Lady Ayame, why not let those three go?" I said. "I will stay and help you."

"Nonsense! You are my guest. You shouldn't have to prepare your own sleeping space. We have little left to us, Lady Himiko, but we have not lost everything."

True, I thought, regarding the old woman's noble bearing with admiration. *Your village has become a burial ground, your noble rank is a drop of water in the sun, and hunger sleeps across your threshold, but you have kept one treasure: your dignity. I will not rob you of it.*

"My lady, I never intended to offend you," I said. "It's simply that I would rather bathe later, but if you *insist* I go now . . ."

"Insist!" She raised her hands in protest. "Didn't I just

say you're my guest? I would never do something so—so *discourteous*." She gave me a hurt look.

I hastened to apologize, which mollified her immediately. "What a silly misunderstanding we've had, Lady Himiko! If you don't want to go to the spring, please stay here and keep me company while I look after the house. You'll see there really isn't *that* much to do, so you can leave it all to me."

"Of course." I inclined my head deferentially, but I think we both knew how things would sort themselves out once Kaya and the children were out of sight.

I was right, and soon I was helping the old noblewoman make space for us in her poor home. As we worked, she began to chatter happily, words pouring from her with the joy of fresh water freed from the confinement of a dam.

"Ah, Lady Himiko, you have no idea how good it feels to be able to talk to another adult," she said after we had finished the task and were sitting together in the shade of a venerable oak tree. "Isamu and Yuri are good children, yet they *are* children. There are times I find myself looking forward to my Nazuna's next visit more for the conversation we'll have than for the food she'll bring."

"Lady Ayame, forgive my curiosity, but . . . if you miss Nazuna so much, why don't you and the children live with her, among the Inoshishi?" I asked. "Since she's there already, part of a household, it's clear that the boar people don't object to folk from other clans joining their settlement."

Lady Ayame's face became a flint. "You sound like her.

She always asks us to travel back over the mountain and live under her roof. She says she worries that we will die here, if we stay, but we have not budged from this land since the day the Ookami destroyed all we knew, all we loved, and we are not dead yet."

"*Yet,*" I thought, remembering the children's thin limbs and pinched faces.

"When we were with the boar clan, one of their young noblemen told me that they were the last village before we'd reach the Ookami settlement, but he also said that they were the second clan the wolves attacked," I said quietly. "Now I understand his words."

"Yes, we were the first of their conquests," the old woman said, her gaze seeking ghosts. "Nazuna told me that young Lord Ryu sent a messenger to the boar clan giving them the choice of battle or surrender. The wolf chieftain gave us no such choice, and no warning before the onslaught. He wanted us to *become* a warning to the other clans. Our fate was the reason the Inoshishi chieftain gave up without a fight."

She bent her head, and tears dropped onto her work-worn hands. "If I can do one thing before I die, it would be to make Yuri and Isamu see that Nazuna's mother was *not* a shameful coward. When the Ookami attacked and we saw that our men would not win that battle, she tried to gather *all* her children and get them to safety. I"—Lady Ayame's voice caught—"I told her to take Nazuna and go ahead. I promised I would come after her and bring the little ones, but . . ." She could not go on.

"But you are a hawk." I spoke hoping that I could find

the words to let her know that I understood her heart. "A nobly born lady of the Taka clan, and no hawk leaves its nest while one stick remains on top of another. You had faith that your warriors would rally and win the day, so you stood firm."

"Firm?" she echoed. "Foolish. How can I blame my Nazuna for being stupid and stubborn when she has *me* for a grandmother? Thank the gods that her mother had more sense! When she saw that I'd broken my promise, she didn't wait any longer but took her child through the pass and down to the boar clan lands. She died among strangers, but Nazuna was never made to feel like an outcast among the Inoshishi."

"Neither would you and the little ones," I coaxed. She only shook her head.

"We are *Taka,* not Inoshishi. The children and I have managed to reclaim one of our clan's fields. We raise enough food to get by, and we know how to forage for more. It will get easier as they get older and can do more work."

If they survive to get older, I thought, but decided not to press the point any further.

A little while later, Kaya and the children returned. My friend was so relaxed she looked as if the hot spring had melted the bones right out of her body. "You have to go there, Himiko," she said. "It's much nicer than that other one."

"No snakes?" I asked mischievously.

"Why do you think I said it's nicer?"

"Do as your friend says, my dear," our aged hostess urged. "We will eat after you bathe."

"Don't you want to come with me, Lady Ayame?"

"I used the spring this morning. Go, go! It's not too hard to find. The children and I have beaten a path to it, you'll see."

It was as she said: the winding woodland path was easy to follow and soon I was chin-deep in beautifully hot, soothing water. My hair floated around me, my travel-weariness wafted out of arms and legs, back and shoulders, the trees arching above the pool were filled with sweetly twittering birds, but my mind remained a blazing, clamoring knot of anxiety.

There must be a way to convince Lady Ayame to leave this place, I thought. *I have to find it! That woman is dancing with survival, her feet balanced on a single blade of grass above a chasm, but her first misstep will take down* three *lives. She is devoted to Yuri and Isamu, but clan pride and loyalty to the dead are hard ties to sever.*

I crawled out of the water and dressed, preoccupied. Before I rejoined the others, I placed my goddess on the edge of the hot spring and offered her a prayer: "Lady of the sun, lady of the dragon stone, help me. If I can give Lady Ayame an honorable reason to leave her ancestral lands and join Nazuna's new family, I think she'd take it, if only for the children's sake. Have mercy on them, and guide me. Let me find what I seek!"

That night, as we all lay uncomfortably close together in the shelter of Lady Ayame's hovel, I whispered my worries to Kaya.

She failed to see the problem. "Tell them you're a

shaman and that if they don't pack up and leave, you'll make them sorry."

"I can't do that!"

"Why not? Because it's false? Would you rather have these children pay the price for your honesty?"

"Kaya, suppose I do what you suggest: I scare Lady Ayame into going to the Inoshishi and living with Nazuna's family. Fine. But how long do you think she'd *stay* there? Hunger and isolation haven't made her run to a more comfortable life. If I force her to leave, she'll just wait until she's sure I've moved on and then come back."

"Yes, but I doubt she'd drag the children back here with her. And if she dies, it won't be so bad, because she'll do it on her own terms and because—because—" Kaya was suddenly quiet.

"—because she's old?" I supplied.

"I didn't say that." My friend sounded cross. We both knew she had been about to voice those very words without thinking, and she was ashamed of it. "I know that all their lives count, but we'll lose every one of them if we don't find an answer *soon*. We're moving on in the morning!"

"Lady Ayame is strong willed," I said. "The decision to join the Inoshishi must come from her, or it won't endure. How can we persuade a resolute woman to change her mind?"

"How does anyone make you change *your* mind?" Kaya quipped, then yawned. "If *I* had your skills, we wouldn't be losing sleep, trying to untangle this. First I'd summon Lady Ayame's ancestors to talk some sense into her, then

I'd make the spirits fetch that mountain ogre and have him carry the old woman and her grandchildren all the way to the boar clan village. But I'm no shaman, just tired. At least I can solve *that* problem myself. Good night, Himiko." She turned onto her side and was soon asleep.

I lay awake, listening to the sound of Kaya's slow, steady breathing, Lady Ayame's light snores, and the children's uneasy snuffling. *She's right,* I thought. *We have to leave tomorrow. Maybe I'll have better luck persuading Lady Ayame when we pass through here on our homeward road. If she has some secret reason for not wanting to live dependent on Nazuna, I might be able to have her join us and come live with my clan, or Kaya's, or . . .*

The day's long trek caught up with me. I began to lose myself in the first fog of sleep, but before dropping out of the waking world completely, something unexpected happened: my mind opened like a flower. I saw the goddess shining at its heart and heard her sweet voice, answering my prayers.

A spring morning high in the mountains was cold, waking everyone in the little house before sunrise. By unspoken agreement, Kaya and I dipped into our own supplies to provide breakfast for Lady Ayame and her family. When the old noblewoman tried to refuse, out of pride, Kaya stepped in:

"I made this meal. Are you saying that I—*your guest!*— am not worthy to cook your rice?" She put on such an implausible expression of wounded dignity that Lady Ayame cackled and conceded.

"Lady Ayame, we will leave you soon," I said as we ate. "Before I go, there are two things I must do, with your help."

"Name them, Lady Himiko."

"I have told you the name of my clan, but not our history. It is very much like your own: the Ookami attacked us, defeated us, and enslaved many of our people."

"I am sorry to hear it. The wolves' road leads them through here whenever Lord Ryu sets his sights on fresh conquests. We have often watched from hiding as the warriors march over the mountain, and we have witnessed them coming back with captives and plunder."

"Then you might have seen their return from our lands when three of my closest kin were taken as their hostages," I said, and told her the true purpose that had brought Kaya and me so far from home.

Lady Ayame was aghast. "Are you serious?"

"Serious enough to try."

"But you're so young! You should be choosing sweethearts, marrying, having children, not walking into the dragon's mouth!"

I did not ask her where she thought Yuri and Isamu would find *their* mates, if they survived long enough to reach that age. This was not the time. Instead I said, "I gave my word, Lady Ayame. If you cannot make me break it, will you help me keep it?"

"I?" Her hands flew to her chest. "What can I do?"

"You have lived here a long time, since the days before the wolves turned wild. Was there ever a time when your people traded with them, or were able to cross their lands unmolested? Did any member of the Taka clan see the Ookami settlement and speak about it when he came home? If you can reveal anything—*anything* about what's waiting for us at the end of our road, please speak. Your words may make a great difference."

"I . . . I will try." Lady Ayame closed her eyes and summoned distant memories.

Her words confirmed what I imagined: there *had* been better times between the Taka and the Ookami. In her father's day, young men often visited back and forth, all of them convinced that the *other* clan had the prettiest girls. From these scraps of remembered travelers' tales, Lady Ayame stitched together a fine description of the Ookami village and the land around it.

We thanked her so enthusiastically that she blushed with pleasure. "Who would imagine that those old stories would be useful?" she said. "Or this old woman?"

"Oh, *Grandma!*" Yuri gave her a mighty hug. "Don't talk like that. It makes me sad."

"Then I will never say such things again, my precious one," she replied, pressing her cheek to Yuri's. Satisfied, the child released her. "You see, girls?" Lady Ayame said to Kaya and me. "*This* is what you should seek: the blessing of love from your children's children, not the road to a monster's lair. Lord Ryu of the Ookami was rightly named; he is as dangerous as any dragon. But if you are still determined, heed my counsel: when you approach his lair, don't rush in. Watch and wait. Learn which blade will shatter against his hide and which sword has the power to slay him."

"I'm not going to try to kill Ryu," I said. "All I want is my little brother."

"Anyway, Himiko's not good with swords," Kaya put in. "Now, if you want to kill a dragon by dropping a rock on his head . . ."

I shot my friend a nasty look and went on speaking as if she hadn't said a word: "Thank you again for what you've told us, Lady Ayame. Now I have one last small thing to ask of you." I reached into my bag and placed the sacred bronze bell and mirror on the ground between us. "I am a shaman. Let me be the one to offer comfort to your dead."

I chanted for the spirits of the brave hawk people who had fallen to the spears and arrows of the wolf clan. I danced in a field of flowers somewhere between the ruins of the Taka village and Lady Ayame's tumbledown woodland house. Beneath the bright overgrowth of grass and blossoms lay what was left of her clan's ancestral burial ground. If I looked hard, I could see the remains of grave mounds, now little more than grassy hillocks. Had the Ookami knocked them down when they devastated this settlement? I could not bring myself to ask Lady Ayame such a painful question, but I would not be surprised if the answer was yes. What was it she had told us about Ryu's attack? *He wanted us to* become *a warning to the other clans."* To achieve that, he had not hesitated to strike down the dead as well as the living.

I sang for the dead, but the song that the spirits carried to my lips was a song of life. My mirror caught the rays of the ever-living sun and I sang about how joyfully all living things greeted the light of sun or moon and stars. I struck my bell, and I braided the words of my chant with those deep, warm notes to conjure images of kin gathered together to celebrate happy occasions—births, weddings, harvests. I opened my arms and spoke to the hawk clan spirits, setting them free from the graves that held them, offering them a better resting place.

"The earth turns to dust and blows away, the rivers run dry, the mountains crumble," I sang. "But the heart whose spark you kindled with your life, with your love, that is your enduring home. Wherever it dwells, you dwell, and before the day comes when it no longer beats, it leaves behind a new heart that will hold its spirit and your own! The earth turns to dust and sets you free, the rivers run dry and let your spirit bathe in light, the mountains crumble, but the living breath of love carries you higher than any hawk, beyond this place, beyond this earth, this sky, beyond every tomorrow. Let the gods be my witness, this is so, now and forever!"

I struck the bell one last time and let the fading echoes fall around me like cherry blossoms.

Lady Ayame approached me, Yuri clinging to her hand, Isamu walking stiffly beside her, striving to hold back tears. "This was what we could not give them," the old woman said softly. "Lord Ryu's one act of mercy was letting his new slaves bury our dead, but there was no reverence allowed. When the work took too long he lost patience and marched away. I buried the few he left behind, but I never felt my task was done until now. I think"—she gazed over the field—"I think I would like to go tell Nazuna what you did for us, Lady Himiko."

I held her free hand. "She will like that."

Lady Ayame and the children were busy gathering their meager belongings when Kaya and I took up our interrupted journey. Before we parted, the Taka noblewoman advised us to leave the well-traveled mountain path as soon as we saw a pair of rocks shaped like a wild boar's tusks. It was a landmark that Lord Hideki had mentioned too, though his instructions were to go straight through.

"Of course, he was trying to *encounter* the Ookami," I told Kaya. "We've got to circle *around* their valley, find a spot with a good view of what's below, and pray that we haven't picked a place that lies along one of their hunters' favorite game trails."

"Don't speak of game," Kaya said. "I saw *five* fat rabbits since we started down this path, and what could I do about it when my bow's little more than a stick of firewood? I swear, I heard the biggest one laughing at me!"

"You were going to make a new bowstring from Gori's hair," I reminded her. "Why don't you try that with mine? If you don't need a *lot* of it, that is."

"No, thanks."

"Why not? Do you *want* the rabbits to laugh at you?"

"Ha-ha-ha. Very funny. For your information, human hair makes a poor bowstring. It's not durable enough; too stretchy. Sorry to disappoint you."

"*And* the rabbits."

9

THE MOUNTAIN OGRE

Following Lady Ayame's directions and advice, Kaya and I left the main path and plunged deeper into the wilderness high above the Ookami village. We were close enough that the breeze sometimes brought us the faint, smoky smell of cooking from below, but far enough away that we could kindle our own campfire, as long as we kept it small.

The valley where the wolves dwelled was steep-sided and wide. The hillsides bore the scars of many rockfalls, making it look as if some titanic beast had raked its claws through the groves of oak, cedar, pine, and camphor trees. We had to make camp several times as we skirted the settled land. We were seeking a vantage point from which we could observe the Ookami without being detected and make our plans accordingly. How high was their palisade? How well maintained? How heavily warded? Had Ryu's ongoing series of triumphs made him and his people so overconfident about their own security that they no longer kept gate guards? Did the man assigned to the village watchtower take his duty seriously, or was it just a fine opportunity to nap away the day? *Why should I strain my eyes when all I'll ever see approaching us is a stray boar or a curious fox? Who would be foolhardy enough to attack the Ookami? We have conquered them all!*

As we continued to look for the ideal spot for seeing without being seen, we often went so deep into the woods that we could not get so much as a fleeting glimpse of the valley. Many tiny brooks crossed our path, their banks dappled with the hooves of kamoshika and deer, as well as the prints of smaller animals. There were even more signs of game marking our narrow, winding route, a trail so heavily used by the forest creatures that even Kaya's trained eye was not able to tell the difference between them.

"No really *big* beasts, anyhow," she said. "Nothing too dangerous, like a herd of wild boar or the *other* kind of wolves. And no *oni,* either."

"How would you know what sort of footprints an *oni* would make?"

"Hey, I can imagine what they'd be like. I've heard the stories. A monster with taloned feet who's bigger than five men is going to leave a mark even *you* could identify."

"I heard the stories too, and an *oni* is only as big as *two* men," I shot back. "Besides, since we turned off the main path, we're avoiding the mountain ogre's territory."

"I hope someone told all that to the ogre."

At one point, we encountered a stream broad and deep enough for fish to flicker through the water. We crouched on the rocks and tried our luck snaring them with our bare hands. To my own amazement, I caught two young trout, one after the other. Kaya was annoyed to see her hunter's status threatened, plunged wildly after the next set of glittering scales to swim past her, and made such a splash that she wound up empty-handed and soaking wet from neck to waist.

She sat back on her haunches and scowled at me. "Don't you *dare* say one word."

I pretended innocence. "What would I say?"

"That the rabbits aren't the only ones laughing at me now." She sat cross-legged on the rock, chin in hand. "Are you still willing to let me have some of your hair? I want to try making that bowstring after all."

Kaya began her task that evening while I broiled the trout. I watched, fascinated, as she began working with the long, thin strand she'd cut from the back of my head.

"Have you ever done that before?" I asked.

"No, but Mother taught me how to make thread. It's pretty much the same thing, except this is something I *want* to do." She paused and flexed her fingers. "I also hope I'm better at it. Mother said my threads were such a lumpy tangle that you could use them for bird snares."

She did not finish making her bowstring that night and was annoyed with herself all the next day. It didn't help that we stumbled across a full-grown mountain hare that sprang back and forth across our path as if he knew we had no way to bring him down.

"Rabbits laugh, but hares are *sarcastic*," Kaya complained, throwing a rock that the creature dodged with contempt. "I had to stow the bowstring in my bag, wrapped in some oak leaves. It had better not get loose or it'll be tangled and I'll have to start over."

"If that's what you have to do, I still have lots more hair," I said.

"It would be better if I could find something stronger to twist into it. Hmm. Kamoshika hair might work."

We had seen the prints of those short-horned, long-faced, shaggy mountain dwellers, and even caught sight of one as it fled before us, heading for the upper slopes of the valley, and yet . . .

"How will you get kamoshika hair for your bowstring if you can't catch a kamoshika without your bow?" I asked.

"I might find some tufts snagged in a bush. It's spring; the beasts will be shedding." She sounded self-assured. "I'm going to keep my eyes open for that, add it to the bowstring, and the next sassy hare I meet had better watch out!"

Kaya became obsessed with searching the under-growth for bits of kamoshika hair, looking left and right more than straight ahead. I warned her that if she didn't pay attention, she'd trip over a root or walk into a tree, but she ignored me. That was why, when I stopped at the edge of a clearing, she walked right into me and sent us both sprawling.

"*Off,*" I snarled, trying to push myself up.

"All right, all right, stop acting like a tail-singed dog." She rolled to one side, stood, and helped me stand. "It's your own fault for pulling up short like that. What's wrong? Did you see a spider?"

"I saw *that.*" I waved my hand, indicating what could only be called a gift from the gods. The clearing was exactly what we needed. The side facing the valley was screened by a row of young trees, survivors of a small land-slip that had taken down the rest of their grove. It was easy to look between them and get an unobstructed view of the Ookami settlement, but someone looking up from the valley would not be able to see anything on the mountainside but forest. There was also a rivulet running across the open ground, plentiful piles of fallen twigs and branches for campfires, and even a wild mulberry bush.

"Sickly thing," Kaya said when I showed it to her. "I doubt it will bear much fruit."

"If it grows so heavy with berries that all its twigs snap off, we'll never know," I said. "We'll be long gone by that time."

We began making ourselves at home in the clearing. Kaya unpacked her bag and was delighted to find that her half-made bowstring had not become a nest of knots. She sat beside the largest pile of deadwood and resumed work-ing on it. I unpacked my sack as well, taking stock of our food before making a short, exploratory walk through the woods beyond our camp. I hoped to find as many edible plants as possible, for until Kaya was once more able to wield her bow, we would have to depend on our own dwin-dling supplies and whatever we could forage from the land.

I could always go back to that stream where I caught the fish, I thought. *It wasn't too far from here. And maybe I can also . . .*

Mulling over the possibilities, I wandered back toward our campsite, unaware that I had become as distracted as Kaya when she'd bumped into me earlier. That was why I did not notice the mountain ogre lurking behind a tree until I was close enough for one huge, hairy paw to dig into my arm and haul me off my feet.

"Who are you?" he roared, stinking breath hot in my face. He raised his hand high, leaving me to dangle painfully while my shoulder felt ready to tear itself apart. Panicked, I groped for the strips of cloth barely covering his chest. When my fingers tightened on a handful of fabric, I pulled myself close, clinging to him like an infant to its mother. The ripe stench of sweat and rotten meat that radiated from his flesh made my head spin, but I had managed to take the strain off my shoulder, so I bore it.

"What are you doing to me?" the *oni* demanded, goggling at me with heavy-lidded eyes. "Who are you? Don't touch me! Go away! Why do you take my things? Talk! Talk!" He gave me no chance to respond to his warring questions. He shook me so hard that I lost my hold, but he also released his grasp on my hand. I flew into the nearest tree, the breath knocked from my body. He stomped toward me while I struggled to regain my senses, and loomed above me. That was when I saw that his other fist held a club big enough to crush the skull of a wild boar with one blow, a deadly bludgeon now hovering just above my head as the monster repeated his command: *"Talk!"*

"I—I am Himiko," I croaked, my bruised bones aching. "Please don't hurt me."

"Hurt you?" He blinked, then frowned. "You want to hurt *me*. You always do. You lie to me. You promise me clothes and food. You give me *this*." He patted his tattered garment. Was it the remains of a tunic or only a bunch of rags? His loincloth was not much better, as filthy, stinking, and disheveled as everything else about him. "And you put bad things in my food! When I eat what you give me, I get sick. Why do you do this?"

"But I did nothing," I protested, holding out my empty hands. "I never saw you before. I don't want to hurt you. I—"

"*Get away from her, monster!*" Kaya burst through the trees, waving a big stick of firewood. She swung it wildly at the *oni*, who wrenched it away from her as simply as breathing. Then he gave her a backhanded blow with his fist. She collapsed in a splay-limbed heap, unconscious.

"Kaya!" I rushed to my friend's side and took her into my lap, cradling her head in my arms. My fingers glided delicately over the side of her face where the beast had struck her. The skin was already shading from red to purple, but I felt nothing to indicate that he had broken her bones. "Oh, Kaya, my sister, what did he do to you?"

"She tried to hurt me."

Whose voice was that, so timid, so subdued and remorseful? I jerked my head up and saw the *oni* standing as far away from us as he could be without disappearing into the forest. He looked ready to cry.

"She tried to hurt me," he repeated, wringing the haft of his awful club between both hands. "You saw. Don't lie. I had to stop her, didn't I? Please?"

The mountain ogre's bizarre behavior threw me off balance, making me feel as though I'd gulped a bellyful of rice wine. I wanted to scream at him, to berate him for what he'd done. I wanted to draw my wand and urge the gods to make the earth open under his ponderous feet. I wanted to demand why a brutal, heartless monster who might have killed my friend if he'd landed a second blow was speaking to me like a penitent child.

A child . . .

"Yes," I said, making a special effort to speak calmly and subdue any hint of anger. "She did try to hurt you, but she only did it because she saw you hurting me."

"That isn't fair." The *oni*'s shoulders hunched. "I had to stop you too. You were in my place. No one comes here unless they want to hurt me, or do bad things. Once you left a rotting dog right where I sleep. Why don't you stay down there, where you belong? You sent me away when my mama died." His voice rose to a wail: "Why do you come after me? Why won't you leave me alone?" He slammed his club into a tree trunk again and again, sobbing.

My son! My son! See what those cruel creatures have done to you, my sweet little one!

My skin prickled the way it did before a thunderstorm. A mother's ghostly lament filled my head. My lips parted, and I heard myself begin to sing an unfamiliar lullaby. As I sang, I witnessed a shadow with a woman's face take shape in the air beside the ogre who was no ogre at all. The phantom did not touch him, yet her presence calmed him, comforted him, stilled his sobs, made him drop his club and sink to the ground, hugging himself into a tight ball. It vanished with the final note I sang.

"Why do you know that song?" he asked, staring at me in awe.

"I am a shaman," I said. "Sometimes the spirits speak through me. Your mama did not want to see you so unhappy and upset, so she let me help you. She loves you very much."

"She's ashamed of me too," he said, wiping his nose roughly on the back of one hand. "When the other children made fun of me, I hit them, but I was much bigger than they were and it"—he gave Kaya a guilty look—"it was very bad. I'm sorry. I'm sorry I hurt you. I'm sorry I hit your friend."

"I know," I said. Kaya groaned and stirred, but her eyes remained shut. "You can make this better. I am a shaman and a healer. I can make my friend feel better. Will you help?"

"Yes! Oh yes!" He sprang up and scooped Kaya from my lap. Before I could catch my breath, he had her back in the clearing, lying on a pile of leaves and odd scraps of fabric that had been concealed among the trees. Under my direction and with his knowledge of our surroundings, we soon had a cloth soaked in fresh, cold water spread across her brow and another pressed tenderly to her bruised cheek.

The first thing Kaya saw when she opened her eyes was my smile. "Hi-Himiko? You're all right?" She sounded muzzy. "Did I kill the ogre?"

"He is no ogre," I told her. "Just a human being who had the bad luck to be born different." I told her all about his unhappy history: born into the Ookami clan to a widowed mother who realized her son was unlike other children when his body grew so much larger than theirs but his mind lagged so far behind. People either shunned him or tormented him, and when he couldn't understand why they treated him so unjustly, he lashed out in frustration and grief. When his mother died, Ryu's father had him driven out of the village.

"But that doesn't stop some of his so-called kin from seeking him out up here and persecuting him," I said bitterly. "They probably go home afterward and brag about it, claiming that they're heroes who braved the ogre's den."

Kaya laid a hand to her cheek and winced. "Poor fellow. I hope he gave them twice what he gave me. *They* deserve it." She propped herself up on her elbows and looked around the clearing. "So where is he now? Don't tell me you scared him off."

I shook my head. "I asked him to stay out of sight until I could let you know he's a friend. When I call him back, please tell him he's forgiven."

I handed her a new cold cloth and she held it to her face, grateful for the way it eased her pain. "While I'm at it, I'll ask him to pardon me for calling him a monster," she said. "No tusks, no talons, no claws, and his skin's not blue or red . . . I should have noticed all that before attacking an *oni*-that-wasn't. All right, call him. What's his name?"

The corners of my mouth turned down. "He doesn't remember. His mother was the only one who called him by it. After she was gone, the wolves mocked him for so long, so mercilessly, that he couldn't recall a time when he answered to any name but the one they gave him."

"What was that?"

My hands curled into fists. "Oni."

Kaya and Oni made peace between them. It almost took a bad turn when she declared that Lady Badger forgave him, and put on a great show, complete with assorted snorts, growls, huffing, and chuffing. Confused and scared, poor Oni jumped away from her, raising his club in self-defense against the demon badger in girl's disguise. I had to soothe him and scold Kaya simultaneously, but no real harm was done.

Once Oni understood Kaya's sense of humor, he was enchanted by it. Her funny stories sent his robust laughter booming out over the Ookami valley as the three of us ate a frugal dinner and watched the sun go down. I tried vainly to make the two of them be more inconspicuous, in case we attracted the unwanted attention of Ryu's clan.

"Oh, don't worry about that, Himiko," he said, still chortling over Kaya's tale of how Lady Badger punished the five laughing rabbits. "They already know I'm here. If I make noise, that's nothing new. If they see a fire, they think it's warming no one but me. They only come to my place when they want to bother me, but they won't do that now. This is planting time. They have to work all day and then they are so tired they sleep all night and let me be." He grinned. "I love planting time."

"I hope they're so exhausted that they slumber more deeply than the dead," Kaya said to me. "It will make your task easier to accomplish."

"It will be a while before I make the attempt. I can do nothing until I discover where Noboru sleeps," I answered.

"Next I have to plan how to get in and out of the Ookami settlement, and only *then* I can try stealing down there and carrying him off."

"You won't be going there alone, remember?" She nudged me with her elbow. "I didn't walk all this way to miss the best part, when you find your baby brother!"

"You might have to wait up here to see that, Kaya. If I fail, I might be captured. If that happens, I want you to go back to my people and let them know what happened."

"I will *not*. What kind of friend would I be if I let you face the dragon with no one to guard your back?"

"Kaya . . ."

"No, no, don't you give me *that* look! It turns you into an old turtle with a gassy gut. Try to argue with me and I'll pluck out your tongue and feed it to crows!"

A loud whimper from Oni silenced Kaya before she could add to her joking threats. He had grown more and more agitated while listening to our conversation and now he howled his wretchedness to the stars.

"Why are you fighting with Himiko, Lady Badger? Why are you talking about going down there, to where *they* live, and about being captured? You must not let that happen! You will be their slave, and have to work hard all the time or get beaten. I don't want them to beat you! I'll kill them if they try!"

I stood behind Oni, leaned against his back, and put my arms around his hulking shoulders. "Hush, don't be afraid," I murmured in his ear. "Kaya and I aren't really fighting. We're just disagreeing about something."

"But she said she was going to take your tongue and—!"

"Kaya says a *lot* of things." I shot her a *Now see what you started?* look that Oni could not see.

She paid it no heed. "That's because *Himiko* never listens to enough of what I say. But you don't need to worry, Oni: no matter how much the two of us argue, we'll always be friends." She smirked at me. "Except *some* people have a hard time understanding what real friends are willing to do for each other."

I drew breath to tell her she was not going to accompany me into the Ookami village to save Noboru, but realized it was precisely what she wanted me to do. Instead I smiled tightly and said, "A real friend would clean up for all of us after dinner, don't you agree?"

"Why, Himiko, what a lovely offer!" Kaya chirped. "You're a real friend after all!"

That night, as I waited for sleep to find me, I heard Oni moving restlessly on the heap of leaves that made his bed. I tried to shut my ears to it, wanting to believe this was the way the lonely giant always settled down for the night, but I soon had to accept that his distress was not going to go away unless I did something about it.

I left my bedroll and carefully picked my way around the remaining embers of our fire. "Oni?" I whispered, placing one hand on his back. "Are you all right? Would you feel better if I sang for you again?" I didn't know if I could recall the lullaby his mother's spirit had placed on my lips, but I knew other tunes to soothe a frightened child.

"Himiko . . ." It was difficult to hear him. Even with so little light, I could see he was sucking on his fist for comfort. "Himiko, why were you and Kaya talking about going down there, where *they* are? Why won't you stay here, where it's safe? Why won't you stay with me?" He sniffled in the dark. "What did I do wrong?"

When I was small and the world became scary and bewildering, Mama would stroke my back to calm me. That simple, tender gesture could banish more demons than the chants and dances of a hundred shamans. Now it was my turn to work that comforting spell on Oni.

I told him everything. I tried to do it in a way that preserved the truth but would not add to his fears. I explained why Kaya and I had left our clans and come so far, though I spared him the fact that my mother's sanity and survival were at stake. I ended by offering him the best gift within my power: "And when we have Noboru and go home, I want you to come with us."

"Me?" One word, yet it held many: *Do you mean that or are you taunting me too? Will I have a home again, or will you abandon me without a second thought? Will you keep your word or, when it's time for you to leave, will you laugh at me for being stupid enough to believe that anyone could ever want someone like me?*

"*Yes*, you," I said. "We need you. You can protect us on the road back, and when we reach my village, you can live under our roof. You can help with the crops, or you can work with my big brother, Masa, in the blacksmith's forge. You'll have good clothes to wear, and you'll share our food."

"Are you sure that will be all right?" Oni asked shyly. "I'm not part of your clan."

"Then I will *make* you a part of it," I declared. "You will be my kinsman, my new brother, a Matsu."

"Matsu . . ." He tasted his future and found joy. "I will be Oni of the Matsu!"

"You will have another name than that. You are no mountain ogre, and when we return I will ask our elder shaman, Master Michio, to ask the spirits for a name that suits you better." I hesitated. "That is, if you don't mind the change?"

He sat up and hugged me with surprising gentleness. "Thank you, Himiko! I've never been so happy."

"I hope you will be even happier, Big Brother."

Two days passed. I spent most of them staring down through the trees, noting the comings and goings of the Ookami. As I'd hoped, they felt so safe from attack that they did not place guards at their gates, but they did have a manned watchtower, probably to scan the surrounding area for signs of wildfires rather than to sound the alarm for invaders approaching.

Their village was larger than any I had known. The palisade of logs surrounding it looked relatively new, and if I strained my eyes I could see what looked like the marks of a smaller, older enclosure within the boundaries of the one now standing. The wolves had prospered on a diet of war and expanded their settlement at the same time they expanded their territory.

Most of their fields were like those of the Inoshishi, terraced up the far side of the valley, though some were set out on flatter terrain. A small river ran between the cultivated lands and the settlement. Inside the palisade, many homes were clustered together in what I thought of as the "old" Ookami village. These were simple pit dwellings. Grander, more imposing houses stood apart from these, with a comfortable amount of open space separating each from its neighbors. Tall, thick wooden pillars raised them even higher than the homes of my own clan's aristocrats. What a view they must have had!

There were a few additional structures built in the same elevated style as the nobles' houses, but these looked more weathered, and lifted their thatched roofs above the "old" settlement. I presumed they were storehouses, though for all I knew, some of the impressive, newer-looking buildings served the same function. The Ookami needed somewhere to stow the food they seized from their subjected clans.

While I studied the wolves in their lair, Kaya and Oni became fast friends. The clearing where we camped was the gentle outcast's favorite refuge, but it was not his only one. During the years of his exile he had made himself many safe places throughout the dense mountain forests. Though his mind was limited in some ways, in others it was extremely inventive and keen. Condemned by his own clan to live like an animal, he became a very *clever* animal, maintaining countless storage places in hollow logs, between tumbled boulders, and in deep, artfully concealed holes in the ground. Most of them held food, but some hid a few surprises.

"Himiko! Himiko! Look at what Oni gave me!" Kaya came running into the clearing, waving a long piece of rawhide. The big man came trailing after her, rubbing his head and looking both pleased and embarrassed. "Isn't it *gorgeous?*" she gushed, falling to her knees so I could get a better look at what had sent her spirit soaring.

"It's very . . . nice?" I faltered.

"It's not 'nice,' Himiko, it's a *bowstring*! Or it's going to be. You know how hard I've been trying to spin a new one from your hair, and how badly that's been going. Oni saw me working on it, and asked why I was all scowls and growls. Did you know what a good hunter he is? He uses a spear to go after deer and kamoshika, and after he eats the meat, he scrapes off the hides and puts them away until he needs them. Well, when I told him my troubles—why *does* your hair tangle so easily?—he took me to the place he keeps his animal skins and gave me *this*." She hugged the brown scrap to her heart. "It's still pliant, and I can make a good bowstring out of it in no time!" She turned to Oni, her bruised face alight with gratitude. "I will be your friend *forever*."

"You are both my friends." Oni spoke with unusual formality, like a man taking an oath before the gods. "You'll see that I can be a good one."

"Oh, you're already good enough," Kaya said lightly. "And once I can use my bow again, I'll show you what a good friend *I* can be. We'll have a feast of game to celebrate Noboru's rescue!" She cocked her head at me and added: "How did it go for you today, Himiko, keeping watch on the wolves? Are we closer to making a move? Were you able to catch sight of him anywhere down there?"

My discouraged expression put an end to her cheerfulness. "I'm too far away. I can see people and I can distinguish children from adults, but I can't see their faces clearly. I'm going to have to move downslope tomorrow, stay high enough to be able to look into the village but be close enough to pick Noboru out of the crowd."

"I don't like that idea. What if you get *too* close and someone spots you? Remember the watchtower!"

"We're going to have to deal with that sooner or later," I reminded her.

"You should let me do it, then. I know how to move through the forest unseen; you don't."

"And I know what my little brother looks like. Do you?"

"I will once you describe him to me!" Kaya said, and when I tried to ignore her demand she persisted until I gave in.

When I was done, I said, "There. Now do you think that gives you enough information to let you pick him out from among every other child in the Ookami village?"

"*Yes!*" Kaya said so hotly that we both understood she meant, *Um . . . maybe?*

"Listen, let's compromise. We can *both* go down the mountain tomorrow. You'll help me move as soundlessly as you do, and I'll recognize Noboru. Is it a bargain?"

Kaya accepted readily, but Oni looked so disturbed by what had just happened that I asked if he was feeling well.

"I don't want you to go," he said. "Not you, not Kaya. She was right: it will be dangerous. Don't go!"

We assured him that he was worrying over nothing, that Kaya was skilled in woodlore, that we would turn back if we so much as glimpsed the tower watchman turning in our direction. Our encouraging words seemed to comfort him, and since he raised no further objections, I did not think he needed to say outright that he was content with our plan.

Kaya and I decided we would make an early start the next morning, but when we woke up, we discovered that someone else had made an earlier one. Oni's shout of triumph split the sweet spring dawn as the big man came striding back into the clearing with his club on one shoulder, and on the other . . .

"Noboru!" In the space of a single breath I was out of my bedroll, on my feet, and reaching avidly for my little brother. Oni scarcely had the chance to set him down before I grabbed him and pulled him down into my embrace. "Oh, Noboru, it *is* you! It *is*!"

Laughter and tears shook me. I hugged him so close that he had to squall his protests straight into my ear to make me let him go. I was still stunned and half deafened when he looked at me with large, awestruck eyes, reconsidered, and flung himself back into my arms.

Kaya watched our reunion in open-mouthed astonishment. "How did you *do* that, Oni?" she asked. *"Magic?"*

He chortled gleefully, like a child who knows he will soon be given a new toy as a reward for doing something wonderful.

"It was easy," he said. "You were sleeping when I left. I went down into the village. I used to go there sometimes, to take things to eat, but I don't like it, so not too much. No one stops me if they see me. They don't want to come near me unless they're with a *lot* of other people." He shifted the club on his shoulder and added: "It helps them stay away when they see *this*."

"So you just . . . *walked* into the village?" Kaya was confounded. He bobbed his head, his grin growing impossibly wide. "But—but once you were inside, how did you know where to find Himiko's little brother?"

"I didn't, but I knew who did. Lord Ryu is chieftain, and chieftains know everything. I went into his house. He was asleep too, and his family." Telling about his midnight adventure made Oni very excited. He began to speak faster and faster, everything pouring out at once: "I got down next to him, and I took my knife and held it to his neck, and I put my hand over his mouth, and he woke up and wanted to shout and bite me, until he felt the blade touching his skin, and then he lay still."

I took this the wrong way: "You killed him?"

Oni's expression said *I thought you were* smart, *Himiko!* "If I killed him, he couldn't give me Noboru. And he did that, so why would I kill him after he gave me what I wanted? Oh! This is funny: Noboru was right there in Lord Ryu's house! We didn't have to go anywhere else to find him. I told you it was easy!"

"It would've been easier if you'd killed the wolf while you had the chance," Kaya grumbled. "What kept him from raising an alarm as soon as you were out of knife-range?"

"I thought of *that* too." Oni was growing more and more self-satisfied by the moment. "I made Lord Ryu walk out of the village with us, all the way to the edge of the trees, and then I hit him. I hit him harder than I hit you,

Kaya, and when he fell down, I put Noboru on my shoulder and we ran and ran and here we are!" His grin had grown impossibly wide. "And we can all go home."

"Quickly," I said. "Unless you cracked Ryu's skull open, he's going to come back to his senses, and when he does . . . We have to leave *now*." I held Noboru with one hand and grabbed my travel bag with the other. Kaya followed my lead.

"Why are you in such a hurry?" Oni asked in his small, frightened voice. "Are you going to run away from me? But you said I could come with you! You called me Big Brother! You promised that I—"

The arrow whizzed out of the trees and hit him in the throat with a sickening sound. Oni dropped his club and pawed at the feathered shaft helplessly, the whites of his eyes showing. A second dart took him in the back, a third in the chest. They were coming from all directions. He dropped to his knees, then pitched sideways, and still the arrows found him.

I threw Noboru to the ground and shielded him with my body. He shrieked, terrified, and I whispered countless bits of nonsense to calm him, swearing that everything would be all right, that I would not let anything happen to him, that we were going home to see Mama. When he tried to wriggle away and look around, I clapped one hand over his eyes and sang to keep him from hearing Oni's gasps and groans. Kaya was calling my name, but her voice was growing fainter, swallowed by the sound of a struggle somewhere among the trees.

A hand closed on the back of my neck with a grip like

a falcon's claw. I was hauled away from my brother, whose small face crumpled with grief as he stretched out his arms to me. An instant later, he was snatched up by one of the hard-faced men now swarming the forest clearing. His cries receded rapidly as he was carried into the woods until all I could hear was a ghost's mournfully fading "Himiko! Himiko! Save me!"

I struggled in my captor's grasp and got a hard slap for it. A second man joined us and whipped a length of thin rope around my wrists, then shouted back over one shoulder, "We have her, my lord!"

Ryu of the Ookami stalked into the clearing, a bow in his hands. The arrows in the quiver on his back were fletched with the same-colored feathers as the first one to strike Oni down. His face was as handsome as I remembered it, and as hateful. He paused to glance at my fallen friend's body and muttered, "Still breathing? Tsk." I tensed when I saw him draw his knife.

"Leave him alone!" I yelled. "Coward! Let him die in peace!"

He gave me a sidelong look. "Welcome, you troublesome girl," he said. "You haven't changed much, have you? Still pretty as a summer rainbow and foul-tempered as a winter storm. You can't imagine how shocked I was to wake to this beast's ugly face and hear *your* name on his lips!" He indicated Oni, whose only sign of ebbing life was the slight, fitful clenching and uncurling of his thick fingers. "Did you use your beauty to make the poor simpleton serve you? Is that why he came barging into my house, holding a sword to my neck, stealing what belongs to me?" He made a disgusted sound. "I should thank you for it. We ought to have rid ourselves of this monster a long time ago."

"*He* is not the monster!" Pushed past my limit by Ryu's callous words, I made a sudden, enormous effort to wrench free of the men holding me. I kicked and twisted violently, taking them both off guard long enough to break away and throw myself between Oni and Ryu. "You . . . will . . . *not* . . . touch him." I spoke with a warrior's fiery courage and a menacing tone that did not make empty threats, but deadly promises.

The young chieftain backed away three steps before he realized what he was doing. Then he glanced nervously at his men, to see if they had noticed the fleeting shadow of fear that had crossed his face when he met my gaze. He had once fled from me in terror, and I could read on his face how close he had come to doing so now.

Ryu threw back his head and laughed, too loud and too long for it to be natural. "Don't be frightened, little princess," he mocked me. "I won't touch your beloved. We will leave him here, but you may say good-bye if you're quick about it."

I shut my ears to his spite and stroked Oni's cheek softly with the back of one of my bound hands. Leaning close, I began to sing his mother's lullaby.

His eyelids fluttered. A faint smile made his face beautiful. "I remembered, Himiko," he whispered. "You won't have to give me a new name; I remembered. I am Mori . . . Mori . . . Mori . . ."

Mori: Forest. He died where he had lived, and where his spirit had always belonged.

PART II
WOLVES

10

BINDING A BIRD'S SONG

They took all I had.

They took my bell and my mirror. They took my little brother Noboru and the life of my friend Mori. They took my hope of saving Mama and my dream of seeing our family reunited. They took my right to say no.

As the last breath left Mori's body, Ryu barked an order. His men dragged me upright and gave me a hard shove between my shoulder blades, sending me staggering in the direction they wanted me to go. I never had the time to utter a single word to comfort my friend's spirit or let him know that now he was free.

The Ookami warriors who had Kaya in custody were waiting for us not far from the clearing. She was furious, but I was relieved to see that she looked otherwise untouched. When she tried to speak to me, one of the men slapped her face, deliberately aiming for the livid bruise

Mori had given her. I could do nothing to ease her pain or help dry her tears.

The men in charge of Noboru must have gone ahead of us, because I did not see my little brother again that day. Kaya and I were marched down out of the mountains and brought through the gates of the Ookami village as curiosity-seekers crowded around us, pointing and muttering. We attracted puzzled looks, leers, and even one or two pitying glances.

We were taken to one of the pit houses in the center of the village and pushed roughly through the doorway when we didn't move fast enough for our captors' liking. I failed to duck and banged my forehead so hard that a burst of stars dazzled my eyes. Dizzy from the blow, I lost my balance and fell forward, taking the impact on my right side. The Ookami warriors laughed at me as I sprawled in the darkness.

"Stop your yapping, you flea-fouled curs!" Kaya shouted at them. The same man who had slapped her earlier growled a curse and would have stormed into the house to do it again, but his companion grabbed his arm.

"That one might be prettier without a bruised face," he said. "How are we going to find out if you keep hitting her?"

"You *care* what the girl looks like, Hiroshi?" The first man laughed crudely and shook off his grip. "Well, I guess you would, at your age. Wait until you've got whiskers on your lip instead of milk before you talk about such things to a *true* man. Next you'll be claiming you want to marry her!"

"I would, if Lord Ryu ordered me to do it," came the

measured reply from the younger warrior. "He *did* order both of us to stow them here and stand watch. Nothing more."

Something ugly crept into the first man's voice: "Why don't *you* stand watch and let me have a little fun?"

"*Or* I could leave you to your 'fun' and go ask Lord Ryu if that was what he had in mind for these girls."

"Then do it, you double-tongued snake!" the older guard exploded. "He'll strip the skin from you for deserting your place, wait and see! If you'd fought in half the battles I have, you'd know our chieftain doesn't care how we treat our slaves."

"Maybe I haven't seen as much fighting as you, but I did see what happened in the ogre's clearing today," the one called Hiroshi said. "Lord Ryu *knows* one of these girls. Who's to say he doesn't know the other one as well? Can you say for certain that he doesn't have plans of his own for them?" He finished with a meaningful: "What happens to anyone who touches *his* property?"

The first guard cursed louder, calling Hiroshi countless names, but he soon subsided into grumbles, then sullen silence. I wished that I could have thanked the younger man for how cleverly he had protected Kaya and me from the unthinkable. He had given me an unexpected realization that not all of the Ookami were as vicious as their leader.

We spent the day awaiting our fate. Though we were free to converse, we were so beaten down in spirit by our capture that we maintained mutual silence. That was a mistake. I should have spoken. I should have shared my grief for Mori's death with Kaya. I should have told her of the relentlessly growing sense of responsibility and guilt in my soul. I should have let her know how hopeless, helpless, and useless I felt, and I would have listened to her speak about her own fear, sorrow, and despair.

Such talk had the power to cleanse our minds of their swiftly gathering shadows. A rushing mountain stream is clear, healthy, and full of life, but a stagnant pond soon chokes on the uncleanliness it breeds. It would have been better for us both to talk.

With dull, indifferent eyes I stared at the doorway and watched the daylight fade. I wondered where my little brother was, and if he had stopped crying. I prayed that he had not seen Mori die, though I knew it was impossible for him to have missed all the violence that had devastated us that day. Was he in Emi's care? I implored the gods to make it so. If he could be with our stepmother and her son, Sanjirou, he would be comforted even if they were all slaves.

Slaves like us.

The world beyond the doorway of our prison became noisier as the day turned to evening. I heard the bustle of people returning home from the fields, the sounds of neighbors greeting neighbors, dogs barking to welcome their masters home, children squealing happily at play and being scolded for neglecting their small tasks and errands.

I caught snatches of excited chatter from villagers who were only now finding out about their chieftain's victory over the "mountain ogre." Silently I urged the gossipers to walk faster, taking their witless jabber far from where I had no choice but to hear it. Only once did a woman's voice murmur "But he wasn't a real *oni,* was he? His mother was my friend. He was such a sweet-faced, gentle child . . ." I yearned toward her kindhearted words, willing her to linger, but she moved on.

The dying day also brought the Ookami slaves back into the village. Five of them came into our hut, all women, filling the cramped space with the smell of mud from the planting fields and the reek of sweat. Three of them looked about the same age as my mother, one was a thin, white-haired elder, and one was a young girl with an old, old face and the rounded belly of a mother-to-be.

"Wonderful," she said dryly, regarding Kaya and me. "As if we weren't crowded enough already. Where do you two come from?"

"Maybe the wolves marched off to another war while we were working," one of the older women said, snickering. "A very *brief* war, if they're back in a day's time."

"A very *small* war, if they couldn't bring back any more plunder than these." The pregnant girl waved a hand at us.

"You rattlejaws! Are your heads filled with pebbles?" the old woman shouted. "Try shutting your mouths and opening your ears, for a change. Didn't you hear the talk that's everywhere out there?" She gestured at the doorway. "Remember the uproar at dawn when they found their chieftain stretched out cold as a fish?"

"He should have stayed that way," one of the other women muttered.

The old one ignored her. "And remember all the tumult when he came to and started yelling for his men to grab their weapons and go haring off into the mountains after the fellow who'd done that to him? Well, they found him, they killed him, and they brought these two back as trophies. All hail the 'brave' wolf chieftain, who needs a whole war party at his back to murder just one poor, child-ish outcast!"

"*Shhh!* Don't talk like that about Lord Ryu. You'll get a beating."

The old woman was undeterred by the warning. "Good. Maybe I'll die from it. I've lived too long already."

"This isn't living," the pregnant girl said somberly. She squatted next to Kaya and began removing the bind-ings on her hands. "How long have they had you in here, stranger?" she asked in a more caring tone.

"Since morning." Kaya rubbed feeling back into her freed wrists while the girl turned to undoing my bonds.

"And you just sat here, tied up like pigs for slaugh-ter? You didn't even *try* to release yourselves?" She was in-credulous. "What are you, a pair of princesses who expect someone else to do everything for you?"

I gave a snort of laughter. Kaya echoed it. Before long, we were holding our sides as we roared with the absurdity of it all. When we paused to breathe again, we told our new companions our names, our clans, and all that had brought us to this point.

"And just to set your minds at ease, we didn't wait for someone to help us do *everything*," Kaya concluded, point-ing at a reeking pottery vessel in one corner of the house.

The pregnant girl pinched her nose shut. "Phew. Thanks for the reminder. Whose turn is it to empty that thing?"

"Mine, if you'll tell me where to do it," I said.

"No, better let one of us take care of it this time. If you try to find the right spot now, with evening coming on, you might not be able to see where you need to go and take a tumble into the ditch."

One of the three middle-aged women volunteered for the unsavory chore. I watched her walk out of the house without a single word of challenge from our guards. When I questioned this, the old one said, "Why should they care about her comings and goings? It was pretty obvious where she was headed."

"But what's to stop her from dumping that pot in the ditch and running off?"

"Ha! How about starvation? A woman alone in the mountains hasn't got a chance. Do we look like we know how to find food out there, or even the path home?"

"That's why we don't usually have guards at our doorway," another motherly lady spoke up. "If we ran away, where would we go? We know it and the Ookami know it."

"Fear makes a better tether than rope and a better wall than wood," Kaya said under her breath.

"What about the men?" I asked. "*Their* lodgings must be guarded."

The pregnant girl shook her head. "The ones who aren't too young or too old to make a run for it have other bonds holding them here. Our masters had a reason for never taking a strong male slave without taking his family too."

More ropes, more walls, I thought. *The wolves are cunning.*

"The only reason those guards are here is on account of you, my ladies," the old woman said. "I don't know what Lord Ryu has in store for you or when he will choose to do it, but while you are here, you are part of our household and we will look after you as well as we can. You must be hungry. Soon it will be time to eat. If the guards permit it, you can come with me to the cookhouse to bring back the evening meal for everyone else. That way, you'll know where to get your food."

"Thank you," I said sincerely. "But please, don't call us 'my ladies.' How can there be any differences between us here?"

"I would rather call you and your friend 'my lady' than call these Ookami dogs 'my lord,'" she replied, holding her head high. "At least *you* deserve the honor. You are chieftains' daughters and you, Lady Himiko, walk the shaman's path. My mother raised me to respect the spirits and those who serve them. I will not change now." She made it plain that it would be no use arguing the matter with her; she was not going to budge.

"Very well, if that is what you want," I said. "But it will be the only difference between us."

"Oh, really? Tell that to Tami!" she replied archly, and indicated the mother-to-be in our midst. We all laughed.

The old woman's intention to take us to the cookhouse came to nothing. When Kaya and I tried to follow her out of the house, our guards ordered us back inside. Even the younger man who had stood between my friend and his churlish comrade spoke curtly to us, barring our path with his spear. We had no choice but to let the other women bring us our dinner. There was not much of it—rice gruel with a few vegetables—and it was indifferently cooked. I felt too disconsolate to eat more than a few mouthfuls.

How long will we be kept here? I wondered. *Will we never be allowed outside? I would welcome the opportunity to work in the fields, no matter how hard the labor, if it meant being able to see the sky, taste the wind, and feel living earth under my feet!*

I cupped my hand to the inconspicuous bulge in my sash. There were still two precious things the Ookami had not found and taken from me: the wand of cherrywood that had once given me such breathtaking hope by bursting into miraculous bloom, and my cherished image of the shining goddess whose arms encompassed the sun.

O my beloved lady, hear me, I prayed. *Show me the way to cast off this darkness that has dropped black wings over my soul. Bring me light!* I opened my spirit to her presence, desiring a vision where I might again find her and be comforted, but none came.

Our first pair of guards was replaced by a second while we were eating. When we were done, Tami took our dishes back to the cookhouse for cleaning. She returned carrying two thin bedrolls.

"Good thing I thought of this," she said, smiling as she dropped them at our feet. "We couldn't have you sleeping on the bare ground."

"Thank you," I said. "We lost all of our gear when we were captured. I don't know if the Ookami men left some of it behind or brought everything with them."

"Well, I know what I won't see again," Kaya groused. "My beautiful bow and arrows, abandoned in the woods like that? It's a disgrace."

"They turned their backs on more important things than your bow," I reminded her gently.

Her brow creased as she recalled our murdered friend. "Not even a handful of earth scattered over him . . . The gods will repay them for that!" Her indignant shout brought one of our new guards darting in.

"Shut your mouth and go to sleep, or else!" he bawled.

"Or else *what*?" Kaya's wrath was aroused. Her boundless energy had been penned in for a whole day and wanted some outlet, even a fight she'd lose. "You'll hit me? I've been hit before. Try it, coward, but you'd better get some of your friends to hold me still because otherwise I'll hit back, *and* kick, *and* bite! Even if you do have the spine to fight me on your own and you win, you'll still be the one who'll have to explain to Ryu why you broke *his* prisoner!"

The guard spat at her feet. "I don't have time to teach manners to a wild brat." He seized the pregnant girl's arm and yanked her toward him so suddenly she was too shocked to scream. "And I don't have to break *you*."

He was right about that. His ruthless strategy put a stop to Kaya's defiance as abruptly and totally as if he'd tossed a noose around her neck and pulled it tight. My friend lowered her head, mumbling an apology. Satisfied, the guard released his hostage and returned to his post.

I did not sleep well. Even when I did manage to doze off, my dreams were a jumble of fitful, torturous images that buffeted me with the force of a gale. I woke up exhausted and went through the morning routine with invisible stones tied to my arms and legs. The only thing that snapped me out of my daze temporarily was when I began putting my hair up, only to have Tami tactfully tell me that slaves were not permitted to dress their hair in the style of free women.

"It's to set us apart," she explained. "But frankly, I think it's because these Ookami sows are afraid we're so much prettier than they are that we'll steal their men." She gave her swollen belly a sour look and added: "They can keep them."

Breakfast was a tepid repetition of dinner and I ate even less than the night before. While I gazed idly at my congealing portion of rice gruel, I noticed the old woman leaning against the doorframe, talking to our guards. She came back grinning and knelt between Kaya and me.

"You can start singing a happier song, my little birdies," she told us. "You're being given room to spread your wings. We are all going out to work in the paddies today. It's a heavy day's toil, but—"

"Thank the gods!" Kaya exclaimed. "I was getting worried that the wolf chieftain intended to bury us in this house."

It was a cheering experience to be let outside. I reveled in the morning light and looked all around as we made our way through the Ookami village. The old woman slipped between Kaya and me so that she could talk to both of us at the same time, identifying every important building and every notable person we passed.

"And would you look at the size of *that* thing?" she demanded, indicating one of the larger structures.

"Is that the chieftain's house?" I asked.

"Oho, that *would* please him, but it's not. No, my dear,

that is the Ookami shrine. It's where their shaman lives, where they worship their ancestors, and where they gather for festivals. And over there's the well, and there you can see . . ."

I was not really listening to her. My mind was elsewhere, and my eyes had no time to spare for gawking at buildings when I needed them to be alert for the sight of Noboru, Emi, Sanjirou, or any of my other captive kinfolk. The Ookami settlement was large, but surely I would encounter at least *one* familiar face! And if I didn't meet any of my clan while still inside the village walls, how could I fail to do so once we reached the fields?

Our group did not walk alone that morning. The pair of sentinels who had been our night watchmen were now replaced by six armed men who formed a vigilant, defensive ring around us. Their leader's head never stopped moving from side to side, as though the village streets were a breeding ground for demons ready to leap out at us the instant that he let down his guard.

What is he searching for so keenly? I mused. And then I found out.

We were almost at the settlement gate when the man appeared from behind one of the massive pillars supporting the watchtower. He was shabbily dressed, and his hair was tied back in a plain cascade rather than arranged in loops over his ears. From what I had learned that morning, this was the mark of a slave. He had the worried look and urgent gait of someone frantic to get where he was going. He was so preoccupied by his errand that he did not notice our approach or heed the lead guard's first irate command for him to get out of the way and out of sight as well.

A second shout did seize his attention just enough for him to pause and turn toward us. That was how I found myself gazing at the face of one of my brother Masa's closest friends, a Matsu slave like me. Our eyes met, and he recognized me too.

"Lady Himiko?" Shock, disbelief, and denial warred over him.

I was about to let him know that he had not lost his mind, that he was seeing me here, sharing his bondage, but I did not have the time to do more than open my mouth before the Ookami guards broke ranks and charged. Two took hold of my kinsman, pinning his arms, while the leader roared abuse in his face. He emphasized every rude word and crushing insult with a blow to the man's face, his chest, his stomach, until the guards immobilizing him were left with a barely conscious deadweight sagging between them. At a terse gesture from their leader, they dropped him and came back to where the remaining three had formed a closer wall around Kaya and me.

"What did he do to earn such a beating?" my friend whispered. I could only shake my head in silence, nauseated and revolted by what we had witnessed. I wanted to run to the fallen man's side and begin tending his wounds and bruises, but since there was little hope of that, my second desire was to get out of the gates and far enough from the wolves' den so that I could pretend that I had seen no more than a bad dream.

Those were my two wishes and neither one came true. The leader of our guards pointed at me and snapped, "Take her back to her place and keep her there!" The brawniest of his men took me by the arm and whisked me away. Kaya made a grab for my hand, but was too late. The remainder of the guards moved in to close ranks around her and the other women, herding them out of the village while I was returned to the dark and lonely house.

I was flung through the doorway without explanation and left to myself. The man who had brought me back took sentry duty. I sat in the middle of the floor, hugging my knees and staring out past him at a world that was going on without me.

Why did they attack that poor man? I cried inside. *What did he do? And—O spirits, help me!—why am I being punished too?*

The shadows grew shorter. Midday came, and with it my guard's relief. I roused myself from my misery when I heard the voice of his replacement: it was Hiroshi, the young man who had been Kaya's champion when we were first shut up under this roof!

He has a good heart, I thought. If I spoke to him, he might be willing to give me answers . . . *if he has any to give. I won't know if I don't try.*

I overheard the two Ookami trading a few friendly words before the big guard left. I waited until I was sure he had gone, then cleared my throat to speak.

"Are you all right in there, girl?"

Hiroshi's question was so unexpected that I was struck off balance and could only stammer, "Wh-wh-what did you say?"

"I was asking if you were all right. Do you have drinking water? Has anyone brought you a midday meal?" He spoke in a voice so low that I had to edge to the doorway in order to hear every word.

"I think there's still some water in a jar over in the corner," I told him.

"Good. And what about food?"

"I had breakfast; that's all. It doesn't matter. I'm not hungry."

"That is *not* good," he said firmly. "I was taught to eat every meal you can get because you never know when you might not be able to get any. I'll stop the next person who walks past and send them to bring you something to eat." He glanced at me quickly and smiled, then snapped back to keeping his eyes on the outside world.

"I told you, I don't want anything," I said. "Even if I did, you might get in trouble for helping me."

"For giving food to a hungry girl?" He made a derisive noise. "I don't think so."

"Then you're wrong. I've already made problems for other people this morning, though don't ask me what I did; even I don't know."

There was a pause, and then: "Ohhhhhhh. I see what you mean. I was told about the incident when I was sent to stand watch here." He clucked his tongue. "Poor man, he must have had his mind on other things or he would have turned tail and run instead of greeting you. Yesterday Lord Ryu let it be known that it's a grave, punishable offense for any of your clanfolk to approach you, speak with you, or even acknowledge your existence. I overheard a messenger delivering his words to one of the houses where Matsu slaves are lodged. *'Make her a ghost,'* was what he said."

I digested this news carefully. "I'm to be cut off from my people. . . ." *My people, and my family,* I thought, forlorn. The one aspect of my captivity with the power to make the rest of it bearable was the prospect of being reunited with Noboru, Emi, and Sanjirou. Ryu had torn that away from me.

And how soon before he robs me of still more that I cherish? What about Kaya? He has let us stay together so far, but will that last? The thought of being separated from my dearest friend, the sister of my spirit, made me feel like I'd swallowed thorns. The pain was so intense that it stole my speech and left me dead silent.

"Girl?" The young guard sounded concerned by my unnatural stillness. "What's the matter in there? Are you crying? Listen, it's not going to be so bad, you'll see! Lord Ryu's got a nasty temper, but it dies as fast as it flares up. All of us know how the giant mountain hermit humiliated him, laying him out cold and taking that little boy of his. He could only kill the big man once, so he's making you suffer for his embarrassment too. Trust me, this won't last. He'll forget he gave that order, or the men called to guard duty will forget to enforce it, or you'll find a way to make Lord Ryu change his mind altogether. I'll bet you could do that easily, eh, a pretty girl like you?"

His words were intended to encourage and cheer me. Instead, they kindled a smoldering rage. "Oh, *could* I? I know what kind of persuasion you expect me to use! Hear me: I would turn my pretty face into a demon's mask before I'd let Ryu touch me. I would sooner be sealed alive in a burial mound, with slime to drink, mud to eat, and a thousand poisonous reptiles for company than do what you suggest!"

"All right, all right, shush, stop that, people can hear you!" My outburst sent the young guard into a panic. *"Please* be quiet, or someone's going to repeat what you said to Lord Ryu and then we'll both be up to our necks in the muck! I'm sorry I offended you. Forget I said anything! I'm begging you—"

"I'm done," I said. And that was the last that I did say until Kaya and the other women came home that evening.

Kaya did not need me to tell her why my unfortunate Matsu kinsman had been given such a beating by our guards. As soon as I was hustled back to the house, the old woman told her everything. She was still shaking her head over Ryu's unjustly severe orders throughout dinner and until it was time to go to sleep.

"Do you think he'll try to part us too?" she asked, mirroring my own fear.

"I don't know. I hope not." My words sounded feeble. After less than two full days of captivity I was already broken in spirit. The burden of so much failure, affecting so many lives, was horrendous. I needed distraction from my bleak thoughts, but I had been shut away from the possibility of life's small joys and diversions. I could only look inward, to darkness.

"Himiko, what's wrong with you?" Kaya put one arm around my shoulders. "You sound ill, and you hardly took a bite of food this evening."

"It tastes awful," I said, avoiding the real question.

"Yes, but it's all we've got and I doubt we're going to get anything better. If you're not sick now, you will be unless you eat."

"I'll do better tomorrow."

My friend gave me a doubtful look. "Be sure you do."

Things improved slightly the next day. I was permitted to join the rest of the women laboring in the paddies. I had done that sort of work at home, though always with the freedom to rest whenever I liked. As a slave, this choice was taken from me. My clothing became soaked with sweat, the hem of my dress heavy with mud. My long hair fell forward as I bent over the furrows, rooting the young rice, and trailed in the water. I tried tying it back, but it still got wet and filthy at the ends.

"Take off your sash and wrap it around your head," the woman working next to me said. She pointed to the cloth she'd used to bind up and cover her own hair.

If I did as she suggested, I would have nowhere to hold my wand and amulet of the goddess. "Good idea, but too late for me to try today," I said as cheerfully as I could. I showed her how much of my hair was already drenched and dirty.

"Oh, you're right. Silly to coil wet hair with dry, eh?" She went back to work.

It was good to be out in the sun, even if its warmth only fell on my bent back. I would have enjoyed it more if I hadn't been on edge, worried about accidentally encountering anyone from my clan. I did not want to be responsible for even one more person being punished on my account, thanks to Ryu's inhumanity. Whenever I looked up from the mud, I became intensely alert, scanning the fields. If I so much as imagined I saw a kinsman, I turned away sharply, or hid behind Kaya. By the time we were sent home I was almost as tired from my evasive tactics as from the actual fieldwork.

The next day was the same, and the next, and the next. I became so used to the routine that I hardly noticed when there was no longer a guard assigned to the doorway of our house. When Kaya pointed this out, I said, "So what? The whole village is our guard now."

That was true. The two of us had become familiar faces to the Ookami. A few even knew us by name. On days that we were sent to the river to bathe, at least three of their female elders accompanied us to patrol the banks and chase off any young men who came to leer at us or shout indecencies. When we sat outside our house on balmy evenings, a few Ookami girls would sometimes greet us, chat with us, and ask our pregnant friend shy questions about what it felt like to carry a child. They did not speak to us as mistresses to slaves, but as maidens close in age to one another. If our lives had followed a different path, we might have been friends.

There were also Ookami men as caring and courteous as the guard who'd saved Kaya and comforted me. They never insulted us or made inappropriate remarks. I think that when they looked at us, they realized that if the war between our clans had ended differently, their own sisters, daughters, sweethearts, and mothers would be the slaves. Knowing that not all of the wolves were heartless creatures was a consolation, though a very small one. It did nothing to drain the bitterness of captivity.

Every morning when I arose and every night when I lay down to sleep, I prayed fervently to the spirits of sky and stone, earth and air, beasts, birds, and all that drew breath: *Help me, save me, free me! Let me escape and grant that I can flee with all my family, my friends, and every soul the Ookami have subjugated! I am nothing without you. The wolves have left me powerless. Rescue me, O spirits, and I will serve you and praise you forever!*

I offered these prayers silently, from the depths of my heart. I yearned for an answer, whether it would come as a dream, a vision, or a visible miracle. If I begged the spirits for their aid long enough, would a bolt of lightning strike Ryu's house? Would a multitude of the very wolves that were their guardian spirits sweep out of the forests and tear the Ookami warriors to pieces? Or would the shadow gateway open as my spirit prince Reikon leaped into my world, leading an army no mortal warriors could ever hope to vanquish? Again and again I prayed: *Help me, save me, free me!* Again and again and again, into emptiness.

Spring flowers bloomed and faded. Planting the fields gave way to hoeing them to keep down the weeds. The moon's face went through its complete cycle of change three times as the days grew warmer and the light lasted longer. Fireflies danced in the twilight and soon cicadas would fill the trees with their droning, but my days remained the same round of tasteless food, thankless labor, and restless, dreamless sleep.

From time to time, my path crossed Ryu's. I would see

him looking at me as I went out to the fields or fetched water from the well or was busy with other chores. He never said one word to me, silently relishing my humiliation. His sly, gloating smile never failed to jolt me into anger, though the impulse to act on it always died quickly. What was the use? He controlled everything. He controlled me.

On a humid summer evening when the earth still sighed with the burden of the day's heat, Tami felt the first pains of childbirth. We had all been lolling outside the house, straining to catch the faintest hint of a cooling breeze after a hard day's work. Then a sharp cry escaped our friend's lips, she bent forward abruptly, and in that moment our weariness vanished as we all rushed to her aid.

Two of the middle-aged women helped Tami to her feet and began helping her walk back and forth in front of the doorway. The third set to work with a fire-twirling stick and some kindling rags, making a fire to see us all through the night. The old woman scurried inside to prepare a place for the girl to lie down when the time to deliver the baby came. Kaya flew off faster than one of her own arrows to draw pot after pot of fresh water from the village well, working as swiftly as the lowering darkness allowed.

I was left to one side, with nothing to do. Kaya had not waited to have me pick up another water pot and go with her to the well. The old woman had not asked me to help gather dried grass for Tami's bedding. Our fire-starter needed no one's help, but the other two women had not told me to stay close, in case they needed me to relieve one of them from all that pacing. I had not even been requested to find one of the Ookami midwives, whose knife would be needed when it was time to separate mother and child. Why?

I looked at my idle hands. How thin they had grown! Some shamans had the skill to read messages from the gods in the pattern of cracks that formed when they tossed animal bones into a fire. Now I read the answer to my question in the way my own bones stood out so gauntly through my skin.

My appetite never had come back to what it was before Mori's death. The less I ate, the more Kaya worried about me. She tried many tactics to get me to take more food, but I had excuses to thwart every one. Finally, after the moon's face had gone through its full changes nearly three times, she stopped commenting about how little I ate. Had my stubbornness conquered Lady Badger's tenacity?

No. A wise badger does not make a den with only one doorway. Instead of trying to make me eat more, Kaya turned her efforts to making me work less. She drew the other women into her plan as well. It was not difficult: they were already doing exactly the same thing to help Tami save her strength for the challenge of childbirth. They also banded together in exactly this way when the old woman fell ill for a few days. Because we were all together in the fields, no one cared if some worked much more than others as long as our assigned task got done.

But I'm not sick! I protested silently. *I'm not sick and I'm not expecting a baby, so why am I pushed aside as if I were weak and worthless and . . .*

Understanding came in a flash as bright and sudden as lightning leaping across the summer sky: *I've* made *myself look weak. They think I've become too feeble to do anything helpful*

for our friend, so they ask nothing of me. Nothing: not even my
skills as a healer or my calling as a shaman.

I'll show them I can be strong again, but that will take time. I
need to let them see that I am useful now.

I leaned back against the wall of our house, closed my
eyes, and clapped my hands to summon the attention of
the spirits. I began to chant the spell that would be the
child's guide from the land of the unborn into the mortal
world. When I finished, I saw that Tami and her two help-
ers had paused in midstep and were staring at me. I stood
up and approached them, laying one hand on my friend's
belly, the other on the small of her back. As calmly and
steadily as I could, I began asking her all the questions that
would help direct a successful childbirth.

She looked bewildered to find me speaking so confi-
dently and remained tongue-tied until I laughed and said:
"I may be younger than you, Tami, but I'm still a shaman.
I don't blame you for forgetting that, considering the way
I've been acting. I have been a part of births, and I can tell
you many stories about them."

"Good ones, I hope," Tami said with a forced grin.

"*Only* good ones." I looked at the other women. "And I
think I'm not the only one with knowledge to share."

My words had a wonderful effect on our housemates.
They all began to chatter about their experiences giving
birth and dispensed plenty of advice for things Tami could
do to make the process easier and control her pains. Kaya
was the only one with nothing to add, though she did help
by telling funny stories to entertain us all.

It was a very long night. We reassured Tami that a first

birth could take a long time while the child hesitated over leaving a place of warmth and safety for an unknown adventure. We took turns walking with her and rubbing her back when she lay down for a rest.

When the pains overtook her, I encouraged her to yell as much as she liked: "Louder! Louder! It will make you feel better. Go on, see if you can wake up every one of the wolves! The women will understand and if the men complain, I'll—I'll—well, I'll hand them over to the women!"

The stars faded and the sun goddess looked over the mountains to find everyone in our household cloudy-headed from the continuing vigil. Tami's baby was taking its time, though we all agreed it would come soon.

"Not soon enough," Tami said, panting. "If only it weren't so hot!"

The old woman patted her hand. "It will be even hotter in the paddies today, and the flies will be biting. Be grateful that you'll be in here, out of the sun, living the life of a grand lady while the rest of us are out there working." She cackled at her own joke.

"You're leaving me?" Panic choked Tami's voice.

"What choice do we have, my dear? But we'll ask one of the Ookami women to look in on you and bring help when the time comes."

"No, we won't," I said. I knelt beside Tami's bed and folded my arms. "I am staying right here."

"Himiko, you'll get in trouble," Kaya said, looking concerned.

"I'll take that chance and any consequences. Just one thing: before you leave, can you bring more water?"

Kaya began to argue with me, but dropped it when she saw that I wasn't going to give in. She refilled our largest pot with fresh water and set it down within easy reach of Tami's bed, along with a bowl and a wadded-up piece of cloth. When I picked it up and unfurled it, I saw that it was a man's tunic.

"Where did this come from?"

"A generous wolf who wants us to have something nice and clean to wrap this little cub," she replied airily.

"Did you *ask* him to be so 'generous'?"

"It must have slipped my mind. I was in a hurry." Brash and triumphant, Lady Badger flashed me a smile and was gone. The other women followed.

Soon after, Tami's pains began to come more frequently and more intensely. I filled the bowl with fresh water, dipped rags in it, and wiped her face and body, using one of our bamboo plates to waft coolness over her. Her cries brought a number of inquisitive Ookami women to our doorway. They all looked startled to see me there with her and fled before I could ask them to fetch a midwife.

"It's happening, Himiko!" Tami exclaimed, groping for my hands. She squeezed my wrists so tightly I thought she'd snap the bones. Her cries changed, growing deeper, turning to growls and curses. When she released me, I staggered to my feet and ran for the door, yelling for someone, *anyone* within sound of my voice to bring a knife.

"Ah, so it is true!" An Ookami man with a toad's squat body came swaggering up to me, his pockmarked brow bunched up with disapproval. "Here you are, where you have no business being. Get to the fields, girl!"

"My friend is having a baby," I said, matching him scowl for scowl. "I'm staying here to help."

"You're doing no such thing. I was sent all the way here from the paddies because Lord Ryu himself noticed you were missing, and I'm not going back without you. Your friend can have her own baby. It's what women do!"

"Women and pigs," I said, looking him straight in the eye so that he would not be able to dodge my meaning.

He tried to slap me, but he was awkward and missed. I grabbed his hand and pulled it down to his side sharply. He was so taken aback by my boldness that his eyes bulged out, making him look more like a toad than ever. At that moment, Tami loosed a horrible scream and howled my name. The man jumped. "May the gods have mercy!"

I dug the fingers of both hands into his shoulders so close to the neck that it looked like I was throttling him. "Do you know who I am?" I demanded, eyes blazing.

"You're Lady—Lady Hi—you're Himiko," he stammered.

I felt him shudder and tightened my fingers. He was a grown man and could have broken my grip on him easily, but I was using more than my hands to hold him.

"Do you know *what* I am, as well?"

"Y-you're the Matsu princess Lord Ryu rescued from the *oni*."

I rolled my eyes in disgust. "I'm sure that's what *he* says. Your Lord Ryu spits on one truth and hides another: I am a princess of the pine clan, but I am also a shaman, and I can call the spirits of *that* girl's pain"—without letting go of my shivering captive I tossed my head to indicate the interior of our house, where Tami lay—"and have them bring it home to you!"

"You can't—you can't—you can't—" He could barely get the words out of his mouth.

"Do you want to find out? Because if you do, know this: once I cast that spell, I can't undo it. Her pain will not end until she gives birth, and *neither will yours!*"

Another shriek from Tami tore through the hot summer air. The Ookami man's knees gave way, and he sagged toward me so abruptly that I had to let him go. He recovered his balance and took two steps back, raising his hands in a gesture that was part reverence, part surrender.

"Forgive me, Himi—my lady Himiko," he said. "Please forget that I ever troubled you. I will pray to the gods that your friend enjoys a safe and speedy delivery, free from pain, *all* pain! I will return to Lord Ryu and tell him that I could not find you. I will see to it that his displeasure falls on me and me alone. I will—"

"You will bring me a knife."

Tami's son was big and healthy, with a thick head of glossy black hair. His lusty cries welcomed our housemates home that evening. Once I was satisfied that the new mother and baby were cleaned up and resting comfortably, I went to the cookhouse to bring back dinner. I knew that if I didn't do that, no one would. They'd all be too enthralled by the baby.

Our newcomer had a vigorous appetite. Kaya became so fascinated watching him nurse that she forgot to put a single bit of food into her own mouth until I teased her about it.

"I'll eat when you eat," she grumbled, then caught sight of my empty bowl. "Didn't you take *any* food, Himiko?"

"She started with as much in her bowl as you've got now," Tami said.

"And it tasted awful," I added, smiling. "But I think I could do with a little more." I pretended to reach for Kaya's portion.

Without a word, Kaya dumped half of her share into my bowl and fended off all my attempts to give it back. "I made a promise," she said, volunteering no further details except: "You don't cheat the gods."

That night, I found my visions again. Sleep came sweetly to me, so deep and comforting that it was like sinking into a pool of honey. I was in the heart of a moonlit grove of willow trees, their supple branches sweeping the ground. Their long, slender leaves were filled with birdsong. Beyond the trees, a stream flowed past, its chuckling water glittering with the reflections of innumerable stars.

I turned slowly, taking in the beauty of the place. As I did, my contentment changed to unease as I became aware that the stream was not following an ordinary course but instead was a rushing circle enclosing the grove completely. I was about to make my way through the trees to the water's edge when a longed-for voice called my name. The willow branches rustled and Reikon had me in his arms.

My beloved, where were you going? he asked, his cheek pressed against my hair. *Why were you running away from me?*

I wasn't doing that, I protested. *It's just that*—I waved one hand at the encircling stream—*I wanted to see if there was some way to cross that: a fallen tree trunk, some stepping stones, even a place where the water runs shallow.*

But why would you need to seek such things? Reikon lifted my chin so that I could not look away from his astonished eyes. *We are together here, after too long a time apart, and I have prepared so many delights to welcome your return. Come and see.*

He took my hand and guided me back to the heart of the willow grove. The grass was spread with a silk cloth like a captive piece of summer sky and a multitude of laden dishes awaited us. My mouth watered at the sight of those delicacies. I sat down and reached for the nearest one, which held a savory-smelling stack of crisp-skinned trout, still smoking from the cookfire.

Reikon moved faster. He snatched the dish from my hand and began plucking bits of broiled fish from the bones and stuffing them into my mouth. He did not do it clumsily or brutally, and he never forced a new morsel on me until I had chewed and swallowed the one before, but there was still no escaping his determination to feed me. When I tried to stop him by stretching out one hand for a bowl of rice topped with vegetables, he took it and repeated what he'd done with the trout. It was the same with the next dish, and the next, until I could not bear it.

Reikon, please stop, I begged. *I don't need you to do this for me.*

But isn't this what you prayed for? he replied. *To be given help, because you could not help yourself?* He tried to feed me another pinch of rice.

I struck his hand away. *You're mocking me! Is this some sort of game you spirits play with mortals? Did it entertain you to hear me call out to you day after day while you stayed silent? And* now *is this your answer, after so long? This ridicule? Then I wish you had never answered me at all!*

Reikon's coaxing smile disappeared. His handsome face turned grave. *How could I answer you, when I could not recognize your voice? My beloved is a warrior who fights with heart and courage, a spear that strikes down cowardly oppressors, a shield to guard the innocent, and sometimes*—the image of the toadlike Ookami was a fleeting wisp in the air between us—*a knife.*

He took my hands and compelled me to stand, leading me to where the willow leaves grew so densely that I could not see what they concealed until he pushed them aside. What were those strange, round objects hanging from the branches? They looked like the work of some clumsy basket-maker who had taken dried reeds and plaited them too loosely. The results were hollow spheres with the open weave of a fishing net, none larger than ripe melons.

Then I saw the birds inside. The green shadows could not dull their bright feathers. I saw flutters of blue and red, orange and green, yellow and white through the pale, interlaced strips. Some of the tiny captives sang as though their world were still as boundless as earth and sky. Some battered themselves against the walls that held them prisoner. Some lay very still, dead or awaiting death.

I turned accusing eyes to Reikon, but all he said was: *Look more closely, my love.*

Mistrustful, I drew closer to the burdened branches. I gazed past the cages that held struggle and surrender until I found the only one that held . . . nothing. The round, woven walls were empty. A tuft of blue feathers wedged between two of the wider-spaced slats was the sole hint that this cage had ever contained a prisoner. On a twig far above my head, a tiny, sky-bright bird filled the grove with a song of victory.

She could not beat down the walls around her, so she did not try, Reikon said softly. *She could not submit to imprisonment, so she did not give up. She set her heart on watching for what she* could *accomplish, and when she saw that there was a place where she could wriggle through the bars, she did it. Her song remains her own. If she sings it for us now, that is her choice.* He touched my forehead with his lips. *She did not wait for me to open her cage.*

A breeze stirred the willow branches, making the cages bob and dance. I moved like a sleepwalker, taking each one down and cracking it open. The birds took flight, even the ones I thought were dead. The grove filled with song and the glorious sound carried me from vision to waking. I lay on my bedroll, staring up at the roof of our house, still seeing the marvels of the spirits' realm.

"She did what she *could* do," I whispered to myself. My heart beat like the wings of the birds I had set free.

"Huh? Did you say something, Himiko?" Kaya's muffled voice brought me all the way back to our own world.

I edged closer. "I said that tomorrow night you're going home."

11

THE WOLF'S DEN

Kaya was a hunter from the tips of the fingers that drew a
taut bowstring to the soles of the feet that could track game
stealthily across mountain meadows, through forests, and
up mountain paths. As a hunter she knew the virtue of silence and soft speech. A loud noise on the trail could startle
your quarry into flight or catch the ear of a beast you did *not*
want to face. I think this must have been the only reason
why she did not blurt "Are you out of your *mind*?" the instant I told her to make her escape from the Ookami village.

She saved that for later. Meanwhile, she acted as though
I hadn't said anything extraordinary. Her sole reaction was
a noncommittal grunt before turning away and beginning
to breathe deeply much too soon.

Faker, I thought fondly. *You'll have plenty to say about this
tomorrow.* And that turned out to be true.

Morning found a sleepy-headed household. Tami's
son behaved like all healthy infants, waking up many times

during the night. We all took turns helping the new mother as much as possible. Tami was the only one who could feed him, but the rest of us could clean him up when he needed it, or stroke his back to help him digest a bellyful of milk. It was a good thing that we were so many under one roof: it allowed Tami to get as much healing sleep as possible and also meant no one blamed me for not doing a fair share that first night. When the baby's strident yowls could not rouse me, everyone presumed I was exhausted from helping his birth, not lost in a vision of the spirit world.

Despite her grogginess, Kaya's mind stayed sharp enough for her to pounce on me when I announced that I would bring everyone's breakfast.

"And *I'll* go with you for water!" she declared. I raised no objection. There was much that we needed to say, and few opportunities to say it without fear of extra ears. As we walked toward the well, she looked at me and asked, "So, did I *dream* what you told me last night or are you simply insane?"

"I told you to escape this place tonight," I said calmly. "You might want to put it off a day or two, but you shouldn't wait much longer than that. You might lose your nerve."

"Himiko, are you *hearing* yourself?" Kaya's eyes darted warily from side to side. There were many people awake and doing their morning chores. The way to the well was busy; so was the cookhouse path. She slowed her pace to maintain our distance from crowds. "How can you talk about running away? Even if we do succeed, what do you think Ryu will do to your family when he finds out?"

"*We* are not going anywhere, Kaya," I said. "Only you."

She stopped in her tracks. I had to take her by the elbow and urge her along. "People are staring," I murmured. "Keep walking before they start wondering what's wrong with you."

"What's wrong with *me*?" Kaya whispered back fiercely. "Better to ask what's laid a nest of crazy eggs in your head!"

"There's nothing crazy about this," I said, my voice firm. "I've thought it all through and you're going to *listen* to what I have to say. You *have* to escape, Kaya. You have to do it, because you can and I can't. The forest is your second home. You can find food and water and a way back that *won't* make you cross paths with any of the villages subject to the Ookami."

"So can you." Kaya sounded deeply distressed. "Give me time to find a way to do it so no one's punished for our escape. I *will*! We came here together and we'll leave together. I'm not leaving my sister behind."

I took a long breath. "Kaya, if I weren't here, would you try to get away?"

"Try?" she repeated with a wry grin. "I'd have eaten one of their awful dinners and been gone before breakfast!"

"So you *could* do it? Could you run off, elude the wolves, return to my village and then to your own before harvest time comes?"

"Yes, of course. I've noticed that there are some places along the village wall where people have dumped broken jars and other trash. I could get to the top of one of those rubbish heaps and climb the rest of the way over the palisade, easy as shinnying up a tree. And it would be no problem leaving our house after sundown. The night Tami's pains began I went to the well and back unchallenged.

There weren't more than two or three Ookami about and not one of them questioned me. I guess they saw the water pot in my hands. But that doesn't mean I'm going to—"

"Yes, you are," I said. "You must. You have to go back to my people and let them know what's become of me. I told them I'd be back with Noboru by harvest time, remember? His return would have cured Mama's madness, I'm convinced of that, but now . . ."

"The sentence against her will be carried out if she can't be healed," Kaya said gently. "Himiko, I don't see what good it will do for your mother's case if I return to your people alone and empty-handed."

"You underestimate yourself, Kaya," I said with a faint smile. "You will find the words to make the Matsu elders delay the death sentence. You will make Lord Hideki into your ally, your sword, and Mama's shield. Above all, you will tell everyone that you saw Noboru here, alive and well. And once you have done that, you will go home."

"First you want me to abandon you and next you want me to abandon your mother?" Kaya sniffed scornfully. "Who do you think you're talking to?"

"A very loyal Badger." I touched her arm. "You want to save my mother so badly that you forget your own. She knows that you're strong, brave, and independent or she never would have let you go adventuring this long. She has faith that you'll come back, but she isn't going to wait forever. She's been informed that you'll return in the autumn. How will she feel when you don't? What will she do when she discovers you've been enslaved by the Ookami?"

Kaya's eyes opened wide as she pictured the answer.

"She'll come after me. She'll lead our warriors here, against a clan that's much bigger than ours and much more used to war. If she does . . . she'll lose."

"Now do you understand why you *must* go?" I asked.

No reply came. Perhaps it was because we'd reached the well and there were too many people who might overhear us. All I could do was hope my friend now saw her path clearly.

She did. She was gone the next morning.

When Kaya's disappearance was discovered, four Ookami warriors stormed into the millet field where I was working and hustled me home, leaving my housemates and the rest of the slaves nearby stunned and speechless. I was flung through the doorway, where I found Ryu waiting. There was no need to wonder why he was there. I gave silent thanksgiving that we were alone. Tami had recovered quickly from childbirth and was doing lighter work in the cookhouse, carrying her baby with her in a sling.

I knelt on the dirt floor and faced the dragon.

"We will find her, you know." Ryu looked down his nose at me and spoke without the slightest hint of irritation. "If my best hunters haven't got the ability to track down one fool of a girl within a day, they might as well lay down their spears and choose husbands."

"May the gods bless their marriages with many children," I muttered under my breath.

"What did you say?"

"Nothing you'd like to hear."

He frowned, then forced a chuckle. "This is your doing,

isn't it? You haven't got the courage to try running away yourself, so you persuade your feather-brained friend to do it. When she's caught, you stay safe while she suffers for it."

"She won't be caught."

This time Ryu's frown stayed. "You are a troublemaker, Himiko. You stir up the muck at the bottom of a clear stream so that no one can drink from it. I'm going to put a stop to that, before you do some real harm."

"If you're so afraid of what I can do, you have a sword and I have a throat." I looked at him directly, steadily. My lips were dry, my heart beating fast. I knew I was taking a dangerous gamble, but I had to keep all of his thoughts of punishment focused on me.

Ryu's eyebrows went up. "You think you're *that* important? How funny. I'll save my sword's edge for a worthy opponent, not a spoiled child. I've made the mistake of giving you too much liberty, but that won't be difficult to correct." Without warning, he grabbed me by the shoulder and hauled me outside, through the village, and all the way to the foot of the ladder leading up to the chieftain's grand house.

"Climb," he said.

I did as I was told, but behaved as if I were graciously accepting an invitation, not obeying a command. I did not wait for him to join me on the platform at the top of the ladder before I walked through the doorway with my head held high.

"Where do you think you're going?" Ryu seized me again. This time it hurt. He shifted his grip on my shoulder and gave me a vicious shove forward so that I tripped on the hem of my field-stained dress and sprawled on my face.

When I raised my head from the floorboards, I felt a trickle of wetness trailing down the side of my nose. I touched it and saw blood.

"Oh! You're hurt!" A young woman rushed to help me sit up. She was very plainly dressed and carried herself so humbly that I believed I was meeting a fellow slave. "Let me get you some water and a bit of cloth for that." Her broad, sallow face showed sincere concern for my injury.

"The gods preserve us, Chizu, is there no end to your stupidity?" Ryu roared at the young woman so ferociously that she threw one arm across her face as though expecting a blow. "It's bad enough that you've turned the brat into your pet, but do you intend to treat every slave I give you like an honored guest? Bah. This is what I get for thinking you could learn. My mother was right: a stone was never born to sing."

"I'm—I'm sorry, my lord husband," Chizu replied, still shielding her eyes from his contemptuous stare. "I didn't know. I thought—"

"You *can't* think. Why do you try?" He snorted. "This girl is Himiko of the Matsu clan. Get her a new dress and make sure she bathes before she puts it on."

"Yes, my lord husband." Chizu's protective arm slowly lowered. "Thank you very much. She will be a great help to me."

"A help to *you*? Do you think I brought her here as a gift for *you*?"

"No, my lord husband." The young woman's head drooped. "I was mistaken. Now I see how pretty she is— much prettier than I. I hope she will make you very happy."

I sucked in my breath loudly in disgust, but not loudly enough to be heard over Ryu's disdainful laugh. "It's a good thing that Mother runs this house and not you. A chunk of firewood has more common sense than you! This creature is conceited enough already. Why would I want to add to her arrogance by making her my woman? She doesn't *begin* to deserve that honor." He fixed Chizu with a cold look that as good as added: *Neither do you.*

His timid wife flinched and asked for his forgiveness. Ryu did not bother to acknowledge her apology. "Once you've gotten her bathed and dressed, she will be strictly in my mother's charge. If you want the girl to help you with some task that's too overwhelming for you, tell Mother and she will approve it, or not. You will have only one remaining duty concerning Himiko: she is not to be allowed the company of anyone who is not an Ookami. *Anyone.* Can you handle that without making a mess of it?"

Chizu touched her brow to the floor before answering: "I'll try my best, my lord husband."

"That's what I'm afraid of."

I didn't know which sickened me more: Ryu's spiteful disrespect for his wife or Chizu's spineless deference to her mean-souled mate.

The wolf chieftain left the house to tend to other business. Chizu tried to speak harshly to me, the way she presumed Ryu would approve, but she was not born to be a petty tyrant. *Please* and *thank you* and *if you wouldn't mind* cropped up in every other sentence as she took me to the river for my bath and back again to don a dress that didn't reek of sweat, soil, and fertilizer.

The interior of Ryu's house was different from my father's. It was newer and much larger, though it was difficult to see exactly how large it was unless you viewed it from the outside. Inside, a series of artfully woven and dyed cloths hung between slender poles, dividing the big space into many smaller ones. Chizu took great pains to point out which ones were the family's private sleeping rooms and to let me know that I was never to set foot in them uninvited.

"Oh, and this is the little boy's place," she added, showing me a tiny curtained-off area between the room she shared with Ryu and the one his mother occupied. "You'd probably better stay out of this one too."

Just then there was a clamor from outside. We peered around the curtains and saw my brother Noboru come running into the house, his back laden with kindling wood. A bird-boned woman with fog-colored hair came huffing and puffing after him, though she was not *too* breathless to stop her constant stream of talk.

"—disgraceful, the way those useless lumps lost a trail that a blind pig could follow! They'd have found her soon enough if *someone* I could mention told them that failure gets rewarded with a whipping, but nobody listens to me."

Noboru dropped his bundle of sticks and brought her some water. "*I* listen to you, Auntie," he said earnestly.

"Hmph. Well, you're better than nothing. And if you *do* listen to me, why can't you remember not to call me 'Auntie' when we're under this roof?"

"I'm sorry, Aun—Lady Sato."

"Good boy." She patted his head.

"Um . . . I think you might want to go into your room now, Himiko," Chizu whispered. "Please?"

I yearned to call my little brother's name, but held back. We were now under the same roof, and that would have to be enough for me, at least temporarily. Being able to find Noboru instantly would be a great advantage if—no, *when!*—we made our own escape. But if I broke Ryu's rule about speaking with none but the Ookami, he might separate us, and he certainly would make Chizu suffer for it. I could not risk so much to gain so little.

With a silent indication of consent, I withdrew toward the back of the house to the curtained space where I was supposed to sleep. I tried to move as quietly as possible. It was bad luck that Chizu chose that moment to sneeze loudly.

"What's that? Who's lurking there?" Lady Sato did not wait for an answer to her shrill questions but came swarming down on her daughter-in-law's hiding place. "Is this how you welcome me home, you mannerless thing? Why didn't you—? Oh!" I had retreated silently enough, but too slowly: the wolf chieftain's mother caught sight of me and gasped in surprise.

"Himiko?" Noboru peered at me from behind Lady Sato's flaring dress. His uncertainty changed to joy in a heartbeat. "Big Sister, you're here! You didn't leave me!" He ran into my arms.

Chizu groaned and covered her face with her hands.

Lady Sato gave the young woman a peevish look. "*Now* what are you whining about, you mouse?" Bit by bit, Chizu told her mother-in-law about my introduction to the household, including the ban on my speaking to anyone but members of the wolf clan.

"And now *this* has happened, and I'm going to be blamed for it!" Chizu concluded with a whimper, indicated Noboru and me.

"As you should be," Lady Sato said, imperturbable. "If you had come forward to greet me when I returned home, that would have given the girl enough time to get out of sight. You really are a bungler, Chizu. I told my husband it was a mistake to encumber our only son with such a bride, but *he* knew better. *He* said that you were almost as nobly born as Ryu, that your father had promised him many rich gifts for the honor of uniting our houses, and that the women of your family have as many sons as there are seeds in a gourd." She eyed Chizu's flat stomach meaningfully and remarked: "A *ripe* gourd, not a hollow one."

I saw the tears roll down Chizu's face as she received her mother-in-law's piercing attack in silent dejection. What sort of childhood had created such a woman? How had she been turned into a living ghost, as weak and lost as a single drop of milk in a bottomless pond? Who had robbed her of the strength to love herself, and to demand the love of others?

Spirits, hear me! I prayed. *Bring truth to the words I am about to say. Yet if you choose to leave me with the burden of a lie on my lips, I accept it. I cannot find the spell that will mend this woman's broken spirit in a day, but I can give her at least a day of shelter from her tormentors.*

"Lady Sato, you are wrong," I announced with conviction.

"When spring returns, your daughter-in-law will give you a grandchild."

Ryu's mother scowled so intensely that the hairy mole between her eyebrows vanished. "A *wise* slave shuts her mouth unless her mistress wants her to speak."

"I am more than a slave, my lady," I said, holding my ground. "I am a shaman, and the spirits command my voice more than you ever will. They have given me visions, revealing what is hidden, and I tell you that Lady Chizu is going to have a son!"

Lady Sato's thin lips moved as if she were chewing a tough piece of meat. Finally she spoke: "Nothing happens in this house without my knowledge. I will find out soon enough if what you say is true or false and you will be treated accordingly. For the time being, I'm going to believe you, because it will mean we didn't make a *totally* worthless bargain when we took *that* one into our family." She waved a hand at Chizu, who was still gaping in shock over the great blessing I had just prophesied for her.

"Meanwhile, I have made a decision," she went on. "My son will not be told about this accidental meeting between you and your little brother. Just see to it that it doesn't happen again."

"Thank you, Lady Sato." I pressed my face to Noboru's downy cheek. Who could say when I might have the chance to hold him like that again? "You have given us a gracious gift."

"Hmph. I have a bit of a reputation for being very generous to those who walk with the spirits. My son does not

approve, but I feel that a *capable* shaman should be rewarded."
She took Noboru from my arms and gave me a hard look.
"And a lying slave should be punished. Now get out of
my sight."

I made a quick gesture of reverence and hastened
to obey.

It did not take long for my new dress to become as homely
and work-stained as my old one. Lady Sato's kindness did not
last. The way she viewed things, the world was divided between the strong and the weak, conquerors and conquered,
masters and slaves. Those who lost wars lost everything,
and those who won were entitled to command. She always
had plenty of heavy work for me to do, with summer heat
making each chore twice as taxing. She treated me as a slave
first, a shaman second, and a princess . . . not at all.

One day, she startled me by letting me sleep until well
past the time to make breakfast for the family. I woke up to
find her kneeling at the foot of my bedroll, a bowl of millet
porridge in her hands, a smile on her face. I began to apologize for shirking, but she signaled for silence.

"Enjoy your food and then go back to sleep if you like,
my dear," she said. "Or get up, if that's what you'd rather do.
The day is yours. I've sent my son off with a hunting party. He
didn't want to go, but I have my ways." She winked. "While
he's gone, why don't you and your little brother spend some
time together? Poor child, it's very hard on him to know
that you're so nearby and yet he's never allowed to share
your company!"

I rubbed sleep from my eyes, wondering if this was

part of a vivid dream. It *seemed* real enough. "Lady Sato, why are you . . . ?"

She laughed at my confusion. "And they say that we old people are forgetful! I once told you that a good shaman must be rewarded. Your words have been proved true and this is how I have chosen to show my appreciation."

"My words . . . Oh! You mean that Lady Chizu is—"

She nodded with satisfaction, followed by a thoughtful look. "Why do you sound so surprised? You were the one who told us she was pregnant."

I met her challenge boldly. "I'm not surprised, I'm merely half awake."

"Hmmm." She looked as if she were going to say more about it, but changed her mind. I was permitted to enjoy a day of freedom and delight with Noboru. It was over much too soon, and my life under Lady Sato's rule returned to the same exhausting routine as before.

I must admit, there *was* one heartening difference: as soon as Ryu heard that his wife was expecting their first child, he stopped browbeating her and sometimes even tossed a careless compliment or two in her direction, like throwing scraps of gristle to a dog. Chizu was pathetically grateful for the change and insisted on giving me all the credit for it. She could do nothing to break her mother-in-law's power over me, but found countless small ways to make my days brighter, everything from leaving a ripe peach beside my bedroll to "forgetting" her husband's orders and sending Noboru to me with an unnecessary message whenever Ryu was out of the way.

Chizu was also always willing to help me with my

chores, whenever she could do so without her mother-in-law spying on her. Lady Sato had certain fixed ideas about how a chieftain's wife should act. Sharing the household slave's work was definitely *not* a part of this, but Chizu was clever and found her own modest ways of dodging the older woman's rules.

One of my chores was to wash the family's clothing. Chizu told me to go to one particular bend of the river, thickly overhung by willow trees. She insisted that the flat rocks I would find there were ideal for scrubbing and beating the dirt out of clothing. It was really no different from any other spot for doing laundry, but it *was* so well concealed and out-of-the-way that she could meet me there and shoulder half the task.

As we worked, I asked her a question that had been on my mind since the day I was dragged into Ryu's household. "Lady Chizu, I've noticed that each of the Ookami noble families have at least *three* slaves to serve them. Your husband is their chieftain, so why am I the only one who works for you?"

"It wasn't always this way, Himiko. We used to have five slaves, but Lord Ryu gave them to his most favored counselors right before he brought you home. He said"—she looked ill at ease—"he said that your friend's escape was *your* doing and that you needed more work and less time to make mischief."

"At least that explains why I'm busy from sunup to sundown," I remarked, wiping my brow with a piece of wet laundry. "And it also probably explains why Lady Sato is so snappish. I'll bet she hates being reduced to owning one measly slave instead of having five to boss around."

"That's true." Chizu sighed. "But she had to accept her son's decision. All she can do about it is pick at him for everything else."

"That poor, mistreated man," I said with a flat voice and a straight face. Chizu raised one brow and gave a nervous giggle.

Summer steeped the land in heat, with gusty rain showers filling the rice paddies and irrigating the fields and fruit trees. The earth was patterned in shades of green, and the prospect of an abundant harvest made everyone in the Ookami village more friendly to one another. Ryu was more smug than usual, strutting among his people as though he were personally responsible for how well the crops were growing. I wondered how long it would be before he began taking credit for the rain and sunshine too.

Every evening it was my job to serve the family their dinner, then I retired to my sleeping chamber to eat my own. Once I was safely out of sight, Lady Sato called Noboru to come from his room, sit beside her, and share the meal.

One night, after this had happened, I overheard Lady Sato lavishing fond names on my little brother and coaxing him to eat the best morsels from her own plate. Because the inner walls of the house were flimsy curtains it was easy for me to catch every word. It made me happy to know that even though he was far from his true family, Noboru was not condemned to a life without affection.

Ryu did not share my feelings.

"Must you treat that Matsu brat as if he were a member of this family, Mother?" I heard him growl. "Remember he's a slave like the rest of them!"

"I suppose you'd rather have this little one out in the fields?" came the sarcastic reply. "I'm sure he could weed all the paddies in a day! Hmph. You never were very good at thinking *sensibly,* Ryu."

"And how do you intend to act toward him once my son is born?" Ryu countered. "I will not have Katsuro believing that a captive is his equal!"

"May the gods help us all, you've *named* the child?" Lady Sato shrilled. "And a boy's name too, when there's no way you could know if you'll have a son or a daughter? The gods will punish you for being so arrogant, but they'll make the child suffer for it as well. Could you *be* any stupider?"

Ryu made an impatient sound. "Do you really think I would do anything so foolish? As soon as I knew Chizu was finally doing her duty as my wife, I went to Master Rinji to find out about the child. He read the future signs and told me I will be the father of a strong boy!"

Lady Sato's cackle sounded like someone shaking a basket full of pebbles. "'Master' Rinji? That miserable excuse for a shaman couldn't predict water in a rainstorm! He stutters through the chants, trips over his own feet when he dances, and as for being able to heal anyone—! Old man Ta had a swollen belly from eating bad meat and Rinji spent half a day trying to help him give birth!"

I couldn't help myself: I laughed out loud.

In an instant, Ryu was standing in the doorway to the narrow sleeping quarters, his face livid with rage. "How dare you eavesdrop on us!" The next thing I knew, he was roaring for Noboru to go to his sleeping chamber at once while he pulled me out of mine. I caught a flash of my little brother's disappearing form and heard him crying in fright just before Ryu jerked me upright and pulled me behind him, into the presence of his wife and mother.

"Is *this* how you train an upstart girl?" he shouted at Chizu. "Letting her think it's acceptable to listen at corners so that she can go blabbering our business to the whole clan?"

"My lord husband, I'm sorry." Chizu wept without making a sound, tears washing over her cheeks. Her skin looked pale green. "Please forgive me. It's my fault. I—"

I could not stand to witness any more. "It is *not* Lady Chizu's fault!" I exclaimed. "But it will be yours if all this bullying makes her sick while she's carrying your baby."

"You insolent *snail*. Is this the only way to shut your mouth?" Ryu raised his fist.

"No!" Chizu tried to spring to her feet in order to prevent her husband from striking me, but swayed dizzily and nearly fell. Ryu reacted at once, letting me go and catching her. She looked stunned by this unaccustomed display of caring, but only for a moment before she was messily sick all over him.

Lady Sato watched all of this with a dry little smile. "Oh, *well* done, my son. Your father's spirit is *so* proud of you, I'm sure. Beating the very shaman who foretold the birth of your child? Yes, *that's* the way to win the favor of the gods! And there's your reward." She waved one hand at his befouled tunic.

Ryu helped Chizu sit down before tearing off his clothes and throwing them in my face. "Wash that, bring me something clean to wear, and fetch cold water to bathe your mistress's face!" he snapped.

"In that order?" I asked archly.

This time Chizu was too weak to interfere when Ryu slapped me.

"Fools," Lady Sato muttered. "I am trapped in a house of fools. Didn't I *tell* you not to strike her, Ryu? Now she'll use her powers against the baby!"

My cheek stung, but I swallowed my tears. "I would never do such a thing, Lady Sato."

"And I would never spread wings and fly," Ryu sneered. "*Think,* Mother! If she had any power worth naming, would she be our slave? That so-called prophecy was nothing but a lucky guess!"

"Your precious Rinji couldn't even do that much, and yet he's living like a lord under Master Daimu's roof," Lady Sato replied. She turned her scowling face to me. "What are you staring at, girl? Your master gave you orders: obey them! Take care of my silly daughter-in-law first, then bring Lord Ryu a new tunic and scrub this floor while you can still get the stink out of it. You can wash the clothes in the morning." She made a face at her son. "*Another* brilliant idea of yours, telling our one remaining slave to do laundry at night! If she wouldn't have the sense to run off as soon as she was out of the gateway, she'd fall into the river and drown, and then who'd be left to serve me?"

I helped Chizu undress and lie down in her bedchamber before bringing water from the village well for my

chores. Lady Sato and Ryu were still quarreling when I returned, though she paused just long enough to snipe at me
for taking too long. As I cleaned Chizu's face and cooled
her body with wet cloths, I heard the argument grow more
heated. Apparently Ryu could win tribute from clan after
clan without ever achieving enough to satisfy his mother.

Two names in particular kept cropping up on Lady
Sato's sharp tongue. I knew who Rinji was—clan shaman
and *"the only person even less competent than you!"*—but who
was Master Daimu?

The answer came on the breath of a sigh from Chizu's
pale lips. "I wish she wouldn't do that to him."

"Do what?" I asked as softly as I could.

"She always compares him to Master Daimu, and never
nicely. She makes it sound as though she wishes she were
the shaman's mother instead."

"I thought Master Rinji was your clan's shaman."

"Not exactly. He was Master Daimu's apprentice."

"What happened to his master?" I remembered the
death of my own beloved teacher, Lady Yama, and felt a
pang of pity for Rinji. It was hard to lose someone with
whom you worked so closely and who understood some aspects of your spirit better than anyone else, even your family.

"Oh, Himiko, don't look so sad!" Chizu whispered.
"Master Daimu isn't dead, he's just gone. He left us many
seasons ago. The spirits told him to make a great pilgrimage, though he never told any of us why. He will be back
some day." She sighed again. "I hope it's soon. Master Rinji
tries hard but . . . my mother-in-law is right about him. He's
not very good as a healer. If all goes well, I won't need him

to help with the birth, but I feel so sick, and I'm so afraid it means I'll need someone besides a midwife, and if Master Rinji makes a mistake I know I'll be blamed because my husband always takes his side, and—"

I patted her hands, trying to calm her before she became so overwrought that she attracted Ryu's unwanted attention. "*Shhh, shhh,* you mustn't fret. It's perfectly normal to feel sick when you first become pregnant. A few more turns of the moon and it will pass. Remember, I am always ready to help you. Now if you're comfortable, why don't you go to sleep?"

"I am tired," she admitted. She settled down on her bedroll only to bolt upright and beg to know: "Do you think I'm *too* tired, Himiko?" I reassured her that weariness was just as normal as an unsteady stomach during early pregnancy, and she was able to sleep without further worries.

The following morning, Lady Sato kept finding fault with her breakfast. First she demanded a fresh bowl, then a helping of rice gruel scooped from the top of the pot, then the bottom, then the middle. Ryu scolded her for calling me back and forth so many times, not because he felt bad to see me being run ragged but because his mother's fussiness was bringing me into unavoidable contact with Noboru.

"She is *not* to spend any time with the brat," he said. "Is that so hard to accomplish?" He glared at my little brother, who had scarcely begun to eat his breakfast. "Get out of here! Hide yourself! Go!"

"Stay right where you are, boy," Lady Sato commanded.

She regarded her son coolly. "Is this the sort of man you've become? One who starves innocent children?"

"Mother, he can take his food with him."

"And spill it everywhere! Of course, certainly, why not? *You* don't have to clean up the mess."

"Neither do you." Ryu's jaw was tight. "The girl will take care of it."

"Did it ever occur to you that I might have some *necessary* work for her to do today?" Lady Sato was a human rockslide: there was no stopping her once she got going. "Your tunic is still filthy from last night. Were you planning to *yell* at it until it gets clean? And the stench!"

"Himiko!" Ryu shouted at me. "Go wash my tunic at once!"

"Meaning that *I* must clear away the breakfast dishes?" Lady Sato's eyes narrowed.

"Chizu will do—"

"In her condition? Look, she's barely eaten anything! She's going to be sick again, mark my words." (That was only partly true: Chizu wasn't eating because she was too fascinated by her mother-in-law's tirade.) "No doubt you'll want *me* to swab that up too. Why not? It's just another mark of how much you *respect* the woman who gave birth to you."

"How can you claim I don't respect you?" Ryu threw his arms in the air, half mad with frustration.

"What sort of respectful son puts his miserable old mother to work in the very house where she used to have *seven* slaves to care for her?"

"We only had five!"

"Oho, so now I'm a liar? Yes, *that's* how you honor me! Himiko, go to the cookhouse and fetch me whatever the field workers are eating today. *They* will be better fed than I. *They* are valued."

Ryu uttered an incoherent exclamation of exasperation and stomped out of the house.

Lady Sato sat primly in her place until the last reverberation of his feet on the ladder faded. Then she cackled again: "Ha! I thought he'd never leave. Chizu! Stop picking at your food. Either eat it or leave it, but be done with it. Noboru! Stay here and finish your breakfast, then clean the dishes. Himiko! Close your mouth before it fills with flies, splash some water on your cheeks, and pull your hair out of your face. Rinji is a hopeless excuse for a shaman, but until the gods have pity and send Master Daimu home, he's the only one we've got. You will look presentable before him."

"Lady Sato, why must I see the Ookami shaman?" I asked.

"For two reasons: because I am your mistress and I say so! Now let's go."

12

SUMMER SONGS, WINTER DANCES

Lady Sato knelt on the wide, airy platform in front of the Ookami shaman's house and looked around her with distaste. Chizu was hunched over next to her, as though trying to fold her body into itself and disappear. I stood to one side, taking my place in the ranks of the shaman's slaves. There were six of them—three men and three women, none from my clan. They were all gray-haired and wrinkled, but sturdy and well-fed. Judging by their comfortable attitude, they had a kindhearted master. As slaves, they had no choice about the lives they led, yet I got the feeling that even if they had been free, they would have picked this path.

Their master did not share their contentment. He had reacted to Lady Sato's unexpected arrival like a speared frog and had not stopped twitching since. He would have been a good-looking young man if not for his alarming skittishness. Everything about him reminded me of a praying mantis caught in a cookpot—long, skinny limbs and body, goggling eyes, and an air of jumpy desperation. The only difference was that the mantis had some hope of escape. I did not think it was possible to find someone who could arouse more pity than Chizu until I met Master Rinji.

"This is—is a great honor, Lady Sato," he said, absent-mindedly cracking his knuckles. "I have been wanting to congratulate you on the approaching birth of your grandchild—your *first* grandchild, that is, for surely the gods will send your son and his lovely bride many more children. I have offered prayers every day for Lady Chizu's safe pregnancy and delivery, and I hope—"

"Do *they* have to be here?" Lady Sato cut in rudely, jabbing her hand at the shaman's servants.

"Oh! I am sorry. Shall I send them away?"

"*Shall* you?" Lady Sato performed a cruelly accurate mockery of the awkward young man's tremulous voice. "*I don't know. Why don't you ask their permission?*"

Rinji bent his head, his face scarlet, and muttered words of dismissal. They retreated into the house and I was about to join them when a harsh command from Lady Sato brought me up short:

"Where do you think you're going, troublemaker? Come here and sit. I didn't bring you here to enjoy idleness. You're lazy enough as it is! You are the reason we're here, and the sooner I take care of things, the sooner you can get back to doing *real* work."

I sat where she directed, next to Chizu, and wondered what that thorn-tongued old woman was up to. Rinji stole a questioning glance at me, but we were partners in ignorance.

"My dear Lady Sato, it is—it is my heart's desire to help you in any way," he said. "What can I do?"

"Something Master Daimu would never need to do," she replied crisply. "Prove to me that you *are* a shaman and not just a sack of wind. This girl here is Himiko. Her father was chieftain of the Matsu clan until Lord Ryu defeated him. She is no longer a princess, but she *is* a follower of the spirits' path." She pierced him with a hard look. "A *real* one. Unfortunately, her undeniable magic arts led to an argument in our home—the details are none of your business— and it ended with my hotheaded son slapping her. Slapping a *shaman,* the very one who foretold my grandchild's birth! Can you imagine such a thing?"

"Uh . . . what do you want me to do about that?" Rinji asked, squirming. "I don't think it would be appropriate for me to scold Lord Ryu, but if you insist . . ."

"What I need you to *do,* boy, is work a spell to prevent any misfortune from coming to the baby because of my son's rash act. The Matsu girl claims she would never ill-wish the unborn child, but I want to make sure of it. Use your magic to contain hers, and do it now!"

"Now, Lady Sato?" Rinji's eyes darted all around, as if hoping to catch sight of someone to rescue him from the formidable old woman. "It will take me a while to make the preparations. Will you and Lady Chizu be comfortable waiting here, or would you prefer to come inside?"

"We have no intention of waiting. We have too many chores to do at home, chores that Chizu and I will have to do on our own since our one and only slave will be here for the better part of the day."

"I'm sure it won't take me all day to—"

"Do you intend to *rush* through the ritual? You make enough mistakes when you take things slowly. I saw how badly you stumbled when you had to bless the first rice planting this spring! Do this slowly and do it *right*, if you value your position. We are entrusting you with the life of the next Ookami chieftain. If Chizu gives birth to a healthy boy, I will come to you on hands and knees and swear you are a greater shaman than Master Daimu. If not . . ." She did not have to specify the consequences.

Rinji drew his head down between his rounded shoulders like a frightened turtle. "I swear by my ancestors, I will use all my powers to protect Lord Ryu's son."

"That's what I'm afraid of." With an unnaturally large sigh, Lady Sato stood up. "Come, Chizu. We have much to do and no one to help us do it. Do try not to strain yourself, dear daughter-in-law. Who knows what effect that might have on the baby?"

"Er, would you like to have one or two of my servants for the day?" Rinji blurted.

Lady Sato gave him a coy look. "You are too kind, Master Rinji," she said, and took all six.

I stood at the edge of the platform and watched them go. "I'll bet she finds a way to keep them," I said.

"Probably." Rinji shrugged. "I'll be given others. I don't need slaves to do much for me, but they tend the shrine too." His sigh was sincere as he added: "If she does keep them, I hope she'll treat them well."

I tilted my head back and gazed up at the high, peaked roof that jutted out above us. "I was told that your house and the clan shrine are the same building. We didn't have an enclosed shrine in my village. I'm eager to see what it looks like inside."

"Ah? You are?" he asked nervously. "Well, that's good. We have to go in so that I can, er, fulfill my promise to Lady Sato. This way, please."

I followed him into the cool shadows of the building. Everything I saw enthralled me. The first thing I noticed was how new everything was. The roof soared steeply, its thatch still exhaling the fragrance of cut grass, and the supporting pillars still held the spirits of the trees they had once been. I placed one hand against the smooth wood and felt it tingle with the forest's song.

Two corners of the interior were curtained off. When I gave Rinji an inquiring look, he explained: "The smaller one is where I sleep and the larger one is where I prepare medicines and keep the things I use in the rituals. Would that interest you?"

I cocked my head. "Master Rinji, are you this obliging to every Ookami slave?"

My question flustered him. "I—I find it difficult to think of you as a slave, Himiko. Lady Sato doesn't fear slaves."

"Lady Sato doesn't need to fear me, either. I would never curse a child, not even the child of the man who killed so many of my kin."

"Well . . . *she* would." He gave me a hesitant smile. "She left you in my care because you're a shaman, not because you're a slave. I don't believe I need to perform any kind of rite to protect Lord Ryu's child from you, but I must honor my word. I hope I will be able to do it quickly enough so that the experience won't be too drawn out or tedious for you."

I laughed. "While I'm here, I'm free. Take your time."

Rinji was very shy, but the longer we spent together, the more outgoing he became. He brought me into the larger of the two curtained chambers, where he gathered together the necessary ingredients for the ritual he'd promised Lady Sato. My heart lifted with joy to find myself once again surrounded by the tools of my calling. I was familiar with everything he would need for casting such a spell and began lending him a hand without asking his permission. He did not object. In fact, he seemed relieved to have my help. As we worked side by side, he began chatting happily about the years he had spent as an apprentice, and of how his one dream was to see Master Daimu's return.

"I'm glad to hear that your clan won't object to having two shamans," I said, recalling the ploys Master Michio and I had had to use to conceal my status as his equal.

"Oh, that's not going to happen," Rinji said with a shrug. "When Master Daimu returns, everything will go back to being the way it was before he left."

"You mean you'll be nothing more than his apprentice again?" I was taken aback. "Won't you miss being your own master and having your clan's respect as a shaman in your own right?"

"Miss it? I'd welcome the change with open arms!" His cheerful tone vanished. "Why did Master Daimu have to go? There was so much he didn't have the chance to teach me before he left! He claimed that I was smart enough to be able to fill in the gaps myself by studying the things I *did* know, but he put too much faith in me."

He gestured at the bundles of dried herbs and the other ingredients for potions and poultices. "I know how to seek out all the right plants and how to prepare them properly. It's the one part of my calling that I love beyond all others. When I'm in the forest or walking along the side of the fields, seeking roots and flowers and seeds, I'm at peace. I feel so much satisfaction every time I mix a new batch of medicine, because I know that the work of my hands will relieve pain, cure an illness, or even prevent one."

I nodded. "I know what you mean, Master Rinji. The spirits have been generous to us, filling this world with the means to heal our sicknesses and injuries."

"The spirits . . . Master Daimu talked about them all the time. He spoke as though they were always within reach of his voice. He could hear them, see them, walk with them." Rinji looked at me with sad eyes. "He told me that I would be able to do the same, someday, but that day never came. The spirits shun me, Himiko. They prove it by making me look like a bumbling fool whenever I try to call upon them to bless our clan, to help our dead find eternal rest, or to guide me through a healing. I would have given up many seasons ago, but Lord Ryu encourages me and Master Daimu will cast me aside if he returns to find that I abandoned our people. How can I let them down? But how can I go on pretending to be something I'm not?" His voice rose, impassioned. "What good does it do to have the best medicines if you lack the skill to use them? What's the use of being a shaman in name only, when your people need help, not make-believe?"

He suddenly realized what he was confessing and looked away, embarrassed. "Did you need proof of how much the spirits despise me?" he said with an awkward laugh. "They loosened my lips so that I've humiliated myself before—before—"

"Before a slave?" I laid one hand lightly on his arm. "But you said you don't think of me that way. I am a shaman, like you. I will seal away everything you told me just as you will perform the rite to seal Ryu's unborn child from harm."

His thin mouth twisted into a self-mocking smile. "You'll do the better job of it."

To be a shaman is to be a healer. To be a healer is to share the sufferer's pain so that you feel driven to end it, but not all pain afflicts the body. I knew what I had to do.

"Master Rinji, would your teacher ever have accepted you as his apprentice if he thought you were unworthy of becoming a shaman?" I asked.

He thought about it, then slowly shook his head.

"Then hear me, please: my brother Masa is a blacksmith. When he began his apprenticeship it only took him ten days before he could use all of his master's tools, but that didn't mean he was ready to forge a sword. He had the talent; he needed his teacher's guidance to show him how to *use* that talent." I tightened my hold on his arm. "Your teacher was called away before he could finish your training. You don't know when he will return. My training as a shaman is complete . . ." I paused, knowing the full significance of what I was about to suggest, feeling uncertain about going on.

"You . . . would teach me?" Hope and possibility lit Rinji's face.

"If you wouldn't consider it dishonorable to learn from a captive," I said, pleased that my misgivings were groundless.

He seized my hands and pressed them to his chest. "Dear Lady Himiko, it would be the greatest honor in the world!"

Before we could begin planning how I could continue Rinji's training without anyone finding out, he had to cast the spell he had promised Lady Sato. We agreed that he would not attempt to build a wall around my powers but instead would petition the spirits to shield Chizu's infant from *all* harm until the day he was born.

It proved to be a dreadfully unimpressive display of the shaman's art but an excellent opportunity for me to observe where Rinji's strengths and weaknesses lay. He knew all of the steps of the ritual and performed them meticulously, but he sounded like a small child reciting words he did not understand. There was no heart in his chanting, no emotion in the movements of his dance. When he struck the sacred bronze bell to conclude the ceremony, it made a hollow, wooden *thunk* instead of a deep, resonant chime.

"How was that?" he asked when he was done.

"We have work to do," I admitted.

"A lot?" He looked dejected and ready to hear the worst.

"Not as much as you might expect," I said tactfully. "You are like a good, sturdy house that only needs a new roof to be perfect." *A roof and a fire on the hearth,* I thought. When Rinji had performed the rite, the air within the shrine remained lifeless; the spirits he sought were still far beyond his reach.

Rinji and I schemed out the best way for me to become his secret teacher. It proved to be remarkably simple: Lady Sato longed for the days when she had commanded a whole household of slaves; Rinji had them. Her greed and envy showed plainly in her eyes when he brought me back to the chieftain's house and claimed his people.

"Are you *sure* you've done everything possible to protect my grandchild?" she demanded. "I told you not to hurry. In fact"—an unpleasantly insinuating tone slithered into her voice—"why don't you have the girl stay with you overnight? Don't you deserve to have someone young and pretty waiting on you for a change? And she carries herself so elegantly! Even with that bad leg of hers, she manages to move gracefully. It's a pleasure to watch her; a pleasure you should enjoy for as long as you like, dear Master Rinji."

"Er, thank you, Lady Sato, but I would not want to annoy Lord Ryu by taking his property without his permission, especially overnight," Rinji replied.

"Never mind *him;* he hasn't touched her!" Lady Sato snapped. "Take her away with you now, before he comes home. Once he sees how comfortable it is to have the servants that *should* be ours, he won't raise a peep of protest."

Rinji shook his head. "I don't want to antagonize my chieftain."

"Do you *hear* yourself, you infant?" There was no more *dear Master Rinji.* "A *real* man wouldn't think twice about the consequences for keeping this girl!"

"Please let me finish, Lady Sato," the young shaman said. "I am as eager to enjoy more of La—of Himiko's company as any man, but I'd rather do it without stirring up needless problems. Send her to me on those days when Lord Ryu will not notice her absence and I will send you my people in exchange."

Lady Sato stopped glowering and became attentive. "Your slaves are not invisible and this village is full of gossips. How will we excuse this arrangement?"

"You will make a sacred vow to have your girl tend the shrine once every five days in exchange for the wolf spirit's favor and blessing on your unborn grandchild. I will accept this, but I will also take pity on you—a venerable noblewoman and her pregnant daughter-in-law forced to shoulder the girl's chores. For that reason I will send you *my* servants whenever you send me yours. The wolf spirit will be satisfied and the gossips can chew on their own tongues. Agreed?" He gave her an innocent smile.

"Why, dear, dear Master Rinji, you astonish me! I had no idea you were so clever."

The young shaman looked my way. "I can be clever enough with the right inspiration."

"Well, what do you know?" Lady Sato leered. "The fox cub has teeth after all!"

I did not have to pretend to blush.

I spent the rest of the summer and autumn tossed this way and that between doing what I loved best and toiling through mindless labor that sapped my strength and my spirit. During the four days when I was condemned to serve under Ryu's roof I found my waking moments gradually taken over by black thoughts: had Kaya reached my village safely? Had she been able to convince the elders to hold off on my mother's punishment? If so, how long would they be willing to wait before deciding that I was never going to return? Or had they already carried out the sentence? Was Mama alive or dead? I did not dare turn to the spirit world for an answer, afraid of what I might learn, afraid that I might lose the gods' tenuous favor for trying to find out something I was not supposed to know.

Every fifth day saved me. I woke up joyful, my mind free of everything but happy anticipation. Sometimes I was wakened by a ferocious hug from Noboru. We were allowed and encouraged to be together on days when I went to the shrine. Lady Sato was always in such a good mood, looking forward to being mistress of six slaves instead of one, that she became extremely charitable toward my little brother and me.

On those mornings, I had a special ritual to follow, one that had nothing to do with the spirits. First I served the family breakfast, cleaned up after the meal, and stepped out onto the house platform to scan the village. Ryu had to leave before I could do this, but he was not the only person who had to be out of the way. After the field workers, slave and free, went out to tend the flourishing crops, there were not many people left except the old, the ill, and mothers of young children who were usually too busy to grow meddlesome. The fewer eyes to see me go to the shrine, the fewer tongues to wag about it.

Of course it was impossible to dodge *every* witness. Luckily, Lady Sato had a way of extinguishing any spark of gossip before it started a blaze. She didn't want her son hearing about her six-slaves-for-one arrangement. The busybody who tried spreading scandal about "Master Rinji's shameful infatuation with a mere *slave*" soon got a visit from Lady Sato. I don't know what she said or did to stamp out the talebearing, but it worked!

The hardest part of my cherished fifth days was forcing myself to *walk* to the shrine. I wanted to grow a hawk's wings and fly! It was a pleasure to teach Rinji. He was a wise and willing student, eager to perfect his skills as a shaman. I had never been a teacher until now, and I found that I loved it. When I was Yama's student, there were some lessons that were harder to learn than others, but a source of immense satisfaction when I conquered them. When Rinji mastered a new skill thanks to my instruction, I felt an even greater sense of triumph.

The harvest season drew near. Daylight faded earlier and nights became more chill. The fireflies winked out one by one, gone until summer came again. I prayed that the next time I saw their tiny lights it would be from the platform of my own house, Mama alive and well beside me, Noboru in her arms.

Crops ripened in the field and the people reaped them, singing. The air grew thick with the dust and chaff of grain being threshed. Chizu's belly began to "show" the slightest bit, yet enough to attract countless women, young and old, who filled her ears with stories of childbirth. Most of them wanted her to be reassured about what lay ahead, but there were always some who took twisted delight in scaring the timid young woman with exaggerated tales of agony and tragedy.

"What's *wrong* with those people?" I complained to

Rinji during one of our lessons. I was seated on the floor of the shrine, waiting for him to demonstrate the thanksgiving dance he would perform for the gods as part of the autumn festival. "I wish I could sneak into every last one of their houses and fill their water pots with frogs!"

He chuckled. "What's stopping you?"

"I'd run out of frogs."

"Would you like me to do something about it?" he offered. "I know how to brew a potion that makes a person's stomach . . . loose. If you tell me who's been upsetting Lady Chizu, I'll find a way to add a bit of that potion to their drinking water, and then—"

"—and then their whole family will suffer. Really, Master Rinji, sometimes you sound just like a bad little boy." I tried to frown, but it turned into a giggle.

He laughed with me, then became serious. "Is that how you see me, Lady Himiko? As a little boy?"

"What?"

"It must be easy for you to think of me that way. We're close in age, but you're so high above me that you have to stoop down to see me."

"Master Rinji, how can I be above you? You always call me *Lady* Himiko when we're alone together, but you know I'm a prisoner of your clan."

"You were born a princess of the Matsu; my parents were commoners. You are a fully fledged shaman, a master of the spirits' path; I am your humble student. You weren't always a slave, and I implore the gods to bring the day when your captivity ends"—he took a deep, shuddering breath—"even though I know that will be the day I lose . . . a friend."

His earnest words, his grief-stricken look, the disquieting twist our conversation had taken all set me on edge. How had we gone from joking about plopping frogs into water jars to this? Why was he staring at me with such yearning and such dejection?

My brother Aki's ghost rose before me. I saw his face as I remembered it from the days when he first loved Kaya's sister, Hoshi, but Father forbade him to court a girl who was not a member of our clan. Aki lacked both the strength to defy Father and the power to deny his heart. It tore him apart and made my spirit ache to see his suffering.

Now Rinji's face wore the same expression. He called me *friend,* but I could hear the unspoken truth behind that innocent word! It scared me. I wanted to flee. I wanted to hide. I could do neither one.

What I should have done was speak honestly to him. Who knows what would have happened if I had overcome my fears and done so? But I had no idea of what to say or how to say it, so I took the one path out that I *could* see: the path of distraction.

"But Master Rinji, how can this be the truth?" I asked, trying to keep my words light. "One of the first things I taught you was the proper means to use for approaching the gods when seeking a great favor. I know you can do it exactly as I showed you, so why am I still a slave, unless . . . ? Oh no!" I clapped one hand to my chest as though I had just experienced a revelation. "I must have taught you the *wrong* ritual, and this is your kindly way of telling me so. Will you forgive me?"

My stomach churned as I waited for his reaction. In

my anxiety to decoy Rinji from any thought of being more to me than a friend, I had thrown together a heap of nonsense that sounded false, stilted, and shameful, all at the same time. A child would not believe a word of what I had just uttered. A man would fling my weak ploy back in my face with contempt.

And what would a true friend do?

Rinji laughed weakly. "Forgive you? I must! If I refuse, I may find a frog in my water pot tomorrow."

The tension left my body so completely that I nearly toppled over where I sat. "Well, I'm glad to know that I taught you *that* lesson right. Now let me see you dance."

He went through the motions of the harvest ritual sloppily, but I did not bother to correct him. When he was done, I mumbled some vague comments about his style and a few trivial suggestions about the way he held the sacred bronze mirrors. Their purpose was to catch the light of the sun and multiply it so that the people would not lack warmth during the winter to come.

"I can show you what I mean better than tell you if you'll let me have your mirrors," I said. "May I?"

He handed me one, but only one. "Wait," he said, and went into the curtained room that was his workshop and storeplace. When he emerged, he had a third mirror in his hand. "Use this."

I stared at the polished surface of the sacred mirror given to me by my teacher. The Ookami had taken it when they killed Mori and took Kaya and me prisoner. I never dreamed I would see it again, let alone hold it.

"I have your bell as well," Rinji said solemnly. "Lord

Ryu gave them to me. He was afraid to destroy such holy objects. I think—I think he was also afraid of you."

I turned my mirror slowly, feeling it come to life in my hand. It danced delicately with every golden thread of autumn sunlight that entered the Ookami shrine. It took the light and wove it into song.

I was so entranced by the mirror's spell that when I heard Rinji tell me, "Take them both with you, your mirror and your bell," I believed I had fallen into a dream. He had to repeat himself three times before I realized I was awake and that he was offering me a great blessing.

I placed the mirror over my beating heart and lowered my eyes. "It isn't possible. I have nowhere to keep them safe from discovery. I couldn't bear to lose them again." *And if Lady Sato's prying eyes find these treasures, she may insist on searching me down to the skin while her vile son watches,* I thought. *I can be parted from my mirror and my bell. I can watch Ryu crush my wand into splinters. But if he takes my lady of the dragon stone and destroys her, I will die.*

Regretfully, I tried to give him my mirror. He seemed disappointed that his gift was being rejected, but reached out to accept its return. Abruptly he froze, hands outstretched, then pulled away as though he'd touched fire. He stared at his hands as though seeing them for the first time and murmured, "I can't." Meeting my gaze, he repeated: "I can't do it, Lady Himiko. I can't take your mirror back again. I don't know why. Something forbids it; something I can't name."

He bit his lower lip and closed his eyes. *"You must take what they give you, Himiko,"* he said. His voice had changed. It sounded as though it came from the depths of the earth, from the heights of the sky. *"You must find a way to guard what is most precious to you, by wisdom and not by guile. If you fail, you were not meant to keep even one of your treasures."*

I trembled to hear his words. When he opened his eyes again, he looked shaken and confused. "Rinji?"

He blinked in the light. "What happened to me?"

"They spoke through you, Rinji," I said, overwhelmed by the happiness I felt for him. "The spirits touched you and let you bring their message to me. You *are* a shaman!"

"Oh." He was still bewildered. "Just like that? Well . . . good, I suppose. Do you think it will happen again?"

"I know it will."

"Will it be the same, next time? Will I be taken by surprise again?" He grew visibly nervous at the thought of the spirits lying in wait for him.

"Don't worry about that. You have the training you need to call out to them. Do it with reverence and strength so that they recognize your worthiness. They are less likely to force their presence on those they respect." I paused, then added: "How do you feel?"

"I'm . . . not sure. Happy? And a little bit empty as well." He looked at me. "You'll keep the mirror?"

"And the bell," I said. I wanted to hug him, but held back. I would not risk having him misinterpret it as anything more than a friend's joy for his good fortune.

He fetched the bell from his workroom. I ran my fingertips lovingly over the familiar designs decorating its bronze sides. Rinji smiled.

"I'm glad you're going to keep them. They change everything, don't they? The bell turns air into music, the mirror plays with light, the spells they help us cast can change our lives." Seeing how his strange speech startled me, he said: "I'm speaking for myself, Lady Himiko. The spirits haven't returned. You know, I'm not always the gawky, stammering creature Lady Sato bullies."

"I never thought you were." I held my bell and mirror high. "You can change that too."

He shook his head. "There is only one thing I want to change." The awkwardness between us was back, but he quickly broke its spell with a loud, artificial laugh. "One thing *besides* my clumsiness when I perform the harvest dance. Weren't you about to show me the right way to hold the mirrors?"

"Yes, right away!" I think we were both grateful to tread down our uneasiness beneath the steps of the dance.

Ryu forbade me to attend the harvest celebration. I expected that. The festival had too many enjoyable opportunities for me, and his own pleasure depended on denying mine. Luckily, the village became such a turmoil of feasting, drinking, and revelry that no one noticed one drably dressed girl peering out over the festivities from the edge of a house's front platform. I had an imperfect view, but good enough to let me see how ably Rinji danced for the spirits. How proud I was!

After his dance ended, I retreated into the house. I wanted to use my precious time alone. There was a narrow space at the back of the house between the cloth partitions of the family's storage space and the outer wall. I stood on tiptoe and reached into a spot midway between two of the roof beams and carefully removed a small, tightly wrapped bundle. Once the knots securing the fabric were undone, I was free to gaze at my treasures: the shining mirror, the glowing bell.

"I wish I could dance with you," I whispered. "Maybe I'll take you with me the next time I go to the shrine. Rinji will understand. It will only be three more days until then. I'll need to find a way to carry you secretly when I leave the house. Thank the gods no one saw you when I first brought you here! Lady Sato was too busy scolding her borrowed slaves, so she didn't notice what I was hiding up my sleeves. I'd tuck you into my sash, but you're too bulky. It would be easier if Rinji wasn't so set on refusing to let me keep you at the shrine." I sighed and wrapped them up again. As I tucked them back out of sight under the eaves, I thought: *Perhaps I should ask him again; he might have changed his mind.*

Rinji *had* changed his mind, but not in any way that helped me. On the third day after the harvest festival—the fifth since our last meeting—one of his slaves arrived at our doorway with a message for Lady Sato. I was cleaning up after breakfast while Chizu played a clapping game with Noboru. We heard everything.

"What is your master up to, sending you here so early?" Lady Sato snarled at the man. "Lord Ryu might have still been home! You tell Master Rinji he's lucky that my son is working at the main village storehouse. The boar clan's yearly tribute arrived at dawn, and he's busy making sure those wretches haven't tried to cheat us."

"My lady, I apologize, but I am only carrying out my master's command," the messenger said. "He wants you to know that he no longer wants anyone but his household slaves to tend the Ookami shrine." He did not wait for a reply, leaving Lady Sato gape-jawed behind him.

It did not take her long to recover. Her wrath broke over me like a thunderstorm. "What did you *do* to him, you idiot?" she bellowed, slapping me so hard that my teeth clacked together.

"Why did you hit Himiko?" Noboru cried, throwing his small arms protectively around me.

"Get out of my sight or you'll get the same!" Lady Sato shouted, raising her hand. Chizu carried my little brother away before her mother-in-law could make good on the threat. The two of them stayed hidden, leaving me to face the infuriated woman on my own.

"How did you manage to ruin everything?" Lady Sato demanded. "What kind of girl hasn't got the sense to know how to keep a man? Do you think it's enough that you have a pretty face? Don't flatter yourself! Men get used to such things, and there are always prettier girls around to replace you. Is that what happened? Did someone else catch his eye and did you *let* her?"

"Lady Sato, I never—"

She didn't allow me to defend myself. "What games did you play? Did you try coaxing gifts from him? Did you sulk and pout when he wouldn't give in to your wheedling ways? Or did you decide you were too good to be his bed-partner unless you were also his *wife*? The nerve of you!" This went on for some time.

By the time Ryu came home, my life had been given an entirely new shape. Lady Sato's anger was voracious, devouring any scrap of my happiness it could find. There would be no more stolen moments with Noboru for me. She made it clear that if she caught us together, even by accident, he would be the one to bear the punishment. Furthermore, I was now to be confined to my tiny part of the house, except when I was actively engaged in obeying orders.

Ryu was mildly surprised when his mother informed him of the way things would be from then on. "I've noticed you treating the girl a little *too* nicely every few days, more like a favorite than a slave. I thought I'd have to speak to you about correcting that, but it seems you've realized your mistake without my needing to say a word."

"If the day ever comes when *you* have to tell *me* how to deal with a slave, start building my tomb," his mother spat. "I'm done with showing her any consideration. She doesn't deserve it and acts like it's her birthright. Her problem is she still thinks she's a princess. Hmph! I'll teach her otherwise. Princess of pig-droppings, that's all she is."

Ryu laughed and hugged his mother so heartily for this that she had to shove him away or be smothered.

Lady Sato's new rules were strict and soon became even more so. My life was utterly stripped of joy, but that was not enough for her vindictive spirit. When there was work to do that forced me to leave the house, she accompanied me, her hawk's eyes alert for any glimmer of kindness I might encounter on the way. One of Rinji's slaves greeted me by name and she threw a stone at him as if he were a stray dog. Hiroshi smiled at me in passing, only to have Lady Sato call him all sorts of shameful names. She meant to bury me alive, and the final clump of earth that she dropped onto my tomb was forbidding Chizu to have any dealings with me at all.

"You're a mud-puddle person, Daughter-in-law: every-one steps all over you," she said, smiling when Chizu winced at the insult. "You don't know how to handle an insolent slave. Ha! You don't even know how to handle an obedient one! I've heard you talking to our *princess* as if she were your girlhood friend. Ridiculous. I remember when you *were* a girl, and I could count the number of friends you had in this village on a snake's fingers! From now on, if you need *Lady Himiko* to do anything for you, tell me."

"But . . . what if you're not here?" Chizu ventured.

Lady Sato folded her arms. "I will be."

I met the first snowfall of winter with a heart as bleak as the empty hillside fields. I was an insect caught in a drop of poisoned amber, a prisoner of Ryu's longstanding resentment against me and his mother's younger bitterness.

Lady Sato was a master of spite, an artist who was always finding new ways to improve and adorn her grudge. If I gave any sign that I was becoming accustomed to my dreary existence, she produced a fresh means of torment. When I no longer seemed to care that she and Ryu were the only ones speaking to me, she took to giving me her commands in the form of grunts and brusque gestures. It would have been funny, except that when I failed to understand precisely what she wanted, she would take it out on Noboru.

Oh, my poor little brother! Lady Sato still treated him with fondness, unless she wanted to punish me by punishing him. He had no idea why the woman who fed him the choicest bits of meat from her own dinner would suddenly scream abuse in his face and send him to his chamber with no food at all. Sometimes he would cry until dawn. I lay on my bedroll, listening to his sobs and imploring the spirits to send him pleasant dreams.

My own dreams became nearly as tedious as my life. Night after night, I escaped to that otherworldly realm where I had last seen Reikon. No matter where I walked, my steps inevitably brought me to the willow grove where my spirit prince had shown me the caged birds and given me renewed strength. The cages were still there, but all the birds were gone. The grove was silent. From the time I closed my eyes to the moment I awoke, I stood among the willows, calling Reikon's name in vain.

It was a hard season. I overheard Ryu tell Chizu to wear two cloaks when she left the house, for the baby's sake. Lady Sato claimed that the winter had come earlier than usual and would freeze the life out of the land. That was when she started speaking to me again. It was not compassion, but because she wanted to be certain I would not misinterpret her will when she ordered me into the mountains.

"The mountains?" Ryu said the first time his mother told me to go there. "What are you doing, sending her *there*?"

"I want her to bring me some acorns," Lady Sato replied huffily. "There are no oaks growing anywhere near our village."

"What are you going to do with acorns?"

"Er, I'm making something special for *your* wife, to help her deliver *your* baby safely, when the time comes."

Ryu looked ready to pose more questions, but a ferocious scowl from Lady Sato persuaded him that some battles were not worth fighting. "Have it your way, Mother," he said with a shrug. "But give the girl something to wear over her dress. I don't care what you do to her as long as she doesn't die from it."

Lady Sato complied by finding me the shortest, most threadbare cloak in the whole village. As I draped it over my shoulders before leaving on my errand, she said, "If you even think about using this as a chance to run away, the only question will be whether your little brother is punished *before* or *after* our hunters follow your tracks in the snow."

From that time on, she found me chore after chore that could only be accomplished among the frosty branches of the mountain forests. At first her assignments made *some* sense, such as seeking acorns where oak trees grew. But after a while she began giving me tasks that could be done closer to the Ookami settlement, like gathering firewood.

"I want *mountain* pine!" she shouted at me one night when Ryu had gone to confer with his counselors about plans for the spring sowing. "It burns better. And I *will* know the difference if you try to trick me with anything less."

Chizu peeked out the doorway. "But it's dark already, Mother-in-law, and so cold," she said plaintively. "We have enough wood for the night, don't we?"

Lady Sato did not like being thwarted. "*I* run this household and I say we need kindling. There will be plenty of small branches for her to gather. The cold will inspire her to work diligently, and the moon is full. She'll be back with the wood before my son comes home, if she isn't lazy."

Chizu actually found the courage to begin a fresh protest, but I would not let her sacrifice herself to Lady Sato's temper for me. "I'm on my way," I said, and was down the ladder as fast as I could go without tumbling down the slippery steps.

I moved through the village in the breath of the winter wind. I was glad to go. Lady Sato thought she was afflicting me with her capricious demands, but I greeted each one with secret delight. I had discovered something wonderful on the day she first sent me to gather acorns and it warmed my spirit better than any fire ever warmed my body.

As I strode along the snowy path, I glanced in the direction of the shrine. Light outlined the edges of the curtained doorway. I had not seen Rinji since I'd spied on him performing the harvest ritual. If he knew what his abrupt treatment of Lady Sato had done to me, he didn't seem to care.

Beyond the village gateway lay fields of white, like clouds come down to earth. All that marred their perfect smoothness were a few threads of small animal tracks, a sprinkling of claw-prints left by the birds, and the occasional footsteps of a lone hunter. The Ookami did not *need* to pursue game in the cold months. Their village was rich, its storehouses fat with the foods they'd provided for themselves and taken out of the hungry mouths of their subjects. Thanks to Lady Sato's mean-hearted whims, I went to the mountains more frequently than any man of the wolf clan.

I let the full moon's beaming face guide me to the place I knew so well, the isolated clearing I had discovered while searching for acorns in the cold. It was smaller than poor, murdered Mori's campsite, but large enough for me. A flat slab of rock was lodged between the roots of two oak trees, its gray bulk tilting up to reveal a wedge of darkness. I smiled and knelt, reaching beneath for the riches the shadows concealed.

I unwrapped the small cloth bundle that held my bell and mirror. I had managed to smuggle them out of the house the second time Lady Sato sent me to the mountains. Though they were icy to the touch from their exile in this lonesome spot, they warmed me better than a summer's day. I wiped the rock clean of snow and set them on it. Loosening my sash, I retrieved my talisman. The clay image of the goddess fit easily into the palm of my hand, but when I placed her on the stone her presence filled the clearing. My wand found its place at her feet.

"I have returned, my dear ones!" I called out, and clapped my hands. "Come to me now, to this place where I am left untroubled, where I have a little peace, where I am free to hear your voices. Father! Aki! Shoichi! Give me your warriors' courage. Yama! Lend me your wisdom. Mori! Remind me that the world is full of gentleness. Hoshi! Let me never become so bitter that I forget to love."

I stood and picked up bell and wand. Serenity settled its wings around me. I relished the quiet, for it let me hear nothing but my own thoughts. The clamor of the Ookami village was far away and the barbed chatter infesting Ryu's household became a distant dream. This was different from the cruel, deliberate isolation Lady Sato had wished on me. This was silence I had chosen freely, silence that was not a wall between mortals but a bridge to take me to the world of my beloved spirits.

I struck the bronze bell three times, letting the separate

tones blend into one another. While the clear note still lingered on the air I took up my mirror and caught the moon's light. "Come and drink, my cherished souls," I said, turning the bright reflection into an imagined pool of silver water. I could feel them near me, all of those I had lost yet never stopped loving. I regretted that I could not offer them a more substantial sacrifice than moonlight and a song.

My voice filled the wintry clearing, climbing the ladder of my frosted breath until it reached the stars. This was no chant I had learned during my apprenticeship with Yama. The words and tune came to me from my heart and I poured them out for the spirits. Faces began to take shape among the branches of the trees as my ghosts came nearer, drawn by the bonds between us that were stronger than death. I could still see them when I closed my eyes, sense them in my blood, feel them taking possession of me and leading me into the pattern of a dance. Singing to the heavens, I swayed and turned, feet stitching the snow with the design of an owl's swooping flight. I do not know how long the magic held me. I only knew that when at last I sank down onto the stone my feet were tired but my soul was content.

"Are they gone?"

The stranger came into the clearing and my breath stopped.

13
Kindness Like a Flower Among the Stones

"Please, don't be afraid," he said, taking a step back. "I won't harm you, I promise." He carried a wooden walking staff, but let it fall to the snow. He held up his hands so I could see he was not concealing any weapon. "Who are you? Where do you come from? Are you lost? Let me help you."

I said nothing. I was lost, but not in the way he meant. His voice echoed in my head like the clear, sacred note of the bronze bell. I recognized it, though this was the first time I had heard it in the mortal world. The moon shone on his face with a light so bright that I could not deny what I saw: though his long hair was unbound and unkempt, though his eyes were weary and his skin dirty from travel, I knew him.

"Reikon?" I trembled as I spoke my spirit prince's name.

"What?" He stared at me, perplexed.

"You aren't . . . ?" My head spun. I teetered where I sat and began to slip sideways from the stone.

He ran to catch me before I could fall. His arms were strong. He smelled of wood smoke and pine boughs. *A spirit of the forest,* I thought, inhaling deeply. Then the unmistakable tang of sweat struck me and I knew he was as human as I.

"I'm all right now, thank you," I said pushing him away. "Forgive me for troubling you. I see you're a traveler. If you don't know this area well, I can lead you to the nearest settlement. I am a slave in the chieftain's house, so I can't offer you hospitality, but maybe he will."

"Ryu won't welcome me," he said.

"Ah! You know the wolf chieftain's name?"

"I am a member of that clan." He made a rueful face. "We grew up together." He did not sound happy about it.

I looked him over from head to toe. Who was this Ookami with the face and voice of my spirit prince? What had taken him away from his clan? Was he a trader? But the wolves did not trade; they took.

Then I recalled the first words he had spoken to me. I had been too stunned by his unexpected presence and his resemblance to Reikon to realize what it truly meant when he asked *Are they gone?*

They.

Anyone could watch me dance. Only someone special would recognize *why.* He knew I was performing a rite for the spirits and he had sensed them all around me. There was just one person he could be.

"Master Daimu?"

"Did the spirits tell you who I am?" His smile was beautiful, free of any trace of mockery. "I wish they would tell me your name too." .

I answered his smile with my own. "I am Himiko of the Matsu clan. My father was our chieftain. He is one of the spirits for whom I danced."

Daimu's face darkened. "So Ryu's greed took him traveling that far away?" He closed his eyes, like a man who is near the end of exhaustion. "I hoped he would be sated by the conquests he'd already made when I left. I expected too much of him." He looked at me with pity. "Your village, Lady Himiko . . . it still exists?"

"Yes. He didn't destroy it as thoroughly as the hawk clan's settlement."

Daimu's black brows rose. "How do you know about their fate?"

"My friend Kaya and I found a noblewoman of the hawk clan living near the ruins of their village with her two grandchildren."

"Ah! Lady Ayame," he said, nodding.

"You know her?"

"When I first set out on the road, I encountered her and the little ones. I am glad to know they're still alive, but—" He paused.

"—you don't like the thought of them living so close to the edge of survival?" I finished for him.

He looked uncomfortable. "Himiko—Lady Himiko, I am afraid to tell you this, but . . . my homeward road took me past the hawk village ruins. I searched the area carefully and found the shelter Lady Ayame and the children were using. It was deserted. I could not find them anywhere. I am afraid they are gone."

"Thank the gods!" I exclaimed, clapping my hands.

He gave me such a strange look that I had to explain why I seemed to be rejoicing over the loss of those three innocents. "Master Daimu, set your mind at ease. Lady Ayame has a third grandchild, a young woman named Nazuna, who married into the boar clan. If you could not find anyone near the hawk village it means the lady agreed to accept Nazuna's invitation to share the safety of her household." I did not think he had to know my part in changing Lady Ayame's mind. The credit belonged to the spirits, not to me.

"I don't understand," Daimu said. "How did you and your friend come to be in the Taka ruins and meet Lady Ayame? Did you manage to escape from the rest of the captives Ryu brought home after defeating your people?"

"I can explain everything, Master Daimu," I said. "But would you mind if I did so while we walk back to your village?" I rubbed my arms. "It's gotten colder since I came here."

"Oh! What a fool I am; I never noticed. Forgive me, please." He removed his cloak and threw it over my shoulders before I could refuse it. The warmth of his body still clung to its ample folds. "Let us return."

He waited patiently while I wrapped my bell and mirror and hid them under the rock once more. We worked together, gathering Lady Sato's firewood, but when we had enough, he skillfully prevented me from carrying it by requesting that I take charge of his traveling bag instead. It was small and light, nowhere as heavy or awkward as the armful of branches he had to bear. All the way back to the Ookami settlement I talked and he listened, telling him about Mother, Noboru, and all the rest of it. By the time we reached the foot of the ladder leading up to Ryu's house, he knew what had brought me down this path and how far I was from fulfilling my mission.

As I set my foot on the ladder's first step, I turned to him and said, "You should give me the firewood now, Master Daimu. It's my job to bring it in."

"You have better work to do than that, Lady Himiko," he responded gravely. "I hope to see you accomplish it. Go ahead. I will bring the kindling."

"I'll get in trouble if you do," I protested. "I wouldn't care about that, except I won't be the one punished for it. My brother—"

"I know." He cut me off. "I lived near Ryu's family for too long. Their ways are painfully familiar to me. But they know *my* ways too, and I do have some sway over what happens in this clan." He made a regretful face and added: "Not enough to put a stop to some things, but enough to affect others. I promise you that neither you nor anyone you love will suffer because I wanted to help a fellow shaman."

"Is that how you see me?"

"Isn't that who you are?" he countered.

"If you ask anyone in this house—in this village—they will tell you that I am their chieftain's captive; nothing more."

My words brought a slight, gentle smile to his lips and the winter moon made him seem even more like an otherworldly being. "Then they must learn the truth that you and I already know, Lady Himiko," he said.

Seeing him like that, wearing silver light like a garment and a blessing, I had to wonder: *Who are you, really? You seemed to come out of nowhere when I danced for my lost ones. I have walked into the spirits' realm time and again. Have you chosen to enter mine at last, Reikon? Or are you truly Daimu, a mortal like me?*

As I expected, my empty-handed return was greeted by a shriek of outrage from Lady Sato, who began berating me viciously for being lazy, scatterbrained, defiant, and a host of other faults and crimes. She was so wrapped up in her attack that she did not notice the sound of a second pair of feet making the ladder creak until keen-eyed Chizu let out a gasp, clapped one hand to her mouth to hold back a cry of astonishment, and pointed wildly at the doorway.

"Good evening, Lady Sato." Daimu stepped across the threshold and dropped the load of wood.

The very sight of him had the magical power to transform everyone still awake under Ryu's roof that night. Lady Sato cut off her ranting so sharply that I think she bit her tongue. For the first time since I'd known her, Chizu looked completely tranquil, relieved, and happy, safe in a world where everything was suddenly all right.

As for Ryu himself, I saw his face turn very pale, then flush before returning to its natural color. He was seated with his wife when I came in and had been enjoying the spectacle of Lady Sato giving me that unexpectedly interrupted tongue-lashing. Now he had gone from relaxed and smug to fully alert, defensive, and tense as a stretched bowstring.

Lady Sato was the first to recover. "Master Daimu!" she cried, raising her hands to the heavens. "Thank the gods, my prayers are answered!" She rushed forward to greet him, shoving me out of her way as she burbled blessings. "Come in, sit down, eat and drink with us. Himiko! Bring refreshment for Master Daimu! Go!"

"That will not be necessary, Lady Sato," Daimu replied calmly. When he smiled at her, she dimpled and giggled like a little girl. "All that I require tonight is a place to sleep."

"Yes, of course, at once!" The old noblewoman whirled to face her son. "Ryu! Wake that incompetent Rinji and tell him to leave the shrine immediately. We Ookami have a *real* shaman once more."

Ryu glowered at his mother and made no move to rise. I saw his hands become fists and imagined from his tight-lipped expression that he was probably gritting his teeth. He opened his mouth to speak, but we never found out if he was about to argue or obey, because Daimu spoke first:

"*Master* Rinji will not be disturbed tonight," he said, his smile gone. "I will not trouble him or any other member of our clan until morning. The only reason I came here, rather than spend one more night sleeping under the stars, is that the spirits saw fit to have me cross paths with Lady Himiko." He nodded at me.

Now Ryu was on his feet, looking ready for a fight. "Is that what she told you to call her, Master Daimu?" He uttered the shaman's title as if spitting out a mouthful of fish bones. "Is she still pretending to be *Lady* Himiko, trying to hold smoke in her fingers? And you believed her, even though you found her gathering firewood?" He chuckled. "Well, maybe you encountered some clans where princesses perform such tasks, but let me refresh your memory: among the Ookami, that's a job for a *slave*."

"Ryu!" Lady Sato was scandalized at her son's pugnacious attitude. "Speak with respect to Master Daimu. If not for him, this clan would have had no shaman at all for *ages*!"

Ryu snorted. "You make it sound as though he's been our savior since the world was born. The only reason he stepped into Master Ku's footprints so early was the old man's eyes failed and he picked the wrong mushroom to eat."

Lady Sato ignored her son's additional scorn for Daimu's teacher. "So what?" she snapped. "That doesn't change the fact that he is our protector and guide. It used to be that our chieftains were also our shamans, but your grandfather was the last man who could fulfill that calling. He saw that your father would never be able to speak with the spirits, so before he died, he saw to it that Master Ku was there for us. You turned out to be as great a failure as your father when it came to such vital matters, so you ought to be grateful Master Ku had the presence of mind to train Master Daimu, and that Master Daimu was so quick to learn a shaman's skills, and—"

"Enough!" Ryu roared like the dragon for which he was named, the mighty presence whose stirring beneath the mountains caused the earth to tremble. "Why don't you just declare him to be a god?" He turned to confront Master Daimu. "Welcome home," he gritted, and stalked off to his sleeping chamber.

Despite Lady Sato's insistence that Master Daimu sleep in the chieftain's house, he graciously declined. His refusal sent her into a panic that would have been comical if it had not also upset poor Chizu.

So much tension and uproar in this house is not good for her baby, I thought. I would have intervened, but nearly anything I could have said or done would only make things worse. I had to be content with sitting beside Ryu's timorous wife and putting my arm around her shoulders in a gesture of comfort while her mother-in-law was too distracted to notice. Chizu gave me a thankful look.

"Master Daimu, how can you even *think* of leaving us tonight?" Lady Sato cried in distress. "What will people say tomorrow when they find you have returned but that you did not stay in our house? We will be shamed! I will give you anything you desire, but please don't go!"

An odd expression crossed Master Daimu's face. "Will you, Lady Sato?" he asked. "Will you give me anything I wish?"

"Who would not? You have no idea how happy we will all be to have you among us again." She clasped his arm. "Say that you have changed your mind and will sleep here!"

His mild eyes were filled with regret. "I am sorry, honored lady, but no. There is nothing I desire that you have the power to give me. I cannot share a roof with anyone who ill-treats a shaman by word or deed."

"Tsk. Don't listen to Ryu; his anger eats his common sense. I will make him apologize to you!"

He gently held her back before she could suit the deed to the word. "I was speaking about you, Lady Sato."

"Me? But how . . . ? I never! What did I do? What did I say? I swear by all the gods, I have only the highest respect for you and all those of your calling!"

"And I am sure you believe that." Given their respective ages it was strange to hear him speaking to her like a father who is genuinely disappointed in some misdeed his favorite child has committed. "You will need to realize the truth for yourself, but in the meantime, please do not worry: I will be discreet. No one will know that I would not stay here. I will sleep in the shadow of our village shrine, a fitting place for me to let the spirits know that I have returned."

He slipped away into the night, leaving Lady Sato silent, humbled, and so abashed that she did not even try to lay the blame for what had just happened on me.

The next morning, the wolf village awoke to a miracle: their beloved shaman, Master Daimu, had returned! He was simply *there,* as naturally as air or sunshine. No one could recall seeing him enter the village, least of all the lazy watchman, who had most likely been dozing in his tower under several layers of cloaks when Daimu and I passed through the gateway.

He stood on the platform in front of the shrine, Rinji at his side, and hailed his clanfolk one by one as they emerged from their homes and happened to glance in his direction. I was in the midst of it: Lady Sato had sent me to fetch water while she and the rest of her family had their breakfast. Soon the settlement was criss-crossed by people running here and there to spread the glad word. Houses echoed with exclamations of surprise and rejoicing. A crowd gathered at the foot of the shrine ladder and grew until it contained nearly every one of the wolf clan. Infants and the old were brought along. Even a few of the sick insisted that their families carry them there.

Only the slaves hung back. Some drifted uneasily around the edges of the mob. Some peered warily from the shelter of their lodgings. Most kept entirely out of sight until they might know how this news would affect their captive lives.

I went back to Ryu's house with the water. I was not

about to let Noboru be punished for my absence, but I was also determined to return to the shrine and hear what Daimu had to say. As I entered the house and put down my water jar, the Ookami chieftain greeted me with a familiar scowl.

"What took you so long, girl?" he thundered. "And what's all the racket out there?" He did not wait for my reply but got up and pushed me aside to stand on the platform, one hand shading his eyes against the winter glare. He could not see the shrine from where he stood, but he was not a stupid man. An ugly curse burst from his lips.

"Mother! Chizu! Stay here. Your *precious* shaman's stirring up hornets. Don't move until I come back." With that, he was gone.

Chizu obeyed him, of course, but Lady Sato was out the door almost the instant that Ryu was at the foot of the ladder. She was a nimble old woman, especially when she had the chance to witness something exciting. I followed her at a safe distance. Meek little Chizu didn't attempt to stop me. It would not have mattered had she tried: I was going back and no one would stand in my way. I melted into the crowd of Ookami gathered in front of the shrine just as Daimu raised his arms to call for their attention.

"My people, as you can see, I have come home at last," he said. This simple declaration was met by prolonged cheering from the crowd. I caught sight of Ryu in the throng. The young chieftain's jaw was set. He looked ready to bite chunks out of a sword blade.

When the happy uproar finally subsided, Daimu spoke on: "I have missed all of you. I left because I was deeply troubled by the path our people were taking, a path that led from conquest to conquest, destruction to destruction. I turned to the spirits, seeking the right road, and saw that if I remained to oppose what was happening, it would tear our clan apart. How could I bring harmony between gods and mortals then? They took pity on me and blessed my departure."

"But Master Daimu, why were you so unhappy?" a voice came out of the crowd. "We *won!*"

Daimu's expressive eyes became sad. "There was a time when the clans we conquered were the conquerors. It is easy to claim that success is proof of the gods' favor, but those are fools' words. The gods are more ancient than the mountains, the spirits have always dwelled deep in the heart of the land, and the land is old. Her bones are wisdom and memory. We dance like gnats on a single breath of the gods, but if we make our dance of cruelty and oppression, the gods hold back their sustaining breath and we fall."

An uneasy silence fell over the crowd. In that time of stillness, I saw Ryu climb the ladder to the shrine. "Is this what you've learned on your pilgrimage, Master Daimu?" he demanded. "To call your people fools? You seem to have forgotten who we are: we are the Ookami, the wolves of the mountain! We are born to hunt together and to keep faith with one another. The only wolf that leaves the pack is too old, too sick, or too cursed by madness to live with his kin. Which is it for you?"

Master Daimu lowered his eyes. "You can see for yourself that I am young and well, Lord Ryu. If you think that I am afflicted with insanity, perhaps you would feel safer if I went away again. Say the word and I'll go, never to return."

A flash of cruel joy showed in Ryu's face at Daimu's offer, but it was short-lived. The crowd burst into wild wailing. Countless voices shouted pleas for the chieftain to stop Daimu from leaving, including those of his finest warriors. Some of those entreaties sounded ominously like threats. The Ookami were not prepared to lose their trusted shaman a second time, and if Ryu were to blame for it . . .

His moment of triumph vanished. He had only one choice.

"I spoke poorly, Master Daimu," he said, his voice harsh and brittle. "Stay."

The Ookami shaman bowed his head. "That is my heart's desire, Lord Ryu. I have eaten strange food and drunk strange water for too long, but at least my journey has taught me lessons of value gathered from those who serve the gods in other clans. I am happy to share these new ways with our people."

"We do not need any new ways," Ryu snapped.

"If that were so, we would still live as we did in the time before we knew the gods at all," Daimu countered. "I have journeyed very far and I have seen clans even more prosperous than ours. Surely you cannot deny they are doing *something* to earn so much favor from the spirits?"

"I don't know anything about that," Ryu grumbled. "We can make our own good fortune. We are the Ookami, and—!"

"Yes, the wolves of the mountain. So you said." Daimu's charming, gently mocking grin gave the people permission to titter softly at their pompous young chieftain. Then his whole manner changed. His smile vanished and he became a thundercloud bristling with bolts of lightning. "I know who we are, what we are, and what you have made us become. I know who I am too: your *shaman*! I walk the borderland between worlds, keeping the balance, calling on the gods for help and mercy, and keeping the ghosts of the vengeful dead at bay! You rule this clan and preserve our lives, but I choose the path that will earn us the blessings of the gods! It is not an easy path to find or follow. Do you want to take that task from me?" He plucked the sacred bronze mirror from his belt and thrust it within a finger's span of Ryu's face. "Then take it! Take it now, or stand out of my way!"

Reflected sunlight from the mirror lashed across the chieftain's eyes. He staggered backward, dangerously close to the edge of the platform. Rinji gasped and rushed to seize Ryu's arm before he could fall. His cheeks burned red with humiliation at being rescued. Rinji earned a glare for what he'd done, not gratitude.

"Calm yourself, Master Daimu," Ryu said coldly. "Keep to your path and I will keep to mine. We will see which one gives better things to our people."

"So be it." Daimu put away the mirror and raised his hands. "If the new ways I bring home please the gods, let their blessing be a gift to our clan, but if the spirits are displeased, let their curse fall on me alone."

Ryu showed his teeth. "Agreed."

◆ ◆ ◆

All that day, the Ookami settlement hummed with talk about the shaman's return and his confrontation with Ryu. My chores took me out and about in the cold, but my ears burned every time I overheard someone mention Daimu's name. Everyone was eager to discover how he would change the old ways.

They did not have long to wait. The very next morning, as I was serving breakfast, we heard Rinji's timid voice come faltering through the cloth-hung doorway. "L-Lord Ryu? Lord Ryu, sir, would it be too much trouble to speak with you?"

The wolf chieftain frowned. "What does *he* want so early in the day?" he muttered. "Himiko! Tell him to come back later."

I did as I was told, but when I stepped outside to greet Rinji, he looked as if he'd seen a demon. "Oh! You know? How—? Never mind. Do you have anything to bring with—? No, no, that's a foolish question. All right, follow me."

"Master Rinji, what are you talking about?" I asked.

Before he could reply, a heavy hand closed on my shoulder as Ryu surged out of his house and yanked me aside. "How long does it take you to deliver a simple message?" he snarled.

Rinji misunderstood that the chieftain's words were meant for me. "My—my apologies, Lord Ryu. I will be brief. Himi—Lady Himiko is to come with me to the shrine."

"Is this a joke?" Ryu's eyes blazed. "It isn't funny."

Rinji shook his head violently. "It is what the gods want, my lord. Master Daimu told me so."

"I do not believe that she is what the *gods* want," Ryu replied, curling his lip. "Let your master amuse himself with some other slave girl. This one belongs to *me*."

"No," I said quietly. "I may be a captive of this clan, but I do not belong to anyone."

"Shut your mouth, girl!" He raised his hand to strike me, but I was too quick for him and, with a scornful look, dodged the blow. He was about to try a second time but Rinji flung himself between us and dragged Ryu's arm down.

"My lord, *please*!" he cried. He jerked his chin toward the ground. A crowd had gathered at the foot of the house ladder—a tiny crowd, but one whose members were watching Ryu's every move with the highest interest. "They followed me here from the shrine," Rinji murmured. "They saw Lord Daimu send me here and asked him what it was all about. He told them that among some of the other clans he visited in his travels, the spirits were happier to be served by a man and a woman together, and that you were the one chosen for the task."

"Ridiculous." Ryu shook off Rinji's grip, but made no further move against me. "He made up that nonsense to excuse his own desires. If it's truly the spirits who want a woman to wait upon them, let Daimu pick one of the female slaves already tending the shrine."

Rinji blushed deeply. "He said it had to be Lady Himiko because—because only a chieftain's daughter is worthy to approach the gods. I'm sorry, my lord, but . . ." His voice trailed away under the long, hard look Ryu gave him.

At last, the wolf leader broke the silence. "Very well. Take her. I will not oppose our *revered* shaman. He might threaten to run away and hide again. But tell him that she is forbidden to enter this house or speak to anyone dwelling under my roof. If I must obey what he claims is the will of the gods, then *he* must obey the command of his chieftain."

"Yes, Lord Ryu. Thank you, thank you." Rinji hurried down the ladder, making frantic motions for me to come with him. The few people watching us chattered breathlessly among themselves.

As we walked to the shrine, Rinji spoke to me, but it was no true conversation. Every word he uttered was an apology. He begged my pardon for having failed to appreciate the help I'd given him in mastering the shaman's art. He implored me to forgive him for the brusque way he'd ended my visits to the shrine just because I'd wounded his pride. He humbly asked that I set aside any ill will I might feel toward him for his part in what awaited me.

"And what might *that* be?" I asked sharply.

He was startled by the forcefulness of my question and the unshielded anger behind it. "Why—why, becoming Lord Daimu's woman," he stammered. "I cannot blame him for wanting you, but unless you want him too . . ." He bit his lip and seemed uncomfortable in his own skin. "I will be leaving the shrine. I cannot bear to live there, so close to you, when I know that he has the power to own what I could never—could never—" He shuddered. "But I will always be a friend to you, Lady Himiko, if Master Daimu allows it."

I stared at him, unable to believe what I was hearing. "Master Rinji, we were friends, once. You wanted more than that and I did not. *I* made that choice and no one else will ever make such choices for me. I will fight to defend my right to choose—with my words, my strength, my prayers, even with my life. If you want to be my friend again, I would welcome that, but it must be *your* choice, not something that depends on Master Daimu's permission."

He turned his face from me. "You think I'm a coward," he said bitterly.

"I didn't say that. I know it isn't easy to be strong, not for anyone, but—"

"Then you pity me." He looked me in the eyes and for an instant I saw such a look of anger that it was like a blow to the chest. "Keep your pity, *Lady* Himiko," he said, and sealed his lips for the rest of the way to the shrine.

He left me at the foot of the ladder. I climbed it to find one of Master Daimu's female servants awaiting me. "Welcome back, Lady Himiko," she said with a warm smile. "I am Ashi. Let me show you to your room."

She brought me to a private sleeping chamber with a single bedroll. There was nothing in it aside from a new dress, a belt, and a few hair ornaments. I turned to Ashi and asked, "Where does Master Daimu keep his belongings?"

The older woman was taken aback by the question, but recovered quickly. "In his chamber, of course. He is a very tidy man." She picked up the dress and shook it out. "May I help you change, Lady Himiko?"

I moved in a daze while Ashi took my old, soiled garment and slipped the new gown over my head, though I did retain the presence of mind to conceal my wand and my amulet until I could tuck them back into the folds of my new sash. This was not what I had been expecting. After all of Ryu's ugly insinuations I was certain I would be forced to share Daimu's quarters. I wished I could have enjoyed the feeling of clean clothes and having my hair being put up in neat loops again, but I did not know whether to be relieved or to be even more on guard.

Daimu had me brought *here, as if I were no more than a bale of rice,* I thought fiercely. *He thinks he owns me, so there's no need for him to rush anything. He feels that he can wait.* My expression was grim and determined. *May the gods witness my words: he is going to wait* forever!

Once she had my hair properly arranged, Ashi said, "Is there anything else I can do for you, Lady Himiko? I know you are a little familiar with the shrine from the days when you came to help Master Rinji, but there is a difference between living here and only visiting."

"Where is Master Daimu?" I asked.

"I'm sorry, I don't know. As soon as he sent Master Rinji to fetch you, he told the rest of us that he was going out because he wanted you to become accustomed to your new home without any distractions."

This is not *my home,* I thought. *And it never will be.*

Although I told Ashi that I did not need anything more from her, she would not leave my side. *Is she my new guard?* I mused.

One of the other female servants brought me food and drink. She and Ashi served me and cleared away my dishes, but did not eat in my company. When I invited them to do so, they shook their heads. "Slaves don't eat with their masters."

"Slaves don't own slaves, either," I said. They didn't

know how to react to that and coped by claiming they weren't hungry.

Daimu came home in the early winter twilight. I was helping Ashi sweep the shrine floor, in spite of her constant protests, so he found us arguing while we worked. When she saw him, she exclaimed, "I'm so sorry, Master Daimu, I tried to stop her, but she insisted!"

He smiled. "I'm sure she did."

"I'll bring your dinner right away," the older woman said, and scurried off, leaving the two of us alone.

"Welcome, Lady Himiko," Daimu said, keeping his distance. "Have you had a good day?"

"No." I bit off the word short and pursed my mouth.

"Really?" He tilted his head. "What has displeased you? Your room? Your clothing? The food? I want you to be content here."

"Then you're going to be disappointed."

Daimu met my flinty expression with regret. "I understand, Lady Himiko. You want to be free. If I could grant you that, I would do it in a heartbeat."

"I want more than *my* liberty, Master Daimu. If my people are slaves, I am not free."

"You mean your family? I was told that your stepmother and two of your brothers are with us. I could try to—"

"I mean my *people*," I repeated. "My clan should not be in bondage to yours."

"Who should?" he asked softly. "In my travels I have seen many clans who live on the labor of their war captives." He sighed. "I grew up with this way of life. It should be natural to me, yet somehow I cannot accept that it is a *good* way."

"But you still own slaves," I pointed out. "Six of them."

"They served my teacher, Master Ku, and are a part of the shrine. I do not have the power to free them, only to send them away. That would place them in the hands of other masters. At least if they remain here, I can see to it that they are well treated. Slavery runs deep into the life of many clans, including the Ookami, like the taproot of an oak. One person cannot pull it from the soil."

"Then he should break off a branch," I said. "Or a twig, to show that he *wants* to make a difference in the way things are. Anyone can *talk* about changes."

He stepped closer to me. "I wish I could do more, Lady Himiko. For now, I can only promise to think about your words. Meanwhile, how can I bring back your smile? When we met, you did not look at me so coldly."

"When we met, I thought you had a kind heart." I restored the original distance between us. "You saw me dance for the spirits and treated me with the respect one shaman owes another. But today you let me know that you see me as nothing more than a slave among slaves; property, not a person."

"How can you say such a thing?" He was genuinely distressed. "I brought you here to save you from that sort of treatment in Ryu's house."

"That's not the tale others tell about why you ordered me here."

He grasped my meaning at once and the harsh shock it gave him was plain to see. "You mean Ryu. I expected him to spit poison when he lost his hold over you, but I didn't think you would take his words seriously."

"Was he wrong?" I wanted to believe it, but stubbornly held on to my doubts.

"I've given you your own room here, and two of the women here will attend you constantly. You will never be alone with me."

I cast my eyes to either side. "We are alone now."

"For the last time, I swear."

"My attendants are your slaves. You can command them to leave us whenever you like."

"In that case, I will have to find other ways to prove the truth: that the sole reason I brought you here is to serve the gods."

"Maybe you'd better find a way to let your clan know that," I said. "Ryu won't be the only person to claim you took me under your roof to please yourself, not the spirits. Remember, sometimes it's not enough to tell the simple truth; you must make it convincing. If the people think you use the gods as an excuse for your own desires, they will lose their respect for you as a shaman."

My advice surprised him. "You care about my reputation?"

"Ryu would love to see you covered in mud and dragged down to his level. I care about thwarting him."

Daimu smiled. "I'm glad you're honest with me."

"I hope you're honest with me too."

Ashi returned with our dinner, which she had brought from the central cookhouse. The shrine could contain a few small fire-holding vessels to keep off the cold, but the building was too important, too sacred to risk the larger, more frequent flames needed to prepare meals. A guarded silence enveloped Daimu and me as we ate, and it remained settled over us like a bird's wing until we went to our separate chambers.

As I prepared for rest, I saw Ashi laying a bedroll across the entrance to my quarters. "Is that where you sleep?" I asked her.

"It's where I sleep tonight, and where one of my friends will sleep tomorrow. We all share a cozy little house in the shadow of the shrine, but Master Daimu has requested this arrangement." She chuckled.

I made a doubtful face. "What's so funny about it?"

"As if a miserable, weak woman like me could keep a strong young man like him out of your room if he *really* wanted to get in? Even if he *weren't* my master? What could I do? Shriek and slap at him, as if he were a lizard trying to climb my skirt? But he still insisted that we play this game. 'She will be able to sleep peacefully, knowing someone stands between her and me,' he said. Oh my, men are all the same when they're trying to be gallant: silly things. But at least they can make us laugh." She stretched out on her bedroll and yawned. "Good night, Lady Himiko."

I slept well that night, although it was not on account of the "watchdog" at my doorway. The muted chime of a bronze bell lured me from my dreams. I rose, dressed swiftly, and followed the sound, stepping over Ashi's snoring body. The floorboards of the shrine were like ice under my naked feet. The sun had not yet risen, but gray, watery dawn light filtered through the roof and crept in at the edges of the door curtain.

Daimu knelt in the center of the shrine, holding the

bronze bell high. His softly chanting voice was as clear and sweet and resonant as the bell's soul-stirring note. The skin of my forearms tingled to hear him, and a thread of fire trickled from the back of my neck all the way down my spine. I shuddered with joy as I sensed the presence of the spirits, summoned by Daimu's spell.

He spoke to them with love, awe, and gratitude. His prayers were respectful requests for the welfare of his people. Some were mentioned by name—the sick, the sad, the broken. I heard him mention Ryu: "O gods, let him be the good man who dwells in the dragon's heart! Let him find wisdom!"

Then I heard him speak my name: "Spirits, you know what a great gift I have brought you by having Lady Himiko enter your holy place. All I ask in return is that you show your thanks by granting the chief desire of her heart. Protect her, body and soul. Preserve her family and her clan. Provide her with the countless blessings of freedom and peace." He struck the bell once more and set it down. His prayers were finished.

I stole back to my room before he could look around and realize I was there.

Later that morning, over breakfast, Daimu asked me, "How will you spend the day, Lady Himiko?"

"I—I hadn't thought about that," I replied. "What do you want me to do?"

"What would *you* want to do if this were your home? You no longer have to obey anyone but yourself."

I laughed. "Then it's nothing at all like my home. Mama, Emi, and Yukari were always finding work for me to do. My teacher, Lady Yama, was also very keen about giving me chores."

"Was she the one who recognized your calling?"

I nodded. "She said I had a talent for gathering plants and preparing salves and potions." I cast a sidelong glance at the curtained room containing all that the Ookami shaman needed to care for his clan and serve the spirits. "Will you trust me to make medicines for you?"

"Trust you?" He thought I was joking.

"Your warriors took the lives of my father and two of my brothers," I said, unsmiling. "It would be easy for me to avenge them by making a 'cure' that kills."

"You would never do such a thing." He spoke with conviction and led me to the room where dried herbs, roots, and the rest of his supplies awaited. That was the beginning of my work assisting the Ookami shaman.

On the fifth morning of my new life, Daimu told me, "I'm going away today. Don't worry if I'm not back before nightfall."

"Where are you going?"

"Not on another pilgrimage, if that's what you're afraid of," he teased.

I put on a fake haughty expression. "As if *that* would bother me! Just tell me if there's any specific chore you need me to do while you're off chasing butterflies. *Some* of us want to do *necessary* work."

"Then perhaps it's time *some* of us left this house to find that 'necessary work,'" he rejoined, grinning. "You've done nothing since you got here but brew potions and mix remedies. It's time you put them to use. This winter has brought us a heavy share of sickness. Too many people are afraid to bother me with their aches and pains, and some who are too ill to leave their homes still don't dare to send for me. Go to them, Lady Himiko."

"You think they'll allow me to tend to them?" I asked. "You may trust me, but will they?"

"Why not? After all, I was speaking of the slaves."

That was enough for me. I gulped my breakfast, packed an assortment of cures and treatments in a large basket, and set out to find the people who most needed my help. I went from house to house where the slaves lived and discovered more than enough sufferers. My appearance always startled them until they stopped being fascinated by my fine new dress and looked at my face instead.

"Himiko?" There would be a moment of dread as they recalled Ryu's ban on speaking to me, but I was soon able to set their minds at ease:

"The wolf clan shaman can overrule their chieftain. It's safe for me to share your company; Master Daimu will protect you. Now tell me what hurts."

I did not return to the shrine until after dark. My only regret was that the day did not contain enough time for me to visit all the people in need of my care. I consoled myself by thinking about how much good I had managed to accomplish, and how much more I might do tomorrow.

Daimu was waiting for me. He was seated on the floor with Ashi at his side, setting down his dinner. She frowned when she saw me.

"About time! I was afraid you were going to eat cold rice."

"Let that be the worst thing that ever happens to me,"

I said cheerfully, taking my place opposite Daimu. As the older woman handed me my plate, I thanked her and added: "Ashi, why don't you sleep under your own roof tonight?"

"Lady Himiko?" Her brows knit in confusion and she looked to Daimu for help. He only shrugged.

Later on, after Ashi left us, he spoke to me: "Are you sure about this?"

It was my turn to shrug. "You trusted me to make medicine for your people, even if I'm not the one to give it to them. Now I must trust you."

"Thank you," he said solemnly. "I want to be worthy of that trust, Lady Himiko."

"And I want you to call me Himiko, Master Daimu; nothing more."

"Because you want me to remember that some think of you as my slave? I never—"

"No." I held up one hand to silence him. "Because I want you to think of me as your friend."

"Then you must call me Daimu."

"I will, except when there are others present," I said. "It wouldn't be proper, then."

His smile was so very much like Reikon's that it made me draw in a short, sharp breath of wonder. I had crossed into the spirits' realm in my dreams many times since coming to the Ookami shrine, but I had not encountered my lost prince there even once. "Still defending my reputation?" he asked.

"As a friend should do," I replied.

"In that case, I have something to give you . . . as a friend." He stood and went into the storeroom, returning with a small bundle. Placing it in my hands, he said, "This was the reason I left the village today. I wish I could have done it sooner."

I felt the chill of cold metal through the cloth and knew what I held even before I unwrapped it. The shining bronze surface of my mirror winked at me the instant that I pulled aside one corner of the fabric, and the sturdy, graceful shape of my bell conjured memories of its music.

"I thought you should have these close at hand, now that you can use them openly again," Daimu said.

I laughed through tears of joy and gratitude. "How funny! This is the second time I have received this gift under this roof from an Ookami shaman. Master Rinji was kind enough to restore them to me once. May the gods be praised, I won't have to hide them anymore!"

"Rinji . . ." Daimu sighed. "I don't know why he left the shrine. He said he had no true calling as a shaman, but I know that isn't so. I hope he'll come back."

I touched his hand lightly with my fingertips. "So do I. He was also my friend."

14

THE BONE SEEKER

Winter waned. The snow melted even from the upper slopes of the mountains and the sun grew stronger. Each day I found more and more joy in the new life I had been given. Even if I did not have my freedom, I was still free to follow the way of the spirits and perform the functions of a shaman. I compounded medicines, made offerings, and lifted my voice to invoke the goddesses while Daimu called upon the gods. When the earth waited to receive her first plantings and the Ookami held their great spring celebration, I danced.

It was a strange time for me, a time of contrasts as vivid as light and darkness. I lived both free and captive. I could come and go as I wished, but only inside the village walls, and even so, there was still one house where my presence was forbidden. I could not set foot outside the settlement gates, for Ryu had grown warier and doubled the guard in the watchtower. Did he fear that I no longer cared about rescuing my family and that I might take advantage of Daimu's lenient ways in order to save myself? Or was he having second thoughts about the security of his clan? Spring was opening the roads that led the Ookami to victory over their neighbors, but those roads ran both ways. Was Ryu troubled by Daimu's warnings that today's conqueror might become tomorrow's captive? I did not know.

I lived both happy and heartbroken, because although I was following my heart's chosen path, I was still far from home and no closer to fulfilling the task that had brought me to the Ookami village in the first place. Noboru remained a captive. So did Emi and Sanjirou. So did I, and I did not dare to think about my mother's fate. For all I knew, Kaya had failed to persuade our elders to delay carrying out their verdict and she was already dead. I could not face such black thoughts. Whenever they arose, I sank myself in work, exhausting my body in order to exhaust my mind.

Daimu could not understand why I volunteered to be part of the spring planting when I didn't have to do so. "We have enough hands for this labor," he said.

"Slaves' hands, and I am still a slave," I reminded him. "And among the Matsu, every able-bodied person helped plant the rice, including my father."

He considered this. "Our own chieftain should follow such a good example."

"Don't hold your breath waiting for that to happen," I said. "Some things never change."

But some things did.

Spring was a season of joy, but also a season that bred illness and injury. Winter food supplies dwindled before fresh food could be found, giving many villagers bellyaches and sluggish bowels. Work in the fields became more intense, which led to aching backs and a host of accidents when the people were clumsy or simply unlucky wielding their iron tools.

It was at this time, when Master Daimu seemed to be constantly busy with one healing after another, that I was first approached by one of the Ookami women. She came to the shrine seeking help for her husband, who had cut his foot while hoeing weeds from the millet field.

"Master Daimu isn't here right now," I told her. "He's taking care of one of your elders who's got a bad fever."

"I don't want to wait for Master Daimu," she told me. "I want you."

Mystified, I went with her and was soon treating her husband—changing the bandage, cleaning the wound, and covering it with a layer of herbs to speed healing. When I was done, I asked how she'd known I could help them.

She rolled her eyes as if I'd asked *Why is water wet?* "You are a shaman, Lady Himiko. Who ever heard of a shaman who wasn't also a healer?"

"But I am not an *Ookami* shaman. I am a member of the Matsu clan."

"What's the difference? You've been working among the slaves and not all of them are Matsu, yet your cures and spells still heal them."

"To be honest, I did not expect an Ookami family to trust me."

She waved away my words. "We did not trust you as a Matsu girl, but as a shaman. We have been watching you,

Lady Himiko. We saw you perform the chants and the dances for the spirits. Nothing bad happened. We also see how our Master Daimu respects you. That's good enough for us."

It was good enough for many other Ookami as well. Daimu warned me that I was going to drain my strength, trying to take care of every sick or injured person who sent for me. "Try telling some of them to wait another day."

"Some can't wait," I replied. "And some of your people are too highborn to accept any delay in getting what they want. The only ones who would *have* to wait for my help are your slaves, and I will never allow that."

"I thought you might say that." Daimu handed me a small cloth bag tied with twine. When I closed my hand around it, it gave off a heady, beautiful scent.

"What's this?"

"Herbs and dried flower petals. When you go to bathe in the river, wet it and use it to scrub your skin. It will revive you and give you energy."

I took his hand in mine and squeezed it gently. "You are always doing kind things for me, Daimu. When you returned my bell and mirror, it was only the beginning. How many times has Ashi or one of the others distracted me from my meals long enough for extra food to appear on my plate? Why have I found pretty beads scattered across my doorway, just waiting to be strung into a necklace? I know that birds' nests don't appear out of nowhere, filled with nuts and dried fruits, and yet that's exactly what was waiting on top of my bedroll when I went to unfurl it three nights ago. And now this."

He looked down at our clasped hands. "I'm not doing anything special; I'm being selfish. It makes me happy to see you enjoying such small things. Your smile becomes pure."

"What do you mean, 'pure'?"

"Free of hidden grief, free of ghosts. I know that you can never be completely happy while you live here, so far from your home, under Ryu's rule. I can't break the walls of your cage, but if I can widen the spaces between the bars—"

I remembered my vision of caged birds among the willows and my grip on Daimu's hand tightened so violently that he winced. "Who are you?" I whispered without realizing how bizarre that question would sound.

"Himiko?" He looked bewildered and worried about me.

I closed my eyes tightly and took a long, cleansing breath. "I'm sorry," I said. "I don't know what made me ask you such a thing. I must be more tired than I thought."

"You should rest," he said, and helped me to my feet even though I was perfectly capable of doing so myself.

I slept late the next day, drowning in my dreams. I saw myself back among my people, welcomed home by the living and the dead. We met in the shadow of Grandfather Pine, even though the Ookami had torn down that ancient tree when they conquered our village. Countless arms enfolded me. Father's smile was a blessing. Mama stood to one side, balancing Noboru on her hip and smiling tranquilly. Not a trace of her wild madness remained.

Aki was there too. He held me close and ruffled my hair as though I were still a child. *How does it feel, Little Sister?* he asked, beaming at me. *How do you like being in love?*

What are you talking about, Aki? I protested. *I'm not in love!*

Oh, but you are! You're just not ready to admit it. You're like a little tower of pebbles stacked one on the other. They stand firm, until someone adds a single grain of sand to the top and then—! He made the clattering sound of their fall and flashed his fingers in my face so suddenly that I gaped and woke up.

"Big Sister?" A small voice, well known and well loved, sounded shyly in my ear as I lay curled up sideways on my bedroll. "Big Sister, are you asleep?"

I rolled first onto my back, then to my other side and saw him: my little brother, Noboru. My eyes went wide.

"Yes," I said faintly. "I think I must be dreaming. How else could I be seeing you here?"

"I brought him, Himiko." Daimu spoke from the doorway to my sleeping quarters. "Early this morning I went to the chieftain's house and spoke privately with Lady Sato. It's simple to get her cooperation when she's happy, and she is *very* happy having plenty of servants at her beck and call once more. We agreed that there is no *good* reason to keep the child away from his beloved sister, so long as Ryu doesn't find out." He scratched the back of his head. "Lady Sato doesn't have a very high opinion of her son's judgment, it seems."

I took Noboru into my arms and held him as though monsters were striving to tear him away from me. "Is that why she let you bring him here secretly?" I asked. "Because she scorns her own son?"

"Well, there is another reason," Daimu confessed. "It's because she's become a little—just a little!—afraid of you."

"What?"

He spread his hands. "You are a shaman, Himiko. You have openly served the spirits with all of our people to witness it. The village hums with stories of all the healings you have performed. Some of your patients tell tales about how you cast out multitudes of demons and banished evil ghosts from afflicting the sick. You have become a formidable girl."

"But I never did anything like that," I protested. "It's nothing but lies!"

"I know, but those lies make other people pay attention to the liars. If you can't fight gossip, use it." He indicated Noboru. "I did."

"I don't suppose Lady Sato fears me enough to set us free?" Daimu shook his head. "But enough to help me be with Noboru?" He nodded. "Every day?"

"As long as Ryu doesn't find out," Daimu reminded me.

I hugged my little brother and smiled. "That will be good enough for now."

But it wasn't good enough for Daimu. A few days after he first brought Noboru to me, he took us to a small pit house far from the center of the village. He refused to reveal his purpose, but I suspected what it must be, and who dwelled in that drab hut.

He paused just outside and called: "They are here."

A fast-moving bundle of energy shot out of the doorway and Noboru and I were knocked backward by our unruly half brother, Sanjirou.

"Big Sister! Big Sister! It *is* you! It *is*!" He was taller and scrawnier than when I'd last seen him, but that had been a long time ago. Even though his eyes looked too old for a child, slavery had not yet broken his rambunctious spirit. He threw his arms around my neck and nearly dragged me to the ground with the force of his embrace.

"Sanjirou, stop that!" My stepmother Emi stuck her head out of the small house. She looked haggard and her hair was heavily streaked with gray. "Someone will see." She made quick motions for everyone to come inside, where we had to huddle close together. Only then did she manage to take me into her arms for an awkward hug.

"Oh, my dear Himiko, how good it is to see you!" she cried. "I missed you so much."

"I missed you too," I said, choking back a sob. "Are you well?"

Even in the dimness of her tiny house, my stepmother's smile was radiant. "I have never been better. So, what they say about you must be true: you are a wonderful healer. You restore me, body and spirit, just by being here."

I drew back enough to examine her with my eyes. "*Do* you need healing, Mother?" I asked.

She laughed. "Ah, little Himiko, so serious, so grown up! No, my precious one, you don't have to worry about me. I am not ill or hurt, and my Sanjirou enjoys excellent health in spite of all the work our masters pile on such a young child."

"I'm *not* a child," Sanjirou declared. With a look of pride directed at Noboru, he added: "I am the *man* in this house!"

"It's not a very big house," Noboru observed. The next

instant, my little brothers were tussling in the dirt while
Emi fluttered over them, ineffectively trying to put a stop
to their harmless brawl.

Once the boys settled down, Emi, Daimu, and I spoke
about the future.

"You will be able to come here whenever you like,"
Emi said happily. "This place isn't much, but Sanjirou and
I have it all to ourselves, so it's better than our former lodg-
ings." She gave Daimu a grateful look.

"It's also surrounded by other slaves' quarters and out
of the way," he added. "None of the Ookami have any business here. Even if any of my people did notice you, they'd
think you're tending the sick, not visiting your family."

"Can I come back to visit too?" Noboru asked plaintively.

Sanjirou shoved him. "You'd better! But you can't tell
anyone about it, all right? Swear!" The two boys immediately began constructing a bloodthirsty oath of total secrecy,
calling on the gods for the slow, painful, bone-by-bone destruction of anyone who broke it. The rest of us had to clap
our hands across our mouths to keep from laughing.

That evening I waited until Daimu and I were alone
before speaking to him about the events of the day. I had already thanked him, but there was so much more I needed to
say, or my heart would burst from holding back the words.

"Daimu . . . ," I began, and all at once I found myself
speechless, helpless, and trembling. What strange magic
stole my ability to utter a single sound? Why was I drowning
in a flood of feelings that swirled around me and dragged
me deeper into myself? I felt my face blaze with shame. *He's*

staring at me, waiting for me to speak, but I can't. I can't! *O my sweet goddess, aid me, open my lips, lend me your light! I can't see the path I need to tread and Daimu is waiting. He'll think I'm nothing but a fool!*

I tried again: "Daimu, I know I've already thanked you for bringing my family back together. I can never repay you for it, but—"

"Please don't say anything more about it, Himiko," he asked, his voice low and rough. "I didn't do this to earn your thanks. You must never feel that you are in my debt. Some gifts have no value unless they are freely given—not to get something in return, not to settle an obligation, but given from the heart."

"From the heart," I repeated, and leaned forward to touch my lips to his.

How could I not love Daimu? He trusted me, he believed in me, he cared about me more than he did about himself. I could not deny that he was attractive, but Ryu was just as handsome on the surface. Age would dull their eyes, steal the gleaming blackness from their hair, and mark their faces, but Daimu's spirit would still shine as brightly, then as now.

Our first kiss opened our lives to each other. In the tender warmth of the springtime evenings we sat together on the platform of the shrine, watching the sunset paint cherry blossoms over the clouds, and spoke. Each new thing he told me about his childhood, his years of growing up and suddenly knowing he was meant to serve the spirits, his fears and failings, bound us more closely. Every secret I shared with him became the petals of a windflower, opening one by one even in the chill of autumn to reveal a golden heart.

When I told him about the first time I had entered the spirits' realm and met Reikon, he smiled sadly. "Is that why you care for me, Himiko? Because I look like him?"

I wished I could have put my arms around him and driven that question from his lips with a kiss, but some passer-by might look up at the shrine and see that. Instead I shook my head and said, "Spirit or mortal, you are the only one for me."

Those sweet days filled my life with contentment and hope. Daimu and I became inseparable, though we took great care to conceal our true relationship from his people. Ryu was wise enough to fear the power Daimu had over the spirits, but who knew what would make his resentful nature flare up enough to destroy his common sense?

One morning, Daimu announced that he was going into the mountains for fresh leaves, shoots, and blossoms to replenish our medicinal supplies. "I'm sorry that I can't bring you with me, Himiko," he said.

"I'm sorry too," I replied. "It's been too long since I wandered the forest! How long will you be gone?"

"I'll be back by sundown." He gathered up an armload of empty sacks and went away.

I was left behind in a deserted shrine and an almost deserted village. Ashi and the other slaves who tended the shrine with me were gone. The good weather and the good fortune of the wolf clan made Ryu decide it was time to break ground on a new rice paddy, high on the slope where the sun lingered longest. It was a project that demanded the hands of every healthy worker, slave or free, and I overheard Ashi tell one of her friends that Ryu himself was going to labor with everyone else. I muttered a wish for him to fall on his face in the muck, just as he'd done years ago, when I pushed him into our moat back home.

As I swept the shrine floor, I enjoyed the peace of being by myself, attended only by my thoughts. When I was with Daimu, I found it hard to think about anything but him and how the two of us might create our future. The hushed, rhythmic *ksh-ksh-ksh* of the broom sent my mind wandering down many roads, each unrolling before me like a tightly coiled rope that is suddenly released, each becoming hopelessly tangled in a snarl of questions that I could not answer:

How could we get away from the Ookami? Would Daimu even consent to leave his people again? What would we do about bringing Noboru with us? How could we take him and leave Emi and Sanjirou behind? And most frightening of all to contemplate, if somehow we did succeed in escaping the wolves of the mountains and making our way back to my own clan, what was to prevent Ryu from hunting down his shaman and his property? What would stop the Ookami chieftain from taking vengeance by turning my home into a worse wasteland than the ghost lands of the hawk clan?

I knew the answer to that final question, at least: nothing.

I swept harder.

"Master Daimu? Master Daimu?" A young girl's voice climbed the ladder to the shrine long before her face peered through the doorway. "I beg your pardon, Lady Himiko, but where is Master Daimu, please?" She wove and unwove her fingers nervously.

"Gone to the mountains to gather herbs," I told her. "Is something wrong? Maybe I can help you."

"Oh!" She looked as tense and jumpy as a rabbit when the fox prowls near her warren. Everything about her said *Let me run away!* "I—I—I don't think you *can* help. My mother told me that on the day you became a keeper of the shrine, Lord Ryu forbade you to come back under his roof."

"Lord Ryu?" My brows came together. "You serve him?" I was not familiar with any of the slaves who had replaced me.

"Yes, my lady. Me and my mother and my sister and Father and Uncle and Auntie and two cousins."

I made a sound of amazement. "It must get crowded." I wanted to calm her down, so I tried making a joke. "And I'll bet it's going to be even more tightly packed once Lady Chizu has her baby."

"That's just it, Lady Himiko," the girl said in a panic. "She's having the baby now. I mean, she's *trying* to have it. Her pains began last night, but they weren't very strong. This morning, Lady Sato told Lord Ryu there was no cause for alarm just yet, and to go ahead with making the new rice paddy. But then, as soon as everyone had gone to the fields, Lady Chizu began to scream *dreadfully*! That was when Lady Sato had Auntie take the little boy out of the house and sent me for the midwife."

"It's a good thing you were there instead of in the fields," I told her, privately thankful that Noboru would not be caught up in what might become a tragedy.

"Uh? Oh! That's because I'm Lady Sato's personal maid." She did not look thrilled by the "honor."

"If you brought the midwife, why do you need Master Daimu?"

The girl's eyes grew huge as an owl's. "Because something is wrong, Lady Himiko. The baby—the baby won't be born. He's all upside-down, coming feet first, and every time the midwife tries to make him turn around so he'll come out the right way, he fights her and slips back wrong way 'round. Lady Sato says there must be a demon at work inside Lady Chizu and she wants Master Daimu to cast it out before— before—" She covered her eyes with both hands and began to sob.

I put down my broom. "Has Lady Sato sent for her son?"

The little maid looked up at me with red-rimmed eyes and sniffled. "No, Lady Himiko."

"Good." Without another word I moved to fill a basket with everything that I might need to help Chizu.

As soon as the girl saw what I intended to do, she became even more upset, begging me to reconsider. "If Lord Ryu finds out you were in his house, I'll be blamed for it!"

"Then I'd better see to it that Lady Chizu has her baby before he comes home," I replied evenly, starting down the ladder.

I found the chieftain's household in chaos. Chizu's groans were punctuated by long shrieks and some of the ugliest curses I had ever heard. Where had that timid creature learned such words? How I wished Ryu were here just long enough to listen to some of the things she was saying about him!

The midwife was not much older than I. According to the maid, she had not been summoned until early morning and it was not yet noon. In spite of that, she already looked exhausted. She added to the din by shouting orders at the two strong, older female slaves who were forcing Chizu to pace back and forth even though her pains seemed to be coming very close together. The time for that helpful practice was not now, with the birth about to happen. The only reason I could imagine for inflicting it on the suffering mother-to-be was that the midwife had run out of ideas for turning the unborn child and hoped a brisk walk would do the trick.

The women supporting Chizu were shouting pleas for mercy to the spirits. Were they sincerely petitioning the gods for help or only trying to make everyone present remember how ardently they prayed? If things went wrong and Ryu wanted someone to be at fault for it, they could hide behind this: *You must not blame us for the loss of your wife and child, my lord. We never once stopped begging the spirits to save them!*

Lady Sato had no breath left for prayers. She was too busy scolding everyone in sight, berating the midwife, the slaves, and even her helpless daughter-in-law. "Where is my grandson? Why don't you stop playing games and bring him into this world *now*? Do you think he can wait forever? Hurry, you lazy things!"

I had seen enough. "Let her lie down!" I called out from the doorway. All eyes fixed on me. Lady Sato turned as white as Chizu.

"What are you doing here? My son said—!"

I ignored her, striding into the house to confront the slaves. "I told you: let her lie *down*." They obeyed.

The midwife knelt beside me, her brow starred with sweat. "The child is—"

"—coming the wrong way. I know." I stroked Chizu's forehead. "You'll be all right," I told her gently. "You must relax and not worry anymore. Soon you'll have a fine, healthy baby."

"I won't, I won't!" Chizu moaned. "I'm going to die! Ah, it hurts so much, I wish I *would* die now!"

"And I wish you wouldn't say such nonsense," I told her. Turning back to the midwife, I said: "You tried turning the baby and it didn't work?"

She nodded. "He keeps squirming back, no matter what I do. I have attended other births where the same thing happened, but the babies always let themselves be guided into the right position. There's a trick to this one, and I can't figure it out. If my mother were still alive, she might have the answer, but she died of an autumn cough before she could finish instructing me." She regarded me with a faint glimmer of hope in her eyes. "Have *you* ever seen such a thing? Do you know how to fix it?"

I lowered my voice so that Chizu could not hear me say: "I've delivered other children, but I've never experienced a birth like this." My chin came up sharply; I held the midwife's gaze. "But my teacher instructed me in *all* kinds of healing, and I know what we should try."

I laid out potions and salves made from bearleaf and wolfberry and motherwort. These were medicines to give a laboring woman strength, to keep her from losing too much blood, and to make a barrier between her and the evil spirits that brought fevers that killed many new mothers. Lady Sato tried fussing at me; I barked threats and commands until she understood who was in charge. The slaves were sent to fetch fresh water, which was soon infused with fragrant herbs. I had them wash Chizu thoroughly but quickly. There was no time to lose.

"Now, let's see if this child is stubborn enough to defy two of us," I told the midwife, and together we took on the daunting job of turning the unborn baby and keeping him in the proper position for an easy birth. We shared the task, the midwife maneuvering the infant, me holding him steady. Chizu's stomach rippled with labor pangs, but she was finally able to put all of her efforts into bringing her child into the world.

"All right," I said, breathing hard. "It feels like he's given up. Chizu, you're going to get up and squat now. Everyone else, be ready!"

"I . . . am . . . *more* than ready," Chizu panted. The two slaves helped her into position, linked their arms behind her, and let her squeeze their free hands as hard as necessary. There was a grunt, a gasp, a yowl, and then the midwife was holding a tiny, squalling, outraged infant boy in her arms.

As soon as Lady Sato heard that she *did* have a grandson, she tried to snatch the newborn from the midwife before anyone had a chance to cut the cord linking mother and child. She hovered over us, urging haste, whining about how cruel we were to keep her waiting, and making a nuisance of herself. The midwife was attempting to wash the baby, I was preoccupied with guiding Chizu through all that came after a birth, and the slaves were struggling to prepare a comfortable place for mother and child to rest. Lady Sato managed to get in everyone's way at once.

I was at the end of my patience. Chizu's difficult labor had taken almost all of the young woman's strength, and I did not like how bloodless her face still looked. Desperate to get rid of her, I suggested: "Lady Sato, don't you think you should go to your son and tell him he's a father?"

She compressed her wrinkled lips, disdaining my proposal. "Hmph. He'll find out soon enough." Then, reconsidering, she made an imperious gesture at her maid, who was still shaking from having witnessed such a hard birth. "You, girl! Go to the fields and give Lord Ryu the news." With a squeak of distress, the maid dashed out. Lady Sato immediately stretched out her hands for the child.

"My lady, he should be with his mother first," the midwife said.

"He'll be with *her* soon enough," the old woman declared. "Now give me my grandson."

I sprang up and swooped over the newborn, lifting him from the midwife's arms to place him tenderly on Chizu's belly. He squirmed, eyes closed, and opened a small, toothless, hungry mouth until his mother guided him to her breast. He began to feed steadily. Chizu's face shone with love.

"Look at my son, Mother," she said to Lady Sato. "See what a fine boy he is! I thought I would not live to know his face, yet here we are."

Thwarted, Lady Sato glared at her daughter-in-law, but her anger had no effect. Chizu was in a world of her own, where there was only room for two.

Needing a target for her temper, the chieftain's mother turned on me. "A fine shaman *you* are!" she exclaimed, folding her arms. "Interfering in matters that don't concern you and failing to carry out your own duties. How are the gods going to bless this boy if they don't know he's here? And what about the house, eh? Do you think it will purify itself? I can practically smell the evil spirits lurking in the shadows!"

"My apologies, Lady Sato," I said. "I will begin the rites at once."

"What rites?" Ryu stood on the threshold, the little maid cowering at his side. When he saw me standing with his mother, his face became a mask of rage. "What are *you* doing here, against my specific orders? Inexcusable! If Daimu thinks he'll be able to spare you the consequences of this—!"

"Husband, please don't speak so to Lady Himiko!" Chizu spoke in clear, forceful tones, free of all timidity. "Your son is waiting to greet you."

"My son?" That word worked a great enchantment, melting away the wolf chieftain's furious expression. He moved cautiously to where his wife lay cradling the infant in the crook of her arm, and knelt at her side. For the first time I saw Ryu without his pride, his coldness, or his arrogance. As he gazed at the newborn in utter fascination, the only emotion filling him was love.

Chizu began to whisper to him while he caressed the

baby's downy cheek with a fingertip. I could not hear what she said, but I soon found out. Looking grave and chastened, Ryu stood up and returned to me. "You saved my son's life."

"She and I"—I indicated the midwife—"are both glad we could help your wife and your son."

"Thank you for that." He spoke grudgingly, as if the words were slivers of stone between his teeth, painful to spit out. "If . . . if you were to return to this house, you would not be treated as a slave. You and your little brother would live as honored members of our household. Your closest kin would share the same privileges. All of your past offenses will be forgiven and your place among the Ookami will be secure."

"My place here is already *too* secure," I said, striving to restrain my true feelings. *He is* trying *to be kind,* I thought. *He means well, but . . .* "Isn't that always true for a slave?"

"I promise, you will be treated as if you were freeborn Ookami!" Ryu cried. He must have thought it was the greatest favor he could bestow. "Master Rinji will be this clan's next shaman. He'll need a wife. None of my people would dare look down on you then."

"So Master Rinji is still following the spirits' path?" This was interesting news. "He has not entered the shrine since—for some time."

Ryu was perplexed. He was probably expecting to hear me thank him profusely as I accepted his "generous" reward for my services. Instead I was questioning him about Rinji. "He—he has been serving the gods elsewhere, with my approval. I'm surprised he was not sent for today, once it was known that *Master* Daimu could not be found." He gave his mother and the little maid a hard look. "At least he does not go wandering off when his help is needed."

"Send for Rinji? Bah!" Lady Sato rejected the very idea. "I don't know why you continue to support that boy. He's no shaman; he's a mosquito, buzzing in the ears of the spirits. The only time they answer his prayers is when he irritates them so badly they'd do anything to make him fly away! Now as for Master Daimu"—she smiled at me sweetly—"Master Daimu and his dear Lady Himiko—"

"His?" Ryu frowned.

"Well, as good as his," the horrible old woman said lightly. "Everyone who isn't blind knows it. The two of them keep a respectable distance from one another in public, but they can't control the look in their eyes. How sweet it is to see young love in springtime! Tsk. And here you stand wasting your breath, Ryu, offering the girl the same honors she'll enjoy without your help the moment she marries our real shaman! My poor son, if you only knew how foolish it all makes you sound."

I wanted to grab Lady Sato and shake sense and discretion into her. Her gabbling tongue was destroying all the goodwill I had gained from the wolf chieftain for saving his wife and son.

"I should go back to the shrine," I said calmly. "Lady Chizu will need a tonic to help her milk come in." I kept my eyes averted. If I looked at Ryu directly, he might take an innocent glance as mockery, defiance, or a challenge. I could sense him seething with anger stirred up by his mother's careless speech. He was looking for an excuse to make me pay for that. I would not give it to him.

"Thank you for your trouble, Lady Himiko," he said in a flat, frigid voice. "There is no need. The midwife will see to everything from now on."

"Yes, Lord Ryu," I said, and left the house without bothering to gather up my supplies. No doubt they would be returned to the shrine without the need for me to linger in hostile territory.

Daimu came home before the sun set, as he had promised. The Ookami village was already loud with the sounds of festivity as he climbed the ladder to the shrine. The people were rejoicing over the birth of their chieftain's son, a celebration that would really get under way the following morning. Ashi brought me the news that Ryu had decreed a day of festivity and feasting. Not even the slaves would work, and everyone would receive as much food and rice wine as they could swallow.

The noise of early revelry did not have any effect on my beloved. He looked oddly distracted and mournful. *Perhaps he hasn't heard the good news about Chizu's son,* I thought, but even after I told him, he remained distant, his mind elsewhere. All through dinner, Ashi and the other servants chatted happily with me about the birth, but he remained closed in on himself, picking at his food.

I waited until we were left alone for the night before I chose to deal with what was wrong. "Where are they?" I asked bluntly.

My question took him by surprise. "They? What 'they' are you talking about?"

"The herbs. The flowers. The roots. You told me you were going into the forest to find new ingredients for our remedies. You came home empty-handed."

A wistful smile curved his lips. "You are too observant and too clever, Himiko. I should have known better than to try lying to you."

"Is the truth you're hiding from me such an awful thing?"

"Not at all. It's just that I've gotten into the habit of concealing this from the rest of my clan. You see, when I was a little boy, my uncle went away." His smile deserted him entirely as he spoke on. "Went away . . . that's what I was told. When I was older, I learned the real story: he had been exiled from the clan for a great crime."

"What was it?"

"Being different. Being so different that the wolves—the brave, *brave* wolves were afraid of him. He's a big man, a giant, very strong, but he can act as impetuously and uncontrollably as a child. My mother told me how hard it was to speak with him and be understood. His mind didn't work quickly enough to satisfy those who didn't love him.

"But *I* loved him." Tears brimmed in Daimu's eyes. "He was always kind to me. I missed him. That's why, as soon as I was old enough, I went into the mountains and found him. I can't tell you how happy I was to see that he was still alive and well, able to survive in the wilderness. And he remembered me, even though I was grown up! I told him that I had become the Ookami shaman and had the power to bring him home again, but he also remembered the cruel treatment he'd gotten from our clan. I couldn't overcome his fear, so I told him I would come back to see him often."

My pulse was beating rapidly at the base of my throat. *A big man, a giant, very strong, too different to be tolerated in this cowardly village . . . Mori! No . . . no, it mustn't be him. O gods, please let Daimu be speaking of some other man!*

"Is that where you were today?" I asked, dreading the answer. "With your uncle?" My hands curled tight as I willed him to say *Yes, and it was very good to see him alive and well.*

Instead, what I heard was: "That was my plan. I go back every spring, to see how he's getting along and to ask if he needs anything. I'd visit him more often, but he begged me not to do it. He was afraid our clanfolk would find out and trouble him more than they already did. Some of our young men think it's great fun to track down my poor uncle and torment him, can you imagine that?"

I could, much too easily. I said nothing.

"I was very eager to see him again," Daimu went on. "I almost didn't leave on my pilgrimage, because I was worried about him. I begged him to come away with me, but he refused. New things terrified him. When I offered to stay, he insisted that I go and swore he would be all right in my absence. He had great faith in the spirits; I suppose that's because he lived so close to so many of them, up there in the forest. But when I went seeking him today, I couldn't find him in any of his usual haunts. I'm going to go back tomorrow and try again. Maybe he moved farther up the mountain. I only hope—"

"You will not find him," I said, and told him of his gentle uncle's fate. I spoke without emotion, as if I were recounting one of the ancient stories about the gods. I did not dare do otherwise or grief would choke me. "He was a brave man, Daimu. You say he was afraid to return to this place, but when I told him about Noboru, he didn't hesitate: he went into the village, into Ryu's own house, and brought my little brother to me. Your uncle had a hero's heart."

"If that is so, it must have been slumbering for a long time," Daimu said. "Something awakened it. I think it was you." Before I could deny it, he went on: "I knew my uncle very well. I told you he feared change, so what would have the force to make him set aside his old, deeply rooted terror of the village in order to go down there and rescue your little brother from Ryu's control? Do not discount your powers of persuasion and command, Himiko. I believe you have the gift to charm people with a greater magic than any shaman has ever mastered. The gods alone know what you will achieve with such a gift someday."

"If I do have such powers, why can't I use them on Ryu?" I asked.

Daimu looked grim. "Because your enchantments touch the heart, and he has none."

All that night, he did not sleep. Grief transformed his bedroll into a nest of thorns. He sat beside it, murmuring prayers. I urged him to rest, but it was no use. He thanked me for my concern, told me not to fret about him, and suggested that I take my own advice.

"No," I said stubbornly. "If you're not going to sleep, neither am I." I tried to be true to my word, only to slump against his shoulder and doze off until dawn.

I woke up in my own bedroll, alone. Daimu was nowhere to be found. Neither were any of the servants. The angle of the sunlight streaming in through the shrine doorway told me that the day of celebration was well under way.

I hurried outside, seeking him. I made my way through clusters of strangely subdued Ookami. Where were the cheers of celebration, the cries of revelry? I saw mats spread everywhere, laden with food, but no one was eating. All heads were turned in one direction, all faces anxious and ashen.

A dreadful thought struck me and my hand went to the precious amulet in my sash. *O Lady of the Dragon Stone, light of the sun, merciful one, grant that no harm has come to Chizu or her child!*

I emerged from the ghostlike crowd to find Daimu standing at the bottom of the ladder leading up to Ryu's house. The wolf chieftain looked down at him from the wide platform, attended by several of the highest-ranking Ookami nobles. Lady Sato was at his right hand, Rinji at his left. I gave thanks to see that there was no sign of sorrow on any of their faces, though the younger shaman was nibbling his lower lip so feverishly that I expected it to bleed at any moment.

As I took my place at Daimu's side, I saw that he was breathing hard and that his skin was flushed. I laid a soothing hand on his shoulder and my touch made him shudder.

I had never seen him so transformed. What was happening here? What had I missed?

Ryu's pitiless laughter from above brought my answer: "There you are at last, Lady Himiko! Have you come to hurl mad accusations against me too? Master Daimu insists that I murdered his uncle, the exile known as Oni. What next? Will I be guilty of *murdering* the pig we'll roast for my son's birth feast?"

"Can you deny you killed him?" Daimu shouted. "Can you swear on your newborn son's life that you are guiltless?"

Ryu's face paled. "How *dare* you! I am our chieftain; I *protect* our people. Oni was left to live unmolested for years, as long as he left us in peace. *He* was the one who chose to attack this village by night and kidnap an innocent boy! What did you want me to do before I acted, Daimu? Wait for him to steal another victim? To *kill* a child? He was dangerous! I did what needed to be done."

"Oh yes, you are the great hero!" Daimu's bitter sarcasm was a slap across the wolf chieftain's face. "Tell me this: Did you *need* to leave my uncle's body unburied, to become food for scavengers? How did *that* protect our people?"

"Silence!" Ryu roared. "Today is dedicated to rejoicing over the birth of this clan's next chieftain. You are our shaman; your job is to shield all of us from unseen evils, from threats that cannot be fought with sword or spear. You should be performing rites of purification, ceremonies to attract the gods' blessings. Instead you rant about the unburied dead. You will bring a swarm of jealous ghosts upon us!"

I could stand no more. "Lord Ryu!" I called out, raising

my arms high to draw every eye to me. "Lord Ryu, hear me! There is only one ghost whose vengeance you should fear. Give Mori's spirit what he should have had many seasons ago!"

"Ah, Lady Himiko." The wolf chieftain smirked and spoke to his nobles: "There she stands, giving commands as if *she* ruled this clan. And yet the moon's face has not changed more than four times since she went clad in rags, emptying the night soil pots in my house!" He burst into laughter.

To his chagrin, none of the nobles joined in the joke. One said, "My lord, she helped Master Daimu perform the springtime rites. We trusted her to bless our crops, and they are already flourishing."

Another added, "When my daughter coughed so hard that she could not catch her breath, Lady Himiko healed her. The child has enjoyed perfect health ever since."

Even Lady Sato spoke up, saying, "Is this how you speak to the shaman whose powers gave me my grandson? Are you *trying* to offend the gods by making fun of their devoted one? Shame on you!"

Their chiding words were backed up by murmurs of agreement from the Ookami around me. One bold soul shouted, "Hear Lady Himiko! Oni's ghost must be appeased!"

Ryu glared at everyone, a man betrayed. Then an idea came to him, for his narrowed eyes opened, his expression relaxed, and he smiled graciously. "Lady Himiko understands that my words are not to be taken seriously. There is a special bond between us now. She remembers all the honors that I offered her for helping bring my son into the world! If she did not choose to accept them . . ." He spread his hands. "Let it be as she says: let there be a grand funeral to lay Oni to rest, body and spirit. It will be a royal burial, at my expense, and I will stand before his tomb to ask forgiveness for us all."

"Only one person here needs to beg my uncle's ghost for pardon," Daimu muttered for my ears alone.

"True, but this is likely to be the best we can expect from Ryu," I whispered back. Aloud, I said: "Thank you, my lord. With your help, we will raise a fine monument for Mori, placate his spirit, and—"

"When?" Ryu asked abruptly.

I tilted my head. "How . . . how can I answer that? You are the one who must give the order to build the tomb. How long do you think it will take to complete?"

"How can I answer that before you bring back Oni's bones?" he replied with a thin, mocking smile. "What good is a tomb that holds nothing?"

"You want us to find his body after so much time has passed?" I objected. "His remains will be scattered by now, maybe even destroyed by birds, by animals, by—!"

"But you are a *shaman,* Lady Himiko," Ryu said, still with that taunting expression. "Perhaps even a greater one than our own Master Daimu, to hear the stories." He spared a moment for quick, cold glances at the nobles who had spoken in my defense. "Is anything impossible for someone with your gifts? Let the gods show their favor for you! Bring home Oni's bones."

I ignored the scorn behind his words. "You'll trust me to go into the mountains?"

"Trust you not to run away, you mean? Ha! I think I can do that . . . unless your feelings for your kinfolk here have changed. And you will not go unattended. Master Daimu should be a part of this. If the gods refuse to guide one of you to his uncle's remains, that is their privilege, but if they turn their backs on you both . . ." His shoulders rose and fell slightly. "Let's hope that doesn't happen. I would hate to ask what such bad luck meant for all of us. So, do we have an agreement?"

I stood straighter. "We do. I will bring back the bones."

"Excellent!" Ryu grinned. "But you must not leave until after we have enjoyed this happy event. Eat! Drink! My wife has given me a son!" He waved one arm imperiously and the people returned to their celebration with renewed enthusiasm.

I looked at Daimu. His jaw was set and his eyes were burning coals of anger. He stalked away from the scene of rejoicing and I followed. He did not stop until he stood in the shadow of an Ookami noble's lofty house. With a wordless cry of frustration and disgust, he struck one of the massive supporting pillars with his fist.

"I *knew* it!" he exclaimed. "I knew that serpent would find a way to slither out of this. He never meant to make amends to my uncle's ghost! Now if any misfortune comes to this clan, he won't take the blame. He'll say it's our fault for having failed to bring back Uncle's body for proper burial."

"*My* fault," I corrected him. "I am the one who must seek the bones."

"No. You can't go into the mountains alone."

"I've done it before," I said. "Not *these* mountains, but still . . . I'm not afraid to do it."

"But I am afraid to let you go, not for Ryu's reasons, but for my own. We will make this trip together."

I was on the point of replying when we were interrupted by the sound of a distinct, artificially forced cough. Someone had come after us and wanted us to be aware of his presence.

"Forgive me, Master Daimu," Rinji said. "I came after you to offer my help in finding Oni's remains. I didn't intend to eavesdrop."

Daimu's anger was gone. He embraced his former apprentice wholeheartedly. "Rinji! It's been too long, my friend. Please tell me that you've changed your mind about coming back to the shrine. I need you!"

Rinji looked at his feet. "I know that's not true."

"What are you talking about? Of course it is!"

"You have Lady Himiko." He stole a quick glance at me before averting his eyes again. "She's a better shaman than I could ever be."

"We are not in competition, Master Rinji," I said, taking his hand. It felt cold and clammy. "We work together, not for ourselves, but for the spirits."

He shook his head briskly. "No. I don't belong there anymore. I wouldn't want to intrude on the two of you there."

"Intrude?" I exchanged a furtive look with Daimu. Lady Sato claimed that the whole village was aware of the love between us. No wonder Rinji was staying away! He had tried to become more than my friend, but I turned him down.

I'd done so gently, but that did not erase the hurt, merely diminished it. Many people had told Rinji he would never be Daimu's equal as a shaman. Now he must also feel as if he would never equal him as a man.

Pity overcame my common sense. "But, Master Rinji, you wouldn't be intruding at all!" I exclaimed, clasping his hands. "You mustn't believe every piece of gossip you hear."

He raised his eyes to mine. "Then the two of you are not—?"

"We are *friends,* Rinji," I told him.

"We are your friends too," Daimu added, as eager as I was to ease his apprentice's unhappiness. "Come back."

"Oh!" His smile was wonderful. "I'd like that, but— but I can't. I mean, I can't live at the shrine anymore. Lord Ryu sent for me this morning. He said that he wants to build a second shrine for our village, one dedicated to the wolf spirit alone. I'm to be in charge of every part of the project. I need to sleep near the site, in case the wolf wants to enter my dreams and tell me his desires."

"We must give the spirits what they want," I agreed. Secretly, I was relieved that Rinji would not be living in the shrine again. "But even with your new responsibility, it would be good to speak with you more often."

"You'd like that? Really?" I felt his fingers tighten in mine. "Even though I stopped your visits to the shrine before Master Daimu's return?"

"You must have had a good reason," I said, wanting to encourage the shy, hopeful look in his eyes. "Let's not worry about what happened in the past. Many things have changed since then, haven't they?"

"I pray that's true, Lady Himiko. I would welcome change. Now please . . . when do you want us to leave this village and begin to search the mountain?"

Daimu intercepted the question before I could reply: "Thank you for the offer, Rinji, but think: it might take days to find my uncle's bones, days you should be spending at the site for the new shrine, waiting for the wolf spirit to speak."

"I wanted to help . . . but I guess you would know what's best, Master Daimu." With a final squeeze of my hand, Rinji released it with much reluctance and declared, "I'll come see you as frequently as I can. Thank you, Himiko; thank you." He hurried away.

"There goes a happy man," Daimu remarked. "And all it took was telling him a lie."

"I have no idea what you're talking about," I said haughtily, which was *another* lie.

"Then what you said to Rinji was true?" Although we were out in public, the Ookami were all elsewhere, joyfully participating in the birth celebrations. No one was near us to see Daimu lovingly twirl a strand of my hair around his fingers and tug me closer to him. "You and I are friends, and nothing more?" It was a good thing that he already knew the answer, because I was too embarrassed to respond. Then, in a more serious tone, he asked: "What do you think will happen when he finds out the truth?"

"If he really is your friend and mine, he'll be glad for us. If not . . ." I sighed. "Do we have to talk about this now? We should get started on our search."

He agreed with me about that, but said, "This isn't something that's going to go away."

"I know." But I hoped it would. I hated painful confrontations. I liked Rinji, even if I could not share the feelings he had for me, and I felt sorry for him. That was why I told such a lie.

I meant well. I was trying to be kind when I should have been honest. In that moment I spared his heartache, but I sealed my own.

15
Knowing What the Gods Desire

I stood in the middle of the clearing where Mori had died and slowly sank to my knees. I was tired in body and soul from a day spent searching every part of the sweet-natured giant's old campsite. Daimu was still somewhere out there in the surrounding forest, moving in gradually widening circles, seeking his uncle's bones. We had found nothing, not even the smallest glimmer of a white finger bone in the thick, new growth of spring.

I rested my face in my hands and sighed. What creatures had come to this lonely place and done such a thorough job of devouring poor Mori's body? Even wolves left bones behind. *Had* there been wolves here? Would they have dragged away a man's remains, taking it elsewhere for their grisly feast? I lifted my face and blinked in the waning sunlight. Soon it would be dark and we would have to go home.

I heard Daimu's approach through the underbrush. He

entered the clearing looking disheveled, his hair a tangle of leaves, his expression the image of complete discouragement.

"Nothing," he said. "I found nothing." He knelt beside me and lifted my hand to his cheek, then kissed me tenderly. "We should head back before darkness comes."

I nodded dully. "We'll have more time to resume our search tomorrow," I said, getting back onto my feet.

"There won't be any more searching." He was a beaten man, deadweight on my arm as I helped him stand.

"You don't think Ryu will allow it? He hasn't got the right to do that, or the power!" I objected. "He might be able to forbid me from coming back here, but how can he stand against his clan's shaman? You're not his prisoner."

"You mistake me, Himiko. Ryu would *like* to see us both come back here again," Daimu said. "And again, and *again*, every day in all weathers, until our forays become a ridiculous joke he'll share with everyone in the village. People like watching others fail. It makes them feel better about their own shortcomings."

"If we return without your uncle's bones, that will count as a failure too."

"But an honest, simple one, soon forgotten."

"Like Mori?" I couldn't help myself. I wanted justice for that mistreated man.

My word stung. Daimu looked at me with pain in his beautiful eyes. I tried to apologize, but he prevented me. "No, you're right. I surrender too easily. I haven't got your strength of spirit, Himiko. I worry too much about how things will look to others. We will come back tomorrow, and the next day, and as long as it takes until we find him.

And if we never do . . ." He sighed. "Let us pray that does not happen. If we could locate even a single bone, it might be enough to deflect his rage and resentment from my clan. Otherwise, I fear it's just a matter of time before my uncle's ghost stops wandering the spirits' realm and swoops down to make us suffer for our neglect."

"I can't imagine Mori taking revenge on anyone," I said. "Not even on the man who killed him. He was such a gentle person."

"Yes, when he was alive. But now?" Daimu shook his head. "The dead have always envied and resented the living."

I thought of Aki, whose love for me had never faltered. I pictured Father, who had cherished me, in spite of his sometimes gruff, hardheaded nature. Now the grinning image of my brother Shoichi was standing with them before me in the mottled shadows of the trees. How he had loved to tease me! Yet it was never done with malice. Little by little, I realized that my memories were becoming something different. I was not merely recalling my father and brothers, I was *seeing* them. In the next breath, sweet Hoshi's ghost joined the gathering of my lost loved ones, her affectionate smile as warm as any embrace. I heard her speak: *Dear Little Sister, now you know what it is to find the true love of your life. I am so happy!* Last of all, Lady Yama appeared, her white hair streaming with starlight as she said, *My Himiko, see how your gifts have thrived! How proud I am of you, dear child.* There was not a hint of jealousy or rancor in any one of them. They faded from sight, leaving behind nothing but their love.

"You're wrong, Daimu," I said, slowly coming back

from the place where my unbidden vision had taken me. "Your uncle would never take revenge on his clan, no matter how badly they abused him in life. That kind of meanness isn't in his nature, not even now, and it never will be. But that doesn't mean we have the right to ignore what his spirit needs to rest in peace."

He put his arms around me. "Then it will be as you say: we'll come back tomorrow. We'll explore every part of this mountain, seeking him, and if that isn't enough, we will search farther still. Above all, we will pray that the gods pity us and guide our steps where they need to go."

"The gods . . ." All at once I pushed away from him with both hands. "The gods!" I cried. "Daimu, we're fools! We've been seeking Mori's remains with weak, human eyes. No wonder we've failed! Why haven't we sought the spirits' help and guidance?"

He gave me a crooked smile. "Because you are right again, my love: we're fools. But we can correct that tomorrow."

"No, we'll do it *now*." I did not wait for him to consent. Glancing around the clearing, I sought the spot where Mori's body once lay. Time had passed, blurring my memory of that awful moment, but I put my faith in the guiding power of the spirits who inhabited that place and felt drawn to one particular patch of ground. Here I knelt, folded my hands in my lap, closed my eyes, and waited.

Himiko? I don't know how long it was before that small voice came to me, a firefly presence in my mind. *Himiko, why did you come back?* A child stood alone in the darkness, toying nervously with his fingers. He was young, but already tall and as sturdily built as the trunk of a great tree. *Have you come to punish me? Did I do something wrong*

again? I try to be good, but I'm always so clumsy, and it's hard to
understand. . . . He wept, as vulnerable as a newly hatched
baby bird.

A phantom image of the forest clearing took shape
around us. I sensed that my calm seeking had brought me
into a place where the spirits' world overlay our own. There
was no need for me to speak as I stretched out my arms to
the little boy, taking him into my lap. *You did nothing wrong,*
dear Mori, I comforted him. *I came back because I wanted to see*
you again, that's all, and to bring you home.

Home? His eyes grew large, brimming with tears. *At last?*

Yes. That's where you belong. Would you like that, Little
Brother?

He snuggled against me. *Will I see Mama again?*

You will. She's waiting for me to bring you back to her. I stroked
his thick, coarse hair. *Tell me where to find you and we can go.*

He knew what I meant. Some things did not need to
be explained in the realm of the spirits. We stood and he
took me by the hand, leading me out of the clearing to the
base of a broad-bodied oak tree. It looked no different to
me than any of its companions, but the child Mori insisted
I go closer, to where a patch of wild briars seemed to grow
against the tree's flank.

Here we are, he said cheerfully. He placed one plump
hand on the thorns. Their sharp points were as insubstan-
tial as his flesh, so there was no way they could do him any
harm. It would be another story when I sought out the living counterpart of those prickles in the real world. *This is*
where she hid me.

Lady Badger. She came back. She was going back to her home, but she stopped long enough to visit me. She was very unhappy when she saw what they had done to me—the birds and the animals of the forest. I tried to tell her it was all right; I didn't mind. I was used to their company. He sighed. *She cried anyway. I think it was because they had taken away so much of me and made a mess of what was left.* He looked at me. *My mama didn't like it when I was messy, either. You girls are funny about that kind of thing, aren't you?*

Yes, I said through my own tears. *Yes, we are.*

When she stopped crying, she gathered everything together and put me here, between the tree and the thorns. Do you want to see?

Not yet, Little Brother, I told him, wiping my eyes with the edge of one sleeve. *In a little while, when I am able to take you from this place and bring you home.*

His loving, grateful smile was the only farewell he gave me before he faded away. I opened my eyes and sobbed.

Daimu was with me before I could take a second breath. I clung to him, my body shaking with misery. Not even the touch of his lips to my brow could console me. "My poor Himiko," he said tenderly. "You found him."

Night began to fall while we were on the path back from the mountain, but we were able to reach the settlement before full dark. As soon as the sentries recognized us and proclaimed the news of our return, many villagers came running to meet us. Some brought lights. They were probably expecting us to be empty-handed, but when they saw what we carried, their cries roused more of the Ookami.

Torches multiplied almost as fast as exclamations of awe tinged with fear. By the time Ryu made his way to where we waited, it felt as if the entire wolf clan was standing witness.

We could not cross the threshold of the Ookami village; we carried the dead. What we did, before everyone assembled, was lay out the bones with care and reverence. Some small pieces were missing, but the larger ones could be set in their rightful places. The birds of the air and the hungry creatures of the wilderness had laid them bare. Torchlight played over the eyeless sockets of Mori's skull, and his ribs stood out like the limbless trees of a plague-struck forest. When we were done, we folded our hands and looked steadily at Ryu. There was no need to declare we had fulfilled our quest. The bones had their own eloquence.

"Bones . . ." Ryu stroked his chin, staring at the fleshless remains. "But are they *his* bones? How do we know that for sure?"

"See for yourself, my lord," Daimu replied, holding back any show of emotion. "Look at their size. My uncle was no ordinary man." He looked over one shoulder at me and raised his voice so that everyone there would hear him say: "And his bones were found by no ordinary woman!"

Calmly, proudly, he began to recount all that I had told him about how Mori's own spirit had chosen me to discover his resting place. Ryu listened in tense silence, but the Ookami whispered excitedly among themselves, many pressing forward to try and catch sight of the long, bleeding tracks of briars that scored my hands.

The young chieftain stooped for a closer look at what

we had brought back. He did not dare touch the remains; he would not risk bringing the taint of death into his home, where his newborn son slumbered. Finally he nodded. "It would be a terrible thing if our forests had been haunted by two such monsters. This must be Oni's body."

"His name was *Mori*," I said. "And he was no monster."

"I didn't ask to hear your opinion," Ryu said fiercely. "You may serve the gods and have some *small* gift for healing, but remember: you are a captive! A slave!"

"Well, she shouldn't be!"

I never found out who shouted that protest into the stillness of the late spring night. All I knew was that as soon as those words took flight, their sentiment was echoed by one voice after another.

"How can we hold her? She's a shaman, favored by the spirits! If we keep her prisoner, the gods will avenge this insult!"

"She's a healer beyond compare. If we don't show her the proper honor, she'll turn her skills against us, and our children!"

"She saved the life of our chieftain's wife and son. She commands the powers of life and death!"

"She opened the gates of the other world to bring back Oni's bones. If we don't please her, she'll summon forth the spirits of all the dead to attack us!"

"Set her free, Lord Ryu! Free her before she *takes* her freedom and destroys us!"

"Release her, or we'll be facing the wrath of the gods!"

"Even Master Daimu bows before her. Let her go!"

"What difference will it make if we have one slave more or less? We can't sleep secure at night if she remains a captive. The spirits will punish us if we do nothing!"

"Enough, enough, *enough*!" Ryu bawled over the din. The voice that had commanded an army to devastate the clans around his own was loud enough to quell the uproar raised by his people. Panting for breath, he glowered at the crowd. "Do you *hear* yourselves? You're infants, whimpering at shadows!"

An older man came forward. He was dressed in silk, the sign of the nobly born. His gray hair marked him as one who had served Ryu's father and was now compelled to give his allegiance to Lord Nago's son.

"My lord, hear your people," he said gravely. "Remember, I was there when your father visited the Matsu clan, seeking an alliance. I saw you leave our meeting with Lady Himiko, and I saw you return. On that day you started out well pleased at the chance to spend time with such a lovely young girl, but you came back drenched to the skin, reeking with mud and other filth, so furious you couldn't speak. She was no longer in your company. We never asked what happened between the two of you that day, but I can guess: she humiliated you somehow. She wounded your pride so deeply that you cannot let go of that day, even after so many more have passed."

"Be quiet," Ryu grumbled. He would not look at the older man. "You know nothing about this. I am chieftain of this clan, and—!"

"—and she is a shaman who has proved her power!

Yesterday, in front of us all, you declared that you *protect* us. Then do it! Stop treating Lady Himiko as the girl who wounded your pride. Give her the respect she deserves as one who speaks with the spirits. Lord Ryu, do not tempt the gods!"

A great roar of agreement went up from the Ookami, sweeping away all possible arguments Ryu might have raised. He was not stupid; he read the signs. If he wanted to keep his place as chieftain, he would have to concede.

"Lady Himiko . . ." He pronounced my name so quietly, in such rough tones that at first I was not sure if he had spoken to me at all. His back was bowed in defeat. "Lady Himiko, you have your freedom. You can return to your people tomorrow. No one will stop you. May you have . . . a good road."

"My lord," I said, making a brief gesture of respect to him. "My lord, with your permission, I would like to stay here for a little longer." I hooded my eyes, avoiding Daimu's gaze. "I cannot go home yet."

Ryu's spine straightened. His head lifted like a dog's, catching the scent of prey. "And why is that, Lady Himiko?" he demanded. "It's about the brat, your brother, isn't it?" He curled his lip as he looked at the gray-haired Ookami nobleman. "That's what brought her here, you know," he told him. "That's why Oni died, trying to steal one of *our* rightful hostages, for her! Shall I give her what she wants? Shall I send the Matsu chieftain's son back to his clan, free to grow up and assume his father's role? Free to reach manhood and raise an army? Free to march against *us,* some day?"

The older man's face flushed. "I do not ask for that, Lord Ryu. We must hold on to our hostages, especially those from the more distant lands we've conquered. It guarantees peace."

"Oh, good. For a moment I wondered if this girl's magic had turned *all* of your blood to milk," Ryu sneered. He looked at me again. "Lady Himiko, I gave you your freedom. Stay or go."

I met his stare with defiance. "I will not go before I can take my brother Noboru with me. I will not leave this village without him, or without my other brother, and my stepmother as well!"

"Is that the only thing keeping you here?" Ryu regarded Daimu and drawled. "How disappointing."

My beloved ignored the jibe. "Lord Ryu, how much longer do you want us all to stand here, watching the night pass? I need someone to bring me a suitable container for my uncle's bones until you can make arrangements for the funeral you promised him."

"It shall be done, Master Daimu." The wolf chieftain's friendly expression was thin as an eggshell. "I understand your eagerness to spread out your bedroll. These sweet spring nights will soon turn very cold for you."

He gave a series of terse commands, and soon two young men came rushing up with an empty clay storage jar. How they trembled as they handled the giant's bones!

I patted one of them on the shoulder. "Can you find an empty house to shelter this until Mori's tomb is ready? We cannot keep his remains in the shrine."

He tensed at my touch. "We'll do our best, Lady Himiko," he answered quickly. They hoisted the jar and dashed out of sight.

Ryu chuckled. "See how fast a man can run when fear drives him! I should learn a lesson from those two: fulfill Lady Himiko's wishes swiftly, or live in terror of her *powers* striking you down. My people, hear me! At dawn we will begin work on the grand tomb for Daimu's uncle. Our work will be everything the gods could desire. Oni's spirit will be sent to its eternal home royally, with all the rites, honors, and sacrifices fit for our greatest chieftains! He will enter the other world dressed in silks, heaped with riches"—Ryu held my eyes as he concluded—"attended in death."

PART III
DRAGONS

16

BONES AND CLAY

"What did he mean by that?" I asked Daimu as we walked to draw water from the well. Our contact with Mori's bones meant we needed to be purified before we could serve the spirits again, a cleansing ritual as simple as it was essential and compulsory. "What did Ryu mean when he said your uncle's spirit would be 'attended in death'?"

"It was a command to our village pottery-maker," Daimu explained. "She'll have to begin work on the clay figurines that will share the tomb with my uncle."

"Figurines?" This was something unfamiliar to me.

"We cannot send our most important people to the spirits without the comforts they enjoyed in life. The potter and her apprentices will make images of everything my uncle will need in the next world: food, a house, many servants . . ."

"We Matsu don't do such things," I said, watching him drop the empty water vessel into the depths of the well.

"You mean that your chieftains, nobles, and shamans go to the spirits in poverty?" Daimu was so astonished, he nearly lost his grip on the rope.

My pride was hurt on behalf of my kin. "We bury them with other types of offerings: pots and bowls, glass beads and ornaments, sometimes bronze mirrors. I wouldn't call that *poverty*."

"Yes, but without servants, who looks after their needs in the spirits' realm? If they have to do everything for themselves, how will they be recognized as worthy people?" He pulled up the filled vessel and set it on his shoulder as we pointed our footsteps toward the shrine.

"Maybe the spirits think that truly admirable people need no one else to take care of them. They stand on their own, independent and capable."

"Do you think our ways are wrong?" Daimu looked genuinely concerned about my opinion.

I set his mind at ease: "Your ways are right for your people. I am not entitled to criticize them, and the gods would punish me for arrogance if they thought I was mocking Ookami customs just because they are not the same as what we Matsu follow."

We could not enter the shrine in our present condition, so we turned aside at the house where Ashi and Daimu's other servants dwelled. They were waiting for us, having witnessed our return with the giant's bones. No one had to tell them that we would need to perform a purification rite; they knew, and had readied everything we would need. They had even fetched and filled three additional water pots.

With the women's help, I was soon cleansed and fit to stand before the gods once more. I entered the shrine with my heart singing, happy to feel the sacredness of that consecrated space surrounding me. My bare feet slid across the smooth floorboards as though they did not need me to lead them into a dance of gratitude and rejoicing. Mori's bones no longer lay abandoned in the wilderness! He would be laid to rest with royal honors and his spirit would know lasting peace.

When Daimu returned from the conclusion of his own purification rite, he found me dancing. "Celebrating your freedom?" he asked.

I paused in midstep. "I was thanking the gods for helping us find your uncle," I said. "But I should thank them for that as well."

I moved to resume my dance only to have Daimu's arms encircle me and hold me close to him. His breath stirred my hair. "Will the gods punish me if I *don't* thank them for setting you free?"

Turning around to face him, I frowned and said: "Maybe they won't, but I will! How can you say such a thing? Do you want me to remain a slave?"

"I want you to remain *here*," he responded. "With me, forever."

"Daimu . . ." His words made me irrationally afraid.

"Don't speak of this, Himiko." One of his fingers rested on my lips, light as a kiss. "Nothing either of us can say has the power to untangle what must happen. You have to go back to your people, bringing Noboru home for your mother's sake. That will be hard enough to do, but even if you can achieve it, would you leave your stepmother and your other little brother behind?"

"No." I nestled against him, inhaling a fragrance of clean water and pine boughs. "No more than I could ever leave you."

He gave a glad cry and clasped me so close that I felt as if the gods were about to take pity on us and make us a single person sharing one heart and one spirit. Then he let me go, and the enchantment was broken.

"We will find the answer we seek, my beloved," he said, beaming. "As long as I know that you don't *want* to leave me, now that your freedom is restored, I'll strive with everything I have to discover a way for all of our desires to come true. Your family will not be slaves any longer, your mother will be saved, and you and I will be—"

"Together," I said, framing his face with my hands. "Always."

The next morning, Rinji appeared in our doorway shortly after Daimu and I had eaten breakfast. The servants were almost as overjoyed as we were to welcome him back, from which I guessed that he had been a very kindhearted master. That made me glad because I liked him.

Rinji was eager to do well, to live up to Daimu's faith in him, and to earn the respect of his clan and the favor of the spirits. He was also still haunted by his teacher's exceptional skills and reputation. I wanted to tell him *Stop worrying about how brilliant Daimu is and how badly you fear to have him outshine you. You are not Daimu. Be* Rinji, *and kindle your own light!*

That morning the three of us enjoyed a friendly visit. Daimu and I were careful to behave as though we were only friends while in Rinji's company. It was not difficult: he was my friend as well as my beloved, and I looked forward to the day when I might be able to introduce him to Kaya. What would Lady Badger have to say about him? Would she feel jealous, having to share her place in my heart? Somehow I thought she would understand and give us her blessing. She would always be my dearest friend and companion, but if the gods allowed, Daimu would become my husband, the father of our children, the spirit whose hand would never let go of mine in this world and the next.

"You should see what's happening at the burial ground, Master Daimu!" Rinji exclaimed, his eyes bright with excitement as he told him the news. "Lord Ryu must have rallied the workers before dawn. They've already laid out the boundaries of Oni's tomb and are nearly done digging it as deep as it must go."

"Not Oni's tomb, Master Rinji," I said patiently. "A man named *Mori* will rest there."

"Oh! Excuse me, Lady Himiko, I'm sorry!" he cried, deeply upset by his error. "It's just that everyone else calls him O—by that name."

"Which does not make it *right.*"

"No, certainly not, forgive me. Why am I so stupid?"

"I have a better question for you, my friend," Daimu said, clapping him on the back. "Why are we still *Lady* this and *Master* that when there is no further difference among us? We are all shamans, all walking the same path."

"Daimu is right," I said. "You have been entrusted with the care of our village's new shrine. As soon as the wolf spirit visits you and makes his wishes known, it can be built. I wager it will become at least as important as this one, if not more so. We must be Rinji and Daimu and Himiko to one another. High-sounding titles have no place between friends."

Rinji smiled hesitantly. "You helped me find confidence once before, La—Himiko. Now you and Daimu renew that gift. I have something else to tell you, but I was afraid to do so until now. I thought the news would make you angry, and that you would blame me for something that was never my idea."

"Well, tell us!" Daimu exclaimed with an encouraging expression. "How bad can it be?"

"That's just it: I don't know," Rinji said. "When the tomb is finished . . . I am the one who will perform the burial rites for your uncle. Lord Ryu wants it so." He glanced anxiously from Daimu to me, expecting an outburst.

"Is that all?" Daimu's smile remained unshaken. "Then I must thank Lord Ryu for this. He's doing all of us a great kindness. By having you send my uncle's spirit to the next world, he is letting the whole clan know he has full trust in your abilities. He also gives me the chance to mourn Uncle without distraction, as a grieving nephew, not as a shaman concentrating on executing each step of the ritual exactly."

"I . . ." Rinji scratched his head. "I have never had to

carry out the duties of a funeral. You taught me all about it when I was your apprentice, but this is an *actual* burial."

"You mustn't worry," Daimu reassured him. "Just remember our lessons. The way we comfort the dead is always the same."

He was wrong.

Mori's tomb was rising rapidly. Daimu took me to see the progress that was being made on building the great, square-sided mound that would hold his uncle's bones. The Ookami burial ground lay far enough from the settlement to keep the dead at a safe distance from the living, but close enough to make the trek there reasonable. It was situated on flat land in the lee of a small hill that hid sight of the graves from both the village and the cultivated fields set out along the opposite side of the valley.

I shielded my eyes from the sun and studied the mound. "It looks almost ready," I remarked.

"You're right," Daimu said. "Yesterday I came out here to speak with the workmen. They told me that the stone lining of the interior is done and that all they're waiting for are orders about the placement of the grave goods and clay attendants."

"I wonder how much longer that will take," I mused.

"What's the hurry? Uncle has waited patiently this long. A few more days aren't going to bother his spirit."

I dropped my voice so that the workers would not be able to overhear. "A few more days and Ryu will be able to turn his full attention to me again. Daimu, I think he's going to grab the first chance he gets to send me away. He hates me for many humiliations, and we just gave him a new one: he wanted me to *stay* a slave."

"What's wrong with that man?" Daimu muttered. "You saved his wife and son!"

"He hates that too. No one likes being indebted, but it's worse when the person to whom you owe so much is the same one you think of as your enemy."

"He's a fool, then."

"No, he's smart; too smart. It won't take him long to realize my freedom has given him the best weapon he could ever hope to use against me. I have no further place in this village. I do not belong to this clan. I am not an Ookami slave. I am not necessary as a hostage. He's going to send me away, and I will leave here empty-handed, without my brother Noboru, without my kin."

Daimu spread his arms without thinking, wanting to hold me close and drive away anything that could bring me hurt or sorrow. Love made him forget where we were and who would see us, but I was aware of the workmen's idle, curious eyes. In order to dodge his embrace, I had to pretend to stumble away from him. Unfortunately, I caught my heel on the hem of my dress and fell in earnest, sprawled across one of the lesser graves.

"Himiko!" Daimu cried. As I began to fall, he lunged forward, trying to save me from such an ill-omened accident. He only succeeded in tripping himself. He landed with his face in the dirt of the burial ground.

A loud gasp went up from many throats. The tomb builders witnessed our mischance, horrified, but not one of them made a move to approach us. We had to pick ourselves up and brush the dust of the dead from our clothes.

"Don't worry; we're not hurt!" Daimu called out to them. They averted their eyes. Daimu gave me a half smile and whispered, "How do you like being invisible?"

"Why are they acting this way?" I asked.

"They're afraid our bad luck is contagious. They don't want to risk catching a curse."

"What if we'd been injured? Would they *leave* us where we fell?"

"Not forever. If they even *suspected* we needed aid, they'd find a way to bring someone from the village—someone who wasn't here for the accident. It would be safe for him to see us and take care of us."

I stared at the workmen, still annoyed at their callous behavior. "Those men need to learn the difference between respecting the dead and being so afraid of them that it paralyzes you."

"They're not the only ones," Daimu said. "In my travels I encountered many clans. One thing they all had in common was that very fear."

"Hmph." I raised one eyebrow. "If I could make people believe I had the power to raise ghosts, I could rule more clans with a single word than Ryu does now with a thousand swords." My tone made it clear that I was not serious.

"You'll need to wash your clothes first, O mighty ruler," Daimu said, joining in the joke. "You have a stain that looks like a giant salamander is trying to climb up your backside. Give your dress to Ashi when we get home."

"I have a better idea," I said. "I haven't gone to visit Emi and Sanjirou for several days and I miss them. She'll be glad to have the chance to tidy me up, the way she did when I was small."

"Do what makes you happiest."

I could not go to Emi's out-of-the-way house immediately. Daimu and I *had* taken a tumble in the burial ground and that meant we *did* need to cleanse ourselves. Once again the servants helped us, and soon I was bathed, combed, and clad in the shabby dress I wore when tidying the shrine, ready to depart.

"I'll be back soon," I told Daimu, my stained dress in a neatly folded bundle tucked under one arm.

"Take your time." He sounded preoccupied, and his eyes were fixed on something only he could see.

"Don't miss me *too* much," I said dryly, and left.

I was not gone very long, but in that short time, everything changed.

"Lady Himiko? What's happened? Are you ill?"

I staggered through the Ookami village, hearing many voices clamoring to know what was wrong with me. How could I tell them the truth? How could I make them see that a ruthless demon had reached up from the core of the world to tear the ground from under my feet? They would think I was out of my mind.

"Leave me alone," I muttered, slapping away any hands that tried to hold me back. "Let me pass. I have to see Master Daimu. Get out of my way." I reached the shrine ladder and half climbed, half crawled my way to the top. My head throbbed and burned, and although my eyes were dry, despair blurred my vision.

Daimu was where I'd left him, seated on a mat in the center of the floor. He was all smiles. "Back so soon, my love? Wonderful! I have excellent news for you: I've found the answer to your worries about being sent away. After my uncle's funeral, all we need to do is—"

"They're gone, Daimu." The words nearly choked me. "Emi and Sanjirou are gone. They were taken away this morning, while we were at the burial ground. A woman who lives next door to their house told me what happened and why. I didn't believe her. It was too horrible. I went to the pottery-maker's workshop to find out if it was Ryu playing a hideous joke, but when I got there—when I got there—" An invisible fist tightened around my chest and I fought to breathe.

"Himiko, what are you saying?" This time Daimu was able to catch me before I collapsed. He scooped me up like a child and carried me into my sleeping chamber, where he kicked my bedroll open and set me down. I tossed my head, begging him to let me speak, but he had gone to fetch a bowl of water. I watched him crumble a pinch of dried herbs into the bowl before he slipped one arm behind my neck, helped me raise my head, and set the cool liquid to my lips. I drank only a few swallows before shoving it away and sitting up on my own.

"Let me speak, Daimu. The words will poison me if I don't get them out."

"Yes, I understand," he said earnestly, his eyes on mine. "Tell me everything. You went to see the village pottery-maker, the one who's crafting the figures for my uncle's tomb, and . . ."

"There will be no servants of clay to accompany Mori into the spirits' realm," I said, forlorn. "He will be given six human escorts to serve him there: a man, his two wives, their son and daughter. She's only ten years old, but the potter tells me she was chosen because she—she loves to dance and will be able to entertain your uncle's spirit."

"A child . . ." Daimu looked sick to his stomach. "And—and the sixth?"

"Emi," I said. "My second mother. Daimu . . . the family that has been picked to die are also Matsu. Each sacrifice Ryu chose belongs to my people."

Daimu's fingers knotted in my hair. "I know that this practice happens in other clans. I never saw it done with my own eyes, but I was told about it on my travels. Having human slaves go into the tomb instead of clay figures is supposed to be a sign of the supreme importance of the person being buried."

"My clan never did any such thing," I said. "We never even buried clay images. I told you that."

"We use *only* pottery figures to accompany our dead," Daimu said. "What demon's whisper gave Ryu the idea of sacrificing human beings?"

"No demon but the past. Your image-maker is an old woman. She told me that she recalls a time when the Ookami chieftains left this world in the company of those who had served them best while they were alive. Oh, Daimu, I don't

care if Ryu received this awful idea from the gods themselves; I just want to stop him!"

"How?" He looked at me, wanting an easy answer.

"I—I don't—"

He could not wait for me to think. "We could appear
before the people and declare that this sacrifice has made
the spirits angry! We should put on our most impressive
clothes and ornaments, dress the shrine servants in finery
to accompany us, carry as many mirrors as we can grasp or
hang from our necks! I'll tell everyone that I had a vision in
which fire consumed the entire village the moment a hand
was raised to sacrifice the slaves!"

"Daimu, we can't do that," I said sadly. "If we betray
the trust that the gods have given us to be their faithful
servants, they will abandon us and our people. Our lives
will turn to chaos."

"I know," he said. "Even when I was telling you that plan,
my heart was crying out that it was wrong. I never would have
been able to do it." A hopeful afterthought came to him. "Do
you think Rinji could do it?"

"Would you sacrifice him like that? He's our friend."

Daimu hung his head. "I'm sorry. I'm not myself.
The thought of those people dying for nothing—your
stepmother—that child—!" Now he was the one who
needed comfort.

As I held him in my arms, I felt a change come over me.
My wild anguish for the fate of my condemned kin faded,
replaced by a strong sense of determination and conviction. *Tears will not save them,* I thought. *Tricks that bargain with*

the goodwill of the gods will destroy us all. And as for going to Ryu and begging him to change his mind about this dreadful plan . . . I know better than to waste my breath on that. There is only one way to rescue the sacrifices.

I said nothing to Daimu. It was not the time for confidences. I did not want him to know my plans. Ryu hated him and would be ecstatic for the chance of making him suffer with me if my scheme failed. I refused to give the vindictive wolf chieftain such a gift.

"Hush, my love," I murmured as though he were a wakeful child. "Your uncle would never want others to die for his sake. Let's pray his spirit finds its way into Ryu's dreams and gives him no peace until he sees how terribly this path of his must end. Believe in the mercy of the gods."

"Do you?" he asked weakly. "Even after all the tragedies your clan has suffered?"

"I do," I said. It was no lie, though if he had insisted I explain how I could still have faith in divine compassion when my kin and I had lost so much, I would not have been able to find the words.

I cannot use a sword to shoot an arrow. I cannot use words to account for what I feel about the spirits. I accept this.

But I also accept that there are times when I cannot wait to find out which path leads me where the gods desire. I must clear the way and create my own.

By the time Mori's tomb was ready, I had learned much about the preparations for the human sacrifice. It was easy to find out whatever I wanted to know, such as where my kin were being kept and what measures were being taken to prevent their escape. The Ookami themselves provided the information willingly. Now that I was no longer a slave, they saw me only as a respected shaman and were eager to share conversation. From what I gathered, it was considered a mark of great favor to be in my company.

Lady Sato confirmed this. Ryu's status-hungry mother sent daily invitations for me to visit her. I ignored nearly all of them, making one exception because I wanted to see how Chizu and the baby were doing. Now, however, I made it a point to go to Ryu's house, taking pains to make sure he would be absent. My aged hostess's love of gossip was a gift from the gods. She confirmed everything that I had already heard from other Ookami and gave me the priceless knowledge that my younger brother Sanjirou was allowed to remain with his mother until the day of her death.

Thank the gods! I thought. *This will make it easier to free them both at once.*

There was a burdensome price to pay for every scrap of information Lady Sato provided: I had to endure the meanness of her company. She was one of those disturbing souls who took more pleasure from other people's bad luck than from their own good fortune. Her tongue wagged eagerly over the impending funeral rites, especially the matter of the sacrifice.

"My dear Lady Himiko, it's always so nice to have you in our humble home," she greeted me. "And I must say, every time you come here, it is an inspiration to see what a brave face you wear! I know that if *my* kin were being sent to their deaths so soon, I would not be able to bear it. I would lie down on my bedroll and never get up again!

Of course I have a *very* sensitive, sympathetic nature. It's a curse. If only I could be as aloof as you!"

I smiled. I would not let her think that her words had the power to touch me. "You mistake me, Lady Sato," I said as pleasantly as I could. "If I came here and revealed my true feelings about the fate awaiting the chosen captives, it might upset the baby."

"Oh, you needn't worry that something as trivial as a girl's tears will bother our little hero!" Lady Sato lifted her chin and smiled. "Arashi has a warrior's spirit and grows stronger every day. He takes after my father that way, as well as bearing his name." She beamed at Chizu, who was seated between us, happily nursing her child. "You will have my blessings forever, dearest Daughter, for choosing to honor that good man. And to think my own son would have named the child Katsuro. Where did he get such a name? Thank the gods *you* are more thoughtful of an old woman's feelings." There was not a trace left of the old woman's former contempt for her daughter-in-law.

"It was an easy choice, Mother," Chizu said placidly, never taking her eyes from the baby's face. "I have heard your father's virtues praised by many people. Names are important, especially one that a future chieftain bears."

"Who would have suspected you to be so wise, my sweet girl?" Lady Sato gushed. "When my son conceded the privilege of naming the child to you, in thanks for bearing a son after going through such a perilous delivery, I confess that I had my doubts. I feared you might give the precious boy an ill-omened name."

"How could I have done that?" Chizu asked.

"By naming him after anyone cowardly, malformed, weak minded, sickly, lazy, too fat, too skinny, too smart for his own good"—she counted off a list of forbidden conditions on her fingers—"or after a person who failed to enjoy a long, healthy life. And think of how awful it would have been if you'd chosen the same name as one of our male captives! We don't want my grandson's fate linked to a slave's!" She gave me a look of feigned compassion. "Especially not one of the Matsu slaves escorting dear Master Daimu's uncle to the spirits' realm."

"Yes, Mother." Chizu shifted the infant to her other breast and sighed. "Poor things. They don't have much longer to wait. Didn't you tell me that the tomb is finished?"

"Indeed. The burial will take place in three days. I don't see why there has to be such a wait, but Rinji—I beg your pardon, *Master* Rinji—told my son the spirits wish it to be so."

"Great events require the gods' approval," I said quietly. "It's best for us if we ask them to choose auspicious days."

"Well, Master Rinji took his time getting an answer! He *claimed* there was some disturbance at work preventing him from speaking with them." Her tone implied that the real cause for the delay was Rinji's fault.

"I believe that," Chizu said. "There's been a strange sensation in the air for a few days now. I keep waking up in the middle of the night with my skin prickling, and not just when Arashi cries. It feels like something's wrong, but I don't know what it is."

"If you don't know what's the matter, then everything

is fine," Lady Sato said crisply. "My goodness, Chizu, you have the silliest fancies."

"She might be right, Lady Sato," I said. "Such things exist: premonitions."

"Don't tell me you've had the same *oh-dear-something's-wrong-but-nothing's-wrong* feelings, Lady Himiko?" She tried sweetening her patronizing words with a solicitous manner.

"If so, I haven't noticed," I told her. "Other things are on my mind."

"Of course they are." She patted my hand. "This waiting must be so dreadful for you, but at least now you know when it will end. I think we'll all be glad to have Oni's funeral behind us."

"Will I have to attend the ceremony?" Chizu asked with a little shudder. Arashi sensed the tension radiating from his mother and began to fuss.

"Don't worry; you can stay home. The burial ground is no place for a new mother." Lady Sato looked at me again, grinning so wide that I could see her gums. "I do hope *you* will be there, Lady Himiko?"

"You can count on that, dear Lady Sato."

Three days . . .

It was not a long time, but I had been making plans ever since I'd learned of Ryu's heartless intentions toward my people.

It must be after nightfall when I take them from their prison, I thought, pacing the floor of my sleeping chamber. *Once I lead them out of this accursed village, I'll give them supplies and directions for the long journey ahead and set them on the right road for home. After they're gone I'll make sure that they aren't tracked and brought back. This must be carefully timed.* *Rinji had great difficulties discovering the divinely approved day for Mori's interment. Ryu would not dare postpone the ceremony and risk angering the gods. Setting them free on the eve of the funeral would be best, but cutting it close. If I can set things in motion the night before that, they'd have a greater head start and it would still be close enough to the ceremony to make hunting them down impossible. All right, it's settled; with the gods' help, that's what I'll do!*

What I meant to accomplish sounded as simple as a child's game. *How* I would be able to accomplish it was not. There was one factor on which everything depended: the Ookami guards.

Two of them stood between my condemned kin and freedom: one stationed at the doorway of the isolated old pit house holding them, one in the village watchtower. During my conversations with Lady Sato and the other Ookami, I learned that the fellow assigned to the nighttime sentry post was a high-ranking noble's son. He was an easy-going, apathetic young man who would have been beaten for his idle nature if he'd been lowborn. The wolf clan gossips nattered over how surprised everyone was when Lord Ryu entrusted the security of the settlement to such a loafer.

"Maybe he thinks it will give that slug a sense of responsibility," one of them said.

"And maybe he'll doze off in the dark when a fire breaks out and we'll all die in our sleep!" came the reply.

I listened to their fretting and smiled to myself, thanking Ryu for putting that lazybones in the watchtower.

The guard on night duty at the house was another

story. The Ookami rumor-mongers liked telling me all the faults of the men who minded the captives by day, but they had nothing bad to say about the lone warrior who stood watch at night. When they brought his name into our conversation, I gave a little start: *Hiroshi! The same Hiroshi I know, or another one?* Some praised him honestly for his many virtues, but he was a grave disappointment to Lady Sato.

"*That* boy," she said with a derisive sniff. "Oh, how *seriously* he takes himself, as if he belonged to the aristocracy. Everyone knows his father was an ordinary farmer. The spirits chose to give the lad a handsome face, so he probably thinks he can attract the attention of some nobleman's ugly daughter and marry his way into a better family. Ha! Good luck to him!"

Other tongues were kinder, speaking of his stainless reputation, of how courteous he was, how dutiful, how brave. I wondered which reports to believe until the night I stole near to the pit house where my kin languished. I wanted to take the measure of the man I would have to outwit if Emi and the others were going to survive.

I crept along the side of the run-down old house and tried to peer at him without sticking my head completely around the corner. It was no good: there was only a crescent moon to light the darkness, so I had to crane my neck farther before I could make out his face.

If I can just get a quick look before he spies me . . . , I thought. Then I saw him, and no longer had to wonder. *He is that Hiroshi: the young guard who saved Kaya from his brutish partner, the same one who was kind to me as well, when I was left alone. I have to get him out of the way when it's time for the escape, but whatever means I use, he must not come to any lasting harm. What shall I—?*

"You!" The young guard's voice rang out, interrupting my thoughts. He leveled his spear in my direction. "I see you! What are you doing here? Explain!"

I moved out of hiding. "I'm sorry," I said, approaching him with my hands spread wide so that he could see I carried nothing worthy of suspicion. "I didn't intend to cause trouble. All I wanted was to see where my clanfolk are being kept."

"Lady Himiko?" He stood straighter, and though the moonlight remained faint, I could see his look of sympathy. "You've come to say good-b—to visit them?"

"If I may."

"I guess so." He rubbed the nape of his neck. "I don't have any orders forbidding it, but you should have come in the daytime. If you hadn't spoken up and shown yourself right away, I might have thrown my spear, and then . . ." He shivered.

"These people will die in just a few days. They are my kin," I told him. "One is my father's widow, my second mother. Her death will leave my brother Sanjirou an orphan."

"So that's the little boy's name," Hiroshi said, half to himself. "Sometimes I bring him and the girl a bit of dried fruit or a morsel of honeycomb. She thanks me for it, but he never accepts anything I offer him."

"He's a chieftain's son," I said. "What you see as a small kindness, he sees as taking a bribe from his enemy."

"Oh. Well, I wish he'd change his mind. I'm on duty when the prison—your clanfolk get their evening meal, and they're never brought more than six bowls of food. No one cares if Sanjirou stays with his mother while he can, but I think Lord Ryu doesn't really like it. He won't pick a fight with the boy, but he won't make it comfortable for the lad to remain here. I'd feel better if he'd share my dinner with me, but . . ." He shrugged.

"Perhaps I can change his mind," I said, and slipped through the doorway.

The roof of the old pit house had many places where the thatch had fallen or been pulled away by the weight of many winters' snows. Weak glints of moonlight filtered through the gaps, just enough for me to catch a glimpse of Emi's face before she embraced me.

"Himiko!" she cried, pressing her cheek to mine. "I thought I heard your voice out there. My darling, I'm so glad you've come. Listen, you must persuade Sanjirou to leave this place. He's starving, but too much like his father to admit it."

"I am not," came a sleepy protest from the darkness.

I felt my stepmother's fingers turn to claws in my arms. She dropped her voice to an urgent whisper. "Take him away, Daughter. Do it now or tomorrow but don't wait any longer than that. He must not be here when they come for us. Be sure he's not there when we—when we go into the tomb. Do whatever it takes to keep him from seeing that horror! Tie him up, give him a potion to make him sleep, cast a spell of forgetfulness over him: *anything*, I beg you, but show mercy to your little brother. Save my precious son."

"Yes, Mother." I gently disengaged her grip. "I promise

you, Sanjirou will be spared." Then, leaning close, I murmured in her ear: "And so will you."

I spoke swiftly and so quietly that my awestruck stepmother sometimes had to ask me to repeat the words of hope I brought her. By the time I finished letting her know my plan, we were surrounded by the other prisoners, except for the two children, who slept on. "Now let them know," I told her. "You'll have to do it one by one. The guard must not suspect."

She nodded and obeyed, while I began speaking to my captive kin aloud, concealing the sound of desperate whispers. It did not take long for the whole group to understand my intentions. They could not thank me aloud, but hugs and handclasps conveyed their gratitude.

I was about to leave when I felt a tug at my sleeve. "Hello, Big Sister," Sanjirou said, still drowsy. "Please don't go yet. I miss you."

My arms encircled him. "Little Brother, can you keep a secret?" I asked softly.

His body turned to stone. "I know already," he said in a misery-choked voice. "The daytime guards talked about it. In three more days . . ." He fought back sobs.

I held him tighter. "In three more days, this place will be a bad memory. Hear me, Little Brother. . . ." I told him his part in my strategy for saving our kin. Little by little his despair ebbed away. When he shivered in my arms, I knew it was from joy.

When I finished, I asked, "Do you think you can do this, Sanjirou?" My eyes were accustomed enough to the dark for me to see him nodding vigorously. Then he kissed me and hid himself in the shadows once more.

Everything went as planned. The night before the captives were to escape, I visited them again and slipped a tiny, sealed clay pot into my brother's hands. The following evening, the unsuspecting guardsman got his wish: Sanjirou reluctantly agreed to come outside and accept some of his evening meal. Their truce did not last. My little brother thrust the shared bowl back at Hiroshi shortly after an unexpected uproar within the house distracted the man. By the time I arrived with what my clanfolk would need to begin their march home, he was deep in a drugged sleep and Sanjirou was preening.

We moved through the sleeping village in silence. Not even a dog barked, which was strange, but I was too focused on reaching the great gate to question why. I had my people wait hidden behind the nearest house while I approached the palisade. No one challenged me when I pushed the unbarred wooden gate open just enough for a single person to squeeze through. No sound came from the watchtower, though I wagered that if I were to climb the ladder leading to the sentry's post, I'd hear snoring.

There were no farewells as Emi and the others flitted free of danger, of slavery, of Ryu's life-or-death control over their lives. When the last one was gone I pushed the gate shut and went back to the shrine, grinning at the stars and thanking the gods. It had all been so easy.

So *very* easy.

17

THE BRIGHTEST MIRROR

The shrine was dark and silent when I returned. I moved like a thief, ears alert for any sound from Daimu's sleeping chamber, but he never stirred. We would have many things to discuss in the morning. I knew he would be glad to hear that Ryu's sacrifices were gone, but I had deep misgivings about how he would react to what I'd done to effect their escape.

"Tomorrow," I muttered as I felt my way to my bedroll and lay down. My body ached with exhaustion, as though I'd just come back from a race around the outside of the village. Before I closed my eyes, I murmured yet another prayer for the fugitives, then sought sleep.

It did not come. I twisted this way and that, feeling as if some evil spell had turned the smooth floor and my comfortable bedroll into a layer of river pebbles and broken turtle shells.

I have to force myself to stop thinking about Emi and Sanjirou and the others now, I told myself sternly. *There's nothing more I can do for them until dawn, and worrying won't help them. Ugh, my stomach's churning! I'm going to throw up if I let this go on.*

I curled myself up tight as a fern head and deliberately emptied my mind of everything but the image of a field where deer grazed and summer breezes ruffled the meadow. The trick seemed to work: I began to drift away, only to sit up suddenly, staring into the dark. My stomach felt twice as ill as before and my heart beat wildly. I passed one hand over my forehead; it came away damp with sweat.

I must have heard some unusual noise just as I was falling asleep, I reasoned. *That's what shocked me awake.* But no matter how long I sat there, listening in the dark, I heard nothing: not a single sound. No owl's cry, no flutter of bat wings, not even the chirr and drone and buzz and click of night-ranging insects. Nothing at all.

A storm is coming, I thought, lying down again. *A really big thunderstorm always sucks the life out of the earth before it breaks. It's early in the season for one of those monstrous tempests, but the signs are here. No wonder Chizu complained that her skin was tingling! Mine is too. If there were daylight, I'd probably see all the tiny hairs on my arms and legs standing up like grass blades! And my head feels so heavy. . . . It had better not start throbbing. I'm going to need all my wits sharp when morning comes, or tonight's work will be futile. Dear spirits, show me a little mercy now and I won't ask for anything more until . . .* A shallow slumber washed over me and my prayer remained unfinished.

It was bad to spend a wakeful night, but the vision that now invaded my mind was infinitely worse. I was a child again, a bold little girl wanting to prove myself to my adored big brother Aki by climbing to the top of our clan's guardian, Grandfather Pine. The world was waiting for sunrise as I scaled the venerable tree. Higher and higher I climbed, my small hands growing sticky with resin, my legs beginning to tire, my face scratched by twigs and pine needles. Somewhere in the heights of the pine was a branch that would fail me, sending me plunging to the moment when my dreams of becoming a hunter would shatter and my path to becoming a shaman would begin. The dream-child I had become knew this, sharing my waking self's every memory. And knowing this, the child in the pine tree hesitated, frowned, shook her head and began to clamber down.

Where are you going, Daughter? Himiko, child, princess, shaman, queen, why are you abandoning me? A golden light glowed in the branches above me. A circle of polished bronze with a blinding shine entranced me. I could not take my eyes away. The voice that called to me from the heart of that luminous mirror pulled me toward it, branch by branch, until I reached impossible heights, balanced on a single spray of pine needles at the airy summit of the tree.

The enormous mirror floated in the sky, my reflection swimming across its surface. As I watched, my dream-child image melted like beeswax and became the self I knew, then shimmered once and dissolved into the goddess I held closest to my heart. She was no longer a simple clay image. Her arms still cradled the golden dragon stone that my infant hand first clasped in the midst of the earthquake marking my birth. Once again she revealed herself to me in all her divine splendor, with the sun's rays spreading wings of fire at her back and the fate of countless mortals in her eyes. I stretched out my arms, yearning for her to come closer, but the sacred mirror drifted high beyond my grasp.

Oh, my lady, here I am! Let me reach you! I cried.

I cannot grant you that, beloved Daughter, no matter how ardently I wish to have you by my side. Her voice was mournful music on the wind. *Evil deeds and wicked intentions blaze across the good land. The soot and cinders from those fires fly up to build a wall that will keep us apart. The air itself is turned to stone. If this goes on, not even the gods themselves will have eyes keen enough to see the purest human soul's reflection in the brightest mirror, and the pathways between our worlds will sink into the hungry sea. Flee, Daughter! When the gods remake the world, dragons dance and mortals perish. Flee, Himiko, before—!*

There was a deep rumble of thunder all around us, and with an awful shriek and groan, the dragon stone in her arms cracked and shattered. Its knife-edged shards rained down, engulfing me in fear and pain. I screamed into the nightmare.

I awoke shaking on my bedroll, breathless and terrified.

Somewhere in the distance, I heard the sound of shouting and knew that at least one of the Ookami had discovered that the intended sacrifices were gone.

"Daimu?" I knelt beside him as he slept and shook him by the shoulder. "Daimu, get up; there's something you must know."

He tossed his head, groggy from being wakened so early, and peered at me with sleep-heavy eyes. Before he was fully alert, I poured out the tale of what I'd done the night before to set my people free.

"So that noise I hear—?" he asked, indicating the

swelling sound of many voices coming from beyond the
walls of the shrine.

"It means that their escape is known," I said.

"They'll be hunted down and dragged back."

"No. Not if we hurry. Not if you help me. I planned for
this. They *will* get away."

"And if they do?" he asked as he threw on his clothes
and both of us headed for the door. "Ryu will simply pick
more Matsu captives to take their place in my uncle's tomb."

"Daimu, *please* don't make me waste time explaining!"
I pleaded as we rushed down the ladder. "Everything depends on my reaching Ryu before he can give any more of
his vengeful commands."

"Yes, anything you say. My poor darling, you look haggard. You must have been up all night, worrying."

I wish I had stayed awake, I thought, recalling the horrors
of my dream. *The goddess brought me a message that's eating at
my heart, but I don't dare interpret it completely on my own. I need
to share it with Daimu, but not yet. Not now.*

"I'll be fine," I told him. "Will you promise to follow
my lead? Will you add your voice to mine?"

"I don't know what you've got in mind, Himiko, but
I'm yours."

We found Ryu descending from his house into a crowd
of villagers. Most of them were only half clad, if that. The
uproar surrounding the slaves' escape had yanked them
from their beds more concerned with satisfying their curiosity than covering their bodies. Oddly enough, Ryu was fully
groomed and dressed, as were the five warriors who now
came trotting toward him. A very rumpled and bewildered

Rinji looked on from a distance. Daimu and I joined him at once.

"Himiko!" he cried, his eyes shining. "Did you hear the news? Your people got away. You must be so happy!"

"Not until I'm sure of their escape," I replied, taking his hands. "But you are a good friend to rejoice over this, for my sake."

There was no time for further talk. Ryu was roaring for silence. All chatter ceased. The new day was utterly still, without even the trill of birdsong. It was as if the wolf chieftain's bluster was mighty enough to intimidate both men and beasts.

"Farewell, my people," he boomed once he had everyone's attention. He was carrying a bow and had a quiver of arrows slung across his back, the same weapons that had murdered Mori. "These good men and I won't be gone long, and once we return with the fugitives, I intend to find out who's responsible for their escape. When you see us come back, have a feast waiting. Assemble the rest of our slaves, while you're at it. I want them to see how these useless escapades end. We are Ookami, the wolves of the mountain!" He thrust his bow at the sky. "No quarry ever escapes us! No lesser clan dares to defy our rule!" Wildly cheering people trailed after him and the five hunters as they headed for the village gateway.

"Hurry," I said insistently, motioning for Daimu to come with me as I skirted the crowd in a race to reach the great gate before Ryu and his men. I hardly noticed Rinji running with us until we arrived. "What are you doing here?" I asked. "You have no idea what we're about to do."

"To be fair, neither do I," Daimu remarked. He grinned at his former apprentice. "Himiko will guide us where we need to go, Rinji, but she won't tell us which road we're taking. Is that agreeable to you?"

Rinji swallowed hard, but nodded.

We placed ourselves in front of the gate—Daimu in the middle, Rinji at his right side, me at his left. We made a pathetic little wall, but it would have to be strong enough to hold back Ryu. The young wolf chieftain's self-satisfied face fell when he saw us, then knotted itself into an ogre's hostile grimace. I saw the men in his hunting party stop short and exchange nervous looks at the sight of three shamans barring their way.

"What nonsense is this, Master Daimu?" Ryu demanded. "Step aside!"

"With respect, Lord Ryu, we will not," Daimu replied.

"You have no business keeping me from bringing back what's mine. And you—!" He jabbed a finger at Rinji, who flinched but held his ground. "What are you doing here? You're supposed to be waiting for our guardian spirit's voice. Are you sacrificing that out of loyalty to your old teacher? I was never one of those who called you a fool, but you're in danger of changing my mind."

"My lord . . ." Rinji shrank back, expecting more abuse, only to be ignored as Ryu turned his wrath on Daimu again.

"Do you believe it's safe for you to block me because I would not dare *force* a shaman out of my way? A *real* shaman gives his life to the gods! He doesn't interfere in other matters."

I took a step forward. It was past time for me to speak.

"Lord Ryu, you speak the truth." I made sure my voice reached every Ookami who had followed their chieftain's hunting party to the gates. "A true shaman's calling is to keep the balance of peace and harmony between our world and the spirits' realm. When we see someone about to anger the gods, we cannot stand by. If the spirits punish him and we could have prevented it, we are guilty of shattering the balance between worlds as much as he."

"Meaning me, I suppose?" Ryu narrowed his eyes. "Your arrogance is incredible. If the fugitives I'm after didn't belong to your clan, you wouldn't be here now, trying to frighten me into letting them go."

Daimu spoke: "I am here too, Lord Ryu, and I am not Matsu."

Ryu's scowl became a sneer. "We *all* know why you're here." He jerked his chin at me. "You want me to let the slaves escape because that's what *she* demands. The Matsu girl's a pretty thing—I can't deny that—but pretty enough to turn you into her tame puppy? You bark when she tells you to bark and if you're a *good* dog, you can beg for her favors."

"Master Daimu and Lady Himiko are—are not—You are wrong about them, Lord Ryu!" Flustered and red in the face, Rinji came to our defense. "She is a great shaman, a healer who has proved her skills time and again, including under your own roof! Master Daimu recognizes this and respects it. That's the only bond between them, I swear it!"

"She must be a wonderful shaman," Ryu remarked, eyeing Rinji coldly. "She has the power to lead young men around by the nose and fill their mouths with lies. What will she make you say next, Rinji? That the spirits will destroy me if I don't let her clanfolk escape? By my father's blood, I wish this clan had never needed any leadership but a chieftain's! You shamans use the gods like an old woman uses tales of ghosts and monsters, to scare little children into obedience!"

"Lord Ryu, be careful what you say." Daimu was somber. "You are the one whose word commands this clan. You will not be the only one to suffer for your insolence to the spirits."

"Don't you mean for my insolence to *you*?" Ryu smirked. He glanced back at his men. "Move them aside. We're losing time."

The men made no move to heed his order. They stood bunched together, nervously whispering among themselves. Ryu fumed, but before he could unleash his rage on his hesitant warriors, one of them spoke up: "Master Daimu, we have never known you to lie, or to use your work as our shaman to enrich yourself. If you will swear that the slaves' escape is really the will of the spirits, we'll believe you."

Daimu lowered his eyes in order to cast another surreptitious look at me, then simply said: "It is true."

"*What* is true?" Ryu countered. He strode up to the warrior who had spoken for the others in the tracking party, raised his fist, and laid him out with a single backhanded blow. Looming over the unconscious man, he shouted: "This clan was *nothing* until I came to rule it! I led you on a path of conquest that fills our storehouses with rice and spares you from a thousand different kinds of back-bending toil! Your children are always well fed, you sleep secure, and even the lowborn among you command at least one slave.

That is the truth, and it stands all around you, plain to be seen. Ask that Matsu girl if her clan ever lived so well!"

"Ask me if my people ever sacrificed the living to appease the dead," I said calmly. "Then ask yourselves why the gods allowed my kin to get away so easily. Have you ever known a single one of your captives to escape this village until now?"

My question gave rise to fresh muttering among the Ookami. Daimu hastened to encourage more: "The spirits have not spoken to me directly about what has happened here, but I say they have sent us clear signs to indicate their desires. I know my uncle was a gentle man who never took a human life while he was alive. Why would he want to do so now that he is dead? The slaves who were to die are all Matsu, Lady Himiko's clanfolk. One of them is even her second mother! What does it mean, my people, that the gods did nothing to prevent their escape? What message— what *warning* does this send to all of us about the spirits' wishes?"

Daimu's words were fuel piled on the fire. The murmurs grew louder and more intense until at last they flared into cries of distress that even Ryu's bullying and threats could not smother:

"Lady Himiko is a powerful shaman—Master Daimu says so! She was a slave among us, but the gods set her free. It's proof they love her!"

"The escaped Matsu slaves were her kin, that's why the spirits made them vanish from our village!"

"But what about Oni's ghost? He was promised a sacrifice. He'll haunt us all!"

"You heard Master Daimu: his uncle would never have wanted human blood shed at his burial."

"Do *you* speak for the spirits now? Are you willing to stake our lives on what will happen if we fail to appease an angry ghost?"

"Appease a ghost at the cost of angering the gods? Are you insane?"

"What can be done? The ceremony is tomorrow. Master Rinji had so much trouble getting the spirits to name a day that it must be the *only* time we can bury Oni if we want to avoid his curse!"

"Can't we bury clay figures with him, the way we always did in the past?"

"Not always. My grandmother remembers a time when chieftains were buried with their slaves. And I hear that other clans still do that."

"Lord Ryu *promised* Oni's spirit that living servants would escort him to the other world."

"But Master Daimu said—!"

"It was a promise to the dead! It must be honored. Something must be done."

"Yes, but nothing that will harm any of Lady Himiko's kin! Lord Ryu should pick other slaves to substitute for the ones that the gods carried away."

Soon all of the Ookami were clamoring for Ryu to turn back from the gateway and deal with the disrupted arrangements for Mori's burial. His own men joined their voices to the protests. Even the warrior he'd felled got up again to dare a second blow. The proud young chieftain became a cornered wolf at the hands of his own people.

My pulse was beating rapidly as a dragonfly's wings. It was not enough that I'd succeeded in sparing my clanfolk such an awful, needless death: no other slaves must be allowed to die in their place. I moved closer to Daimu, thinking frantically of what more we could say to prevent this. *O gods, be merciful!*

The answer to my prayer did not come from the spirits, but from Ryu's own lips. *"Enough!"* he shouted, flinging his arms wide and casting aside his bow. "When did the wolves become possessed by the ghosts of whimpering old women? Your mindless talk has turned a simple slaves' escape into a miracle sent by the gods. If I let you jabber on any longer, you'll all be claiming you saw the Matsu fly over the palisade on the backs of eagles!" He spat on the ground. "Very well. You can have it your way: no slaves will die tomorrow when we bury Oni's bones, and if that angers him, I swear I will do everything in my power to assuage his ghost." He glared at them all and added: "I am ashamed to call myself your chieftain."

"Lord Ryu, you are unfair to your people," I said.

"What is that to you, Matsu?" he demanded, whirling back to face me. "Their welfare is *my* responsibility. I must protect them, lead them, and face the consequences when they refuse to follow the best path. You can poison their lives and walk away without a care. *You* are the favorite child of the gods. But tell me this, O great one: if you are so mighty that we must not lay one finger on you or your kin, why were you an Ookami slave until *I* set you free?"

"I never claimed to be anything except a servant of the spirits," I replied evenly. "But not even the greatest shaman in the world can account for why and how the gods choose to reveal their will to mortals."

"Bah! That's just a fancy way of saying that people like you and Daimu and Rinji who claim to speak for the gods are only speaking for yourselves!"

Rinji placed himself between his chieftain and me. "My lord, please forgive me, but . . . you are wrong. Lady Himiko is sincere. She has never once abused her skills as a shaman. She makes no distinction between Matsu and Ookami and members of any other clan when she performs her healings. Her father and so many of her clan are dead, because of us, and yet your wife and son live, thanks to her. She could have let them perish, as payment for her losses, and claimed it was the will of the gods. She did not. Lord Ryu, I beg you—"

"No more!" The wolf chieftain seized his chosen shaman by the neck of his tunic and twisted the fabric tight, yanking him close. "I *showed* this girl my gratitude for saving my son. I gave her and her brother the chance to live among us as free members of our clan, with all the rights freeborn Ookami enjoy. She threw that gift back in my face!"

Helpless in Ryu's grasp, Rinji rolled his eyes in panic but still managed to reply: "She is loyal to her own clan, my lord. That is understandable."

"Understand this: I also offered her a marriage of such honor and prestige that other girls would *beg* for the opportunity!"

"You—you mean you asked her to be your junior wife?" Rinji was trembling.

Ryu's face turned bright red. He had to be remembering

our first encounter, when I was repulsed by the haughty, insolent spirit behind the handsome mask. I had scorned him then in a way he would never forget or forgive. He would not give me a chance to do so again.

"I am not fool enough to embrace the daughters of my conquered enemies," Ryu said stiffly. "I told her she could marry *you*." He shook the young shaman once and let him drop. Gazing at Rinji with cold disdain, he concluded: "She preferred to remain a slave." He strode back toward his house as the people in his path scrambled aside.

Part of the crowd surged after him. The Ookami were left confused and scared by all that they had just witnessed. They would not rest easy until they knew their leader's rage had faded. Of those that remained behind, many looked to Daimu for reassurance that his uncle's ghost would be content without a human sacrifice, or at least would not punish the whole wolf clan for interring him unattended. Some stared at me, as though they expected me to burst into prophecy or perform some astonishing feat of magic on the spot. I saw more than one hand close around a protective amulet worn as a necklace.

I left it to Daimu to soothe his people's worries. I was concerned about Rinji. The unhappy young man had not moved from the spot where Ryu dropped him. I fell to my knees before him and asked, "Are you hurt?"

"Is it true, Himiko?" He had never looked so woebegone since I'd met him. "Did Lord Ryu want you to marry me and you . . . refused?"

"I had to say no, Rinji," I said. "Ryu was going to *give* me to you the way he would give his mother a necklace or reward one of his warriors with a new spear. He was going to use you the same way, as a token of his gratitude toward me. I could not let him treat you that way. You deserve better. So do I."

"Ah." Rinji forced a smile. "Thank you, Himiko. For a while, I was afraid that you rejected Ryu's offer because you hated the very thought of having me for a husband."

"What silly talk! I care for you very much and I cannot thank you enough for your help this morning, standing up to Ryu. My dear friend, you are a hero to me." I pressed my cheek to his.

"Himiko . . ."

"*Lady Himiko! Lady Himiko!*" The little maid who served Lady Sato came running up to us, distraught. "I have a message for you; terrible news!"

"What's the matter?" I asked.

She shook her head. "I can't talk about it where everyone can hear. My master, Lord Ryu, said I must tell you alone."

"What reason could he have for that?"

"I don't know." The girl's face was streaked with tears. "*I don't know!*"

I seized her by the wrist and led her away behind one of the nearby houses, where we could speak privately. Rinji tried to tag along, but I sent him back. "You heard what she said, Rinji. This is more of Ryu's high-handed way of doing things. If she doesn't obey his whims, someone will report it. This village is too full of idle tongues that would be glad to get this girl in trouble and please their lord by tale-bearing."

"Isn't there anything I can do?" he asked plaintively.

"Yes. She's already attracted too much attention and

curiosity. Stand watch and make sure no one intrudes while she and I talk."

"What if they won't heed me?"

"You are the shaman of the wolf shrine! Or you will be, once it's built. Let your people know that they had better *not* ignore you!"

He trailed off reluctantly. As soon as he was out of sight and earshot, I held the girl by her shoulders and demanded, "Now speak: what's the bad news? Is something wrong with Lady Chizu?" I would not add *Or the baby?* for fear of attracting the notice of malevolent spirits.

"No, it's nothing like that." She clenched her fists. "It's not *fair*. He can do anything he wants, because he's the chieftain, but this just isn't *right*!" She stamped her foot in frustration.

"Will you *please* tell me what—?"

"Oh, Lady Himiko, you're banished! Lord Ryu is sending you away. He says you have no more business staying here. You're not one of us, you're no longer a slave, and he—he"—she choked a little as words and furious sobs fought to be heard—"he says he's tired of wasting food and shelter and patience on a filthy *mamushi*. How can he call you something so vile? You're not the one who's like a poisonous serpent; he is!"

"Hush." I motioned for her to be silent. It was for her own protection, even though no one was near enough to hear her say something unforgivable about her master. If she fell into the habit of speaking like a free person, one day she might forget herself in Ryu's presence. He still owned her. Even her opinions were enslaved to him. "What more did he say?"

She wiped her eyes and nose on the back of one hand and sniffled. "He ordered me to tell you that you can stay until after the burial of Master Daimu's uncle. After that, as soon as the tomb is sealed, you have to leave. And—and you can't take any food or water with you on the journey. He said—he said that the spirits will surely provide everything that—that 'their darling' needs." She looked at me, wretched and apologetic. "That's what he told me to say. I didn't have to—I could have pretended to forget—but I'm so used to doing everything he commands!"

"You are not to blame for your master's lack of wisdom and courtesy. You don't need my forgiveness. Tell Lord Ryu that I received his message." She dipped her head once and dashed away.

The crowd of Ookami had scattered by the time the maid and I finished speaking. Rinji was the only person left lingering by the gates. He brightened at once when he saw me. Then he recalled that I had been fetched away to hear *bad* news, for his expression changed at once to a sympathetic, inquiring look.

"You don't look *too* upset," he said by way of greeting. "Can you tell me what she said?"

"I'm not sure about that. Ryu directed her to speak with me alone; I don't know why. If I share the message with you and he finds out, she'll be the one to pay for it." He was downcast, so to divert him I quickly asked: "What happened to the crowd? Where did everyone go? Even Daimu's gone!"

"Some of the people are still deeply troubled by what happened. Daimu swore to them by every oath you can imagine that Mori's spirit will never bother us again, once his bones are buried *without* a human sacrifice, but they wouldn't be comforted. He finally had to bring them to the shrine to perform a rite of protection. As for the others . . ." He spread his hands. "When Lord Ryu left, he took all their excitement with him. They went home to have breakfast before their day's work begins."

He lifted his head and gazed toward the slopes where the Ookami rice paddies lay. Although the sun was climbing the sky at his back, a mass of dark clouds loomed above the mountains in that direction. A thin rumble of thunder sounded in the distance.

"If that weather comes this way, your people might have to give up a day's labor," I remarked.

He shaded his eyes and studied the ponderous movement of the thunderheads. "So that's why I've been feeling so edgy. It will be good when the rain comes and washes all this tension from the air."

"I agree. In the meanwhile, why don't you come to the shrine and share the morning meal with Daimu and me?" I asked casually. *And the news of my expulsion from this village without Noboru, I thought. Forgive me, Rinji, but I could not tell you anything before I let Daimu know. It would be like keeping secrets from myself. He holds my heart.*

The shielding ritual was over and the attendees gone when Rinji and I entered the shrine. Daimu hailed us smiling. "A good morning's work, my friends," he said. "I'll be able to attend my uncle's burial tomorrow with my heart at peace. Have you eaten? I have a bear's appetite! I told Ashi to serve double portions, so there will be plenty for you as well, Rinji."

"I would be delighted." Rinji did not *look* delighted; he looked uncomfortable, and kept shooting troubled glances my way. A slow-witted man could have seen that something was wrong, and Daimu was clever.

"What is it, Rinji? For the love of the gods, don't tell me Ryu's stirred up some fresh mischief about bringing back the fugitives! Not after all we went through to—!"

"No," I said. "He has accepted his defeat as far as that goes. This is not about them. It's about me." Steadily, impassively, I recounted the wolf chieftain's message. Daimu and Rinji were dumbstruck.

My beloved was the first to find his voice. "He has no right to do this."

"He has *every* right," I replied. "I do not belong to this clan."

"But to send you away with nothing—!" Rinji protested.

"I have traveled without supplies before this. At least this is a good season for it. I can take care of myself, and it isn't too far before I'll reach another village."

Thunder grumbled beyond the shrine walls, though there was still no sign of rain. "At least he did not send you away today, with this storm approaching," Rinji said. "He's showing you a little kindness. Maybe he can be persuaded to show more."

"I think the reason he didn't try to be rid of me today has nothing to do with kindness," I said. "The people took my side this morning and forced him to give up the hunt. If he tried to act against me too quickly, they might thwart him again." I gave Rinji a regretful smile. "Now I understand why he insisted his messenger speak to me with no witnesses. If the crowd had still been there and heard about this . . ."

"Then we have to tell them!" Rinji was already heading for the doorway. "I'll gather the people, tell them that their chieftain is about to exile the most accomplished shaman"—he glanced guiltily at Daimu and amended his words—"*one* of the most accomplished shamans they'll ever know. They'll never stand for it! You saw what happened at the gate: not even Lord Ryu's picked huntsmen stood by him against you. The Ookami will—!"

Lightning lit the sky, casting dazzling white patterns across the shrine floor. Thunder crashed and the clouds tore open with gusts of wind and rain. Flash after flash seared the air, each leaving a strangely piercing scent in its wake. Clap after clap of thunder rolled through the village, making a din so loud that I imagined the pillars of the shrine were shaking. The outer world was whipped away in swaths of water riding the breath of the tempest.

I looked out into the storm and knew that the gods had spoken. The people would not set foot out of their homes in this weather. By tomorrow, the scene at the gate would already be fading from their minds as the demands of ordinary life occupied their attention once more. No doubt Ryu was already using the time between now and then to come up with a plausible, compelling way to make his clanfolk accept the decision to send me home. Any hope we had of rallying the Ookami to support me against him was being washed away with the rain.

"We must forget about enlisting your people to help me," I told Rinji quietly. "If I am going to stay, the answer to Ryu's orders has to come from us."

"There can be no 'if' about it," Daimu said. "You can't leave without your brother."

"The little boy who's Lord Ryu's hostage?" Rinji asked.

"He's more than that: he's the price of her mother's life," Daimu replied, and poured out the whole story of the mission that had brought me to the Ookami village.

When he was done, Rinji cried, "Himiko, why didn't you tell me this before? I would have done everything in my power to let you bring Noboru home!"

"And what would that be?" I asked without any bitterness. "If you have some idea that Daimu and I have overlooked, tell us now, before it's too late."

"I could—I could—" Rinji stammered, took a breath, and fell silent, head bowed in defeat.

"It's all right, my friend." Daimu patted him on the back. "I share your feelings. It's painful to be helpless, especially when someone we care about needs us most."

Rinji shook his head slowly. "Oh, Himiko, I wish we had more time. I know I could find a way out of this for you if Lord Ryu would only give you more than a single day among us." He looked up, a spark of hope in his eyes. "Why don't you pretend to be too sick to travel? He couldn't force you to go then!"

"Couldn't or wouldn't?" I replied. "Remember, we're talking about Ryu."

Rinji jumped to his feet. "I'm going to his house right

now! I'll tell Lady Sato what he's done. Maybe she will have the ability to make him remember how much he owes you."

"You'd appeal to his mother?" I raised one brow. "Ryu isn't a little boy anymore."

"Well, then, I'll ask Lady Chizu—"

"Does he ever *listen* to his wife?"

Rinji pressed his lips together. He knew the answer to that. "I don't know what else to try. If Lord Ryu would only show you the gratitude you deserve—!"

"Ryu believes that *I* am the ungrateful one," I said. "You heard him: he offered me the chance to join this clan and I spurned it." I thought it best not to add that I had also turned down his chieftain's suggestion of marriage to the younger shaman. Unfortunately one look at Rinji's expression told me that he remembered this himself.

"He shouldn't hold that choice against you," Daimu declared. "You wanted *unconditional* freedom. Rinji and I can understand that, can't we, my friend?"

His former apprentice made a vague gesture that was impossible to interpret. Abruptly he said, "The storm is passing. I should go." Though Daimu and I pointed out that the rain was falling as hard as ever, he closed his ears to our pleas and left.

Daimu sighed. "He's right, you know."

"What do you mean?" I demanded. "Should I give up allegiance to my own clan? To the people whose blood is mine?"

"Not that. But if you had accepted Ryu's *other* gift—if you agreed to marry Rinji—your troubles would be over. Who makes a better hostage to ensure the Matsu clan's good behavior? A child? Or a princess so powerful she's a shaman in her own right *and* the wife of the shaman entrusted with building of the wolf shrine? Ryu is not stupid. He knows that the strongest bond between clans cannot be based on conquest alone. Your marriage to Rinji would reinforce his rule over the Matsu once and for all."

I turned away from him and walked to the doorway. The world was rain. I heard the boards creak under his approaching footsteps and felt his strong hands close on my shoulders. "I did not say all of that because I want you to marry Rinji," he murmured. "But if it is the only way for you to save your mother, and if you are willing to go through with it, maybe there's still time to tell Ryu you've changed your mind and—"

"Marry me, Daimu," I said.

His hands clenched. "Himiko, there's nothing I want more. I would thank the gods every day of my life if you became my bride, but . . . Ryu won't. You know how he resents me. He'll see it as further evidence that his wishes as chieftain can be overturned, and he won't like that. His idea was for you to wed *Rinji*."

"I do not love Rinji," I replied, warm rain misting my face. It felt like the playful kisses of a thousand spirits. "I love you. If we marry, it will be as you say: I'll have the status of being an Ookami shaman's wife and the right to stay here without having to give up my place among the Matsu. I will have more time to work on freeing Noboru. Above all, I will have my heart's desire." I faced him, my arms wreathing his neck. I had never seen his face so stunned with joy. "Say yes."

He did so without words.

The rain ended by midday. Daimu and I picked our way around the larger puddles to Rinji's small house near the future site of the wolf shrine. My beloved carried a small container of rice wine and I held a bowl half filled with millet porridge, the leftovers of our morning meal. It was nothing fancy, but the food and drink we would share in the presence of a shaman would mark us as man and wife before the gods.

When Rinji came out to welcome us, we made no attempt to hide our mutual bliss. His smile soon mirrored our own, though he had no idea of the true reason for our happiness. "You thought of a way for Himiko to remain here, didn't you?" he exclaimed, clapping Daimu on the back. "Tell me!" If he noticed the food and wine we carried, he must have mistaken them for the makings of a very modest victory celebration.

Daimu and I both put a free arm around his shoulders. "We couldn't have done it without you, dear Rinji," I said. "Your words showed us the way."

"They did?" He was confused, but still smiling. "How?"

"Let's go inside first," Daimu suggested. "You will need to make a few preparations for the ceremony."

"Your uncle's burial?" Rinji misunderstood completely. "All of that is ready. I hope you will be very pleased by how well I honor him, Daimu. I shined my mirror and my bell *twice,* though after that storm I think I may have to do it a third time." He motioned to where the two sacred items rested on a narrow, raised platform against the back wall of the house.

"They look bright enough to me," I said, kneeling as I whisked a cloth from my sash and spread it on the ground. "Daimu, the wine?"

Rinji watched with ever mounting puzzlement as Daimu and I set out the bowl of millet porridge and the small flask of wine. It was only when Daimu asked him for a single cup that he realized what was going on.

"You're marrying . . . *him*?" His voice was harsh and terrible to hear, as though it were emerging from an abyss where demons dwelled. "Just like that? You're not going to give him the reasons—the *excuses* you gave when you pushed me away?" His eyes blazed as he turned to Daimu. "Congratulations, *Master*. You are clearly the better shaman. You know more spells than you ever bothered to teach me: how to change lies into love; how to snare a heart of snow."

"Rinji, please . . ." I rose and grabbed his arm. "I never lied to you. I called you my *friend*."

"You called *him* friend too!" he shouted, pointing at Daimu. "How many meanings does that word have for you? 'Lover' when you speak of him, 'fool' when you speak of me!" He shook me off and barged out of the house, kicking over the bowl of millet porridge on his way.

"Merciful spirits, what have we done to him?" I breathed. "I didn't want him to be hurt. I thought I'd made my feelings for him clear a long time ago, well before I ever knew you, beloved. I was glad to have him for my friend, but there could be no more than that between us. I thought he understood and accepted it. I even believed he was content."

Daimu knelt to scoop the spilled porridge back into

the bowl. "He was satisfied to be your friend because he hoped you would change your mind someday. I destroyed that for him."

"You are not responsible for his heartbreak," I said. "Neither am I. He chose to turn our friendship into his fantasy of love."

"I still regret how badly this has hurt him." He looked toward the open doorway. "He will never agree to perform the marriage ceremony now."

I took the bowl from his hands and raised it to my lips, swallowing a mouthful. "We will have to perform it for ourselves." I passed him the bowl and watched him eat a little of the cold gruel before he picked up the wine, sipped it, and gave it to me. I accepted the small clay vessel and drank. It felt right.

I gave him my hand. "Are you my husband now?" I asked.

"If you are my wife," he replied, smiling. "In all of my travels I never found a clan that did not follow a wedding rite like this, bride and groom sharing food from one dish and drink from one cup."

"We didn't have a cup," I said archly. "Does that mean we aren't wed?"

"You impossible girl," he said fondly, and took me into his arms.

18

SIGHTS BEYOND SEEING

Another thunderstorm blew through the mountains that night, but the day of Mori's burial dawned clear, bright, and very still. I was up early, ready to greet the servants when they arrived at the shrine to serve breakfast and begin the day's work. Ashi appeared with her arms piled high with clothes.

"I borrowed this dress for you, Lady Himiko," she said, unfurling a hemp gown, the correct attire for mourning. "Did Master Daimu remember where his funeral garments are stored?"

"How would I know?" I replied lightly. "Do I look like his wife?"

The older woman smiled at me. "He could do worse."

The servants remained in the dark about how things had altered between Daimu and me. The two of us did nothing to reveal the change in our relationship. We agreed that our new bond should be revealed publicly only when Ryu tried to enforce his order of banishment against me.

"I want to see his face when I tell him that if you go, I go," Daimu said, ending his words with a kiss.

"What will you do if he says 'Good, then go, and may the mountain ogres feast on your bones'?" I teased. "It would be the perfect opportunity for him to be rid of you and set Rinji in your place as this clan's sole shaman."

"Do you think the rest of our people will consent to that?" he replied. "Do you think Ryu's own mother will allow it? Ha! She'll skin him alive with that sharp tongue of hers." More earnestly, he added: "My love, Rinji is a good man and a good enough shaman, but the Ookami fear the spirits too much to settle for that. They have eyes and memories, to see and to recall how much the gods favor one shaman over another by how quickly a sick person recovers or how well we avoid disaster. When they compare his work to yours and mine, he loses the contest."

I could not argue with that, perhaps because I wanted to see the same outcome as he did. We ate our morning meal seated well apart from one another and hardly spoke a word, for fear they would be unguarded words of love.

It was Daimu's duty to fetch his uncle's bones to the burial ground that morning. He had placed them outside the village palisade, to shield the Ookami from any bad fortune clinging to relics of death. Stones were piled over the cloth-wrapped bundle, protecting Mori's remains from being disturbed until it was time for their final interment. As I accompanied him to the cairn, many of the villagers fell into step behind us. They had not been kind to the fallen giant while he was alive, but now that he was dead and had a spirit's power, they were eager to show him respect.

As Daimu began removing the stones one by one, the village potter joined us, along with one of her apprentices, a moon-faced girl who was very self-conscious about her part in the day's solemn event. The potter's hands were empty. A person of her status in the village would not need to carry the larger objects she crafted. That was what apprentices were for. The finely shaped, smooth-sided jar that would house the remains of Mori's body was cradled in the girl's plump arms. She carried it proudly, as though it were a noble's child.

Once the bundled bones were revealed, it was my turn to take part in the preparations. I had a length of silk that had been taken from one of the clan storehouses. The Ookami did not make that precious fabric, but received it in tribute from their subjects. Mori's remains would be clothed splendidly, though the man himself had lived in rags for most of his life. Tenderly I swathed the bones in silk and passed them to Daimu, who placed them reverently in the clay jar.

We resumed our path to the burial ground. A crowd was already there, massed around the walls of the waiting tomb. The people stepped aside when they saw us approach, some of them murmuring empty expressions of sympathy to Daimu as he passed. A group of aristocrats occupied positions of honor, close to the doorway into darkness. They managed to show off their exalted status, despite their plain hemp garments, by how many household slaves they'd brought to attend them. I recognized more than one face belonging to the Matsu clan. When the ceremony began, they would share the best view with their masters. I gave thanks that this would not include the sight of our kinfolk being sealed away with the dead.

Daimu set down the jar on the tomb's threshold and looked around. "Has Lord Ryu arrived yet?" he asked one of the nobles.

"He will be here," the man replied. "When I left my house this morning, I caught sight of him hurrying through the village. He must have had some last-moment arrangements to make."

I searched the crowd too. "Where is Master Rinji?" I asked.

That question took everyone by surprise. Soon we were all glancing here and there, seeking the shaman who was supposed to be conducting the rites for Daimu's uncle.

"Maybe Master Rinji has run into some difficulty," a second highborn Ookami suggested. "He could have sent word to our chieftain, asking for aid, and that accounts for both of them."

"Someone ought to go back to the village and look into this," the first noble said. He gestured at one of the commoners. "You, there! See to it!" The fellow jogged off obediently.

An awkward silence settled over the burial ground. It was made even more uncomfortable by the eerie absence of any sound at all, except for the rustle of hemp clothes and the whispers of the waiting people. Though the gods had sent two thunderstorms in rapid succession, the downpours had not managed to wash away the hovering tension that possessed the earth and the heavens before a tempest.

I looked around and was surprised by how many people had come to witness Mori's funeral rites. "It looks like half the village is here," I murmured to Daimu.

"Maybe more than that," he whispered. "I'll bet that the only ones working in the fields today are slaves. If even a handful of these gawkers had treated my poor uncle with a little kindness while he was alive, we would not be waiting to bury his bones today."

"When he was alive, he frightened them because they couldn't understand why he was so different," I said. "Now that he's dead, they can pretend to be brave, like children patting a dead wolf's fur. I wonder how many of them are here because they still expect to see him receive a bloody sacrifice."

"I hope I never find out," Daimu said glumly. "I have to go on living with these people. May the gods never grant me the ability to see beneath the surface of things. If I had no choice but to see the ugliness that lurks behind their smiling faces, I would become a hermit like my poor uncle."

I gave his hand a quick squeeze under cover of my trailing sleeve. "I know what you mean. I used to pray for the day when the spirits would show me their favor by granting me visions. Now I wish it were not so. When this ceremony is done, I want to talk to you about a dream I had."

"A dream?"

"To be honest, it felt more like a vision. When I dream, it's always with the feeling that I can force myself awake at any time and escape it. In a vision, the gods themselves command me to endure it all. I cannot close my eyes or turn away." The echo of the sun goddess's words fell heavily upon me as I spoke: *When the gods remake the world, dragons dance and mortals perish.* The uninvited memory left me trembling.

"Himiko?" Daimu's concern showed plainly in his face. "What's come over you? You're so pale! Are you well?"

"I'm fine." I made myself smile, but my mind held nothing but the image of a glowing golden dragon stone, its face crackling as tiny fissures radiated across it. I had to make an effort not to gasp for breath. "It's the weather—so stifling! There's going to be another storm soon. We have to begin the ceremony before it breaks!"

"There *is* something strange in the air," Daimu agreed. "I think I'd better take charge. I brought this with me"—he tapped the protruding handle of the sacred bronze mirror tucked into his belt—"because I wanted Rinji to use something special to me when he performed Uncle's burial ceremony. Now it looks like I will need *all* the items necessary for the ritual." He sighed. "I expected better behavior from Rinji, but we cannot linger here forever, waiting for him to set aside his bitterness." He stepped away from me and raised his arms to the massed Ookami: "My people, hear me! It is past time that we began these rites. Some unknown cause is keeping Master Rinji away, so I will officiate, with the gods' permission. Will someone run to the shrine to fetch me what I'll need?"

A boy on the brink of manhood sprang forward at once, eager for the responsibility and the attention. Daimu was in the middle of giving the lad his instructions when a shout rose up from the very back of the crowd: "It's all right,

Master Daimu! You don't need to worry anymore: here they come now!"

Daimu smiled happily at the news. I understood: his shaken faith in his former apprentice was restored.

"Thank the gods, he didn't let jealousy rule him," I said softly. "You and I will have to speak with him later and mend things between us, but at least he's here now. Go and welcome him, beloved. The crowd is so thick, he's having a hard time getting through. Why won't they stand aside? What are they staring at? They'll make him feel self-conscious for arriving late."

Then the mass of bodies parted and I saw the reason why the Ookami had clustered around Rinji: he had not arrived alone. He held a short length of rope in one hand; the other end was tied in a noose around a young man's neck. It was Hiroshi, the good-hearted young guardsman who had stood watch at the doorway to my clanfolk's prison. His hands were tied, his face was hideously bruised, and he staggered dizzily. Ryu walked behind him, a grin on his face, a drawn sword in his hand.

"All praise to the gods!" the wolf chieftain called out, not even bothering to conceal the note of mockery in his voice. "I asked for their guidance and here is the result." He planted his free hand in the center of Hiroshi's back and gave him a hard shove. The unlucky young man tripped and fell into Rinji, who jumped as though he'd touched a burning brand. "Here is the answer to all of our prayers."

Ryu's announcement raced through the crowd, sowing confusion. Hiroshi was a well-liked member of the Ookami clan. Everyone began talking at once, some retreating, some gathering so close to Rinji and his captive that the shaman looked like a rabbit cornered by hounds.

Daimu's voice rose above all others, calling for the right to be heard. "Lord Ryu, what are you doing? This is my uncle's interment, a ceremony that *you* promised to provide to be forgiven for killing him. Is *this* what kept you from being here until now and dishonoring his memory with your carelessness?" He indicated the beaten guard. "What has this man done? What crime is so great that you could not wait to punish it until after we have laid my uncle's bones in the tomb?"

Ryu's victorious smile died. "Watch what you say, Master Daimu. Our clan praises you for your integrity. You don't want them to think you'd twist words and deeds for your own purposes, do you? I did nothing wrong in saving our people from a dangerous, unpredictable exile! I still stand ready to shield the Ookami from all harm, whether from humans, gods, or ghosts! I swore to your uncle's spirit that he would have a sacrifice worthy of our mightiest chieftains, but when the chosen slaves vanished, you made it seem like a miraculous sign proving *her* untouchably high favor with the gods!" He jabbed his free hand and all eyes turned to me. "We all heard you declare Lady Himiko's supreme powers as a shaman, and place her and all her kin high above us, untouchable. Better to have an angry ghost lurking in our midst forever than to shed a single drop of Matsu blood!"

"Master Daimu never said such things!" I countered, but my objection was swallowed by the noise of the crowd. The taut, anxious atmosphere enveloping us made all fears feel more vivid. I understood this down to the core of my bones. My own skin was stinging as if a host of demons were pricking it with thorns. The Ookami were caught up in the spell of terror. The open door of Mori's monument sheltered unseen horrors. The monstrous threat of a menacing phantom rose like poisoned smoke from the simple jar that held his bones. Trapped and rendered helpless by their own wild imaginings, they clamored loudly to be saved.

Before full panic could erupt, Ryu raised his voice again. "My people, calm yourselves! Didn't I say that the gods answered my prayers? Oni's ghost will depart in peace forever, attended by the one responsible for robbing him of his proper sacrifice. Let the tomb receive them both!"

Rinji gave a halfhearted tug at the hemp collar ringing Hiroshi's neck and began leading him toward the doorway and the darkness beyond. My insides were as cold as the stones of winter. As they passed me, I saw how the young man turned his eyes everywhere around him, desperately devouring his last sight of green earth, ageless mountains, towering trees, the faces of his friends and kindred, the graceful procession of clouds across the sweet blue sky, and the glorious light of the sun goddess.

I had not freed the Matsu captives solely because they were my kin. I had done so for *her* sake, to serve the goddess. A mirror that has been once steeped in blood can nevermore shine as brightly. My people were safe because I had given Hiroshi a sleeping potion, by my brother's hand. I thought that at most he would be shamed for carelessness, and I regretted it, though believed it was a reasonable price to pay for saving Emi and the family whose little girl could now grow up in safety. But in that moment I saw the truth in a young man's despairing gaze: I had only exchanged one sacrifice for another.

If that was how it had to be . . .

I leaped forward and grabbed Rinji by the back of his tunic, pulling him aside before anyone knew what I was doing. He lurched into the guard and both of them stumbled into the group of nobles. By the time they were on their feet again, I was standing in the doorway to Mori's tomb, feet planted wide, arms spread high, the palms of my hands pressed against the cold doorposts.

"In the name of the spirits, this cannot—*will* not happen!" I shouted. "What is all this reasonless talk of *stealing* a sacrifice that never should have taken place? My people were not snatched away from this village; they *escaped*!"

"Is that so, Lady Himiko?" Ryu's familiar, despised, taunting smile was back. "The gods had no hand in it? Ah, what a pity: you are not the shaman of shamans after all. You are only an upstart girl sly enough to trick fools into believing in you."

"Lord Ryu, watch your words when you speak about Lady Himiko's powers." Daimu's voice was low and threatening. "I will swear on my life that she can look into the other world, walk with the spirits, receive their counsel and their warnings, and intercede with them on our behalf. Compared to her, I am a child."

"A child misled by a pretty face," Ryu said tartly. "You have my sympathy. I came very near to making a similar error not *too* many years ago. And we are in good company." He approached the captive guard, jerking Hiroshi's halter from Rinji's hands. "What reward did she give you for turning you back on your duty?"

"My lord, I *told* you what happened." Hiroshi's tone was pleading. "Right before dawn on the morning of the escape, two men found me sleeping outside the house where the slaves were kept. When they brought me to you for questioning, they testified that it was so hard to wake me, that at first they thought I was dead. I wanted to explain myself, but I couldn't; I didn't know what had come over me. You ordered the men who'd found me to gather the others and told me not to worry about anything more. You were so gracious to me, then! So merciful! Don't you remember?"

Ryu made a disgusted face. "You expect anyone to believe such tales? This girl stole your brains, not mine!"

"My lord, if I offended, why did you let me go?"

"Because I was going to bring back the fugitives and spare your family the pain of seeing you disgraced. But when I met defiance at the gates of my own village"—he gave Daimu a hard look—"this outcome became inevitable for you."

The wolf chief looked away from his hapless victim to the waiting people. "He mocked the gods by letting us believe they were the ones who freed the captives. He would have let Oni's enraged ghost avenge the broken pledge we gave him. He sold his loyalty to our clan for a mere girl's embrace." He gestured at me with contempt. "She leaves this village *now*. Drag her away and let the ceremony go on!"

Several large men came out of the crowd and started toward me. They looked ill at ease but determined. It was no trivial thing to lay hands on a shaman, whether or not their chieftain had just reduced me to "a mere girl."

I drew the image of the goddess from my sash with one hand, my wand with the other. None of the Ookami had seen these signs of my art and authority until now. The men hesitated.

"Lord Ryu, you can order me to leave, but I will be the one to choose when," I said steadily. "Believe me, I will not go until I have seen Mori's bones laid to rest and his tomb sealed without this man's blood spilled in needless sacrifice." *And I will not leave your accursed village without my brother Noboru's hand in mine,* I thought, though that would be a different battle.

"Fine. Go or stay, since it looks like my so-called men jump away at the sight of a girl armed with a stick and a stone," Ryu sneered at the embarrassed Ookami who had failed to remove me. "But when Master Rinji ends these rites, this tomb will hold two sets of bones."

I let my arms fall to my sides. "Then it will hold mine."

Under the staring eyes of Ryu's clanfolk, I recounted all that I had done in order to set the chosen slaves free and send them home.

"Men and women of the wolf clan, I know that not all of our customs governing life and death are the same as yours. Master Daimu says that he has visited other clans whose people send human beings into the tombs of their chieftains. But one of the slaves your leader picked for death was only ten years old! How could I let you sacrifice a child? And how could you ever ask the gods for mercy with the stain of so much cruelty on your spirits?"

I went on, taking special care to stress that Hiroshi did not have anything to do with the escape, and offered to demonstrate the effects of the potion that had made him sleep so deeply he seemed to be dead. As I spoke about all that had happened that night, I suddenly realized *why* my kin's escape had been so easy, and the revelation stole my breath for a moment.

"*Two* guards . . . ," I murmured. "There should have been two guards to keep watch over the prisoners by night. Two men were posted at that house by day!" My head snapped sharply to meet Ryu's smug look. "You planned this. Your commands stationed only one nighttime sentry at the door. You picked a well-known idler to stand sentry in the watchtower. He didn't need any sleeping potion to let my kin slip away under his nose! Why isn't *he* here, accused of the same false charges as this man?"

Ryu smirked. "What! You enticed *two* of my guards in one night? Impressive!"

I ignored the slur. "You set a baited trap and watched. You waited. You—you *and* the slave-hunters with you—were all fully dressed and ready to set out after the fugitives, even though the alarm sounded well before dawn! You—!"

"—went to a lot of trouble to snare you?" He chuckled. "You were my slave. I could have done anything I liked with you, at any time. I'm sorry I missed the chance." He sheathed his sword. "Master Rinji, this man is innocent after all. Let him go."

Daimu's former apprentice was so eager to fulfill Ryu's command that in his haste he scraped Hiroshi's cheek with the coarse rope while yanking the noose off over his head. A pair of the attendant nobles had to help him as he fumbled over the knots binding Hiroshi's wrists. The people cheered when the falsely accused prisoner was finally able

to stand before them, free.

"Thank you, Lady Himiko!" Hiroshi cried, eyes shining with gratitude. "How can I ever—?"

I wanted to ask him to pardon me for what he had endured to save my kin, but Ryu did not permit it. He moved with the grace and speed of a striking snake, his hands digging hard into my arms as we stood pressed together in the doorway to the tomb.

"Go, Himiko," he said coldly. "You will not leave this village after all. Here you will stay, under this roof. By your own confession, you stole a promised offering to the spirits, even if only to the spirit of a creature better off dead. Sacrilege is sacrilege. Pay the debt you owe. Go in quietly, and I promise to show you mercy"—he nodded briefly at his sword—"before we seal this tomb."

"You will not touch her!" His voice strong with the spirit of the wolf, Daimu seized Ryu from behind and tore him off me. I saw the beast's fierce soul glowing in his eyes, barely controlled by the man it had possessed.

"Master Daimu, you go too far," Ryu said, and suddenly *two* wolves faced each other on a battleground laid out before an open tomb. "I am your chieftain. I rule this clan. I gave this girl chance after chance to turn away from her stubborn, rebellious ways, but she rejected every one. She has chosen this fate."

"This *girl* is still a shaman," Daimu shot back. "One whose abilities—"

"—make your skills look like a heap of bird droppings,

yes, so you keep saying." Ryu looked as if he were trying to figure out some unsolvable riddle. "Why, Master Daimu? Why is it so important for you to make this clan believe she is a *great* shaman—no, the *greatest* shaman we shall ever know? What makes you so keen to sacrifice your own reputation in order to build up hers?"

"I only say what is true," Daimu replied. "I praise Lady Himiko because I have recognized her gifts." His somber gaze passed over the Ookami. "To ignore what the gods have given us is unwise; to treat the one who embodies those gifts . . . that is dangerous. I am like you, my lord Ryu: everything I say and do is for the sake of our people."

"*Liar!*" Ryu's accusation fell like a blow. "You gave up the truth long ago, for *this.*" His fingers clutched my face.

"Let me go," I said through gritted teeth. I stamped his foot as hard as I could. The wolf chieftain yelped in shock and lost his hold. I ran to Daimu's side, but that was as far as either of us could go. The Ookami were pressing in all around us. If we could break through the crowd, how far could we run?

Run? I would not do that, even if it were possible. *Oh, Noboru! Mama! Kaya, sister of my heart! Will I see any of you again?*

Ryu came toward us, one hand falling to the sword at his waist. Daimu stepped in front of me. "Endanger her, and the sky will not be vast enough to hold all the curses that will fall on you. Harm her, and the earth will turn to flames beneath your feet and spit out your bones into eternal darkness. Kill her, and you will live just long enough to witness every member of your family, every person who shares your blood, every whisper of the Ookami name be drowned in oblivion."

The wolf chieftain's face turned white. Daimu's threats unnerved him, but only for a moment. He showed his people a confident smile and proclaimed, "*This* is the man who claimed that everything he does is for your sake! *This* is how your beloved shaman protects you, by calling on the gods to annihilate us all! Tell the truth, Master Daimu, if you can remember how that's done: the only reason you defend this girl so fiercely is you intend to make her your bride!"

Ryu did not wait for Daimu to respond. He plunged into the crowd and dragged Rinji into the midst of our confrontation. "Tell the people, Master Rinji! Tell them what you told me. Then let the gods decide who should be accursed for treachery, blasphemy, and sacrilege!"

Rinji lowered his eyes, unwilling to look at Daimu or me while he spoke. "This is the truth that I swear to by my life: Master Daimu and Lady Himiko asked me to marry them. They reasoned that if she became his wife, Lord Ryu could not cast her out of this village. She—I think she has some hidden scheme she wants to use against our chieftain—perhaps against us all—but she needed time to make it happen. She has enchanted Master Daimu so deeply that he would do anything for her." For an instant he forgot himself and looked up. Our gazes met and he twitched involuntarily, then flushed red from the neck up and hastily concluded: "If I have lied, may I suffer for it."

Rinji's revelation shattered the crowd. Cries of protest

and condemnation burst out everywhere. Daimu was visibly shaken, turned against by the man who had been his cherished student and his valued friend. He looked so dazed that I wondered if he could hear his own people shouting for his banishment.

"He betrayed us! He lied about the will of the gods just to save *her*!"

Others came to his defense: "Didn't you hear what Lady Himiko said? This is all Lord Ryu's doing, from first to last. He never wanted to honor Master Daimu's uncle. He *killed* the man! Clay grave attendants were good enough for every Ookami chieftain *I* can remember. Why did Lord Ryu suddenly decide to pay *living* tribute to Oni's spirit?"

Many agreed with this: "He's always held a grudge against Master Daimu—anyone with eyes and ears knows about it. Lord Ryu hates having to share his authority with the shaman."

But there were dissenting voices too: "Who cares if Lord Ryu manipulated everything? We should thank him: it let us see Master Daimu's true nature! Our shaman doesn't speak for the gods; he echoes that Matsu girl's wishes!"

"Speak with respect of 'that Matsu girl.' She healed my son's fever!"

"She saved my daughter's hand when it was burned in a cookfire!"

"She saved my *life*! I owe her everything!"

"Then why don't you pay your debt by taking her place in Oni's tomb?"

Small skirmishes flared up. Sharp words led to hard blows. Ryu did nothing to stop it. Every fresh argument against Daimu was like honeycomb melting on Ryu's tongue. He devoured it greedily and looked ravenous for more.

"Why should *any* of our clan walk into the darkness?" one of Ryu's warriors demanded. "If Lady Himiko hadn't interfered, Oni's ghost would be more than content having six Matsu slaves to attend him!"

"Why not?"

"Why not *what*?"

"Why not make that offering, then? There are still plenty of Matsu slaves among us."

"What a good idea! Satisfy Oni's ghost without touching the shaman's girl: perfect!"

"Hey! Hey, everyone, listen to this!" Word of the horrible solution spread among the Ookami. I saw them jostle the nobles in order to grab every slave whose facial tattoos marked them as Matsu. That was bad enough, but then I heard someone exclaim:

"These people breed trouble for us. They're not worth keeping. Let's go back to the village and bring them all!" I watched in horror as a group of men set out to fulfill that ghastly plan.

No! Oh gods, no! My mind screamed in protest. I tried to push my way past Daimu, wanting to catch up with the departing men, but he grabbed my hand and would not let go.

"Himiko, beloved, what are you doing? You can't stop them."

"I can try." My voice broke with pain. "I *must* try. If your kin go through with this, no rite of purification will have the power to remove the stain. They'll sacrifice a dozen Ookami souls for every slave that dies to fill your uncle's tomb!" I struggled to twist out of his grasp. "There may still be a chance to save—!"

And then my body turned to stone. I could not move, could not feel, could not speak or weep or even breathe. All I could do was *see.*

"The dragon!" My voice surged back with the force of a raging storm. It resounded loudly over the land, blasting flocks of crows out of the treetops, sending them in a caw-ing spray of black wings across the sky. "The dragon comes! O my people, hear me, the moment is at hand! The dragon— *the dragon dances!"*

My eyes filled with visions beyond my ability to describe except as fragments of a nightmare. Images of shrieking faces whirled around me. Pale hands made of smoke and water and naked bone plucked at my clothes. I fought my way through a forest, clawed through a wave of earth that came crashing down over my head, staggered over a bridge of fire and into a pit house whose walls were shored up by lifeless bodies. Somewhere a wolf was howling and a child sobbed for his mother until both voices were swept away in a cold wind.

A rock caught my foot and I fell, face in the dirt, graz-ing my forehead. The pain was real, but not strong enough to break the spell upon me. I, who had traveled between the realms of men and spirits, now set my feet in both at once. The wild, disturbing apparitions ebbed, but would not vanish. I stood at the top of the hill hiding the burial ground from the village, but could not account for how I had gotten there. I saw the ordinary world around me, but at the same time . . . something more.

Speak, Himiko! The goddess's voice filled my ears, my mind, my heart. Her face glided over the surface of everything I saw, a translucent flower petal floating across the surface of a pond. *Let them know what stirs from slumber under stone. Show them the path that may yet save them. Speak, dearest Daughter, speak!*

From the hilltop I could see the men who had rushed off so willingly to bring back Matsu slaves as sacrifices. They were already at the village gates. I cupped my hands to my mouth and shouted: "Yes, go faster, bring them! Bring them all! Man, woman, and child, slave and free, *everyone*! No one must be left behind! No one must be allowed to remain under a roof! Drag them if they will not come with you and carry them if they cannot walk, but bring them away, *away*!"

I turned and looked back at Mori's tomb. Blood from my scraped brow blurred my sight. I wiped it aside, streaking my sleeve scarlet, and yelled fresh commands: "Let no one linger! Extinguish every fire! Empty your village! Take nothing with you! Send your strongest men to the rice paddies and have them stand ready to save your precious young crops when the dragon stone shatters! Why do you stare at me? If you will not hear my words, hear *hers*!" I held the clay image of my goddess high and felt her cradled dragon stone turn to fire in my clasp.

A backhanded blow knocked her from my hands. Ryu had climbed the hill to confront me. His sword was drawn.

"Get down from here," he ordered. "This hill is sacred to us. I will not allow a madwoman to pollute it with her presence."

"Ryu, you fool!" Daimu scrambled up the slope and stopped to retrieve my amulet. "Can't you recognize that she speaks with the voice of the gods?"

"I recognize insanity. Or trickery." He looked down the hill at his bewildered clanfolk. "Ignore her! She's trying to deceive you by pretending to hear the spirits. Let her learn that the Ookami are too wise to be led like dogs!"

I hooked my fingers into the folds of Ryu's tunic. My assault was so unexpected that he shrank back, but could not escape me. "Save them, Ryu!" I cried. "There is not much time. Go now, return to your own towering house, lord of the wolves, and when you save your most precious treasures— child, wife, mother—remember Noboru! Let there be no line between Matsu and Ookami when you rescue children! The gods will bless you if—"

"*Get off me, demon!*" Ryu struck my upper arm with the pommel of his sword. Pain radiated through me from shoulder to wrist and I fell back into Daimu's arms. "*No one will heed your ranting! The sacrifice will go on, and I will rejoice to see it.*"

My hand dived for the bronze handle sticking out of Daimu's sash. My fingers whisked the shining mirror above my head, twisting it to catch the brilliance of heaven. Sunlight knifed from the polished surface directly into the wolf chieftain's eyes. He cried out in fury, blinded, and dropped his sword.

"Run, Daimu!" I gasped, clinging for a moment to my heart's chosen one. "If Ryu won't listen to me, you must, or there will be no way of numbering so many dead! Go, before—before—" I crumpled against him. A sigh escaped my lips, and the last remnant of the spirits' presence within me took wing on that breath. My eyes refocused slowly; I saw only the mortal world now.

"Himiko, are you all right?" Daimu slipped one arm around my waist and gazed at me with concern and tenderness.

Why is he still here? I wondered, groggily. *Didn't I tell him—didn't I tell* all *of them to run to the village and save . . . and save . . . ?*

I turned my head slowly back toward Mori's tomb. Not one member of the wolf clan had stirred a single step. All of them stared at me in alarm and astonishment. So many gaping mouths, so many goggling eyes, so many faces that were now gray as ashes! My vision-born outburst had left them overcome with paralyzing awe. They stood frozen, transfixed . . .

. . . useless.

"Why are you still here?" I pushed away from Daimu and shouted at them. My ordinary voice was back. It was nowhere near as compelling as what had leaped from my lips in the throes of vision. Still, I could make it loud and forceful enough for the people to hear. "What are you waiting for?"

Ryu blinked rapidly, recovering his sun-dazzled sight. "I told you, Himiko: my people know madness when they see it."

"But not their own stupidity," Daimu responded hotly. "You are all *fools*!" he thundered at the people. "The spirits

send us a warning and you stand there, heaps of dead wood?"
He uttered a disgusted sound and headed down the hill.

"Where do you think you're going?" Ryu demanded,
his sword once more in hand.

"To heed the gods," Daimu replied, breaking into a run.

"Stay where you are!" Ryu went after him, murder in
his eyes. He slashed at Daimu and a thin line of blood crept
across my beloved's sleeve, but did not slow him. The crowd
near Mori's tomb scattered as the two men rushed past. I
pursued them as fast as I could, though the strain sent pain
lancing through my bad leg.

"Stop, Ryu, stop!" I cried, and with a final effort leaped
to close the gap between us. I landed on his back, clumsily
scrabbling to hold on. He had no trouble shrugging me off
onto an age-sunk grave mound.

"I have had enough of you," he said, raising his sword.
"I should have done this long ago."

"My lord Ryu, you mustn't hurt her!" Rinji rammed his
scrawny body into the wolf chieftain's ribs. The only effect
this had was to send Ryu stumbling three steps sideways.

"Has this girl cast her enchantments over *everyone*?"
Ryu bellowed at the sky. He turned his wrath on Rinji, who
edged closer to me, shaking like dead reeds in a windstorm.
"So you want to play the hero against *me*? You should have
learned better from your teacher and stuck to jabbering
curses." He took a fistful of Rinji's robe in hand and pressed
his sword's point to the base of the young shaman's throat.
The corners of his mouth lifted slightly as he took pleasure from the terror in Rinji's eyes. "You see, Himiko?" he
said smoothly. "You are not the only one to whom the gods

speak. I hear them now! They tell me they are as sick of treachery and ingratitude as I, and that once I've cleansed those offenses from the wolf clan's heart, they'll send me someone worthy to—"

The ground shifted and heaved. Ryu and Rinji toppled beside me across the grave mound. With a rumble of power from the depths of the earth, the dragon raised one paw and smashed it down on the land of the Ookami.

19
THE MARK OF HIS TALONS

The earth lifted and fell beneath me, shuddering through my spine, casting me up and flinging me down. I rolled onto my stomach and tried to get onto hands and knees, but the ground buckled and sent me rolling. I heard a rumbling deeper and more terrible than any thunderstorm and the screech of rock scraping over rock. A frantic commotion of human voices filled the air like a flock of bats, swarming high, swooping low. Howls of wordless horror and helplessness fought to be heard over cries of pain, curses, desperately shouted names, and pleas to the gods for mercy. This was no mere tremor of the earth: it was the true dance of dragons at the heart of the world.

It ended.

The stillness following the quake was nearly as terrifying as the quake itself. I feared that if my heart would not stop beating so hectically, so fast, so uncontrollably, it would shake itself out of my body. My breath raced with the beating of my blood. I had to force myself to hold it for a moment, then inhale slowly and let it go as calmly as I could.

Although I stood up slowly, I was immediately struck by a wave of dizziness. Swaying, I looked around and saw the burial ground transformed into a web of fissures in the earth. Some of the more modest grave mounds had become shallow pits. Most of the taller ones, dedicated to the highest-ranking Ookami nobles, had tumbled down. The heaps of earth covering them had slipped away, revealing the slabs of stone within. I felt a pang of regret for Daimu's sake when I saw that Mori's monument too had collapsed. There was no sight of the jar holding the giant's bones.

We will find them again, Mori, I vowed silently. *You will go to your rest the way you should, with reverence and without the sacrifice of innocent lives. I swear you will have the rites you deserve as soon as I have seen to the needs of the living. Wait patiently, gentle friend.*

I started for the Ookami village, never looking back. I refused to think about what I would see once the path brought me into view of the shaken settlement. My visions did not matter, Mori's fallen tomb did not matter, the devastation I might see at any moment did not matter to me. As I drove myself forward, my mishealed leg aching in protest at the speed with which I moved, my thoughts filled with the one thing in the dragon-shattered world that was as vital as blood and breath: *Little Brother, I am coming. Don't be afraid! Daimu is with you—he must be! He will protect you until I can hold you in my arms and bring you home. Oh, Noboru, be brave!*

A press of Ookami surged around me on the path. Their faces were smeared with dirt, their clothes rank with sweat, their eyes streaming tears. I found myself being shoved and battered back and forth in their midst. If I fell, they would trample me in their haste to get back to their homes.

"Himiko?" Rinji's haggard face appeared out of the crowd. "Himiko, you're limping. Here." He offered me his back and I clambered onto it. There would be time later for sorting out the troubles between us. For now, we had a single goal. His long legs carried us to the forefront of the mob, and my position high on his back let me be among the first to see the work of the dragon.

The palisade was down. Most of the massive log fence that had ringed the Ookami village had become a giant's scattered woodpile. The watchtower leaned over the wreckage at a precarious angle, one leg snapped in two, one a creaking mass of splinters. As we entered the village, I saw that one of the great gates remained upright, but the other had fallen. Four men worked desperately to lift it. I wondered why, until we came closer and felt sick to my stomach at the sight of a pair of legs sticking out from beneath the massive door.

The air was thick with the smell of burning. Many small fires threw ropes of smoke into the sky, but the worst blaze came from the cookhouse, whose thatched roof had become a solid mat of flame. A group of Ookami formed a line between the village well and the conflagration, relaying water jars.

"It won't be enough to put out that fire," I muttered.

"They know," he replied. "They're trying to soak the roofs of the nearest houses, to keep the flames from spreading. Thank the gods that there's no wind!"

No wind . . . and no nearby houses, I thought. There was nothing but rubble surrounding the burning cookhouse. Not a single dwelling was left standing close enough to be threatened by the blaze.

"Shall I carry you to the shrine?" Rinji asked.

"No. I can walk now. Set me down."

He did as I asked, but so slowly that I recognized his reluctance before I saw the doubtful look on his face. "Tell me where you want to go. I'll see that you get there."

"Rinji, I don't need you to—"

"You do," he said, indicating the chaos around us. People were rushing this way and that, choking on the smoke as they called out for help, grasping each other's clothing as they begged for aid.

"Have you seen my father?"

"The roof of my house fell in! I called my daughter's name, but there was no answer and I can't move the beams alone!"

"Can you help me find something to bind up wounds? My husband was hit in the head by a falling timber, and there's so much blood!"

Knots of workers were already laboring over the ruins of houses, shouting into the rubble. An answering voice was cause for cheers, but silence was only a momentary discouragement. As they hauled aside the remnants of pit house roofs they did not pause to ask if the trapped souls within were their clanfolk or their slaves.

The village pathways were thick with debris. Everyone worked at a frenzied pace, not bothering to notice where they tossed the lighter pieces of rubble. A chunk of wood came flying at us. Rinji pulled me out of its way just in time. His face was stern and there was a stubborn look in his eyes as he said, "Where do you want to go?" It was clear that he was not going to let me go alone, and I saw the wisdom in accepting this.

"Ryu's house. Quickly."

He took my arm and strode through the ruins of his village. Storehouses leaned against one another like drunkards. Smashed clay jars poured out the grains that should have fed this clan until harvest.

If there will be a harvest, I thought. No one had listened to the spirits' words of warning. No one had gone to stand watch in the terraced fields. When the dragon twisted his back under the mountain and the thick earthen walls of the rice paddies cracked open like eggshells, no one was there, ready to cram mud into the breaches before everything was lost.

We passed many of the nobles' houses before we reached the chieftain's home. The bulky pillars that supported these grand dwellings were no more than stalks of autumn-faded grass between the dragon's claws. Many had toppled, taking the houses with them. Some creaked and swayed dangerously, as though ready to fall if brushed by a butterfly's wing. Some still stood, but split open like the skin of an overripe fruit. The proud homes of the highborn and the pit houses of the common folk were equals in the blind, indifferent power of the earthquake.

So were the dead: rich or poor, old or young, man or woman. We saw them everywhere. We heard the wailing of those who had loved them, brought them out of the wreckage, arranged their bodies so they no longer looked like broken dolls. I caught sight of one small, cloth-draped shape and could not hold back a cry.

Rinji made an awkward attempt to hug me, but I was already running as fast as I could. Too many ghosts were rising, and I dreaded seeing my brother's face among them.

Rinji caught up to me just as I reached the chieftain's house. It was now no more than a pile of broken timbers, scattered thatch, and swirling dust that blurred the figures moving away from the rubble. Lady Sato was the first to emerge into clearer air, followed by Chizu. Her arms were empty and my heart sank until I saw Ryu come after her, his infant son held tightly and tenderly to his heart.

"Lady Himiko!" He was smiling and weeping at once, and he looked like a man who has witnessed miracles. "He saved them," he said in a hushed voice. "Master Daimu rescued my family, my dearest ones"—his awestruck gaze returned to the baby—"my Arashi. By the time I reached the house, they were already out of harm's way. If I had stopped him, they—they would be—" He began to sob.

"He was wonderful," Chizu said, her face shining. "The house shook and slid and tilted over. The ladder fell and we were too high up to jump, but he arrived in time to set it back in place, climb up, and—"

"Where is he?" I demanded, seizing her shoulders. "And where is my little brother? Where has Daimu taken him?"

"Taken him?" Her look of joy faded. "When the earthquake struck, your brother shrieked and ran to the back of the house, where he sleeps. I tried to go after him, but I was holding the baby, and the house slipped, and I was calling his name, and Lady Sato was screaming that the ladder was gone, and—and—" She trembled, reliving those moments of too-recent terror. Biting her lip, she regained control of herself and went on: "Master Daimu got us out of the house, then saw that Noboru was missing. I told him where the child was hiding. He ordered us to move as far from the house as possible and then . . . he went back."

I stared at her in disbelief, then turned my head toward the demolished house. "No," I said. *"No!"* I flew headlong into the shroud of dust, clawing madly at the ruins, calling the names of my brother and my beloved again and again and again!

"Himiko . . ." Daimu's voice came to me so faintly that at first I thought it was a cruel illusion. "Himiko, we are here . . . back here."

I clambered over the fallen pieces of the wolf chieftain's house, my heart soaring. *He's alive! Daimu is alive, and he said "We are here"! That must mean Noboru is safe too. Oh, may the gods be praised!*

The dust was settling. I followed the sound of Daimu's voice and found him half buried under an open tangle of fallen beams. He smiled weakly when he saw me and shifted his body just a little. The owl-eyed, anxious face of my little brother peered up at me before his mouth twisted sharply down at the corners and opened in a lusty yowl.

Somewhere behind me I could hear Ryu's voice shouting orders. A group of five strong warriors appeared and began to move away the timbers arching over Daimu and Noboru. My brother was the first to be freed. He buried his face against me so deeply that I was sure it would leave a bruise.

Let it leave a hundred! I thought gladly, embracing him.

Ryu dropped to one knee beside us. "The child is all right?" he asked with genuine concern. I could only nod, too happy to speak. "Himiko . . . Lady Himiko, from this moment—now—you and your brother will be treated with all respect and every honor. There will be no more talk of hostages, or banishment, or"—his voice dropped to a shamed whisper—"or sacrifice. You truly are the greatest among shamans. You foresaw this and tried to warn us. It is thanks to you that my family survives. How can I repay such a debt?"

"There is the one you must repay," I said, nodding to where his men had finally extricated Daimu from the fallen house. Two of them lifted him clear while two more removed as much of the quake debris as possible before their comrades set him down. The fifth man removed his tunic and rolled it into a support for Daimu's head.

With Noboru clinging to me, I moved gracelessly to attend my beloved. His eyes were closed, but the lids fluttered when I took his hand in mine. "Did you see them?" he asked softly. "Ryu's family . . ."

The wolf chieftain's shadow fell across us. "They are safe," he said, choking on unshed tears of gratitude. "Master

Daimu, I swear to you by the precious lives you rescued, you may name anything you desire and it will be yours. If your shrine has fallen, it will be the first structure we rebuild. Your marriage to Lady Himiko will be a celebration that this clan will remember forever. Your household's share in our harvests—if the gods have spared our fields—will be twice as great as mine."

Daimu smiled. "Don't promise me *too* much, Lord Ryu. You might regret it. Are you sure you want me to marry this"—he coughed before he could finish the joke—"troublemaker?"

"Please bring him some water," I said to one of the men who had freed Daimu from the wreckage. "This dust is awful; it's choking him and he's covered with it. See how pale he looks? Rinji!" Daimu's former student was with us at once, crouching at my elbow. "Find the best house that's still standing. He should be brought there and made comfortable before we begin treating him."

"Of course, Lady Himiko." Would he always speak to me with such an air of apology from now on? "I'll also see if the shrine still stands, or at least hasn't been destroyed completely. I hope to salvage some of the remedies and the ingredients; we'll need to make more." He glanced at the darkened bloodstain on Daimu's sleeve where Ryu's sword had slit fabric and flesh. "And bandages," he added as he rose to go.

"Rinji . . . wait. Stay with me." Daimu's request rasped from his throat. The ongoing chaos of the ravaged village made it difficult to hear, but I thought I detected a low, eerie crackling in his breath.

"Noboru," I said in a quiet voice. "Little Brother, I need your help." He looked up at me with inquiring eyes but still clung close. "Lord Ryu must stay here for now, but Lady Chizu needs someone strong to stand by her, to protect her and the baby."

"Come with me, Big Sister," he whispered.

I shook my head. "I must stay here too. You're a big boy, and you will be our leader someday soon; you can do this." I gave him a ferocious hug. "I know you won't disappoint me."

"Yes, Big Sister." He still looked scared, but he trotted off.

"Why did . . . you do that, Himiko?" Daimu spoke with his eyes closed. I stroked his brow and tried not to shudder with alarm at how clammy it felt. "Why . . . send Noboru . . . away?" Every utterance was a struggle.

"He's seen enough unhappy sights for one day." I battled tears.

"What's the matter?" Ryu broke in. "Why are you talking like that?" He seized the edges of the slash on Daimu's sleeve and pulled them apart, revealing the wound below. It was hardly more than a nasty scratch, and he said so for everyone to hear. "And this is the only mark on you, Master Daimu, besides some insignificant scrapes and bruises. It's nothing, *nothing*! Look, Lady Himiko is crying! Tell her that there's no need for that. Tell her you'll be well!"

Daimu sighed, then coughed again. A bubble of blood glittered and burst at the corner of his mouth. "She knows . . . truth. Give her . . . your thanks . . . not me. Her vision saved . . . saved . . ." The nerve-racking sound strangling his breath was harsher. The whiteness of his lips stood out in shocking contrast to the thin trickle of red moving slowly down his chin.

I lifted him gently so that his head was cradled in my arms. "Daimu . . . my beloved . . . my only one . . ." The Ookami warrior returned with water and a rag. I tried to help Daimu sip from the bowl, but he shook his head feebly. His eyelids drooped and fell. I used the water to wash his face instead, possessed by the ridiculous hope that its cooling touch would revive him.

"O spirits, hear me," I murmured fervently. "You who dwell in all things, you who heal the wounds that fire and flood, drought and quake inflict upon the earth, heal him. Do not tear my heart away. In mercy's precious name, do not part us now."

"Himiko . . ." Daimu's voice had become the sighing of an autumn wind. "My Himiko . . . you hear the gods more . . . more clearly than I ever did. Hear them now, my beloved . . . my bride. . . ." A last breath, and his spirit flew away.

I saw it go. I swear this by all that I have ever loved, I saw Daimu's spirit rise and cross the shadowy border between worlds. I held his lifeless body in my arms and felt the tears dry on my face as he walked into the willow grove I knew so well.

Reikon was waiting in the dappled shade of the willows' drifting branches. The two spirits drew near to one another, as though some god's unseen hand were moving a mirror closer and closer to the thing that it reflected. But there was no telling which of these two was merely the image and which the reality. Before my eyes they melded into one—the prince of my spirit, the love of my heart, the keeper of my soul.

Do not mourn me, Himiko. The words brushed over me as delicately as the touch of willow leaves. *Do not spend your strength or waste your powers in grief. You know the truth.*

I nodded, neither knowing nor caring if he could see it. I did know: my life's purpose still lay before me. This blessed land, favored so generously by the gods, was shattered into more fragments than any dragon's dance had ever left behind. Clan mistrusting clan, clan battling clan, clan enslaving clan, when it was all the same as mistrusting, battling, and enslaving ourselves!

Now the grove became a swarm of countless spirits. My beloved disappeared into their midst. I called to him by his name as a prince of the spirit world and by the name of the young Ookami shaman who had been mine for such a sorrowfully short time. Reikon or Daimu, spirit or mortal, he had been swept away.

Now the spirits summoned me: *See, Himiko! See what awaits you! See the balance and beauty of the land! Grandfather Pine grows tall and shelters the wolf and the boar, the deer and the hawk alike, in harmony. Death too has its place here, but death within set boundaries. The hawk strikes from above, but sheds blood only to satisfy his hunger. The wolf hunts and kills, but does not slaughter. Remember this, Himiko.*

Remember this, O princess, shaman, queen. Remember this, my cherished Daughter. The sun goddess stood before me. Her arms were empty, but her cupped hands were heaped with the shards of the dragon stone. One by one they rose into the air. One by one, they joined together as I watched and as she spoke: *Become what you have always known you could be. Become the healer, the counselor, the comforter, the one who builds a path between worlds. Become this vision and this memory. Bring this teaching to every clan your life will touch until your touch makes all clans one.*

Fascinated by the glittering fragments, I stretched out my fingers to touch one before it could reunite with the rest. I scarcely brushed its jagged edge, but that slight contact was enough: a long cut opened from the tip of my left hand's smallest finger to the base of my wrist.

I cried out in pain and found myself in a world where a village lay in ruins, an unknown path lay before me, and the only one I could ever love as my soul's other self lay dead in my arms.

20

AWAKENINGS

We put out the fires. We rescued the living from the wreckage of their homes. We repaired the fields. We shared food and water and shelter without asking the person eating from our bowl *What is your clan? Are you highborn, lowborn, free or slave?* We began to rebuild the houses and the storage shelters. We buried the dead.

I said my last earthly farewell to my beloved two days after the earthquake. There would be no elaborate ceremonies and no extended period of mourning. The needs of the living took precedence over the peace of the departed. Daimu would have understood that. Ryu supervised the rebuilding of Mori's tomb, putting four men on the job as well as himself. They salvaged stones from the fallen monument, and though the result was modest, it was a proper resting place that Daimu shared with his uncle's bones.

Rinji performed the funeral rites. I could not have done it without breaking down. The calamity that had befallen his people left him deeply altered. All of his hesitancy and self-consciousness were gone. He carried himself with quiet dignity in the presence of the gods and with true humility, not cringing self-abasement, among the Ookami. Even Lady Sato noticed the change and spoke to him with respect, though she looked a little peeved to have lost her sarcasm's favorite target.

When the ceremony was over, Rinji approached Noboru and me. We were both weeping, taking comfort from one another. The Ookami who attended the interment kept their distance during the burial rites and headed back to the village without speaking to us afterward. I think this was partly out of respect for our grief, partly because they had all become a little afraid of me.

Rinji waited patiently until my sobs subsided and I indicated I was ready to talk. I thanked him for how well he had invoked the gods and even managed to give him an encouraging look as I said: "Your teacher would be very proud of you."

"I hope that *both* of my teachers feel that way." He glanced after the departing villagers. "Lady Himiko, it would be a great kindness if you could visit our pottery-maker today. She is beside herself with misery because she wasn't able to work fast enough and make enough attendants for Master Daimu and his uncle."

I smiled faintly. "She provided more than enough, and in such a short time. Mori had no one to look after him while he was alive, and Daimu took care of himself when he was on his long pilgrimage. She shouldn't fret, but I will speak with her anyway."

"I could do that for you, Big Sister," Noboru said.

"Thank you, Noboru; that would be good. Why don't you run ahead and see to it now?" With a nod and a grin, Noboru was on his way. Rinji and I watched him go.

"He's a fine boy," Rinji said. "You should be pleased that he's so eager to set the potter's mind at ease. It was a miracle that the earthquake spared her firing oven. She's going to need it." He sighed. "So many burial vessels for her to make, so many funeral rites for me to perform."

"Not so many as that." I wiped away the last of my tears and gazed at the monument. "I will help you bury your kin."

He looked surprised by my offer. "How can you? Now that Master Daimu has been buried, you and Noboru will leave us soon."

"We have been gone for so long, will a few more days make much difference? You and I will be able to comfort the dead and the living more quickly if we can work together. I think—I *know* this is what I should do"—I could not take my eyes from Daimu's resting place—"for his sake. I hear him telling me, *'Himiko, my people need you.'*" With an effort, I turned away from the monument. "But my mother needs me too. It's my duty as her daughter to go back, yet if I forsake my duty as a shaman, I will regret it forever. Oh, Rinji, if there only was a way that I could accomplish both!"

"May the gods grant that there is."

The next day, as I was thinking about preparations for the journey home, Rinji came to tell me that he had sent a messenger to the Matsu clan with word that I would return with Noboru before summer ended. "A message! Such a simple solution!" he said happily. "I should have thought of it right away."

"And I," I said.

"I'm glad you didn't. This way—helping you even a little—I feel I'm finally able to begin atoning for what I did to you and Daimu."

"Rinji, I forgave you for that."

"I wish I could forgive myself." He sighed again.

Seeking to distract him, I asked, "Who did you send? Someone reliable, I hope. Someone who knows the way to my village?"

He brightened. "I sent Hiroshi. You have to agree, he's the right man for the job. He's never traveled to the Matsu lands, but his brother-in-law made the journey many seasons ago, with our old Lord Nago. He told his family so many tales about the trip that Hiroshi swears he'll be able to find his way there with ease. He's ready to do everything but sprout wings and fly, to serve you."

"Does Ryu know you did this?"

"If he doesn't like it, I'll take the consequences."

Hearing him speak so calmly, without a hint of his old timidity, I had to smile and say, "You are very brave, my friend."

"Brave as a cornered rat. You know how we're all living, these days. If he does discover what I've done, I have nowhere to hide, so I might as well pretend I'm standing up to him out of courage."

Rinji was trying to make little of his newfound valor, but he was right about one thing: there was no longer any way for him or me or Noboru or Ryu and his household to avoid one another.

By the greatest luck, the Ookami village shrine did not collapse in the earthquake. Ryu's family moved into it at once, bringing Rinji, Noboru, and me. Lady Sato was much too pleased to have all of her slaves *and* the shrine servants attending her. When it was their turn to serve on the house-building crews, she took it as a personal attack and an attempt to steal her property.

Everyone in the village took part in the reconstruction efforts, unless they were too old, too young, too sickly, or recovering from the injuries they had sustained during the quake. Some worked on the actual process of raising a house: digging holes, felling trees, shaping lumber, gathering thatch, and everything else. Others saw to it that the laborers were well fed, had enough water to drink while they worked, and that their tools remained in good condition.

I . . . did nothing. Although I worked with Rinji, caring for the spirits of the dead, it was not a task that took up every moment of my days. Unlike Lady Sato, it did not feel natural for me to be idle in the midst of so much unfinished work. I accepted the fact that I would not be of any use when it came to the heavy labor of home-building, but whenever I tried to take my place in the ranks of the water-carriers, or the cooks, or ax-sharpeners, I was turned away.

"Lady Himiko, you mustn't do this sort of work. It isn't fit for you."

"We have more than enough people helping us already. You should go back to the shrine and ask the gods to bless us with success in erecting this new house."

"If you are busy working here, who will guide us? Who will decide what we should do next? Who will settle all the problems that have arisen since the great disaster?"

"Our shaman shouldn't dirty her hands washing dishes."

"Our leader shouldn't waste time hauling water from the well."

It did me no good to tell them that I was not their leader, and that while I was a shaman, I was not *their* shaman anymore. From the earliest moments of my grief for Daimu's death, the Ookami had left me little time for tears. They implored my forgiveness for having ignored my vision-sent warnings. They swore they would not make that mistake a second time. They begged me to tell them what the future held, and when I explained that I did not control when and what the spirits told me, they refused to believe it.

I reminded them that their chieftain was alive, strong, and capable. He had taken charge of all rescue and restoration efforts, as was his right and duty toward his people. They chose to hear, *Lord Ryu is following* my *direction and obeying* my *commands!*

If that were only true! Though the quake had changed Ryu's heart and opened his eyes, it had not turned him into a lump of beeswax for me to shape in any way I liked. It purged him of his resentment, his haughtiness, and the petty grudges that had once filled his spirit with a *mamushi*'s venom, but it had not driven out his dreams of further conquests. That task remained for me.

On a summer day when heavy rain made it impossible for the wolf clan to do anything but take shelter in their overcrowded houses, old and new, I decided it was time to settle all of the unresolved matters between me, Ryu, Rinji, and the rest of their clan. While Chizu and the baby napped, and Noboru helped Lady Sato weave ramie fabric for the new clothes all of us needed so urgently, I discreetly asked Ryu and Rinji to come with me.

I led them to the back of the shrine, where I had once again set up the cloth walls of my sleeping quarters, now shared with Noboru. I motioned for them to sit, but before they were properly settled, Ryu blurted out: "Don't leave us yet, Lady Himiko, please!"

I was taken aback. "What are you saying?"

"I thought you wanted to speak to the two of us because you were going to announce your departure." When I shook my head, he looked embarrassed by his outburst. "I'm sorry. Of course you are free to leave at any time—you and all your kin. It's just that . . . we still need you *and* them."

"It was good of the Matsu to stay on and work with our people, even after Lord Ryu gave them their liberty," Rinji said. "I'm surprised they didn't leave at once."

"They're waiting for Noboru and me," I said. "For some reason, they don't want to go home without us."

"It's a mark of respect," Ryu said. "They are like the Ookami: they don't want to tempt the displeasure of the gods after seeing the proof of your powers."

I lowered my voice. "I did not *cause* the earthquake, Ryu."

"No, but the gods sent it to punish us for our offenses against you and your kin: the attempted sacrifices, the slavery, the war that took the lives of your father and brothers—"

"Then why did the quake bury at least two Matsu along

with the Ookami? And why are more of my people suffering from wounds and broken bones?" I shook my head. "The disaster did not come as a punishment. It came because . . . it came. Such things happen. I do not believe that the gods release the dragons of this world against us as penalties for our wrongdoing. If that were so, would there be a single person left alive? Your people are not suffering *because* of how they treated me and mine. The Ookami are as precious to the spirits as the Matsu, or any other clan. The gods see none of the differences between us, the differences that we created ourselves."

Ryu looked solemn. "You are right, Lady Himiko."

"Lord Ryu, Master Rinji, we must help the people see the truth as well. The Ookami treat me with *too* much deference. They see me as their leader *and* their shaman."

"Is that such a bad thing?" Rinji attempted a jest, but Ryu was not laughing.

"It is," I insisted. "The people should be guided by those who can lead them best, not those who terrify them most. Otherwise they will face a future forever torn by war." I turned my hand over and contemplated the long scar across my palm, relic of the shattered dragon stone's sharp touch. I had given up trying to understand how a wound received in a vision could leave a scar in the waking world. Instead I decided to concentrate on the lessons it might teach me, and that I might teach to others.

"Lord Ryu . . ." I dropped my voice so low that it was almost lost in the sound of the rain. "Lord Ryu, you are not happy with the way your clan has flocked to me." He tried to protest, but I raised my scarred hand and silenced him.

"I do not blame you. *You* are their chieftain, always striving to shield them from hunger and hardship. How have they repaid your care?" He did not need to reply. His look of bitter disappointment spoke for him. "Yet you still want me to stay?"

"We must rebuild," he said. "We have lost too much of our stored food, too many of our rice fields have been ruined, and if we cannot repair and replant them soon, we risk losing too much of the growing season. If you give the word, the people will work better and more swiftly to satisfy you than to obey me. I will not see my clan starve, Lady Himiko."

I lowered my eyelids. "Is that why you are planning to send warriors against the boar clan soon?" I asked.

"How did you—?"

I lifted my gaze and saw how deeply I had unnerved him. "Your people force me to be idle, and idle ears hear rumors. Is this one true?"

"People in this clan talk too much," he said sullenly. "I wasn't going to *war* against the Inoshishi. Why would I? They're already our subjects. I only wanted to make a show of our strength when I tell them they must raise the level of their tribute and send it earlier. I have to begin making up for the stored supplies we lost in the earthquake."

"You must not do this," I said. "Unless he's a fool, the boar clan's chieftain will wonder why you're making such demands. How can you prevent him from dispatching spies over the mountain? When he finds out how badly the Ookami have been weakened by this disaster, he won't send you tribute: he'll send swords. Other clans will do the same.

You no longer have the strength to defeat them all, no matter how well you fight."

He saw the terrible truth in my words. "Then what *can*
I do, Lady Himiko?" he asked in desperation. "I have met
with my counselors and taken stock of our supplies. Until
the harvest comes, we will be facing very lean times. Many
of our livestock died or ran away during the earthquake.
The fish ponds cracked and drained before we could salvage
them. There's only so much we can gather from the forest,
and because we need so many men to rebuild the houses,
we can't amass a decent-sized hunting party."

"The men you planned to send to the boar clan—?"

"—wouldn't make a difference. Not every warrior is a
good hunter." His shoulders slumped. "Lady Himiko . . . you
have no reason to spare my clan after what I did to yours,
but . . . will you help me now? Ask the spirits to show me
the right path. My people need the support of other clans.
How can we gain that without taking up our swords?"

"It will not be easy," I admitted. "But I don't think it
will be impossible. The other clans need you too. There is
much you can provide for one another and enrich everyone.
You must make them see this."

"I don't know if I can." He looked to me for rescue.
"But you could, Lady Himiko!"

Before I could reply, I heard the sound of feet thud-
ding up the ladder and stumbling through the doorway to
the shrine. Lady Sato began squawking indignantly, Arashi
wailed, and above that racket came the sound of Hiroshi's
voice calling, "Lady Himiko! Lady Himiko, are you here?
I have news!"

I dashed out of my quarters and found the young guard panting for breath while rainwater ran off his reed cape and puddled on the floor. *How did he manage to reach my village and return here so quickly?* I thought. I tallied the days since his departure in my mind and the result was plain: *Impossible! Why has he come back so soon? What's wrong?*

"Hiroshi, are you all right?" I asked.

He dropped to one knee. "Lady Himiko, pardon me; I could not fulfill my task."

"What task is he talking about?" Ryu demanded. "Hiroshi, why are you dressed for travel? Where have you been? Have you encountered any other clans? Did you tell them what happened to us?"

"He's making a mess!" Lady Sato complained, her voice shrill. "Who invited him? Get him out of here!"

Rinji attempted to intervene. "Lady Sato, we must hear what he has to say first. Lord Ryu, rest assured, Hiroshi would never speak one word to betray our condition to another clan. I was the one who sent him on this errand to the Matsu. I am surprised to see him back so soon, but—"

"You sent him to the Matsu?" Ryu was livid. "When we need every healthy man here, to rebuild our village? Why?"

"It was for my sake, Lord Ryu," I said calmly, and began explaining the purpose of sending Hiroshi to my people.

No one was more surprised than I when Hiroshi interrupted me. "Lady Himiko, *please* hear me! You must know why I am here now, when by rights I should still be on the road to the Matsu lands. The girl who shared your captivity when you first came here, your friend Lady Kaya—"

"How do you know her name?" I demanded, astonished to hear it on Hiroshi's lips. "You never did while we were slaves and you were our guard."

"I know it now, Lady Himiko, because that was how her warriors hailed her when she captured me." He pushed his soaking hair out of his eyes. "She is a fearsomely skilled huntress, your friend. I never knew she was watching me make my way through the forest until her arrow thrummed in the trunk of a tree less than a handspan from my head. She promised that the next one would pierce my eye if I didn't surrender."

"How strange," I mused. "It isn't like Kaya to ambush innocent travelers."

One side of Hiroshi's mouth twitched in amusement. "She is also fearsomely skilled in recalling faces, Lady Himiko. She recognized me."

"You say she has warriors with her?" Ryu asked urgently. "How many? Where are they heading? And how does a girl come to be traveling in such company?"

"She is the daughter of a chieftess, Lord Ryu," I said. "Her mother once told me that she intends to have Lady Kaya lead the Shika clan one day. Now it seems she is already leading some of them."

"At least twenty," Hiroshi said. "And they are coming here."

"Then we will be ready for them!" Ryu started for the doorway. "Rinji, help me! We must rally our men, arm them, and prepare for battle!"

"My lord, no!" Hiroshi cried in a panic. "Lady Kaya

told me her purpose in coming here after she questioned me and sent me back here. She does not want war."

"I don't believe that," Ryu maintained.

"You should," said Kaya, stepping in out of the rain.

"I think the sun is coming out," I said to Kaya as we watched the last few raindrops drip from the eaves of the shrine.

"Oh, good," my friend said. "Now the Ookami won't melt when they come outside."

"Some of them don't," I said, indicating the intense conversation at our backs. Lord Ryu was talking earnestly with his counselors, who had come to the shrine in spite of the downpour. Hiroshi and Rinji had fetched those respected noblemen secretly, to discuss the consequences of the Shika warriors' presence beyond the village's toppled palisade. "Oh, Kaya, what's going to happen now?"

She shrugged. "You tell me. From what that guardsman had to say, you speak to the gods more easily than to mortals." She laughed, then abruptly bit it back and regarded me gravely. "I shouldn't make such jokes, Himiko. When I look at you, I see someone different. You've changed."

. I hugged her. "Don't be a silly Badger. I'm still the same."

She was unconvinced. "When I escaped from this village, you were a slave. Now you've risen so high that the wolf chieftain has to strain his neck to look you in the eyes. He calls you *Lady* Himiko with so much reverence, you'd think his life depended on it. Every one of the Ookami nobles acted the same way toward you when they entered this house. How did it all happen? When I finally persuaded Mother to let me *try* to free you, my warriors and I stopped at your village first, to see if they'd had any news. Imagine how we felt to hear your stepmother Emi, your brother Shoichi, and a whole family of your clanfolk tell the tale of how gallantly you rescued *them*!"

"Emi and the others reached home? Thank the gods," I said. "And Kaya . . . what about my mother? Is she . . . ?"

My friend frowned. "Didn't *he* tell you?" She indicated Hiroshi, who was seated with Ryu's family, out of the way of the chieftain's council meeting.

"He scarcely had the chance to let us know he'd encountered you before you arrived and took over."

"Ha! Took over. I like the sound of that. Maybe I'll do it, once we put these wolves in their place. It would make a nice change to have slaves instead of being one."

"No, it would not," I said firmly. "Kaya, *tell* me about Mama."

She put both arms around me. "Your mother is alive and well. From what I heard when we reached your village, her healing began the moment she saw Emi and Shoichi come home with the news that you and Noboru would soon join them."

"So she has been freed of the death sentence?"

Kaya smiled. "Not *officially*, as yet, but she's been out of danger for some time. Say whatever else you like about these old men"—she nodded in the direction of Ryu's counselors—"they're still the fiercest warriors we'll ever know, especially when they're fighting to defend their families." Then the insufferable Lady Badger smirked and added: *"Particularly when one of them is protecting his new wife."*

And that was how I was informed that my mother had married Lord Hideki.

Kaya savored my astonishment. "It seems like the spirits don't tell you *everything*. That will make the trip home less awkward. I'd hate to have to stop every two steps and clap my hands, just to pay you the proper respect."

"How did it happen?"

"I didn't think to ask. Lord Hideki told me that you'd asked him to look after your mother, and I guess that once he did, one thing led to another. Isn't that how these things usually happen?" Before I could reply, she added: "Not that either one of us would know."

I said nothing, holding my secrets for a little longer. Now was not the time to tell her about Daimu.

Behind us, one of the Ookami nobles raised his voice in anger. "What do you mean, we have to let the Shika girl go back to her men? She's a valuable hostage, and the little fool *begged* to be taken, walking straight into our village like that. I say we make the most of her stupidity. We hold her, and when the rest try to rescue her, we capture as many as we can. We need more strong hands to rebuild our houses!"

"*You're* the stupid one," a second aristocrat countered. "That girl is Lady Himiko's dearest friend and a chieftess's daughter! If we touch her, we'll bring down the wrath of the gods *and* a war we can't fight now!"

The first man dismissed these objections with a rude noise. "And where does this mighty chieftess live? Beyond the Matsu lands! I tell you, by the time she sends a war party, we'll have recovered our full strength. The Ookami are more than a match for any clan!"

"We will not face *one* clan, my lord," Ryu said softly. He beckoned to Kaya. "Let these men hear what you told me."

Kaya stood up to face the Ookami counselors. "We did not come here seeking war, O elders of the wolf clan. We came to negotiate the release of Lady Himiko and her brother Noboru. But we did *not* come here in ignorance. I was once your slave. I saw Ookami power firsthand and experienced your way of dealing with anyone not of your clan. That's why, as we passed through the lands of those clans that you conquered, one by one, I also gained their support, one by one. If anything happens to me, my men won't stay to fight; they'll scatter to fetch our allies. You can't defeat us all at once. You couldn't do that even before you were weakened by the earthquake." She inclined her head to them slightly and smiled. "And that, O noble wolves, is why I felt perfectly safe walking into your midst alone."

"In other words, put a scratch on her and you slit your own throat," Rinji remarked.

"I don't believe this," the first Ookami counselor sputtered. "She's bluffing."

"Can we depend on that?" another asked uneasily.

"This is what comes of showing too much mercy to the clans we conquered! We should have reduced them to ruins."

"What good are ruins? Ruins grow no rice."

Ryu left his counselors to their bickering and approached me. "Lady Himiko, it seems the time has come for you to leave us. Apparently it will not do to keep Lady Kaya waiting."

I smiled faintly. "She *can* be impatient."

"My people will be distraught when they hear the news of your departure."

"I hope not," I replied. "They have you and Master Rinji. They will lose nothing when I go. I would like to tell them that, to set their minds at ease."

"After all that my people did—that *I* led them to do against yours, you are concerned for them?" Ryu's expression was filled with remorse. "Lady Himiko, if I spent the rest of my days asking you to forgive me, it wouldn't be enough. That first day I met you, all I saw was a beautiful girl, a princess, and I wanted you the way a child wants a piece of honeycomb. I thought you should feel grateful that I'd noticed you!"

I smiled sadly. "It didn't take me long to teach you otherwise, did it?"

"I hated you for rejecting me. I carried that hate with me for too long. I poisoned my own life, trying to make yours miserable. What I did to you and your people was far worse than anything you ever did to me, and yet here you stand, offering one last kindness to the Ookami! I am ashamed."

"Lord Ryu, I *did* hate you," I said, taking his hands. "I can never forget all that I lost because of your grudge against me. Hating you, it would have been very easy for me to despise *all* your people, but if I'd done that, I would have lost . . ." I could not go on.

"Hey! What are you doing to Himiko?" Faithful Kaya saw my distress and stormed up to confront Ryu.

"It's all right, Sister," I said, recovering. "I was just

asking Lord Ryu to summon his clanfolk so that I can make my farewells more easily."

"You want to take the time to say good-bye to these people?" Kaya looked dubious. "I would've thought you'd just want to *go*." She gave Ryu an accusing look. "Do you *swear* you didn't say anything to make her do this?"

"Lady Himiko is not mine to command," he said wistfully. "She never was."

A short while later, Ryu's message of assembly ran through the village. The people rushed out of their cramped quarters at once. Noboru and I were waiting for them just beyond the timbers of the broken gateway, accompanied by the remainder of the Matsu captives. It had not taken any of us long to prepare for the homeward road. We had come to the Ookami with very little, and we were leaving the same way.

The Ookami response to Ryu's summons was so fast, I had scarcely crossed the village threshold before the crowd came streaming after me. Their cries of distress and pleas for me to stay were so insistent that I had to deal with them at once. I sent Noboru and my freed kindred ahead with Kaya, to join her waiting escort, then turned to speak to Ryu's people. I tried to reassure them that their lives held hope, that the disaster they had endured was not a sign that the gods had cursed them forever, that they had capable leaders with the wisdom to learn from the errors of the past and to guide them onto better paths for the future.

They would not accept my words. They begged me to stay, or at least to promise I would not forget them. Chizu came forward with tears in her eyes, followed by Lady Sato, who carried little Arashi.

"Lady Himiko, I know you must go home, but can't there be a way for us not to lose you entirely?" she pleaded. "No other voice we ever knew spoke so clearly in the name of the spirits! It's not enough to rebuild our houses and renew our fields if we labor deaf to the word of the gods!"

Before I could respond, I felt a strong hand on my shoulder and heard a long-absent voice in my ear: "Tell them you will return." I looked back over my shoulder and saw the serene face of Kaya's mother.

"L-Lady Ikumi?" I stammered. The shaman-chieftess of the Shika clan stood at my back, along with her daughter and the rest of my escort home.

"*Shhh,* Himiko. We don't want the Ookami knowing they could've had a clan chieftess as their hostage. Some of them might get bad ideas."

"But—but—"

Kaya chuckled. "I persuaded Mother to let me come after you, but I couldn't convince her to let me do it alone. Who do you think was responsible for all the clan alliances we made on the way here? Did you really believe the chieftains would negotiate with a mere girl like me?"

"There's never been anything 'mere' about you, Kaya," I declared.

"Nor about you, Himiko," Lady Ikumi said quietly, indicating the massed Ookami. "If I hadn't been here, I'd find it hard to believe that a single word from your lips now would make you the unchallenged ruler of this clan in a heartbeat. And judging from the way my own men are

staring at all this, you could probably take the leadership of
the Shika as well."

"Lady Himiko?" Troubled by my silence, Chizu trembled, still awaiting my reply. "Lady Himiko, have I said anything to offend you?"

Spirits, guide me, I prayed, and walked forward smiling,
to let Chizu and all the Ookami know that this parting was
in truth a beginning for us all.

Epilogue

"Emi, *please* stop fussing with my hair," I said. "It looks perfect."

"Oh, so now you have the power to see the back of your own head?" my stepmother said crisply. "Try putting that over on someone who never wiped your nose for you." She continued twiddling with the arrangement of my looped tresses while Mama and Yukari watched.

"But you've been working on it *forever*!"

"Whose fault is that? This wouldn't take so long if you weren't fidgeting."

"Himiko, let Emi do her work," Mama said with a serene smile. She was her old self again, her bruised mind completely healed with Noboru's return, many seasons ago. "This is a very important occasion. Many high-ranking visitors will be attending the ceremony today. You have to look your best and make a good impression."

"As if she hasn't made enough of an impression on

these people already?" Yukari said. "Our little girl is becoming a legend."

"'Our little girl' isn't even a chiestess yet," Mama reminded her. "Not officially, until after today's formalities. First things first."

"Well, for someone who's not *officially* a chiestess, she's managed to accomplish more than any of our noble guests, chieftains included!" Emi broke in. "I've lost count of how many clans have become part of the alliance, once they learned of her powers."

"Which do not include seeing the back of my own head," I remarked dryly. "If more clans want to forge bonds with the ones who are already our friends, it's because they've seen how we're all thriving."

"Then why did every last one of them send a delegation here to meet *you* before they agreed to join with us?" Emi challenged me. "The stories about your influence with the spirits travel faster than any reports of new prosperity; *that's* what brings them! And they always leave convinced that everything they heard about you is true."

I sighed. "As long as the old way of war dies, let them say what they please about my part in it. I wish they wouldn't tell such extravagant stories about me, but if it lets us extend peace over this land, I'll be happy."

And I'll be happier if we could make even more changes for the better, I thought. *Some of the clans that have become our allies still keep slaves. Will I ever command enough authority to guide them away from practicing such oppression? Can I hope to make my people—all* of *my people—see that we must put an end to the*

things that divide us if we are to be strong and enduring? How can
shattered ground support us? How can a splintered jewel shine?

"There." Emi set down her comb with a little sigh of contentment. "Now you're ready."

My mirror and wand lay on the floor before me. I took my precious image of the sun goddess from my belt and bound it to the mirror's handle with a strand of silk cord that I had set aside when my three mothers helped me dress in the fine robes I now wore. The delicate fabric clung to my body like water as I stood up.

"Hey, what's taking so long?" Kaya stuck her head through the doorway. "Everyone is getting impatient." When she saw me, she gasped. "Himiko, you look *wonderful*."

"Good, because I *feel* awful," I said. "I'm not used to this dress. I'm probably going to trip on it, land flat on my face in front of everyone, and die of embarrassment."

"Don't worry," Kaya replied. "When your clan built you this new house, they made it higher than all the rest. If you trip when you step out onto the platform, you'll probably dive straight over the side and break your neck. No embarrassment there!" She linked her arm through mine and added: "Really, Himiko, do you think any of us would ever let you fall?"

As she led me outside to where Master Michio was waiting, I thought: *This is only the beginning. When I face the evils that still dwell among us, I will not despair if I cannot destroy them overnight. I will set my eyes on the right road and believe that our people will follow me, soon or later. With the spirits' help, change will come.*

Kaya brought me to stand next to Master Michio and stepped aside to join the rest of my assembled family on the platform. Lord Hideki held Noboru on his shoulder. Takehiko and Sanjirou looked very grown up and dignified, though the solemnity of the occasion didn't stop them from "accidentally" treading on each other's toes or sneaking a furtive nudge followed by poorly muffled snorts and giggles. My big brother Masa was grinning proudly. He had never wanted to be our chieftain, and could not have been happier to see me about to accept that honor.

I gazed out over the crowd that had come to witness my official ascension as chieftess of the pine tree people. All of the Matsu were there, as well as the chieftains and nobility of every clan that had agreed to ally themselves with us. They ruled their domains, but by their own consent, my words ruled them. I still could hardly believe it was so.

Master Michio was almost as splendidly robed as I was. He beamed when he saw me. "Is it wrong to tell a great chieftess that she is as lovely as the sunrise?" He pitched his voice so that only those of us on the platform could hear his fond words.

Emi stole close to whisper, "If he thinks you look pretty now, I can't wait to see what he says when we dress you as a bride."

I only smiled and lowered my eyes. Although it would disappoint all of my mothers deeply, they would never have the joy of preparing me for my wedding. My heart had been given with love, with passion, with faith, and without regret. It would not be given again. The one who once held it absolutely in this mortal world now cherished it in the realm of the spirits. Our parting might be short or long, as the gods desired, but it would not be forever. He would not mind the wait.

For now, for him, for the gods, and above all, for the people of my beloved land, I had a purpose to fulfill that would carry me beyond the blessed life of wife and mother. I heard Master Michio clap his hands, then strike a long, resounding note from the sacred bell.

"Come forward, Lady Himiko, our chieftess! In the name of the spirits, come forward, our healer, our guide, our queen!"

I turned to the people and raised my mirror high, so that the goddess's image could be seen. The radiant circle of polished bronze held their faces, the splendor of the sun, and the truth I embraced with all my heart: we dance.

Our breath dances with the wind that carries the scent of spring flowers, sun-touched grass, and the keen fragrance of towering pines. Our feet dance lightly to the joyful music of celebration, or slowly, with deliberate grace, to the measured song of our daily tasks. Our laughter dances defiantly in the face of darkness. Above all, our spirits dance through the beauty all around us, and also—whether we know it or not—through the shadow worlds whose hidden wonders lie just beyond our sight, waiting for us to find the path that will lead us there. In song or in silence, waking or dreaming, by the glorious light of the sun or by the faint glimmer of a single star, we dance.

We dance.

How I Missed the Cat Bus*

I might as well confess: I made several attempts at writing this afterword before settling on the one you're reading now. Sometimes a piece of writing just does not *want* to be written. It's like taking care of a very stubborn toddler, when you discover that "I don't WANNA!" can be expressed passively, aggressively, assertively, rudely, crudely, verbally, physically, silently, loudly, and in so many other ways that it will make your head spin.

The problem with my other afterword attempts was that once I'd decided to write something about *Spirit's Chosen,* I realized that I wasn't working on an afterword but a

---

*The Cat Bus appears in the animated film *My Neighbor Totoro* and is the creation of Hayao Miyazaki. This giant, fantastic, grinning, many-legged feline provides a unique form of transportation for some of the characters in the movie. He can transform his body—opening a door in his side, creating fur-covered seats within, and turning his eyes into luminous headlights. Of course he remembers to include windows. Windows on the Cat Bus are very important. How else would his passengers be able to enjoy breathtaking views of the midnight countryside when he takes to the skies? You never know where the Cat Bus will stop, but if it ever pulls up to the curb for me, I'm getting on board!

lecture. I've given enough lectures—just ask my kids. If I have to take you by the shoulders, point you at a particular character or scene or Author's Message in my book, and declare "There! Look at *that*! Pay attention to it! It's important!" then I haven't done my job as a writer. Worse, it would mean I've decided that you aren't smart enough to make your own choices about what is and isn't important in the books you read. (To say nothing of presuming that what is important to me must be important to you too.)

Wouldn't that be ironic, considering that all my Princesses of Myth books are about girls who strive for the freedom to make their own decisions?

That's why I've made a decision of my own: to set aside all attempts at lecturing, preaching, or teaching a Valuable Lesson (you know, the kind they administer with a virtual mallet on some television programs) and instead invite you to share some of the memories and experiences I gathered during my visits to Himiko's country, Japan.

I've visited Japan twice. The first time, I was accompanying my husband on a business trip. He had to work all day, so I was entirely on my own. I didn't understand, speak, or read Japanese, but I did try to acquire some basic phrases before we left home, such as:

"Hello."

"Good-bye."

"Please."

"Thank you very much."

"Pardon me, but I don't understand Japanese."

"Where is the [insert name of the place I needed to find], please?"

I also picked up some information about etiquette, including:

Women hold their hands differently from men when bowing.

If you want to indicate something with a gesture, do not point with one finger. Use your entire hand.

A little about table manners, especially how you should and should not use chopsticks.

If someone gives you a business card, accept it respectfully, with both hands. Don't just stuff it into your pocket or purse. Look at it and then put it away carefully. It's important.

If you don't speak Japanese, don't ask, "Do you speak English?" People who don't speak English will lose face. Instead, you should say, "I'm sorry, I don't understand Japanese." (And make the effort to say it *in* Japanese. If I can do it, so can you!) At that point, people who speak English will happily do so, and those who don't will still do their best to help you.

I spent almost all of my first trip to Japan in Tokyo. I'd planned to make an overnight visit to Kyoto, but plans don't always work out. I took the train all the way there, got cold feet, and went back to Tokyo the same day. Jet lag was to blame.

I have a healthy spirit of adventure and enjoy exploring, testing my limits, having off-the-tourist-route experiences, and trying new things. Unfortunately, my spirit of adventure wilts when I'm tired. It's a long flight to Japan from my New England home, and jet lag opened the door to countless doubts: "I'll be all by myself in Kyoto and I don't speak

Japanese! What if I get sick? What if I have to call my husband in Tokyo and I can't figure out how to use the phone? What if I go into a restaurant and nobody there speaks English? I don't speak Japanese! How will I be able to order? What if I run out of money? What if I get lost and miss the train back to Tokyo? Oh my gosh, I *still* don't speak Japanese!"

Now here's the funny thing: Before I could go back to Tokyo, I had to cancel my Kyoto hotel reservation.

By telephone.

And . . . wait for it . . . I don't speak Japanese. (Surprise!)

Well, what do you know? I did it. I figured out how to use the telephone, I called the hotel, and I kept repeating my most useful Japanese phrase, "Please excuse me, I don't understand Japanese," until I was connected with someone who spoke English. Mission accomplished!

I was also able to change my return ticket to Tokyo. My train didn't leave for several hours. During that time I managed to visit one of the many lovely shrines in Kyoto, have lunch, and get myself back to the train station without anyone's help. I didn't get lost. I didn't miss my train.

And most important, once I recovered enough from my jet lag to realize that I had faced nearly every one of the fears that had sent me running back to Tokyo, I did *not* repeat the mistake of letting self-doubt keep me from having a wonderful time on my own for the rest of my stay!

Besides taking myself to lots of museums and shrines, I enjoyed some not-in-the-guidebook experiences, including:

Discovering a parade—with dancers, huge drums, and portable shrines—passing by our hotel one night.

Finding my way to the Meiji shrine in Yoyogi Park and

getting *happily* lost among the towering trees when it was time to head back. How wonderful to be in the heart of one of the world's most vibrant, modern cities, yet to feel nothing but the tranquil embrace of the forest! (I also met a very elegant and solemn cat who graciously permitted me to scratch his chin. When you're far from home and you miss the special people in your life, you can call them on the phone. When you miss your cats, nothing but meeting another cat will do.)

Encountering the Harajuku Guardian Angels in the midst of their project to pick up street litter, asking if I could help, and being welcomed. (Once again, I do not understand Japanese, but we managed to communicate anyway. They gave me a baseball cap, a T-shirt, and the memory of a definitely *non*-tourist experience.)

Attending a Kabuki theater performance. (And understanding everything that was going on, thanks to the simultaneous translation devices available.)

Collecting some unique—and free!—souvenirs, namely handheld fans advertising different products and businesses.

Having my fortune told at a shrine.

Learning how to use traditional Japanese toilets. (If this doesn't sound impressive, look at photos of these fixtures online. They are also called squat toilets, which should give you some idea. Plus I learned how to use these *while wearing jeans*! Pretty good, eh?)

During some of my visits to shrines, having children (or their parents) ask me to pose with them for photos. As far as I could tell, this was part of a widespread school project. The children were learning English and probably were assigned to practice using the language with people who looked like native English speakers. The photos were the proof they'd done the assignment. One little girl gave me some Japanese postage stamps as a thank-you gift.

Taking my husband with me to visit the Asakusa Kannon temple on his one day off from work. We got lost (happily, again) in the huge canopied maze of shops surrounding the temple and ate sushi at a restaurant where the dishes came around on a conveyor belt. Once in the temple grounds, we heard that a traditional dance troupe was going to perform, so we joined the crowd. The dance was traditional, but the music accompanying them on a boom box was . . . *disco*! A woman next to us remarked, "I wish I'd brought my video camera because they're never going to believe this back home!"

My second visit to Japan was a different experience, though it was another business trip: mine! I was speaking at the World Science Fiction Convention in Yokohama, but before the convention began, I wanted to see more of the country. I spent some time in Tokyo with my family, then set out for Osaka to join a tour group of American fans.

I wish I could share all the beautiful sights we saw. I fell in love with the Japanese Alps. I still remember looking out the bus window at a pair of ancient cherry trees that had been uprooted and replanted to save them from the waters of a man-made lake. Their chances for survival had been slim, but they adapted and thrived. It made me smile. I also recall having our guide point out the rising trails of mist in the mountains, evidence of geothermal activity, and thrilled to hear her call it the breath of dragons.

This trip was filled with special experiences:

Visiting a Tokyo summer festival in the park just across the street from our hotel.

Watching my twenty-something daughter participate in an energy-drink promotion in Shibuya, then have her photo taken for a Japanese magazine. (And no, she doesn't understand Japanese, either, but the patience and kindness of the people running the event made everything work out.)

Enjoying a traditional hot springs bath *and* a gorgeous view on the roof of a hotel.

Wandering into a sake brewery and being permitted to have a taste.

Catching a distant glimpse of Mount Fuji.

Delighting in the company of the tame deer in Nara Park, which is also home to Todaiji, a shrine containing Japan's largest bronze statue of the Buddha. The deer are supposed to be messengers of the gods. You can buy "deer crackers" to feed them, and they know it! They may be tame, but they can also be as bold as they are beautiful.

Attending a dance by the shrine maidens at Fushimi Inari shrine, near Kyoto.

Fulfilling my dream, as a devoted fan of master artist, animator, and director Hayao Miyazaki (whose skill, vision, and heart created *My Neighbor Totoro, Spirited Away, Howl's Moving Castle,* and many other films) by visiting the Ghibli Museum in Mitaka. My one regret? That I could not play on the Cat Bus. Alas, I do not qualify as twelve-or-younger!

Taking part in a bubble-gum-blowing contest in Yokohama.

Visiting a Japanese family who very kindly opened their home to a few members of our tour group.

There are more memories, but I think these will do. If I go on, this afterword will become another book! Let me leave it as it is, a treasure box to hold this collection of keepsakes and souvenirs that I've enjoyed sharing with you.

It also holds one final item, a wish list of the things I would like to do if I am ever fortunate enough to return to Japan for a third time. Here are a few:

Attend a tea ceremony.

Watch a sumo *basho* (tournament).

See more of Honshu, the only Japanese island I've visited so far, but also travel to other islands.

Visit Mount Fuji instead of only seeing the sacred peak from afar.

Travel during autumn or spring, since my two previous trips were taken in the summertime.

Spend more time among the mountains and forests.

Go to the great shrine at Ise.

Take my grandson to the Ghibli Museum. If I can't play on the Cat Bus, I want to watch him do it!

Most of all, travel to Yoshinogari Historical Park and visit the reconstructed Yayoi village. It's the closest I could ever come to sharing Himiko's world. Wouldn't *that* be a writer's dream come true?

If your own dreams include a trip to Japan, I hope you will be able to realize them too.

About the Author

Nebula Award winner ESTHER FRIESNER is the author of more than 30 novels and 150 short stories, including "Thunderbolt" in Random House's *Young Warriors* anthology, which led to the creation of *Nobody's Princess* and its sequel, *Nobody's Prize*. She then traveled to ancient Egypt in *Sphinx's Princess* and *Sphinx's Queen*. Esther is also the editor of seven popular anthologies. Her work has been published around the world.

Educated at Vassar College and Yale University, where she taught for a number of years, Esther is also a poet and a playwright and once wrote an advice column, "Ask Auntie Esther." She is married and the mother of two, harbors cats, and lives in Connecticut. You can visit her at sff.net/people/e.friesner and learn more about her princesses of myth at princessesofmyth.com.